The HEART'S APPEAL

Books by Jennifer Delamere

LONDON BEGINNINGS

The Captain's Daughter
The Heart's Appeal

LONDON BEGINNINGS · BOOK 2

The HEART'S APPEAL

JENNIFER DELAMERE

BETHANYHOUSE

a division of Baker Publishing Group
Minneapolis, Minnesota

Published by Bethany House Publishers
11400 Hampshire Avenue South
Bloomington, Minnesota 55438
www.bethanyhouse.com

Bethany House Publishers is a division of
Baker Publishing Group, Grand Rapids, Michigan

Printed in the United States of America

Library of Congress Cataloging-in-Publication Data
Names: Delamere, Jennifer, author.
Title: The heart's appeal / Jennifer Delamere.
Description: Minneapolis, Minnesota : Bethany House, a division of Baker
    Publishing Group, [2018] | Series: London beginnings ; Book 2
Identifiers: LCCN 2017038828| ISBN 9780764219214 (trade paper) | ISBN
    9780764231452 (hardcover)
Subjects: LCSH: Man-woman relationships—Fiction. | London (England)—
    Fiction. | GSAFD: Love stories. | Christian fiction.
Classification: LCC PS3604.E4225 H43 2018 | DDC 813/.6—dc23
LC record available at https://lccn.loc.gov/2017038828

Scripture quotations are from the King James Version of the Bible.

This is a work of historical reconstruction; the appearances of certain historical
figures are therefore inevitable. All other characters, however, are products of
the author's imagination, and any resemblance to actual persons, living or dead,
is coincidental.

Cover design by Koechel Peterson & Associates, Inc., Minneapolis, Minnesota/
Jon Godfredson

Author is represented by the BookEnds Literary Agency, LLC.

18   19   20   21   22   23   24   7   6   5   4   3   2   1

O magnify the Lord with me,
and let us exalt his name together.

—Psalm 34:3

In memory of my aunt,
Margaret DeBolt Edwards,
a lovely and feisty woman in her own right

CHAPTER

1

Julia Bernay was going to be late. If there was one thing she hated, it was not being punctual. It showed a lack of respect and, if she were honest—which she always was—it made her look bad. She was on her way to a lecture by Dr. Anna Stahl, a physician from America, and she was determined to make a good first impression. After months of toiling away at Queen's College on Harley Street, this was her first real opportunity to interact with London's medical professionals.

Julia had been in London for nearly a year, but the official start to her medical studies had yet to actually begin. She'd come with high hopes of beginning her training right away, only to discover—after failing London University's matriculation exam—that her schooling thus far in life had not been enough. The laws for licensing physicians required that she pass the exam before any course she took at the London School of Medicine for Women could count toward a medical degree.

Queen's College was primarily a school for training governesses, but it also offered the courses needed by women seeking to qualify for a higher education in medicine. Although Julia had given herself fully to her studies over these past months, she was anxious to get beyond standard academic courses and begin training in medicine. Having obtained special permission to attend Dr. Stahl's lecture, she was not going to miss it.

Unfortunately, her plan to take the Metropolitan Underground Railway to her destination had turned out to be a mistake. All around her, the platform was crowded with passengers who had watched three trains come and go because the third-class carriages were too packed to accommodate even one more person.

Julia had bought a third-class ticket to save money, taking the reasonable view that the train would get there at the same time, regardless of which carriage she was in. She hadn't realized that during this time of day, train after train would pass by without her being able to board. Meanwhile, the first-class carriages were only half full.

Now she was in a dilemma, for money and time were both commodities she could not afford to waste. The news she'd received from her benefactor just this week proved that. Mrs. Staunton's letter had sorrowfully informed her that due to a bank failure in Bristol, she could no longer pay for Julia's training. While Julia grieved for the Stauntons as they struggled to reorganize their affairs, this had placed her in an awkward position. She had enough to live on for several more months, because Mrs. Staunton had refused to take back any money already given. Julia could complete her preparation for the matriculation examination, which would allow her to begin studies at the London School of Medicine for Women in October. If she was very frugal, she might even be able to make the money stretch for her first term. But then what? Should she even begin school with no clear means of continuing?

Perhaps she should consider moving in with the Morans. Her sister Rosalyn and her husband, Nate Moran, were away from London most of the year, traveling on tour with the opera company, but Nate's family lived in a large house with room to accommodate boarders. It would be cheaper than the lodgings she had now, if farther removed from the school. It was something she would ask about when Rosalyn and Nate came home for Easter.

All of this assumed she could even pass the matriculation exam. She was still behind in Latin, which was a critical component of the test. With no extra money for a tutor, passing it seemed more daunting than ever.

She might have to consider going back to nursing, but having come this far, nursing could never give her the satisfaction that it had in the past. She would have neither the time nor the money for medical school. She would earn a scant ten pounds per year. Nurses were boarded together in sparse lodgings at the hospital and worked all hours of the day and night. Her goal of becoming a doctor and a medical missionary would be set aside, and Julia could not believe God would allow these dreams to be lost forever.

"Sufficient unto the day," she reminded herself as she watched yet another train pass her by. "The morrow will take care of itself."

She took a deep breath and prayed that the next train would come quickly.

Michael Stephenson stood with his sister Corinna at the entrance to the Underground station while Miss Laura Maynard, the third member of their party, bought a nosegay from a flower girl. He watched as Laura studied the selections in the small, battered flower cart and made her choice, then handed over a few coins to the girl. The flower girl received the coins with a smile and even gave Laura a little curtsy.

Laura held the flowers to her nose and breathed in appreciatively. She was a pretty blonde, slender and charming in an ethereal kind of way. Her light blue cape showed her complexion to advantage, especially with the cart of colorful blooms as a backdrop. The hothouse flowers made a bright contrast to the drab February day. Admiring Laura's beauty and poise, Michael decided he was reasonably content with the idea that she could one day be his wife.

Feeling a nudge in his ribs, he turned to see his sister looking at him expectantly. He realized she'd been speaking to him. "I'm sorry, what were you saying?"

Corinna's gaze traveled pointedly to Laura before settling back on Michael. "I was reminding you about Lady Amberley's annual ball in July."

"As you have every day since you received the invitation."

Getting invited to this ball was the social prize Corinna had spent years striving for. This year it had been granted at last, probably because of Laura's influence. Corinna was bursting with pride and had immediately begun her plans for the event, although it was still months away.

She poked him again. "I was saying that the ball has gained a reputation for being the night when the most fashionable alliances are announced."

"Ah yes, right." It was no surprise that Corinna would refer to an engagement as an *alliance*. He also knew full well what his sister was hinting at. She'd been doing everything in her power to promote a match between Michael and Laura, who was the youngest daughter of the late Viscount Delaford. Such an *alliance* would go a long way toward regaining the social standing the Stephenson family had lost. Truth be told, Michael was committed to the plan as well. The ball was nearly five months away, but he expected to have gained approval for Laura's hand long before that. Even so, he couldn't resist teasing his sister and keeping her in suspense. He patted her arm. "I suspect this year's ball will exceed all expectations."

"Oh?" Corinna's eager expression showed that she'd taken the bait.

"Yes, indeed. I heard the old Duke of Norlington's grand-daughter plans to announce her engagement to that wildly radical member of Parliament, Mr. John Waverly."

Corinna's eyes narrowed. "You know that's not what I was referring to."

Still amused by his sister's social machinations, Michael decided to play the devil's advocate. "But, Corinna, I've only known Miss Maynard a few weeks. Not to mention that she's just come out of mourning for her father."

"That's precisely the point—she is *out* of mourning. There is no time to waste, as she will have plenty of suitors. And the new viscount is much more amenable to the idea of your union with his sister."

This was true. Laura's father, the old viscount, would have been dead set against the idea of his daughter marrying into the Stephenson family after the way Michael's father had dragged it into financial and social ruin. Laura's brother, however, viewed things differently. He saw Michael's trajectory to success, both in prosperity and respectability. Being a young man, he did not have the same memories of the past as his father, nor did he put much weight on them. He was anxious only to get his sister settled in a good marriage.

"Besides," Corinna continued, "you've already spent more time with Miss Maynard than I did with David before we were married."

This remark sobered Michael. Corinna's marriage had been one of convenience, and in thirteen years it had not evolved much beyond that—at least on Corinna's part. A flicker of doubt played at the edges of Michael's mind. Would his marriage end up the same? He pushed the thought aside. He might not actually be in *love* with Laura, but there was nothing displeasing about her. Why shouldn't they be happy together? Besides, he could not forget that Corinna had married a wealthy man as much for his sake as for hers. Still mulling these things over, he gave a murmur of acquiescence.

This was not enough for his sister. She gave Michael a third, sharper poke in the ribs. "Michael Stephenson, I absolutely forbid you to even *think* about marrying Laura Maynard."

Michael started back in surprise. "And why is that?"

Her expression softened to a smirk. "Because you never do anything until someone expressly tells you *not* to."

He couldn't help but laugh out loud.

If the next train was full, Julia would be forced to slip into one of the second-class carriages—or even one of the first-class carriages if necessary. And really, what would be the harm in that? She wouldn't be taking a seat from anyone. Besides, was she not a child of God, intent on giving her life to His purposes? Wasn't everyone equal in His sight? The constant harping on class distinctions might constitute the very fiber of her homeland's psyche, but in Julia's view, it was something that ought to be changed.

If she could get onto one of the other carriages, she did not think anyone would stop her for looking out of place. She'd worn her best day gown for this event. The clerk at the secondhand shop had assured her it was only a year old, not so far out of the current fashions. Everyone waiting for the more expensive carriages appeared to be upper-middle class at best. The very rich people traveled in their personal carriages and would never be caught on the Underground. The designation *first class* was a bit of a misnomer.

The shriek of a train whistle filled the air once more. Overhead, the large globes of the gas lamps swayed as the train pulled into the station.

A collective groan filled the air when those on the platform saw, as Julia did, that this train was also filled to bursting.

This was it, then. Julia had worked hard to get permission to attend this lecture, and she wasn't going to miss it. She began to press her way through the crowd, needing to move swiftly but not draw attention. The third-class carriages were located at the front of the train, closest to the smoke belching from the engine. The first-class carriages were in the center, followed by the second-class section at the end. Julia sent a quick glance toward the station guard. He was conversing with the train conductor over some issue with the engine car, but another guard was eying her from across the platform. Had he seen her standing with the third-class passengers earlier?

Julia paused, trying to look as though she'd been standing here all along. Two women stood nearby. The first was a brunette, tall and striking, if not classically pretty. She stood an inch or so taller than Julia, who at five feet seven inches, considered herself above average height. The other woman was petite, with pale blond hair and a fur-trimmed cape. Her hair was delicately curled into an intricate bun, visible beneath a hat that perfectly complemented her clothes and was set on her head at precisely the most flattering angle.

They were too busy chatting to notice Julia. She overheard enough of their conversation to know they were on a shopping trip. Perhaps they were housewives with husbands who were prosperous merchants or businessmen in the financial district of London called the City. The blonde was detailing three different kinds of gloves she needed to buy. It was more than Julia could imagine buying in a year. Perhaps, Julia thought wryly, if she couldn't pass for one of these ladies, she might be mistaken for a maid who'd been brought along to carry packages.

Whatever issue the officials had been discussing seemed to

have gotten resolved. A platform attendant was now urging people into the carriages and closing the doors after them. Julia didn't have time to reach the second-class section at the back. A surreptitious glance toward the other guard showed he was heading in her direction.

A gentleman who had been standing near the two ladies spoke to them, moving them forward with a polite sweep of his arm. The three of them boarded together, and Julia followed, just making it onto the carriage before the platform attendant closed the doors. With a sigh of relief, she found an empty seat away from the window. Within moments, the train was in motion, hurtling into the tunnel.

Julia had ridden the Underground a few times since arriving in London, but she always found the experience disconcerting. She could not get used to the smoky darkness and the knowledge that the train was shooting at breakneck speed through a tight space. At least this compartment was more spacious than in third class. In addition to being farther away from the smoke, the carriage had proper lighting, and the seats had cushions. There were two other men already in the carriage. Both were absorbed in reading their newspapers and barely looked up as Julia and the others got on board. As no one had challenged her right to be here, she settled back in her seat, confident now that she would arrive at the lecture hall on time.

The gentleman had taken a seat across the aisle from the two women, and they were now engaged in casual small talk. Julia guessed he was just a few years older than she was, or perhaps nearing thirty. He was tall and broad shouldered, with dark hair trimmed neatly at the sideburns. Wearing a perfectly pressed dark suit, he projected an air of affluence and confidence.

Julia opened her copy of *The Lancet* medical journal, planning to make the best use of the travel time by reading. But her attention kept straying to the gentleman and the two ladies he was traveling with, trying to guess their connection. She revised her earlier guess about the women, deciding the tall one must be the man's sister. Their interactions had a comfortable familiarity, and there was a certain family resemblance in height and hair color. The blonde, on the other hand, kept throwing sly glances in his direction, as though to check whether he was paying attention to her. Julia guessed she was not married and had her eye on him.

She wondered if this man was the sort who would find such a woman attractive. He was handsome—even Julia, who paid little attention to these things, could see that. But he did not appear vain or frivolous, as the blonde did. There was a hard-set edge to his mouth. Julia saw determination in him, the kind of man who would be serious about whatever he made up his mind to accomplish.

"Are you sure you won't stop with us at Selfridges for coffee before going on to Gray's Inn?" the blonde asked him. "It would be so nice to have you join us."

"Only on the condition that I be allowed to escape before you two set about your shopping," he returned with a smile. It seemed a genuine, warm smile. So warm, in fact, that Julia's estimation of him went down several notches. Perhaps he was the type to have his head turned by such a woman after all. She supposed she ought to have known. Handsome men always seemed drawn to beautiful women.

Why should you care? Julia chided herself. Today she was going to attend an important medical lecture, and in a few years' time she would be on her way to Africa and a life of service as a medical missionary. She had better ways to occupy her thoughts than to wonder at the private lives of privileged Londoners.

She was just about to suppress her little smile at her own fool-ishness when the man turned his head and caught her looking at him. He must have thought her smile was aimed at him, for his eyebrows lifted and he tipped his chin in acknowledgment. She detected an amused gleam in his eye, as though he were used to having unknown ladies smile at him on the train. She bristled. She was most definitely not that sort of person. How dare he think so!

His eye traveled from her face to take in the rest of her. Julia knew he must be appraising her, noticing the secondhand clothes, the unstylish hat, and gloves that were worn though still presentable. For the first time in her life, she felt an embarrassed self-consciousness. How had he been able to do that with one look?

Was her face growing warm? No. She could not be blushing. Julia Bernay never blushed. That was for hapless females like the blonde sitting in front of her. She quickly averted her gaze, lifting her copy of *The Lancet* and making a point of reading it. That would show him the kind of serious woman she was.

Neither of the women had noticed this little interchange. The brunette said, "You know we would never subject you to something so incredibly tedious as shopping." She spoke with a sarcastic air. "Although you might consider finding a valet who can be a little more creative in your choice of clothing."

The man shrugged. "What would be the point? There's no need to be creative in my profession."

Julia lowered her journal just enough to peek over the top and risk another glance at him. What was his profession? The blonde had mentioned Gray's Inn. He must be a barrister. This was easy to believe. It took no trouble at all to imagine him standing in a courtroom, addressing a jury. He had the kind of presence that turned heads and garnered attention. What would he look like in a barrister's wig and robe? She was sure he would be very imposing.

The train pulled into the next station. Julia could see the platform here was crowded, too. While most of the people vied for the third-class compartments, a dapper man in a fur-collared coat and diamond-patterned cravat strode into the first-class carriage. From the corner of her eye, she saw him send a curious glance her way. She tried to project the casual air of someone who rode in first-class carriages every day, but she needn't have bothered. His gaze traveled quickly over her and settled for a much longer moment on the blonde before he took a seat.

The barrister took a cigarette holder from his pocket and opened it. Julia found this disappointing. She'd read some reports indicating there could be adverse effects to smoking, even though equally as many doctors touted its health benefits.

"Michael, will you hand me a cigarette?" the brunette asked.

He looked at her askance. "Now, Corinna, I don't think David will appreciate me leading his wife astray."

"Then don't think of me as David's wife," she snapped. She held out her hand. "Remember that I am also your sister."

With a sardonic smile, he replied, "Well, since you put it that way . . ."

He rose and stepped into the aisle to give her a cigarette.

At that moment, the train, which up to this point had been rattling and shaking in normal fashion, suddenly came to a screeching halt. It careened sharply to the left, its right side lifting as though loosed from the tracks, forcing Julia and the other passengers to grab hold of their seats to keep from being pitched to the floor. The man Julia knew only as Michael was thrown hard to the left, crashing backward into the carriage window. He tried to right himself, stunned, before he seemed to lose consciousness. As he fell to the floor, his head and neck scraped the jagged glass still attached to the frame. The rest of the glass fell with him, scattering across the floor and mingling with the blood flowing from his head.

CHAPTER

2

THERE WAS A MOMENT OF EERIE SILENCE. Like
Julia, the others were stupefied, trying to come to grips with
what had just happened. Finally, the quiet was broken by
groans and movement as people struggled to right themselves.
One of the gentlemen moaned, "I think my arm is broken!" The
carriage was still tilted to the left. Julia guessed the train had
derailed during its sudden, violent attempt to stop.

"Oh no! Oh no!" cried the blonde, her voice high-pitched and
frenzied, as she stared at Michael bleeding on the floor. Julia
stumbled forward to reach him, alarmed at the quantity of blood
spurting from below his chin. One of the other men crouched
beside him, pulling out a handkerchief and vainly attempting to
staunch the flow of blood.

"You won't stop it that way," Julia said, tugging off her gloves
and shrugging out of her coat for ease of movement. "Step aside.
I'm a nurse."

"A nurse?" He looked at her in surprise, but Julia wasn't about to waste time on explanations. The jagged window glass had sliced deeply into Michael's neck and cut an important blood vessel.

"Do you want him to bleed to death?"

Her bold words so stunned the man that Julia was able to move him out of the way. She took hold of Michael's head. With her other hand, she pinched the cut together and pressed hard, using all her might to force the artery against the vertebral column in his neck. Blood spattered on her hands and gown as she struggled to find the right hold.

"Is he dead?" cried the blond woman, wringing her hands.

"Not yet," Julia answered tersely. She had faced emergencies before, but this was serious enough to unsettle even her. She fought to maintain her own composure as she worked to stem the flow of blood.

Michael's sister looked just as panicked, but she was not cowering as the other woman was. She nearly slipped on the glass and blood as she dropped down beside Julia. "What are you doing? You're strangling him!"

"No, I'm keeping him from bleeding to death. We must keep pressure on the wound until we can get a doctor." She met the woman's gaze, willing her to believe what she was saying. "You must trust me on this, or he will die."

It was a shocking thing to say, but Julia had to make her understand. To her credit, this woman—Corinna, Michael had called her—immediately grew calm. Julia saw her take several deep breaths to steady herself. Corinna nodded. "What do we do next?"

Julia could hear the commotion outside the carriage. "What's happening? How far are we from the next station? We have to find a doctor right away."

The young man who had entered the carriage at the last stop poked his head through the broken window. His gloved hands and heavy coat protected him as he leaned out, assessing the situation. "There is a narrow pathway between the train and the tunnel wall. I see lights coming this direction. Men with lanterns, I believe. We must be closer to the station we just left. That's the direction they're coming from."

"Let's hope there is a medic among them," Julia said.

"We are not going to wait for them to come to us!" Corinna exclaimed. "We are taking my brother out of this carriage right now."

"No! We can't move him. The pressure has to remain constant. In this situation, the blood will not coagulate on its own. The artery must be forcibly closed."

"You will not move?" It was a command as well as a question.

Julia could see Corinna was torn between her desire to remain with her brother and the need to find help. "I'm staying right here," Julia confirmed. She wasn't leaving until she knew Michael was safe.

This was enough for Corinna to make up her mind. "I will find a doctor." She rose to her feet and took hold of the other woman's arm. "Laura, come with me."

Laura was crying, frozen with fear, staring at Michael.

Corinna gave her a tug. "Come along," she directed again, and finally got the woman moving.

"I'll go with you," the man at the window offered. "Other people have already left their carriages. It's a crush out there now, and you'll need some muscle to get anywhere."

Just getting out of the carriage proved to be the first hurdle. Because of the slant of the train, they could only get the door open about a foot before it was stopped by the narrow ledge running the length of the tunnel. But it was enough to allow the young man to squeeze through and scramble up to the ledge. He turned and offered his hand to help Laura and Corinna up and out.

"I'm coming with you," another of the men declared. He was cradling his left arm in his right. "I need help."

It was clear he was in pain. Julia wanted to help, but she could not let go of Michael. But the injured man wasn't waiting for her response. He was already offering his good arm to the other man to help him out of the train.

The man who had initially tried to stop the bleeding made no effort to leave. "I'll stay with you until the doctor arrives," he told Julia.

"Thank you, Mr. . . . ?"

"Carter."

"Can you tell me if the ladies are making progress?" On the floor with Michael, Julia could not see what was going on in the tunnel.

Mr. Carter looked out the broken window. "There are a great many people, but that chap is helping the ladies push their way forward." He turned back to Julia. "If you need me to help, to do anything . . ."

"That's very good of you." In truth, Julia's hands were tiring already. "It's imperative that we keep the pressure on this artery hard and constant. Do you think you can help me with that?"

He knelt beside her. "Just tell me what to do."

He was a large man, with beefy hands well-suited to provide the continuous, strong pressure needed, and he was willing to follow her directions exactly. But even after he was set and she felt confident enough to release her hold, she kept her hands hovering close by, ready to act if Mr. Carter's grip should loosen. There was still some blood escaping from the wound, but it was no longer at dangerous levels.

Miraculously, the lanterns in the carriage were still lit, but they flickered as though they might go out at any time. Julia prayed they would stay on.

Once she was confident that Mr. Carter was keeping hold of

the wound, Julia examined Michael further. He had other cuts on his head and face, but those appeared largely superficial. Opening his coat, she searched his pockets and found a handkerchief. She pulled it out and used it to wipe the blood from the minor wounds. His dark brown hair was thick but felt silky between her fingers as she pushed it back from his face. A short, faded scar ran along one cheekbone, most of it covered by his side-whiskers.

She did a simple review of the rest of his body. His bulk filled much of the aisle. Just a few minutes ago, he'd been so strong and vigorous. Two fingers on his right hand appeared to be sprained or broken. She took out her own handkerchief and wrapped the fingers together as best she could to keep them from further injury. Then she carefully straightened one leg that had bent at an odd angle during his fall. That knee would likely cause him some pain later.

"Your medical knowledge seems quite advanced for a nurse," Mr. Carter said.

"I am also in training to be a doctor."

In the past, Julia had found this pronouncement often drew skepticism. However, Mr. Carter only looked impressed. "Are you really? How astonishing."

The lights finally went out.

Outside, people were still streaming past the carriage, desperate to escape the darkness. Long minutes went by before Julia heard shouting of a different kind. Officials from the Underground had arrived.

"Stay calm, everyone! Stay calm!" an official shouted over the din. "You are in no immediate danger! Let us through! We must evacuate the injured!"

"In here! He's in here!" Corinna stumbled into the carriage, followed by several men. "I've brought the doctor! How is my brother?"

Julia winced at the bright light of the lanterns carried by two of the men. "We've kept the bleeding at bay." She spoke not only to Corinna but to the doctor, who knelt beside her and inspected the situation.

"You did the right thing, sir," the doctor said to Mr. Carter.

"This young lady here showed me what to do," Mr. Carter replied. "She's studying to be a doctor."

"Are you?" The doctor gave Julia a brief, appreciative glance. "This was a good test for you, then."

Corinna looked at Julia with stunned disbelief. "You're studying to be a doctor?"

"Yes, that's right."

The doctor opened his bag. "I've brought clamps to hold the wound shut until we can get him to surgery."

It was difficult for Julia to relinquish charge of her patient. She stayed close, watching as the doctor and an assistant worked to stabilize the wound.

Corinna, too, hovered nearby, her eyes never leaving her brother.

"He's going to be all right," Julia assured her. "We stemmed the loss of blood before any real damage was done."

Julia saw Corinna's lower lip quiver. She knew how relief, when it came, could cause a wall of stoicism to crumble. But Corinna was holding herself firm, if just barely.

"We can move him now," the doctor announced. "Let's get him on the stretcher."

Julia retrieved her coat as the men began moving Michael onto a stretcher that had been passed in through the broken window. "I'm coming with you."

"No!" Corinna exclaimed—rather too vehemently, Julia thought. "He's in the doctor's care now. There is no need for you to come along." It seemed a rough dismissal after all Julia had done. But then Corinna added in a gentler voice, "Thank you.

There are . . . no words." Her voice was raspy, betraying the emotion behind her terse but clearly heartfelt thanks.

It didn't lessen Julia's desire to accompany them, but she couldn't go against the wishes of the wounded man's sister. "You are most welcome. I thank God I was here to help."

Corinna's mouth tightened, but she did not reply. Their attention was drawn back to Michael as the men passed the stretcher through the window to the waiting men outside.

The doctor and his assistant helped Corinna out of the carriage, and they hurried to follow the men carrying Michael. Julia could only watch, assured that at least Michael was under medical care now, as men with lamps led the way for the stretcher bearers. It wasn't long before they were far up the tunnel and out of sight.

"Shall we get out of here?" Mr. Carter suggested. He was holding the last of the lanterns the men had brought with them.

"Yes, I just need to find my things." Julia returned to her seat to collect her reticule and the journal she'd been reading. As she did, her gaze was caught by something on the floor of the carriage. She picked it up. It was a calling card that read: *Michael Stephenson, Barrister-at-Law, Gray's Inn Buildings, London.* It was stained with blood, but Julia wiped it as dry as she could and put it in her reticule.

Mr. Carter struggled to get his girth through the narrow opening of the door, but eventually he made it. He helped Julia up to the walkway.

The tunnel was empty of passengers by now. A crew of railway men had arrived and were beginning to assess how to get the train onto the tracks and moving again. Julia heard a commotion coming from one of the carriages at the front of the train. A workman was shouting to his fellows, "There's a woman in here!"

Julia and Mr. Carter got to him at the same time as several of the men from the railway.

"She's unconscious and hurt, too, I think," said the workman. "I'll need help to get her out."

They followed him into the carriage, which was no easy task. It was crunched from the impact, and the plain wooden seats were broken and jagged with boards sticking out at odd angles. A woman was trapped under one of the fallen beams.

Working together, three men lifted the beam while a fourth wrapped his arms underneath the woman's. She regained consciousness and began to moan in pain as he dragged her out from under the wreckage.

Once the woman was free, Julia inspected her leg. It had been badly mangled by the weight of the board. The shinbone had broken through the skin. The woman was half-delirious, her face contorted and her eyes wide and white with terror. Julia kept up a continuous stream of comforting words as she devised a splint and got the leg set so that the woman could be safely moved. Two men carried her out under Julia's direction, while Mr. Carter led the way with the lamp.

The station was in an uproar, packed with people who'd been stranded by the shutdown. The streets outside were also in confusion, but station officials had been able to commandeer a wagon to take injured passengers to the hospital. They helped the woman into the wagon, but Julia declined to go herself.

Mr. Carter also refused any help, insisting he had no injuries aside from some bruises. "Can I help you home?" he asked Julia after the wagon had gone. "I don't think we'll find a cab, but I can walk you there."

"Thank you, but I'll be fine. I'm sure you're anxious to get home."

"I am, rather," he admitted. "If my wife has heard of the accident, she might worry herself to death before I can assure her I'm all right."

"You must tell her you were a hero today," Julia said. "I'm grateful for all the help you gave me."

"*You* are the hero," he insisted. "We're lucky you were here, miss." He tipped his hat and said good-bye, then set off through the crowd.

It was late afternoon now, the sun nearly setting. Exhausted, Julia sat on a bench, gathering her strength for the walk home. She looked down at her gown, which was torn and spattered with dirt and blood. There would be no salvaging it. Unable to spare any money to replace it, Julia would have to make do with the few plain skirts she owned. But she could not feel any regret over the loss—nothing was as important as the knowledge that she'd saved a man's life.

She pulled the bloodstained calling card from her reticule and looked down at it, rereading the words printed on it. *Michael Stephenson, Barrister-at-Law.* Would she ever see him again?

Yes.

By now, the doctors would have sutured the artery shut and tended to his other wounds as well. Julia knew she had done the right thing by staying behind, which had enabled her to offer critical aid to the other passenger. But this did not lessen her disappointment that she hadn't been able to accompany Michael to the hospital and perhaps even watch the surgery. Tomorrow she would go and visit him. Even though she had confidence in the doctors, she still wanted to see for herself that he was safe and on the road to recovery. Her heart would not rest easy until then.

CHAPTER

3

M ICHAEL WASN'T ENTIRELY SURE how he came
to consciousness. Through the haze he sensed a rus-
tling, as if someone were moving nearby. But even
that whisper of sound made his head throb. Keeping his eyes
closed, he inhaled. In that moment, he knew where he was. He
had stayed the night at his sister and brother-in-law's house before,
and their sheets had an unmistakable scent of lavender and lye.

His nose itched, finally forcing him to move. He reached up
with his right hand to scratch the itch, but somehow knocked
himself in the face instead. Letting out a grunt of pain, he opened
his eyes to discover that his hand was swathed in bandages, his
third and fourth fingers held straight by a splint. He stared at
them, his brain unable to decipher what his eyes were taking in.

"Oh ho, you're awake," said a cheerful voice.

Not entirely sure if he could move, and not much willing to
attempt it, Michael tipped his head ever so slightly toward the

voice, just enough to see his brother-in-law standing to the right of the bed.

With a thumb and forefinger from each hand tucked into his waistcoat pockets, David beamed genially at Michael. He always had the air of a kindly uncle, even though he was only ten years older. "How are you feeling?"

Michael grimaced. Everything hurt. "Like I've been trampled by a horse."

"Horse*power* is more accurate," David replied with a smile.

Now it came back to him. He'd been in the train. Standing up to give Corinna a cigarette. At the memory of his sister, he moved sharply, despite the pain it caused, trying to sit up. "Corinna! Is she all right?"

David placed a gentle hand on his chest, coaxing him back down. "Don't fret yourself. She and Miss Maynard came out unscathed, although you are very much the worse for wear."

"You don't have to tell me." Michael relaxed back into the pillows, relieved to know his sister was safe.

David went to the door and opened it, murmuring a few words to a servant who had apparently been standing vigil in the hallway.

"What . . . happened, exactly?" Michael asked, once David had returned to the bedside. His few memories of the event were split into unintelligible fragments.

"You don't remember anything?" David pulled a narrow wooden chair close to the bed and sat down. The chair squeaked as he leaned forward, his face level with Michael's.

Michael started to shake his head but was stopped by a sudden sharp pain to his neck. "No," he murmured instead. "The last thing I remember was standing up to hand Corinna—"

He stopped midsentence, aware of his promise not to tell David about her smoking.

"You were handing her a cigarette," David supplied. He held up a hand to stop Michael from protesting. "I know all about it. She thinks I don't, and that's a fiction I indulge her. I'm not thrilled that she has acquired this habit, but after thirteen years of marriage, I know where it is best not to challenge her." He gave a smile and a dismissive shrug. "Do you remember anything after that?"

Michael closed his eyes, dredging up what memories he could. "A sensation like a hundred knives being thrust into me."

He reached up again, this time with his left hand, which was uninjured. His neck was swathed in bandages as thoroughly as his right hand was. For that matter, so was his head.

"You look like you've been through a battle rather than a railway accident," David remarked, tilting his head to observe him critically. "Quite appalling, actually."

"Good to know," Michael returned dryly. He tried to give a facetious grin, but even that hurt too much.

"So that's all you remember?"

"At that point, I mercifully blacked out from the pain. Did Corinna give you any details?"

"Oh yes. She filled me in thoroughly. There was a collision in the tunnel. The train ahead of yours had stopped, and the driver hadn't had time to set the warning signal in the passage. The conductor of your train applied the brakes as hard as he could. In the process, the train derailed and threw you against the window."

"Was anyone else hurt?"

"There were other injuries, to be sure, but yours took the prize."

This did not reassure Michael the way David had clearly intended. "There was another woman in our carriage—do you know what happened to her?"

"Indeed I do. She tended to your wounds. You would have bled to death, except that she knew how to close up your artery."

Michael might have thought David's statement an exaggeration, but the searing pain in his neck seemed to corroborate it.

"She was reading a medical journal. Is she a nurse? Is that how she knew what to do?"

"Corinna asked her the same thing. The woman said that not only was she a nurse, but she's also in training to become a doctor!"

The tone of David's voice showed how perfectly aware he was of the irony of the situation. There was only one place in England where women could be trained as doctors, and Michael was working for a client who was trying to put it out of business. The powerful Earl of Westbridge was suing one of the lecturers at the school for libel. There were more factors in the case, but the earl's goal was to shut the place down entirely. This was the most important lawsuit Michael had ever worked on, and winning it would be a major advancement in his career.

Michael swallowed, licking his dry lips. "You're saying the woman who helped me is a student at the London School of Medicine for Women?"

"That appears to be the case."

"Did Corinna get the woman's name or any other information about her?"

"I don't believe so. She was focused on getting you out of danger. As soon as you'd gotten through surgery, she insisted on bringing you here. Since then, our own Dr. Hartman has been tending to you. He was quite impressed with the emergency care that young lady gave you. She probably saved your life."

David launched into a further description of the scene. Michael would never have believed any of it, were it not for the very real evidence of his wounds.

That he had been unconscious through it all, his body carried by strangers through the chaos of the station, was the most unsettling part. He disliked not being in control of any situation, much less having his fate determined by others. At least Corinna had been there, watching out for him. He was grateful for that. As for the woman who had been so fortuitously in the carriage with them—and who was also a student at the medical school—Michael couldn't help but think this was a joke foisted upon him by the fates.

"Where is Corinna?"

"She was lying down, but I've sent the footman to tell her you've come 'round."

The bright sunlight visible through the windows indicated it was around midday. Michael had never known Corinna to be the sort of person to take naps. "Is she unwell?"

"Oh, she's quite well. But Dr. Hartman says that, given her condition, we cannot be too careful."

Condition? Now Michael did sit up, and he didn't care what it cost him to do so. Had she received some sort of injury after all? He turned to look at his brother-in-law, but David had a broad smile on his face.

"David, what are you talking about?"

"Ah, here she is now," David said, as the door opened and Corinna walked in. "We can tell you together." He took Corinna's hand and drew her to Michael's side. "When the doctor was checking her over, he made a most excellent discovery. There will be a new addition to this home come July."

There was no mistaking what he meant. Michael immediately turned his gaze to Corinna. Now that he was looking for it, he saw that her midsection was wider, not her usual slim figure. His gaze lifted to her face, expecting to see joy there—or at least pride. Instead, she looked more pinched and drawn than he could ever remember.

"Is everything all right?" he asked anxiously. "Is there anything we should be worried about?"

"Nothing like that," Corinna returned. "I'm fine."

"No, indeed," said David. "Your sister is as healthy as a horse."

Corinna shot him a sour glance. "What a terrible analogy."

"I'm sorry, my love." David gave her hand a kiss. "You know I couldn't think any more highly of you—especially now."

Corinna tensed, but she made an effort to smile. "We are very happy, of course," she said to Michael. "But how are you?" Pulling out of David's grasp, she sat in the chair by Michael's bed. She laid a hand on his forehead, as though he were suffering from fever and not a cracked skull.

"I won't deny I feel pretty beat up at the moment."

"Dr. Hartman said you would pull out of it, but you still had us very concerned. And of course, Miss Maynard has been positively beside herself with worry. The sight of you on the floor of the carriage, with all that blood . . . I believe she was only half a step away from hysteria."

Michael was trying to take in this information, but he was still thinking about Corinna's news. He realized something that at least partially explained her lack of enthusiasm. "Did David say the baby was due in July?"

"Yes, that's right."

"So Lady Amberley's ball . . ."

He knew immediately from her expression that this was the answer. Her eyes had a gleam of suppressed tears. "I will not be attending."

Michael felt the disappointment behind her words. The invitation to this event was a prize Corinna had coveted for years. And now she would not be able to go. He bet that Corinna had suspected before the accident that she was pregnant but had been denying it to herself, unable to come to terms with it for this very reason.

David gave her shoulder a gentle squeeze. "I've told her there's always next year. They're bound to invite us again. And of course, attendance at a mere party does not compare with the joys of starting a family."

Poor David. He meant well, but those were not the words to console Corinna. Michael could only hope she would feel differently once she became a mother.

Corinna stood up. "I will go and get some hot broth made up for you. Dr. Hartman said you should try to eat something once you came around. I'll also dispatch a note to bring him here—I know he'll want to see you."

"Thank you, Corinna. For everything." He did his best to give her some solace with those few words. He could see her absorb his meaning and give a small nod of acknowledgment. Then she hurriedly left the room.

"I will admit this is a surprise," Michael said once Corinna had gone. After thirteen years, it had looked as though the Barkers were destined to remain childless.

"It was long odds," David admitted. "Corinna doesn't allow me to . . . be as *affectionate* to her as often as I might like."

Michael gasped, then coughed to cover it. The last thing he wanted to know about was the particulars of his sister's private life.

David didn't notice; he was too buoyed by happiness. "Midsummer seems the perfect time of year for a baby's arrival."

"Corinna seems less than excited at the prospect," Michael said. "Do you suppose there is more to it than her disappointment at missing the Amberleys' ball?"

"I expect that's just a bit of trepidation about childbirth. Women don't have it easy in that regard, do they? But with all the advances in medicine, I told her there's nothing to worry about. We'll make sure she has the very best doctor."

The very best doctor.

Michael realized he hadn't asked Corinna for more details about the woman who'd helped him on the train. He would do that as soon as he could. After all, she had saved his life. But he

33

had to admit he'd been intrigued by her even before the accident. She'd had an air of confidence and independence that Michael found refreshing. Her unadorned clothing had only accentuated, rather than minimized, how attractive she was. Who was she, and what would make her want to delve into such a formidable field as medicine? Despite all that was going on with the lawsuit against the medical college, if Michael could see this woman again, he wanted very much to do so.

Julia sat reading the newspaper in the spacious parlor of the town home that served as housing for the students at Queen's College.

In another part of the room, four students sat studying together, throwing out questions and answers from their textbook on natural science. Julia barely noticed them. She leaned over the newspaper spread out before her on the table, carefully scanning each column.

There was a long article describing the accident on the Underground and its aftermath, but there was no further information about those who'd been taken to the hospital.

She sighed, pushing away the paper and leaning back in her chair. Lisette Blanco sailed through the door, moving quickly as she always did. Half French and half Spanish, and only five feet tall, Lisette was a continual blur of energy. She made a beeline for Julia's table and plopped into the chair opposite her. Frowning, she pointed at the newspaper. *"Latine legitur, non quidem hodie."*

Julia looked at her askance, still wrapped up in her concerns over Michael Stephenson and in no mood to translate Latin.

Her withering look did nothing to daunt Lisette, who assumed Julia had not understood her. "I said, 'Shouldn't you be working on noun declensions rather than reading the newspaper?'"

"I'm trying to find information about the man I helped after the accident on the Underground yesterday."

Lisette's disapproval was wiped away by eager interest. "You were there? You must tell me what happened!"

In her excitement, Lisette spoke loudly enough to catch the attention of the other students in the parlor. They stopped their conversation and looked at Julia with curiosity.

Julia told them what had happened on the Underground. One of the students looked shocked when Julia spoke of taking the first-class carriage without a proper ticket. Lisette, however, never batted an eyelash. In fact, she gave an approving nod. When Julia told them about the accident and what she'd done to save Michael, Lisette shouted, "Bravo! Now I understand why you expected to read about it in the paper. You saved that man's life!"

"I'm not interested in personal acclaim. I just want to know what happened to him." She picked up Michael Stephenson's card, which was lying on the table. "I have his card, at least. He's a barrister at Gray's Inn. I'm thinking of making inquiries there."

"A barrister?" Lisette plucked the card from Julia's hand. Her eyebrows flew up as she read it. She extended the card with a look of revulsion, as though it were one of the more foul-smelling specimens they'd been studying in natural sciences. "*This* is the man whose life you saved yesterday?"

It came out like an accusation. "Yes," Julia replied, startled at Lisette's tone. She didn't point out the obvious splotches of blood on the card.

Lisette dropped the card on the table in disgust. "Do you realize this man is one of the prosecutors in Dr. Tierney's libel suit?"

Julia's mouth dropped open in surprise. She knew about the lawsuit, of course. One of the lecturers at the medical school, Dr. Tierney, had spoken at a public rally to repeal the Contagious Diseases Acts. This law directed policemen to arrest prostitutes in ports and army towns and force them to be checked for venereal disease. If the women were found to have any diseases, they were to be placed in a locked hospital until cured. The purpose of the acts was to prevent the weakening of the armed forces through the spread of venereal disease, but in reality they placed terrible burdens on women. Dr. Tierney had stated at the rally that the reason the Earl of Westbridge was so adamant in support of the acts was because his own son had died of syphilis contracted while serving in the army. The earl vehemently denied this claim and brought libel charges against Dr. Tierney and the medical college. The amount he was seeking in damages would ruin the school.

Julia picked up the card and scanned it again. She raised her eyes back to Lisette. "I thought the prosecuting attorney was a Mr. Tamblin."

"Mr. Stephenson shares law chambers with Mr. Tamblin and is assisting him. He interviewed several of us who were at the rally."

"He interviewed you?"

"Oh yes. Asked all sorts of questions about what exactly Dr. Tierney said." Lisette pulled open her reticule and withdrew a card from it. "He even left his address in case we should think of more information to bring to him! Such conceit these men have." She brandished the card. It was identical to the one Julia had—minus the bloodstains. "All that money and trouble they're costing the school, trying to keep women from practicing medicine. I wonder what he thinks now—if they even told him it was a female medical student who helped him." Her eyes lit up with amused excitement. "We ought to go to his chambers and confront him about it—we and *all* of the medical students!"

"I don't think he's there. I went to the hospital this morning, but they told me he'd already been discharged and that his sister took him to her house. I have no idea where she lives."

Colleen Branaugh, another of their fellow boarders, said, "I daresay it wouldn't be difficult to find her address. She's married to Mr. David Barker, one of the wealthiest men in Kensington. Although it's 'new money,' which is supposed to make it somehow less real."

"Money is money," another of the women chimed in, to which everyone nodded their heads in agreement.

"And how do you know so much about Mr. Stephenson's sister?" Lisette inquired.

"Mr. Stephenson interviewed me, too," Colleen admitted. "And I was struck by how handsome and personable he was, despite the fact that he's working on this lawsuit. After all, barristers can't always pick their clients, can they? So naturally I wanted to find out more about him."

"*Naturally,*" Lisette repeated with caustic flair. "Colleen Branaugh, why are you searching for a husband? Would you give up a life you can build for *yourself?*"

"I enjoy reading the society pages, that's all," Colleen replied defensively. "I see no harm in that."

"How can we find out their address in Kensington?" Julia said. If there was a way to find Michael Stephenson, she was not going to pass up the opportunity to see him.

CHAPTER

4

MICHAEL SAT LOOKING OUT his bedroom window. The day was cold; he could tell by the scraps of snow lying along the edges of the buildings and by the way pedestrians tugged up their coat collars as they hurried along the street. But the sun was out, providing a measure of warmth that radiated through the windowpanes.

After four days in bed, Michael was glad to be up for a while. He still felt bruised and battered, and his neck hurt like the devil, but he felt a growing sense of restlessness.

Dr. Hartman seemed pleased with his recovery so far. Having just given Michael a thorough examination, he was now packing his stethoscope and other implements into his bag. "You've come through this amazingly well," he pronounced. "I think we can rule out the possibility of lingering effects."

"Good. I am anxious to return home." Like many London barristers, Michael's work and living quarters were at one of the four Inns of Court—in his case, Gray's Inn.

"I think you ought to stay here for at least another few days," Dr. Hartman advised. "There is no evidence of concussion, but your neck should be given time to heal properly. You don't want to put any undue strain on the sutures and risk opening the wound."

Michael opened his mouth to protest, but he paused when he saw a carriage with Laura's family crest pulling up to the town-house. He'd asked Corinna to send a message to Laura, requesting that she not visit him while he was still recovering. And yet she'd come anyway.

Corinna had told him how frantic Laura had been after the accident. He supposed her response showed how much she was growing to care for him. Still, he did not want her to see him looking like a bedraggled invalid. If that was manly pride, then so be it. Until they were engaged, he wanted to show himself in the best light possible.

Turning back to Dr. Hartman, he said, "I think I am feeling a bit weak after all. Perhaps I ought to return to bed."

The doctor nodded in agreement. "Very wise. Mustn't overdo it."

Michael slowly rose from his chair. His valet, who had been standing nearby, took his arm and helped him settle back into bed.

"Will you just let my sister know that I am resting and should not be disturbed?" Michael said, as the doctor picked up his bag and headed for the door.

"Certainly. I'll be back to check on you again tomorrow."

Even though Michael's restlessness had not abated, for the moment he was content to lie here. There was no reason why seeing Laura couldn't wait a few more days.

Julia paused on the sidewalk as a young woman came out of the Barkers' townhouse. Although still half a block away, Julia recognized the blonde who'd been on the train. She had learned from Colleen Branaugh that this was Miss Laura Maynard. Her brother was a viscount, and Colleen had assured Julia she was either Mr. Stephenson's fiancée or on the verge of being so.

Miss Maynard did not see Julia. She appeared wrapped in her thoughts as she strode purposefully to the carriage waiting at the curb. They must not have been pleasant thoughts, as she was frowning. Was this a sign that Michael Stephenson was not doing well? Had he perhaps taken a turn for the worse? Julia had been worried about so many possible complications—infection or damage from loss of blood among them, not to mention a possible concussion.

When the carriage had pulled away, Julia hastened to the door and rang the bell. The butler answered immediately, looking surprised to see another visitor at the house so soon.

She got straight to the point. "Good afternoon. I'm here to inquire after Mr. Michael Stephenson."

The man's eyebrow went up. "I beg your pardon, miss. This is the home of Mr. and Mrs. Barker."

"Yes, I know that. But I'm here to see—"

She paused. It said quite a lot, that lifted brow. Mostly, it displayed an overblown sense of propriety. Julia smiled sweetly and pulled one of her calling cards from her reticule. Thank heavens her benefactor, Mrs. Staunton, had insisted on getting these for her, saying no proper lady should be without them. Julia had no great wish to qualify as a "proper lady"—she had more important things to do—but if it meant being able to see Michael Stephenson, she would act the part.

She extended the card toward the butler and said in the most polished, polite manner she could muster, "I'm here to see Mrs. Barker. Is she at home?"

Looking mollified, the butler accepted the card. The fine card stock on which it was printed might even have been the reason he invited Julia to wait in the front hall while he went to see if Mrs. Barker was "at home."

"Tell her we met a few days ago on the train," Julia called after him. She saw him pause, but as she was now safely inside, she thought it better to share this information rather than risk Mrs. Barker sending her away sight unseen because she didn't recognize the name.

Julia took in her surroundings while she waited. Everything she could see, from the elegant chandelier to the massive ornate mirror, spoke of wealth. Nearly every square inch of wall was covered with photographs and paintings.

After a few minutes, the butler returned, this time with Mrs. Barker leading the way. Julia half expected the tall brunette to look pleased to see her, if only out of gratitude, but it seemed that surprise had overrun any other feelings. Her demeanor seemed wary as she greeted Julia.

It wasn't the reception Julia had planned on. Nevertheless, she gave Mrs. Barker a broad smile. "As you saw from my card, my name is Julia Bernay. I don't think we were properly introduced on the train." She decided against holding out her hand, as this woman did not appear to be the sort who would appreciate such a bold gesture. "I've come to inquire after Mr. Stephenson. I believe he is staying here with you. Naturally I am curious and most anxious to hear how he is getting on. May I see him?"

Mrs. Barker's eyes widened in surprise. "I'm afraid that's not possible. My brother is not well enough to see anyone at present."

Julia remembered the way Miss Maynard had frowned as she left the house. Perhaps she'd been turned away from seeing her beloved. But Julia wasn't paying a social call. "I certainly would not act in any way to worsen his condition. I merely wish—from professional interest, if you will—to see how he is progressing."

Using the word *professional* might not have been the best idea. Mrs. Barker was likely aware of the lawsuit against the school and Michael's involvement in it. Julia understood how that could cause conflicting feelings. On one hand would be gratitude for what Julia had done, and on the other, embarrassment that the person who had saved her brother's life wished to attend the very school her brother was helping to prosecute.

Mrs. Barker did indeed look uncomfortable. "That really is unnecessary. My brother is under a doctor's care now. Dr. Hartman has been practicing for over thirty years. I can assure you, he has the situation well in hand."

"I'm sure he does," Julia replied, although she had a suspicion that if the doctor was old enough to have been in practice that long, he could well be subjecting his patient to all sorts of outdated and unwise procedures. "I would love to speak to Dr. Hartman. Is he here at the moment? He does not by any chance prescribe bloodletting as a form of treatment?"

Mrs. Barker opened her mouth but then closed it again without speaking, looking too shocked to come up with a reply.

"I'd like to see him try," said a man's voice.

Julia looked up to see Michael Stephenson standing at the top of the stairs. Even from this distance, she could see the glint in his eyes as he looked down at her.

"You underestimate our good doctor, madam," he said. "He's very forward thinking, despite his age."

"Michael, you ought not to be out of bed," his sister chided. "You know what Dr. Hartman said—"

"He said it because I told him to." He began to walk down the staircase, holding tightly to the railing and clearly favoring his injured knee.

It was obvious he'd just gotten out of bed. He wore a dressing gown that looked as though it had been hastily tossed on.

A few locks of his hair stood up at odd angles, which was not surprising given that a generous portion of his head was covered in bandages. Julia thought the effect bordered on comical. It was also unnecessary. The bleeding had come primarily from his neck, not his head.

His sister hurried to meet him, trying to take hold of his arm, but he waved her away. Approaching Julia, he said, "Thank you so much for coming to inquire after me, Miss, er—?"

"Bernay. Julia Bernay."

"Miss Bernay." He repeated her name with a little sigh of satisfaction. "I'm so very glad to make your acquaintance."

He thrust out his right hand, then immediately looked both surprised and mortified to remember it was bandaged and splinted. He began to pull it back, but Julia captured it in her hands before he could do so.

She lifted his hand to inspect the splint. "At the time of the accident, I suspected you had fractured one or more of the bones in your fingers. I see Dr. Hartman located the issue." Gently pressing his fingertips, which were all that were visible of his three middle fingers, Julia was pleased to see the skin changing color, which was a sign of adequate circulation. "The blood is flowing freely. The doctor has done an acceptable job with this splint. In a matter of weeks this hand should be good as new. In the meantime, you may need an amanuensis to do your writing for you."

"I shall be sure to pass along your assessment to Dr. Hartman." There was a hint of amusement in his voice.

They were standing quite close, as she still had hold of his hand, but Julia found herself leaning even closer, anxious to get a good look at his neck. She wanted very much to examine the wound, to study how the doctors had repaired it. But it was fully covered by bandages.

"Is something wrong? Please don't tell me I'm bleeding again."

He sounded genuinely worried, but when Julia looked up to meet his gaze, she saw a gleam of laughter in his blue-gray eyes, and his lips quirked.

She was surprised that he didn't seem to be taking her seriously—unlike Mrs. Barker, who was staring daggers at her. Both attitudes, different as they were, annoyed her. She found it hard to suppress her indignation when faced with people who thought women were unable to be competent physicians. How could these two feel that way, after all that had happened?

She released his hand, giving him a stern look. "I suppose Dr. Hartman has also been watching for signs of concussion?"

"Oh yes. He agrees, as does my sister, that I ought to have my head examined on a regular basis. Isn't that right, Corinna?"

Corinna's mouth pursed, and Michael appeared to be suppressing another grin. It was then that Julia understood that he was not laughing at *her*, but rather that he enjoyed teasing his sister.

"Shall we go into the parlor?" Michael suggested. "There is so much I want to talk to you about."

"Michael, I don't think that's wise," Corinna protested. "You don't want to overexert yourself."

"Precisely why we should go into the parlor and sit down." Without waiting for a reply, he started toward the parlor door, pausing only briefly to motion for Corinna and Julia to precede him. Corinna obeyed, although Julia could see it took effort.

Now it was Julia who found herself amused. She suspected there was a lot of push and pull between these two siblings with such strong personalities. The brother seemed to have won this round. Not for the first time, she wondered what it might have been like to have a brother of any kind, let alone a man such as this.

Julia had never seen a parlor quite like this one. It was so stuffed with chairs, furniture, and bric-a-brac that it was a marvel anyone could move in it. Potted plants competed for floor space with bookcases, small tables, and curio cabinets. The walls were covered with paintings and photographs, just as in the front hallway. It was a splendid display of affluence, but Julia was not impressed. She would never feel at ease living in such a fussy place.

Before any of them could be seated, a robust man with thick black hair and generous side-whiskers breezed in, looking vaguely harried. "Ah, Corinna, there you are. Can you get down to the kitchen right away? The footman tells me Mrs. Teague is having a row with the butcher's delivery boy again, and they need you to intervene."

"Oh, not today, of all days," she answered crossly.

Only then did the man become aware of Julia. "Hullo, we've got company." He gave her a friendly smile. "I'm David Barker. How do you do?"

How he could be so affable when he was married to a woman who seemed to be his total opposite was a mystery to Julia.

Michael said, "David, this is Miss Julia Bernay, the woman who saved my life on the Underground."

Mr. Barker's smile broadened. "Are you really? Well, I'm very glad to meet you. What a good thing you found us. We've been trying unsuccessfully to track you down."

"Have you?" After Mrs. Barker's attitude toward her, Julia was amazed to hear this.

"Yes indeed." Glancing at the grandfather clock in the corner, Mr. Barker added, "I do wish I could stay and chat, but the truth is, I must be off." Turning to Michael Stephenson, he explained, "I've a meeting with an important client at the Royal Exchange, and you know how beastly the traffic is. It will take forever in a cab—but then, one cannot risk going on the Underground, eh?"

Chuckling at his own joke, he gave his wife a swift peck on the cheek and a gentle tug on the hand, indicating she should come with him. "Do go see about Mrs. Teague, won't you?"

"Oh, all right." Corinna threw a stern look at her brother, as though daring him to misbehave in some way while she was gone. "I won't be long."

Putting on his top hat, Mr. Barker nodded to Julia. "Good-bye, Miss Bernay. I hope you will call again."

Seeing the sour look on Mrs. Barker's face, Julia couldn't resist. "Thank you, I would like that very much."

The Barkers left the room, and Julia could hear the front door opening and closing. Presumably Mr. Barker was on his way out, while his wife headed downstairs. She asked, "Does this Mrs. Teague often get into rows with the butcher's boy?"

"Only when there is an important dinner party at stake. I've no doubt Corinna will get them sorted out."

"Mr. Barker seems a genial fellow."

"Yes. He keeps my sister on an even keel."

As he spoke, he reached out and braced himself against one of the high-backed chairs. Julia saw him wince a little, and his face turned ashen.

"You should sit down," she directed.

He did not give her any resistance as she took his elbow and urged him onto the chair. "Thank you," he murmured. "Perhaps I have exerted myself a bit too much."

Julia extended a hand toward the bandage on his neck. "Might I take a closer look? I'm very interested to see how the surgeons repaired the wound."

She could see that an objection was on the tip of his tongue, but instead he said, "I was incredibly fortunate you were in that railway carriage. Dr. Hartman says your quick thinking saved me from losing a lot of blood."

Taking this remark as tacit permission, Julia leaned down to begin her inspection. "I'm gratified to hear the doctor has a good opinion of my work."

She carefully pulled aside the dressing to look at his neck wound. The area was swollen and red, but not from infection. It was normal for sutured skin to look like this so soon after surgery. As Julia studied the stitches closely, she could see the doctor had used great skill and care. "This is impressive," she murmured.

"Are you really studying to be a doctor?" Michael sounded more wary than disbelieving.

She began to replace the bandages. "I will be soon. At present, I am enrolled at Queen's College, taking courses to fill in where my basic education was left lacking. I will sit for the matriculation exam to begin my medical studies at the end of June."

"I suppose your father is supporting you in this endeavor?"

Julia gave a little start at this, and Michael grunted as the sticking plaster pulled at his skin. "I beg your pardon," she said, removing her hands from the bandages. "I have a benefactor. It is not my father."

"He must be quite generous."

Arrested by this comment, Julia did not bother to correct him that her benefactor was a woman. "Why do you say that?"

"I just thought it was a bit odd . . . that is . . . do you typically ride in first-class carriages?"

"I was in a hurry. The other carriages were full." Julia had long ago learned the art of bluster and bravado. It was often the only way to get the doctors in the hospital to listen to her suggestions. She did not hesitate to employ it now. That was all he needed to know. "And yes, my benefactor is very generous," she added for good measure. It was also true. Mrs. Staunton had been more than kind in that regard—while she'd had the wherewithal to be so.

"Can you lean more toward the light?" she asked. "Although Dr. Hartman has been observing you for signs of concussion, one can never be too careful." She leaned forward, her face mere inches from his as she tried to get a good look at his pupils. "Even small bumps on the head can have serious consequences—"

She was interrupted by the sound of the parlor door opening. Irritated, she glanced up, expecting to see Mrs. Barker. Instead, it was the butler.

The smirk on his face irked her even more. "I beg your pardon, sir," he said dryly.

Julia realized that to the untrained eye, this appeared to be a compromising situation. She straightened with unhurried casualness to signal that what she'd been doing was entirely proper and she had not a shred of guilt about it.

Michael sighed. "Yes, what is it?"

"Mr. Tamblin has come to call on you, sir. Shall I bring him in here?"

Mr. Tamblin! The chief legal arm of the man attacking the college was in this house. Julia hoped he would be brought in here, as she wanted very much to see him.

To her disappointment, Michael answered, "No, don't do that. Ask him to wait in the study. I'll be along shortly."

The butler gave a nod and left the room. Michael rose slowly from the chair, looking as though he felt plenty of pain from his injuries. Julia took his arm to help him up. This brought only a smile to his lips. Or perhaps it was a grimace. He leaned heavily on her arm until he found his balance.

"My apologies, but I must spend a few minutes talking with this gentleman. He is my employer, and we are in the midst of—that is, there is a lot going on at the moment." He gave her a sidelong glance. Perhaps he suspected she was aware of his involvement with the lawsuit against the school. "Will you wait here? I am aware—and grateful—that you saved my life. I wanted to discuss—that is, if there is anything I can do to repay you . . ."

Julia looked at him, wondering if he knew what an open-ended and potentially dangerous offer that was. He knew the lawsuit made them adversaries, at least by proxy.

"Yes, I'll wait." She wasn't going to turn down his offer to continue this conversation.

He gave her a brief, grateful smile and left the room.

Alone in the parlor, Julia decided to look around. Many of the objects on the shelves looked like they'd been imported from foreign lands. The Barkers were either world travelers or else they enjoyed buying goods from those who were.

She studied a colorful painting of punt boats along the River Cam with the venerable buildings of Cambridge University in the background. Julia had never been there, but she had seen photographs. From her Latin studies, she recognized the university's motto inscribed on a gold plate attached to the frame: *Hinc lucem et pocula sacra.* She knew it could be translated as "From this place, we gain enlightenment and precious knowledge." Was Mr. Barker an alumnus? Or perhaps Michael?

She wondered what was happening in the study. How she wished she could be a fly on the wall, hearing what the two barristers were talking about! Especially if they were discussing strategies for winning the libel case against Dr. Tierney. Julia toyed with the idea of crossing the hall and confronting them about why they were so willing to bring destruction on a school whose only focus was to help people. She even advanced halfway across the room toward the door before she made herself stop and reflect. Most likely, such an action would only get her tossed from the house.

As she pondered these things, her attention was arrested by a set of carved figurines inside one of the curio cabinets. Drawing closer, she saw that they were chess pieces sitting atop a finely inlaid chessboard. However, the figurines were not in the standard shapes. Instead of knights, queens, and castles, she was looking at the long neck and head of a giraffe with its two short horns, a woman with a pot on her head, and grass huts. Fascinated, she studied the entire set closely. The king had an elaborate head-dress, and the pawns had rings in their ears and broad noses. The entire board was inspired by images from Africa.

It was a timely reminder that Julia should keep her mind focused on her future. She was going to complete her studies, and she was going to Africa someday. Whatever happened with the court case, surely the school would survive. And even if it didn't, she would find some other way to qualify as a doctor before she left Europe. No matter what obstacles lay in wait along the way.

Michael paused before opening the door to the study, catching his breath and giving his head time to clear. He was dismayed at how merely walking across the hall had exhausted him. Used to fending for himself, he did not have the patience to be an invalid.

Aside from the physical stress, his interview with Miss Bernay had muddled his senses as well. While she'd been inspecting his injuries, he'd been overwhelmingly aware of her nearness. Her hands were cool and businesslike, but her touch had affected him with contradictory sensations of well-being and a curious kind of agitation. And she smelled of soap. Not those floral scents favored by most women he knew—just plain, tart, astringent soap. Everything about her signaled that she was a straightforward and practical woman. One who had not the slightest qualms about coming into close proximity with virtual strangers. He'd never had a woman that close to him who did not have some other thing in mind.

All of these things left no doubt that she was every inch the medical professional she claimed to be. And yet this was curiously belied by her physical appearance—a young woman with a trim figure, expressive brown eyes that tended more toward almond-shaped than round, and an angular face softened by full red lips that could draw up into an appealing bow when she pursed them in serious thought—as she'd done while examining him. Even now, Michael found himself smiling at the memory of the butler's face when he'd walked in on them. What did he think had been going on? It was not difficult to guess. Perhaps it would get back to Corinna in one fashion or another. The butler talked to the housekeeper, who talked to the ladies' maid. He ought to be concerned at the possible impact of such gossip, but for now, he merely shrugged it off and went into the study.

Noah Tamblin, Queen's Counsel, had the precise appearance and demeanor of a man befitting his title. With graying hair and a face lined with age, he exuded the dignified wisdom of a man who thoroughly knew the legal system after spending decades working in it. Just now, though, he looked genuinely appalled as he saw Michael. "Stephenson, you look awful."

Only then did Michael remember he was still in his dressing gown with his hair askew and his face unshaven. How odd that he hadn't wanted Laura to see him this way but had completely forgotten about it while he'd been with Julia. "As you can see, I am still convalescing." He lifted his bandaged right hand. "I'd shake your hand, but . . ."

Tamblin shook his head in sympathy. "At least you are up and about. As soon as I found out what happened, I came straightaway to see you, but you hadn't regained consciousness yet. Your sister told me the details. You were lucky there was a nurse on the train who knew what to do."

"Yes, I was lucky," Michael agreed. He reached up to touch the bandages at his neck, thinking of Julia. Tamblin had used the word *nurse* to describe her. It appeared that when Corinna had related the incident to Tamblin, she hadn't included the interesting detail that the *nurse* was planning to one day become a doctor. If she had, what would Tamblin think if he knew the woman in question was even now in the parlor? Would he think an enemy had stormed the gates? Perhaps Michael should view it that way as well. Could it really be coincidence that she'd been on that train with him? Or had she been following him for some reason? That thought was not a little discomforting.

"So what's the prognosis?" Tamblin asked.

"Everything seems to be on the mend." Michael had to stifle a grimace as the various aches he felt everywhere belied that statement. "I expect to be able to return to work in a week or so."

Tamblin gave a nod of satisfaction. "I'm relieved to hear it. You are critical to our work. You are hands down the best devil I've ever had."

Michael had been working hard to make a name for himself as a devil, which was the title given to a junior barrister who did much of the paperwork and kept cases on their slow march through the sludge of the legal system. Success in this arena was a significant step toward furthering his legal career.

Tamblin was still studying him closely. "As I recall, the day before this unfortunate accident, you went to Buxton. What happened? Was it a success?"

"It was." Michael had gone to interview the doctor in charge of a private sanatorium in the countryside where John Morton, the Earl of Westbridge's son, had spent the last three of his forty-five years. Michael had taken a train there. He'd returned home late on the evening before the accident, so he hadn't had time to give Tamblin a report.

Still feeling light-headed, Michael eased into one of the two leather chairs next to the fireplace.

Tamblin took a seat in the opposite chair but leaned forward eagerly as he asked, "What happened? Was Dr. Gale willing to sign the affidavit?"

"Oh yes. Dr. Gale spoke quite freely, giving me an entire list of everything Morton had wrong with him, maladies both physical as well as mental. But nothing at all related to syphilis, of course."

"Hmm, yes. That's good. Another brick in the wall for us."

Tamblin spoke as though he hadn't expected this outcome from the beginning. But why shouldn't he? From the day two years ago when Morton had been found drowned in the pond on the sanatorium's grounds, the doctor had maintained that it was an accident. Morton had not been in control of his mental faculties due to a fever. Morton had been prone to reoccurrences of malaria ever since he'd first contracted it as an army officer in South Africa.

All of this information was public knowledge. But there were also rumors that the real reason for Morton's actions was insanity brought on by advanced syphilis. He might even have deliberately committed suicide. This was the accusation that the Earl of Westbridge was fighting with this libel suit. From Michael's point of view, the whole thing boiled down to nothing more than an attempt to keep scandal from besmirching the family name. To some extent, Michael could respect this. Hadn't he and Corinna spent these past ten years fighting to regain the reputation their own father had ruined? The difference, of course, was that the Stephensons were not trying to hide the ugly truth, only to move beyond it. Although he was working hard to win this case for the earl, Michael suspected there was a good bit of cover-up going on regarding what really happened.

One hint of this was the manner in which Dr. Gale was so willing to lay out in public all of Morton's supposed maladies. Michael was far from an expert on this subject, and yet it seemed to him a blatant breach of confidentiality. The doctor had shown Michael he was ready and willing to do anything to help Lord Westbridge win his case. It was entirely possible he was on the earl's payroll. Or was that merely the cynical view? Perhaps the official version of events had been correct. On the other hand, Michael had noticed that the doctor had been wearing a very expensive waistcoat of embroidered silk, and that he'd pulled out a fine gold watch to check the time as they'd been concluding their interview.

Was it possible that doctors could be bought and sold, as many men in other professions were? Michael had always thought they'd be too altruistic to accept bribes. But perhaps no one was truly immune from the desire for gain. He couldn't help but wonder what motivated Julia Bernay to become a doctor. He would bet that it wasn't money, although he couldn't say how he knew this.

Tamblin rose from his chair. "I don't want to keep you from your rest. We need you back at full strength as soon as possible." As the two made their way to the front door, Tamblin added, "His lordship knows about the accident, and he asked me to pass along his wishes for a speedy recovery. He is aware that your work on this lawsuit has been invaluable."

"Thank you, sir." Michael threw a glance at the parlor door. It was ajar, and he saw that Julia Bernay was still there. She was studying the contents of a curio cabinet.

She turned as Tamblin spoke, and her forehead crinkled. It wasn't difficult to surmise what thoughts would be going through her mind if she'd heard Tamblin praising him for their expected victory over the medical school.

Michael reasoned that it was equally likely that she was unaware who Tamblin was. He had no idea how much she knew of the court case or the people involved. Her look of irritation might merely be caused by the fact that he'd kept her waiting. He certainly had seen a similar look on his sister's face a time or two.

With a few final words, Tamblin left, and Michael gratefully closed the door after him.

"Thank you for waiting," he said as he returned to the parlor.

"Was that Mr. Noah Tamblin?"

"Yes, that's right." He tried to appear nonchalant. "Do you know him?"

"I know *of* him." Now it was clear that her look was one of flat disdain.

He met her stare evenly. "Perhaps now you are sorry you saved my life."

She drew back in surprise. "Never! Don't you know the Hippocratic Oath and its tenet of doing no harm?"

"You are not yet a doctor," he pointed out.

"I will be, and I do my best to live by every principle of the oath now."

He was tempted to admire her sense of purpose, but he was still not entirely sure of her. "So I suppose you keep all of your dealings and associations honest and aboveboard?"

"Naturally."

"You would not, say, have had an ulterior motive for being in the same carriage as me that day? Something to do with this lawsuit?"

This seemed to genuinely surprise her. "What kind of motive?"

"You know of my involvement with a legal matter that threatens the medical school."

"But I didn't know that when I boarded that train. I had no idea who you were. I was on my way to a lecture, that was all."

Her eyes shifted away briefly, and Michael had the feeling there was something she wasn't telling him. "I suppose you ended up missing that lecture."

"Yes. But there will be lots more in the future. Especially after I become a student at the school."

It was not a mere statement, but a challenge. In all likelihood, every other woman associated with that college had the same steely determination. Michael had gleaned that much from his work on the lawsuit already.

"You asked earlier what you could do for me," Julia Bernay said. "How you could repay me for saving your life."

Michael tensed. He couldn't believe he'd spoken so hastily. Although he'd been sincere, he had not intended to couch his offer in such broad terms. "You did say quite plainly that your actions stemmed only from your desire to help," he reminded her.

Her lips pressed together briefly, but the turned-up corners of her mouth indicated this was from amusement. "Are you worried that I shall ask for 'half your kingdom'?"

"Well, I do seem to be at your mercy, just at present."

She looked at him intently. "*Quod in iuventute non discitur, in matura aetate nescitur.*"

Taken aback, he murmured, "I beg your pardon?"

She repeated the phrase. "It's Latin. Do you know what it means?"

"Of course. 'What is not learned in youth is not known when fully grown.'"

"Very good." She spoke for all the world as though she were a schoolmistress. In reality, her pronunciation wasn't very good, although she had spoken the sentence with correct syntax. "Do you know Latin, then?"

Michael stared at her, unable to imagine why the conversation was moving in this direction. "I do."

"I mean, *really* know it. Thoroughly versed in grammar and familiar with the classics."

He couldn't resist. After all, if she was going to boast about her commitment to medicine, he could match her with his qualifications for practicing law. Achieving the highest scores in his major field of study had been an important early milestone in his career. "A thorough knowledge of Latin is indispensable to my profession. I took a first in the classical tripos at Cambridge."

"That *is* impressive." Once more she glanced away, and this time Michael saw that she was looking at the painting of Cambridge that Corinna had bought out of pride for her brother.

"Might I ask why you are so interested in my academic life?"

Her gaze returned to him. "Because I am asking you to tutor me in Latin."

Michael began to worry that his injuries were somehow affecting his hearing. "You want me to do what?"

"In order to pass the matriculation exam, I need to translate a Latin passage and answer detailed questions on Latin grammar. There are other subjects, too, of course, such as algebra and English history. But Latin is my weakest subject."

"I can believe that."

She responded to his deprecating remark with a stinging glare. "So will you do it?"

"But I am not qualified to teach Latin."

"Didn't you just tell me you took a first? Congratulations, by the way. That is an accomplishment to be proud of."

Was she trying to flatter him now? She seemed to be trying every tactic possible. "Knowing it and teaching it are two different things. However, I will gladly pay for a tutor for you." It was the least he could do, and it would be little to pay in exchange for what she had done.

She gave him a look midway between hurt and disappointment. "Would you pay someone else to discharge a personal debt—and a moral obligation?" She shook her head. "Really, Mr. Stephenson, I had higher expectations from a man of your caliber."

This had to be some kind of ruse. He could not believe she was speaking raw truth about her opinion of him, any more than she truly believed the nonsense she was putting forth about moral obligation. Who even spoke of such things nowadays? Michael's life had been about striving to get what he deserved, and working even harder to lay hold of the things he didn't. But this woman gave the impression of totally believing her words. If she was lying, she was better at it than anyone he'd ever met. Given the sorts of people he'd had dealings with as a barrister, that would be saying quite a lot.

"I've already assured you of my deepest gratitude. Why would I offer you a second-rate teacher"—he pointed to himself—"when I can make sure you obtain the best? How would that be neglecting my moral obligation?"

"I do not think you would be second-rate. You can teach me the techniques you used to pass your exam with flying colors. I saved your life. You have stated that you would like to pay me back. It seems to me that such a debt should not be paid by proxy."

This woman had very little in the way of subtlety, yet she was alarmingly persuasive. She would be a worthy opponent in a court of law. He had the feeling she'd used her forceful brand of persuasion to mow down opponents in the medical field in this same fashion. He spared a moment to feel sorry for those men. He should perhaps be glad that his profession was not yet open to women.

Yet he still had one argument left. "Spending time with you will have the appearance of a conflict of interest. It could jeopardize my work. After saving my physical life, will you now ask me to sacrifice my livelihood in return?"

"There is as yet no official connection between me and the School of Medicine."

"Do you know any of the students or teachers there? Have you met them, spent any time with them?"

"I have spent some time with them," she admitted.

"That's really why you're here, isn't it?" he said, seizing on her words. "You're after some kind of retribution."

"Certainly not." She looked sincerely appalled at this suggestion, but Michael had seen enough displays of false emotion in the courtroom to know he should not take anything at face value.

"Then why are you asking me to teach you Latin?"

"I already explained my reasons. This need only be between us. I certainly will not tell anyone else if you think it best." She pierced him with a look that was all fiery challenge.

Absurdly, Michael could not help noticing the freckles along her nose and upper cheeks. It was disconcerting that a woman like this should have freckles. It was not the complexion he normally associated with strong, no-nonsense women.

Heaven help him. He was contemplating an association with someone too close to the adversary for comfort, a woman he barely knew, *and* he would be counting on her to keep a secret.

Nothing good could come from any of this.

He could hear his sister in the hallway speaking to a servant. She would no doubt enter the parlor at any moment. Thoughts raced through his mind, careening into a jumbled mass at the forefront of his consciousness. Interestingly, the effect was not too different from the moment his head had slammed through that carriage window.

First, he did not have the time to be a schoolgirl's tutor.

Second, the tongue-lashing he'd endure from his sister would be as painful as anything he'd experienced in the accident. He'd already seen jealousy—jealousy!—in his sister's eyes, which he assumed could only be on Laura's account. He would have to quell her fears on that subject.

Third, and most importantly, this woman had a personal and contrary interest in the outcome of a lawsuit that was critically important to Michael's career. Spending any time at all with her, much less hour upon hour of giving Latin lessons, would be asking for an exponentially large amount of trouble. Michael was on the verge of obtaining everything he'd been chasing since his father's death. It would be folly to do anything to endanger his ultimate success.

In short, it was entirely out of the question.

Except that she *had* saved his life.

She had appealed to his sense of honor. Somehow, she'd managed to find it, despite his misgivings.

He also realized he *wanted* to see her again, despite the problems it would cause. After all, who wouldn't be fascinated by someone who had saved his life? Especially a woman like this, with so many appealing contradictions?

Therefore, he did the only sensible thing. He threw all caution to the wind.

"All right. I'll do it."

CHAPTER

6

J ULIA HASTENED DOWN THE STREET, dodging the
other pedestrians. She was going to be late for her algebra
lecture if she didn't move swiftly. But it had been worth it.
She didn't know what had inspired her to ask for Latin tutoring
from Michael Stephenson. She only had a sense, deep in her soul,
that this was what the Lord wanted her to do.

Barely managing to squeeze between a streetlamp and a vendor
with a coal-heated cart of meat pies, she turned the corner onto
Harley Street and raced the final half block to the main building
of Queen's College. She pulled open the large oak door and hurried down the hallway, just making it to her seat as Mr. Johnston
was beginning his algebra lecture.

He eyed Julia as she plopped down breathless next to Lisette.
"You are very nearly late, Miss Bernay."

"Yes, sir. Very nearly." With a smile that she hoped was appeas-
ing, she leaned forward, signaling that she was ready to focus on

his every word, ready to learn. She hoped he would not realize that she had neglected to bring her algebra book with her.

He turned to address the class. "All right, we are going to begin where we left off yesterday, on page 161, with some applications for quadratic equations. . . ."

For the past ten months, Julia had focused diligently on her studies, not caring a whit about algebra for its own sake but knowing it was one of the hurdles to overcome in order to get to medical school. But today she found it nearly impossible to concentrate. Her thoughts kept returning to her meeting with Michael Stephenson.

Not only was her mind at ease that he was recovering from the accident, but now things had taken a most interesting turn. She could hardly believe he had agreed to her request. If he truly was doing it out of moral obligation—an argument she'd thought up on the spur of the moment—then he was, at heart, an honorable man. She would not do anything to damage his career, no matter whom he worked for. She could not help thinking that if God had opened a door for her to receive this much-needed tutoring, then whatever it led to could only be for the best. Already her mind was buzzing forward to next week, when they would have their first lesson.

It wasn't until later, when Mr. Johnston had put the ladies in pairs to work together on solving a problem, that Julia began to consider what a challenge it was going to be to keep her future meetings with Michael a secret.

Lisette nudged her and whispered, "So what happened? You must tell me!"

"Things went well." As much as possible, Julia was determined to stick to the truth.

"So you saw him? Spoke with him?"

"Yes."

"*Merveilleux!*" Lisette nearly bounced in her seat from excitement. "Did you point out to him that he is alive today thanks to a woman with medical training?"

"Mr. Stephenson is fully cognizant of the debt he owes me."

"I don't suppose it changed his mind about the case, though."

"We did not discuss the merits of the lawsuit," Julia replied, which was true. "However, I will keep praying that our meeting today will have an impact on him somewhere down the line."

At the mention of prayer, Lisette rolled her eyes. "We don't need prayer!" she hissed. "We need action!"

"Shh!" Julia admonished, pointing to where Mr. Johnston stood just within earshot as he answered a question from a student at another table. Something in Lisette's agitated tone must have reached him, for he turned and glanced in their direction. Julia tapped the paper with her pencil to bring Lisette's focus back to the problem they were supposed to be solving. For Mr. Johnston's benefit, she said just loudly enough to be heard, "In comparing these two functions, I believe the pattern could be that the coefficient for x is minus the coefficient for y. . . ."

Once Mr. Johnston's attention had turned away from them, Julia continued quietly, "Prayer and action are not mutually exclusive, you know."

But Lisette only repeated "Prayer!" with a scoff, adding, "I still say we ought to storm his office."

"What good would that do? They work for Lord Westbridge. I'm sure his lordship could hire any number of lawyers to pursue his ends."

Lisette murmured in disgust, but she couldn't deny the truth of what Julia was saying. They returned to their work, the subject closed for now.

The conversation showed Julia how important it was that she act with discretion. She was going to keep her promise, and she was going to ensure that Michael Stephenson kept his. It would be wrong of her to endanger his livelihood. As a barrister, he had to do his utmost to represent whoever hired him. Still, Julia would continue to pray that her actions could impact the outcome of the case for the better. How this would happen, she did not know, but a few insurmountable odds did not diminish her outlook. That was what miracles were for, after all.

"Michael, you cannot tell me you are serious."

Corinna sank onto the sofa and looked at him, aghast. Michael wasn't sure he'd ever seen her so pale. He wanted to blame it on the pregnancy, but even if that were true, his news could not have helped matters. He was finally well enough to return to his own lodgings, but he had to ask this one favor of Corinna before he left.

A maid entered the room, bringing the tea service, which gave Michael an excuse not to answer right away. He waited until the maid had finished setting up everything and departed, and then he shut the door so that he and Corinna could talk without anyone overhearing.

"Corinna, we cannot deny what Miss Bernay did for me. It was a massive stroke of good luck that she was there—some might even call it providential."

Corinna gave a little sniff. Like Michael, she did not worry overly much about ascribing supernatural causes to life's random situations.

"Aren't you grateful that she saved your only brother's skin?" he asked.

"You know I am." A strained look in her eyes gave more than a hint of the devastation she would have felt if Michael died. "It's just that this situation has brought a new set of worries."

He sat next to her on the sofa. "What worries?"

She set about pouring a cup of tea, her movements smooth, almost mechanical, as she performed the task she'd done countless times. As though she were taking comfort in the routine. Only the slight shake of her hand as she held the cup out to Michael betrayed her true emotions.

"Don't you find it galling that she requires this *favor* of you in return? I don't see anything very altruistic in that."

It was hard for Michael not to point out how often Corinna had done kindnesses with a full expectation of getting something in return. But at the moment he wanted to win over his sister, not roil her. "Whatever her reasons, the fact remains that I owe her a great debt. I found I was . . . well, honor-bound to say yes."

"You are honor-bound to do the job Lord Westbridge is paying you for! Not to play tutor to some woman who wants to hold you under obligation. Won't she try to influence you? Is she trying to find some way to ruin the libel suit? What would that do to your career? To everything you've been working for?"

Michael wiped a hand through his hair. "Do you imagine I haven't thought of these things already? I know what a fine line I will be treading. But she is not actually a student at the medical school, so there is no legal reason why I must keep a distance from her. And consider that she might well have asked for much more than this. It seems a very light thing indeed, compared with what might have been."

Corinna began to pour milk into her tea. "I still don't like it. How will you keep this news from spreading? You can't sit with her in your chambers, and certainly not someplace like the London library. Anybody might see you there."

"I'm glad you and I agree on that point, at least. I would like to hold the lessons here."

Corinna set the little pitcher of milk down with a clatter. "What did you say?"

"Perhaps in this parlor? I wouldn't want to tie up David's study, as he often has meetings there with his clients."

His sister merely stared at him. "I see what you are after, Michael Stephenson. You want to include me in this scheme so that I can say nothing against it."

"It's nothing of the sort, I promise. I thought this might assuage your concerns. You will be able to see exactly what is happening." He took his sister's hand. "I promise I will not throw away the gains we've worked for. But I am asking you for this favor. I beg that you will at least consider doing it out of love for me. If you give me the benefit of the doubt on this, I will be forever grateful."

As much as the two of them enjoyed sparring with one another, Michael knew that whenever he appealed to her in this way, her tender love for him—which bordered on motherly at times, given that she had in many ways fulfilled that role in his life—could not be denied. He saw her face visibly soften, felt her hand relax in his. Were her eyes growing a bit misty as well?

She gave a sigh. "All right. But you cannot meet here on Tuesdays or Thursdays, for those are my at-home days for receiving callers."

Michael exhaled in relief. If he had not been able to persuade her, he had no idea what he would have done. "Agreed."

Corinna withdrew her hand, ostensibly to tuck a stray bit of hair back in her overly tidy bun. He saw a tiny smile break her somber countenance. It held a hint of triumph, which immediately raised Michael's suspicions.

"Corinna, what are you thinking?"

She smoothed the folds of her gown and picked up her teacup. "I was just thinking how marvelous it is that you are up and about. Does this mean you'll be attending my dinner party tomorrow night? Miss Maynard is coming, and she's anxious to see you again."

One thing he knew very well about his sister was that she rarely gave out favors without asking something in return. He'd thought perhaps this one time things had been different. He ought to have known better.

Her request also confirmed that she feared Julia might pose a threat to his relationship with Laura. He had to reassure her that was not possible. "Yes, Corinna, I will be at your party. By the way, did I tell you I am having lunch with Viscount Delaford next week?"

That bit of news changed Corinna's whole demeanor. "You are?" she said eagerly. "Where?"

"At the club. Don't get too excited just yet. Think of this as . . . the preliminary negotiations."

"But still!" Corinna was beside herself with joy. "You and Laura will be engaged soon. I just know it!"

Michael felt almost guilty for so easily swaying the course of the conversation to something that would distract his sister from her worries. But if it kept her from opposing his plans for the Latin lessons, it was worth it.

CHAPTER

7

JULIA WALKED DOWN THE MAIN HALL of the London School of Medicine for Women. Although she had been to the school a few times since her arrival in London, it still gave her a thrill whenever she entered this building. Today was even more exciting, because she was here at the request of Dr. Elizabeth Garrett Anderson. Julia had long been in awe of this woman, who had done so much to advance the cause of women in medicine. In addition to being cofounder of the school and one of its teachers, Dr. Anderson had her own busy practice and worked with several clinics. Julia didn't know why she'd been invited to this meeting, but she hoped it pertained to her plans to enter the school in the fall. She could hardly wait to have the opportunity to learn from teachers such as Dr. Anderson, who had so much knowledge and experience.

The door to Dr. Anderson's office was open. As Julia approached, she could see the doctor was seated at her desk. Another woman sat opposite her, with her back to the door. She was leaning forward, her elbows practically on the desk, and she and Dr. Anderson were in deep discussion.

Julia gave a light tap on the door. "I hope I'm not interrupting?"

Dr. Anderson motioned her forward. "Welcome, Miss Bernay. Please come in and close the door behind you, if you would."

The other woman turned as Julia entered, regarding her with curiosity. Julia returned the look with equal interest. She was a young woman of Julia's age, and her face was covered in smallpox scars. Dr. Anderson introduced her as Lady Edith Morton.

Lady Edith frowned, and Dr. Anderson added, "She prefers to be addressed simply as Miss Morton." The casual way she said it hinted that she considered these niceties irrelevant. "Of course, in another year we'll be referring to her as Dr. Morton."

"Exactly right," said Miss Morton with an air of satisfaction. She extended a hand to Julia. "How do you do?"

Despite Miss Morton's air of self-confidence, Julia could see a wariness in her eyes, as though bracing herself for the usual alarm or distaste a person might show when seeing her scarred face for the first time. But Julia did not hesitate to return her handshake warmly. "I am happy to meet you! I understand you are a stellar student."

"Thank you. It's true—my father made the mistake of over-educating me when I was young."

The bitterness beneath the sarcasm was impossible to miss, a sign that what Julia had heard about the acrimony between Edith and her father, the Earl of Westbridge, was true. Most people believed the earl's anger over Edith's decision to study medicine was the real reason he was trying to close the school. Julia admired Miss Morton for persevering in obtaining her medical license despite the powerful opposition of her father.

Dr. Anderson said, "Miss Bernay, I invited you here in the hope that you can tell us about the accident on the Underground and the events that followed. We have naturally read about it in the paper." She pointed to a newspaper lying on her desk. It was folded open to the same article Julia had scoured on the day after the incident. "However, I've been led to understand by one of your fellow students, Miss Lisette Blanco, that the newspaper lacks certain details that would be of interest to us here at the school."

Lisette had come to see Dr. Anderson? Julia hoped that wasn't Lisette's idea of *action*. She was not entirely pleased with having been put on the spot like this, but she had to admit that the medical school would want to know the story. "I would be happy to tell you about my experience."

Miss Morton was studying her with clear blue eyes that were strikingly set off by her shiny, dark brown hair. She must have been beautiful before her face was disfigured by smallpox. Red bumps, as well as pockmarks, covered fully half her face.

"Does that blemish interfere with your eyesight?" Julia asked, leaning forward to get a better look at Miss Morton's left eye, which sagged at the outer edge from the pox scars.

Miss Morton's brows rose in astonishment.

"Oh! I beg your pardon," Julia exclaimed, realizing belatedly how rude the question must sound. "I truly meant no offense. It's just that I saw several smallpox cases when I worked at the hospital in Bristol. We had a case where a pustule formed on the cornea—"

She was interrupted by Miss Morton's laugh. "Miss Bernay, I like you very much already."

To which Dr. Anderson added, "I can see you have the makings of a true physician, Miss Bernay. Medical interest overrides everything else, including the rules of polite conversation."

"There is no offense taken," Miss Morton assured Julia. "I bear these marks with pride, for it was my illness and the treatments and issues related to my recovery that spurred my interest in medicine. And the answer to your question is no, thank God. My eyesight was spared, even if my face was not."

"Perhaps we might get back to the subject at hand?" Dr. Anderson suggested.

Julia nodded, still feeling a little embarrassed. But Miss Morton was smiling.

Dr. Anderson said, "I was alarmed when Miss Blanco told me one of our prospective students had been involved in the accident. However, I was also impressed to hear of your actions in the aftermath."

"I do feel it was fortuitous that I was on the train that day. I would not have been there if I hadn't been trying to get to that lecture by Dr. Stahl. The Lord does seem to work in mysterious ways!"

"So he does," Dr. Anderson replied, but it seemed to Julia that her tone was noncommittal. Pointing to the newspaper, she said, "This article describes a nurse who splinted the leg of an injured woman. That was you?"

"Yes." Julia felt a little surge of pride that her medical abilities were already being noticed, and she wasn't even a student here yet.

Dr. Anderson absently gave the paper a little nudge as she focused on Julia. "Miss Blanco informed me that you helped another person, too. Someone known to this school. I'm curious as to why that bit of information did not make it into the paper."

"Although we have several theories," Miss Morton interjected.

"Why don't you go over everything from the beginning?" Dr. Anderson prompted.

The two ladies listened with interest as Julia described the accident and the measures she'd taken to keep Michael Stephenson's bleeding in check until the doctor arrived. She explained that, at the time, she had no idea who he was. "Not that it would have made a difference," she insisted. "I will treat anyone in need."

"Yes, that is our calling," Dr. Anderson agreed. "But this brings me to the question I am most anxious to ask. Does Mr. Stephenson know of your forthcoming attachment to this school?"

"Yes."

"And according to Miss Blanco, you went to see him afterward. What happened then?"

Julia described her visit, saying only that she'd briefly seen Mr. Stephenson and was able to assure herself he was recovering well. "This Dr. Hartman seems proficient enough," she declared. Seeing Dr. Anderson smile at this, and added anxiously, "Did I misspeak?"

Dr. Anderson shook her head. "I was simply amused to hear your assessment. Dr. Hartman has a stellar reputation in the medical community."

"Well, I'm glad to hear that," Julia answered with feeling. Perhaps too much feeling, for she saw the other two women trade glances. "I mean, it's criminal for anyone to be mistreated by someone incompetent," she clarified.

"You are correct on that point," Dr. Anderson agreed. "Did anything else happen while you were there? How did they receive you?"

"They managed to be grateful and yet keep a distance at the same time. It is a delicate situation, what with Mr. Stephenson's involvement in the libel suit."

"You are too generous to defend their side," Edith remarked with a scowl.

"I am glad you were able to confirm that Mr. Stephenson's wounds were not ultimately fatal and that he will recover fully," Dr. Anderson said. "If the worst had happened, they might have found an excuse to blame the school for it."

"Oh! I hadn't thought of that! I wanted only to help. I didn't think anyone would try to draw a connection between my actions and the medical school."

"It would have been impossible to foresee. Even so, we are in a precarious position for several reasons. I do not approve of Dr. Tierney's actions or the things she said that brought on the libel suit. I don't think such remarks about a member of the aristocracy can help her cause. However, we cannot remove her from teaching at the school, lest that be seen as an admission that we believe in her guilt. We must do all we can not to harm our chances of prevailing in this suit. In addition, I am on record as having supported the acts when they were passed some years ago."

"You are?" Julia couldn't help but be surprised. She'd assumed all the women here were against the acts.

"I have treated many innocent women who were infected with venereal disease by husbands who consorted with prostitutes— either before or after their wedding night. I have seen their anguish, both emotionally and physically. As distasteful as the measures are, I am willing to support them if it will help eradicate this terrible problem."

Julia turned to see Edith's reaction to this, but her expression was unreadable.

"It's good that things turned out well," Dr. Anderson continued. "I only wish there was some way to keep abreast of how Mr. Stephenson continues on. I worry, lest there be any delayed reaction that might be used against us."

"Perhaps since you know Dr. Hartman, you might find out more information through him?" Edith suggested.

Dr. Anderson shook her head. "I would never ask him to breach physician's confidentiality. I suppose we'll just have to rely on publicly available information and hope for the best."

Julia wanted to tell them she'd be seeing Michael again, but she stayed silent, knowing she was honor-bound to keep her word.

"That woman you helped—have you followed up to see how she is doing?" Dr. Anderson asked.

"I have not," Julia admitted. "I know she was taken to the Royal Free Hospital, so I have no doubt she is getting good care."

"I am going there now," Miss Morton said. "I work as a surgical dresser, and the doctors have been allowing me to visit the patients as well. Would you like to accompany me? We can look in on her together."

"I would like that very much," Julia said, eager to observe how the medical students interacted with the hospital staff.

Miss Morton smiled broadly. "Excellent."

As they were rising to leave, Dr. Anderson said, "Miss Bernay, would you like to come to a *conversazione* at my home in three weeks' time? This is an informal gathering that I hold sometimes with our students. We generally focus on some medical topic that is currently of interest."

Julia was pleasantly astonished by this invitation. "I would be honored!"

Dr. Anderson took out a sheet of paper and wrote down some information. She handed it to Julia. "Here is the date and the address. We look forward to seeing you. And we don't fuss about what to wear."

Julia looked down at the address. It had been scrawled quickly and on plain paper, but even if it had been printed on a gilded card it could not have been more valuable.

"Everything looks fine," Edith pronounced as she and Julia inspected the leg of the woman Julia had helped during the Underground accident. The doctors had replaced Julia's makeshift splint with one made for the purpose, and the flesh wound was sutured and clean.

The woman, Mavis, had been largely silent as they looked her over. She looked at them with dull eyes, the only gleam coming from the glint of tears as they spilled over to her cheeks. She'd been crying the entire time, making no effort to wipe away the tears.

"You should take some beef broth to keep up your strength," Julia told her, reaching for a wide mug that Mavis had left untouched on the bedside table.

"No." Her voice was flat. She turned her head away from the proffered drink.

"Are you in great pain?" Edith asked. Earlier, Mavis had refused a tonic to dull the pain.

"No more than I deserve," Mavis muttered miserably.

"Why do you say that?" Julia asked.

"I'm going to die. I know what happens with a broken leg. I saw it when my uncle broke his. It turns black and green, and then you die. It's judgment on me."

"Not every broken leg leads to gangrene," Edith said crisply. "Certainly not this one. It was treated properly and in a timely manner."

Although Edith's assessment was accurate, Julia saw a deeper problem that medicine wasn't going to address. She took hold of Mavis's hand. "Do you think God is judging you?"

Mavis began to sob, her fingers tightening around Julia's. "I've done bad things, and I'm going to hell for it. God hates me."

"It's true that God wants us to live in a manner pleasing to Him." Julia paused just long enough to allow this to register in Mavis's heart, but not long enough to leave her in condemnation. "However, He is not waiting, poised to punish us at every opportunity. The devil is busy enough doing that."

This comment only caused Mavis's tears to flow faster.

"If she wants a chaplain, we can find her one," Edith said. "You are only distressing her."

Julia didn't reply. She'd seen a person cry like this before because God was healing their heart. With her free hand, she covered Mavis's. "'I am the Lord, that healeth thee.' Will you repeat that after me?"

Mavis looked at her, confused. "What?"

"It's from the Bible. There are many verses that speak of healing. God wants you to be healed and give glory to Him. Shall I share a few more with you?"

Mavis blinked, still looking dazed. She didn't answer, but Julia did not read denial in her expression, either.

"'Bless the Lord, who forgiveth all thine iniquities,'" she continued. "'Who healeth all thy diseases. Who redeemeth thy life from destruction—'"

"I will check on some of the others," Edith whispered to Julia, then left the bedside.

Julia continued to quote the verses that came to mind, adding words of encouragement about God's grace and mercy. After a few minutes, Mavis's grip on her hand began to relax. She lay with closed eyes, but Julia knew she was listening. Edith, on the other hand, seemed to be making a point of *not* listening. She worked her way toward the opposite end of the women's ward, stopping to speak a few words to each patient along the way.

He sent His word and healed them. This was the verse most on Julia's mind as she promised Mavis, who was calmer now, that she'd return to visit again tomorrow. Mavis began to sip at the broth as Julia left.

Julia caught up with Edith as she entered the main hall connecting the women's ward to the ward for children.

"Finished?" Edith's irritation was clear.

"I've found that people will often heal faster if they are in a good state of mind," Julia told her. She wasn't going to apologize for what she'd done.

They began walking down the long hallway toward the wide main stairs that joined the two wings of the hospital. Two nurses passed them, each carrying trays stacked with dirty dishes.

"I'm glad that boy finally stopped grousin' about the food," one of them remarked to the other. "He was only upsetting the others."

"I suppose *Master Crawford* must get very fine food at his mansion in Spitalfields," scoffed the second nurse in agreement. She spoke with an ironic air, for the Royal Free Hospital had been established to care for the poor and destitute.

"Excuse me, Miss Peters," Edith said. "Are you speaking of Roger? What was the problem?"

The nurses paused, evidently knowing Edith but looking perturbed at being interrupted in their duties. "He was moaning that the food we gave him made him sick to his stomach," Miss Peters said. "He's stopped complaining now, though. Finally came to his senses."

"Did he eat the food?"

"No. But his father says he's very particular about what he eats." She said this with a roll of her eyes.

Edith's brow furrowed. "He was complaining about a stomachache, but he says he's fine now?"

"Yes, that's right," the nurse answered impatiently. "If you'll excuse us?"

Edith nodded and seemed hardly to notice as the two nurses hurried off.

"Is something wrong?" Julia asked.

"Why don't we go and take a look?"

Julia didn't know what had arrested Edith's attention. She followed willingly, though, thinking there might be something to learn.

"The boy in question took a bad tumble down some stairs," Edith explained as they walked toward the children's ward. "He fractured his arm and hit his head soundly to boot."

"They've been watching him for signs of concussion, I suppose?"

"That's right. They plan to discharge him tomorrow, but . . ."

She didn't finish the thought. At the children's ward, she went to the bed nearest the door. A boy who looked to be around ten years old was propped up in a seated position. There was a little wooden toy—a cup with a ball and string attached—lying next to him, but he had apparently lost interest in it. At the moment, he lay listlessly against the pillows, his eyes closed.

"How do you feel today, Roger?" Edith said, gently holding the wrist on his uninjured arm to take his pulse. "Miss Peters tells me you were complaining of a stomachache."

Roger grimaced. "I don't like her."

Edith frowned as she let go of his hand, but Julia didn't think she was reacting to his words. "I'm going to inspect your stomach for a moment," she told him.

She began to move her hands over his abdomen, pressing down gently. He cried out in protest when she reached his left side.

She removed her hands. "All done," she said briskly. She pulled Julia aside and said quietly, "I believe he has internal hemorrhaging. The doctor blamed his soreness on bruised ribs, but it may be that his spleen has ruptured. His abdominal area is hard and distended, perhaps from filling with blood. His pulse is fast and weak."

Julia took in this information, amazed that Edith had discovered this problem.

"I've got to find the doctor," Edith continued. "Will you wait here with Roger? Talk to him—we don't want him to lose consciousness."

"Of course," Julia replied, but Edith was already hurrying from the ward.

❧❦❧

"That was a remarkable thing you did," Julia said, as she and Edith walked out of the hospital three hours later. The doctor had confirmed her diagnosis and immediately taken the boy to surgery. Neither Julia nor Edith had been allowed into the operating theatre, but they'd waited until Roger was brought out again. He was going to pull through. "Was it something Miss Peters said that made you want to check on him?"

"Yes. Sometimes internal bleeding can cause colic-like symptoms, but then it dissipates. She said he'd been complaining of stomachache but then stopped. I thought it was worth checking."

"You are very astute for still being a student," Julia told her. "You'll be an impressive doctor one day."

Edith clearly took pride in the compliment. "I also volunteer at a free clinic in Bethnal Green. We deal with lots of injuries there. You did a fine job setting Mavis's leg. If you'd ever like to join me at the clinic sometime—"

"Indeed I would!" Julia answered without hesitation.

CHAPTER

8

"Y OU CANNOT IMAGINE HOW DISTRESSED I WAS!
There was Mr. Stephenson, laid out on the carriage floor
with blood gushing from his neck—!" Laura paused, one
delicate hand raised to her forehead, as though she might faint
even now at the mere memory of it.

She certainly had the attention of everyone at Corinna's elaborate dinner table. This sample of London's elite listened to Laura
with morbid fascination as she described the events in a dramatic
manner that made Michael feel ill at ease. Picking up his wine
glass, he took advantage of the motion to catch Corinna's gaze.
He lifted his brows a fraction to send her a silent question as to
the propriety of having such a grisly discussion in the middle of
her elegant seven-course dinner.

Her response was a slight crinkle of her eyes—her way of
telegraphing a shrug without anyone else in the room noticing.
He supposed she was taking pleasure at this display of Laura's
distress over Michael. He and Laura having survived this terrible

ordeal together would cement them as a couple in the minds of tonight's guests, and that was exactly what Corinna wanted.

"Why, the sight must have been terrible!" exclaimed Mrs. Dalrymple, a wiry old lady who loved nothing more than exciting gossip.

Laura nodded emphatically. "I believe it was only sheer strength of will that kept me from fainting dead away on the spot."

"I am sorry to have caused you so much anguish," Michael said, patting her hand. "Believe me, if I could have avoided doing so, I would have."

"Ho, ho!" chuckled Mr. Dalrymple. "I'm sure you would have, poor fellow."

Laura rewarded Michael for his joke with a smile and a coquettish blink of her lashes.

"Thank heavens you didn't faint, Miss Maynard, or we would never have gotten out of the tunnel and found help for my brother," Corinna declared.

"But we did, didn't we?" Laura answered proudly. "I feel we must also give credit to that kind gentleman, Mr. Browne. There were so many people in that tunnel! But Mr. Browne cleared the way for us because we had to get help to Mr. Stephenson right away."

Despite praising Laura just now, Corinna had given Michael a different story. Laura had been more of a hindrance than a help. She'd been overtaken with panic and near-hysteria. Corinna was the one who'd had the real presence of mind. She'd gotten Laura down that tunnel to the station through a combination of pushing and cajoling, all the while desperate to get help for Michael. This Mr. Browne that Laura mentioned had also offered to take Laura to a cab, freeing Corinna to locate a doctor for Michael.

Michael knew better than to raise any of these points, however. This was Corinna's dinner party, and if she wanted to allow Laura to share the glory for saving Michael, he wouldn't object.

"About that nurse who helped you—what did you say her name was?"

This question came from Baroness Crowder, a spinster bank heiress who had been given a life peerage by the queen because she'd spent so much of her time and fortune on philanthropic causes.

In fact, Julia's name had not been mentioned. Michael had hoped to avoid any detailed discussion of her, lest her medical studies come into the conversation. He ought to have known it would be difficult.

The baroness added, "My second cousin is Miss Nightingale, you know. I believe she would be interested in speaking to this woman. What hospital is she attached to?"

Still trying to think of a roundabout answer, Michael brought a napkin to his lips to buy some time.

Unfortunately, David stepped in to fill the pause and answered for him. "Her name is Miss Julia Bernay. She does seem to be quite an extraordinary young lady. As for the hospital . . ." He turned to Michael. "Did she give you that information when she came here to see you?"

David didn't notice his wife's look of irritation, but Michael did. He also saw Laura frown.

"I don't believe she's working as a nurse at this time," Michael said. He realized that he didn't even know where Julia was from— she hadn't sounded like a Londoner—or where she'd received her training.

"Well, that's too bad." The baroness gave a disappointed shake of her head. "Getting married, then?"

"Married?" Michael repeated, bewildered by this assumption.

"That's why girls usually give up nursing," the baroness said. "They can't do both, since nurses generally live in housing at the hospitals."

"Rather like nuns, aren't they?" Mr. Dalrymple remarked.

"She came here?" Laura asked. "When was that?"

"Only a few days after the accident, wasn't it, Michael?" David supplied. "You were still wrapped up in all those bandages, like an Egyptian mummy."

"But I thought you weren't well enough to see anyone at that time." Laura's statement sounded more like an accusation. She hadn't been happy to be turned away that day.

Corinna interposed smoothly. "Miss Bernay stayed only briefly, just long enough to ask after his health and offer her best wishes for a speedy recovery. You can understand that she would naturally have an interest in how things turned out."

Laura nodded but did not appear mollified. Michael would ensure he spent extra time with her this week and perhaps accompany her and Corinna the next time they went to an art show or some other event. The last thing he needed was for Laura to worry overmuch about Julia. He was a little regretful that he'd agreed to give Julia Latin lessons. He had to be careful to keep these two aspects of his life separate. He had a foreboding that it wasn't going to be easy.

A few days later, Michael stood across the street from the Carlton Club, pausing for a moment to survey the impressive edifice before going inside. It was a long building made of warm brown Portland stone and topped by an ornate cornice. Tall, elegantly arched windows ran the length of its two stories, and it took up a generous amount of the street corner on Pall Mall where it stood.

For Michael, the Carlton Club was a physical representation of what he had been working toward for over a decade. Its members were the conservative power brokers in the city—bankers, barristers, members of Parliament. People with influence, with a finger on the pulse of the nation. This club was also a bastion of social respectability. Above all, it was a place where Michael could become those things, too. Being accepted as a member here had been a feat in itself. Michael's rising reputation was finally erasing the large shadow thrown over his family by his father's infamous dealings and death.

The adage that a person must spend money to make money had never been truer than in this case. As a barrister, Michael was prohibited from advertising his services. Clients had to come to him. Many a young barrister had languished, broke, with no work because he was not yet known. He had to depend on his social connections to help his career get under way. Barristers were officially contacted by a solicitor, and a savvy client knew which barrister he wanted and would make sure his solicitor hired that person.

By working for Tamblin, Michael had grown his personal caseload. Here at the Carlton, he could increase it even more by meeting the kind of people he hoped to take on as clients. He'd already acquired a few important cases since becoming a member here two years ago, and there was promise of more to come as his successes in court added up.

Today, though, Michael was here on a different errand. Laura's brother, the new Viscount Delaford, had accepted Michael's invitation to join him for lunch. The viscount had his own membership at a different club generally preferred by the aristocracy, but for their first meeting, Michael thought it would be better to operate from his own ground. It was a shameless display of status, he supposed, but one that was necessary when trying to impress a peer he hoped to have as a brother-in-law.

He'd set up this meeting weeks ago, before the accident. At the time, he'd been eager to move forward with the match. But now as he looked at the club, preparing himself for the upcoming meeting, he was surprised to realize the idea was not as appealing to him today as it had been. He put it down to his preoccupation with catching up on his caseload and the lingering pain from the accident. These things would pass.

A blast of cold air nearly blew off his hat and sent many people scurrying to their destinations. Pulling his coat collar tight against the bitter March wind, Michael crossed the street and entered the club.

He'd been in the club's excellent library for about half an hour when Lord Delaford arrived. Although Michael had never met him, he was immediately sure who it was. The viscount was not much older than Michael. He was impeccably dressed and moved with the self-confidence of a man born into money and privilege.

Delaford made a beeline toward Michael's chair, and Michael rose to greet him. "Mr. Stephenson, I presume?" He echoed the now-famous catchphrase of the explorer Henry Stanley with a theatrical flourish. Leaning in closer, he added, "I certainly *hope* you are Stephenson. You appear to be the only man under forty in the room, and I'm not prepared to marry my sister off to an old codger."

Michael appreciated the way Delaford sought to put him at ease. His interest in this meeting returned.

After exchanging a few pleasantries, Michael said, "Shall we go in to lunch? There is an excellent soup on the menu today that should chase away the chill from that wicked wind outside."

"Wonderful."

As they ate, the viscount engaged Michael in all kinds of subjects. At one point he remarked, "What in the world are you doing in this club? Now that Mr. Gladstone is prime minister again, you would do better to join the Reform Club."

Others had expressed this sentiment to Michael, although

he was surprised to hear it coming from a peer. Laura had told him her brother had liberal leanings; apparently this was true. Still, Michael didn't give the idea much credence. He figured the political tides were always changing, and it would be folly to chase them. "I'll take my chances. Besides, I know nothing about the quality of their soup."

This quip earned an approving grin from the viscount. "I like you, Stephenson. You are sharp and can't be put in a corner. I suppose that's a necessary trait for success in the legal profession."

"I've found it useful many times," Michael agreed.

The viscount waved a fork to indicate the finely appointed dining room, and by extension, the club itself. "I've been here a few times. It's always congenial. I myself belong to White's. It's been a tradition in my family for generations. Although if I had my preference, I'd belong to the Garrick. A much livelier crowd over there."

A peer hobnobbing with artists, writers, and actors? This was another indication Lord Delaford was a far different person than his father had been.

It wasn't until they were nearly finished with the main course that Delaford said, "Shall we talk about Laura? I'm sure that's why you invited me here today."

Michael decided a neutral approach would be best. "It may seem presumptuous for a man like me to put myself forward as a candidate for her hand."

The viscount weighed this. "Due to your position in life relative to hers? Perhaps. If my father were alive, it would be a different story. He didn't like the idea of commoners marrying into the aristocracy. Unlike him, I am willing to entertain the idea. However, lest you think I am merely some kindhearted soul who sees good in everyone, I will tell you I have carefully researched your history. There are plenty of men pursuing Laura. She is beautiful, they tell me—one can never be the judge for one's own sister—and there is a substantial dowry set aside by our father before he passed away. But although my views are more liberal than my father's, it doesn't mean I am less diligent about making sure my sister marries an honorable man. There are too many rogues and fortune hunters out there. One cannot be too careful."

Michael knew this was only to be expected. "I appreciate that you are performing such due diligence for your sister's sake, sir."

Delaford nodded. "You are, by all accounts, a scholar and an honest gentleman. So much as barristers can be. I also know from my research that you are beginning to acquire clients on your own account, aside from the work you do for Tamblin."

"Yes." These were all facts that would be easy for anyone to learn. But the viscount already having this knowledge kept Michael from needing to blow his own horn.

"I do have one question, though. You seem content to continue at Tamblin's chambers when you are well-positioned to strike out on your own. Why is that?"

This was another question Michael had fielded more than once. "Tamblin's reputation is unparalleled. It is all but certain he'll be appointed to a judgeship soon. At that time, I expect most of his work to come to me."

"So you are prepared to wait."

"I don't think the wait will be long. We expect his appointment within a year. I think of it as strategic planning."

This was true. It was also a way to save money. Establishing his own chambers and hiring a clerk would use up funds that he needed for other things. He was determined to pay back the money that had been given to him by his brother-in-law. David insisted this wasn't necessary, but Michael couldn't live with himself otherwise.

His answer seemed to satisfy Lord Delaford. "I believe your

assessment is correct. I have no doubt you could provide for my sister in the manner to which she's accustomed."

Although the conversation was going well, Michael knew there were deeper subjects to discuss than his rosy financial future. "As you have been looking into my affairs, I assume all aspects of my past are familiar to you? Of my *family's* past, I mean?"

Delaford nodded. "I can see you are a straightforward man who prefers to tackle hard subjects head on." Setting down his knife and fork, he leaned back, not speaking until a waiter who had been hovering nearby whisked away their plates and left them alone again. "Stephenson, in these modern times, many old-fashioned notions are falling away. I can't deny that if my father were still alive, he would refuse even to speak to you. However, I have no such compunctions. Why should I hold you accountable for things your father did? It makes no sense. I believe a man should be judged on his own merits."

"You know there are rumors my father committed suicide."

It was a risky thing to say. Most people believed mental illness was hereditary. But Michael wanted to be sure he knew exactly where the viscount stood on this matter.

Delaford gave him an appraising look but didn't answer right away. He took a slow sip of his wine. As he set the glass back down, he spared a brief look around, as if gauging their distance from the other diners. No one was paying them any attention.

"I am aware of the speculation surrounding your father's unfortunate demise. I believe all that is known for sure is that he broke his neck when he fell off a horse. That is correct, yes?"

Michael nodded. "Those are the indisputable facts."

"So the year I spent at Lincoln's Inn after leaving Oxford was not entirely misspent." Delaford flashed a brief, joking smile before returning to a more serious expression. "Approaching this as a lawyer, I would say that whether your father's death was an accident, in that he had been riding recklessly because he was drunk, or whether he was in fact deliberately trying to kill himself, is a matter of conjecture. I don't believe there are enough concrete facts to make a judgment either way. I also don't deny that the more negative explanation is entirely plausible. There are men who, through bad luck or ill-advised actions, reach a low enough place in life to unbalance their minds, causing them to deliberately inflict pain on themselves or others." He leaned forward, looking Michael in the eye. "But even if this were true about your father, does it necessarily follow that *you* must be such a man?"

Michael met his gaze squarely. "I have spent the past decade doing all I can to restore my family's reputation. I will not repeat my father's mistakes."

This would be exactly what the viscount wanted to hear, but it was also the truth. The last thing Michael would ever do was follow any path that inflicted more pain on his sister. She and Michael had endured enough already.

Lord Delaford leaned back in his chair, relaxing again. "Then we are agreed. I must tell you one more thing, however."

"Yes?"

"My sister and I are only just out of mourning. For propriety's sake, we should not rush into an engagement too quickly. I don't worry overmuch about such niceties myself—although one hates to be accused of bad taste. Also, as Laura's debutante year was cut short by our father's death, this is her first real opportunity to partake of the London Season. Let's give her a bit of time to enjoy it, eh? All those balls and filling up dance cards and what have you. Laura is quite enamored with you, so you have nothing to fear by waiting to declare yourself."

The suggestion that things not be moved along too quickly was fine with Michael. Corinna was anxious to have him settled, and he knew she would feel frustrated at having to wait another few months. He thought he should feel that way, too, but this directive felt almost like a reprieve. He couldn't say why.

Delaford pulled a silver case from his coat pocket. Opening it, he extended the case toward Michael. "Cigarette?"

"No, thank you." As explanation, Michael briefly touched a portion of the bandage that rose above his cravat. The wound still hurt, and he had no desire to increase the pain by smoking.

"Of course. I'd nearly forgotten," Delaford said. "Though I don't know how I could have," he added wryly. "Some days it seems Laura talks of little else."

Michael wasn't surprised that the accident loomed large in Laura's mind. It had never been far from *his* thoughts, either. Physical aches and pains were constant reminders. So, too, was the knowledge that things would have turned out very differently if not for Julia. It was easy to contrast her actions with those of Laura, and for Laura to come out worse for the comparison. But was that fair? Given her sheltered life, she'd never been in such a frightening situation before. Even Corinna, sensible as she was, wouldn't have known how to stem Michael's bleeding. Laura had many good qualities—she was pretty, generally kind, and a competent woman within her sphere of life. Michael ought to be grateful that she was, as Lord Delaford said, *enamored* with him.

Julia was . . . altogether different. She wasn't like any other woman he knew. The whole situation reminded him of a trial where the opposing counsel offered up a surprise piece of information at the eleventh hour. He didn't know what to expect from his future encounters with Miss Bernay, but he was pretty sure they would be interesting. He just had to make sure their interactions did not take his plans in the wrong direction.

CHAPTER

9

THE BARKERS' BUTLER USHERED JULIA into the parlor. Michael Stephenson rose from his chair and greeted her. His appearance was much different than the last time she'd seen him. Aside from the fact that his cravat was tied loosely to keep pressure off his bandage, he looked the picture of a gentleman. His fingers were still bandaged, though, so Julia accepted his polite bow instead of offering a handshake.

The butler withdrew, and Julia noticed he did not shut the door behind him. "Is it just us? I half thought we'd be chaperoned by Mrs. Barker."

"My sister is out making calls, capitalizing on the social cachet she earned at a recent dinner party."

His voice suggested gentle mockery, yet Julia was hard-pressed to determine whether he disapproved of his sister's aims. "I'm happy to hear it was a success."

"Yes." He frowned a little, then seemed to dismiss the matter from his thoughts. "Shall we begin?" He motioned to a table with two straight-backed chairs drawn up to it. "I've set this up for our work."

Julia remembered the table from her previous visit. It had been covered with framed photographs, three or four small plants, a decorative figurine, and a lamp. Everything but the lamp had been removed, and two large books had been laid out—a Latin grammar and a dictionary—along with paper and pens. He had thought of everything.

As Julia placed her own Latin textbook on the table, she saw Michael tug at his collar. "Are you having trouble with your wound?"

"It itches a little," he admitted. "And it is still sore, but I suppose that's to be expected."

She stepped closer to him. "Would you mind if I take a look?"

He removed his hand from the wound and began to smooth his cravat. "That won't be necessary. Dr. Hartman assured me everything is fine."

"When did he last see it?"

"Yesterday."

"Those symptoms could be normal, or there could be an infection setting in. That might have serious consequences if not treated right away. Would you allow me a peek, just to ensure everything is all right?" She looked up at him, aware again of how tall he was. He returned her gaze, and she could see he was wavering.

"You will need to make it quick if you want a Latin lesson. I only have an hour to spare today."

"I promise this won't take long. Perhaps if you would sit down, I could reach it better."

Still looking vaguely uncomfortable, Michael took a seat at the table. Julia sat in the chair next to him, leaning in close as she gently worked his cravat looser to get to the bandage. She caught the scent of the dressing ointment but something else as well. Had he put some pomade in his hair? Whatever it was, it smelled very good. She didn't even realize she'd taken an extra moment to inhale until he tilted his head and looked at her quizzically. From his combed hair to his chin, now smooth from a recent shave, he definitely was more carefully groomed than before. But that was to be expected, since the last time she'd seen him, he'd just gotten out of bed. She remembered how comical he'd looked with his hair sticking up in all directions.

Bringing her mind back to the present, she gently removed the bandage and studied the wound. Her concern had been unnecessary. The red welts around the sutures had lightened to a dark pink, which meant the wound was healing. "Everything looks good," she told him. "No sign of infection."

"That's good to hear."

A hint of a smile played around his mouth, reminding Julia of a different scene: the moment he'd caught her looking at him on the Underground before the accident. Then, she'd wondered what sort of woman a man like him would be interested in pursuing. It had been a rare, foolish tangent for her thoughts to take—and now they were threatening to go that way again. There was no doubt he was handsome, but that wasn't why she was here.

Pulling her thoughts back in line, Julia dabbed her fingertip into the ointment and inspected it, rubbing it between her fingers and giving it a little sniff. "I see he's put linseed oil over the stitches. This is good for now." She carefully replaced the bandages. It really couldn't be helped that her hands should brush against his crisp shirt collar and the smooth silk of his cravat. That her fingertips should be so alive to the sensations startled her, but she did her best to ignore it. "For the itching, I recommend a compound sold by Mr. Baines, the chemist on Gray's Inn Road near the Royal Free Hospital. It is also excellent for healing scar tissue. You might want to apply some to the cuts on your temple." She touched the area—only to indicate the places she was talking about—her fingers running gently along his hairline and the cuts currently covered with sticking plaster. Once again she noticed as she had on the train, that his hair was very fine and soft.

"Mr. Baines," Michael repeated, leaning back in his chair as though to put some distance between them. "Thank you, I will keep that in mind. Now, shall we begin the lesson?"

"Yes!" Julia replied. It was time to focus her attention on the real reason she was here. But there was something she needed to say first. "I want to thank you for doing this. I am appreciative that you agreed to my request, even though . . ."

He finished her thought for her. "Even though you couched it as a debt of honor?"

She nodded. "Quite honestly, I wondered whether you'd change your mind once you had a chance to think."

"Did you? Perhaps because you don't know me very well. I always keep my word." He regarded her quizzically. "Do you?"

He asked the question with a lightly conspiratorial air, as if they were sharing a secret. Which, in a sense, they were. This man could radiate charm when he wanted to. Perhaps it was a good thing that women could not serve on juries. How many of even the most sensible ones could resist this kind of friendly appeal?

"Yes, of course." She reached for the papers she'd brought with her. The sooner they got down to business, the better. "I have here the Latin portion of last year's preliminary exam for the University of London."

"How did you get hold of that?" He sounded suspicious, as though she'd done something underhanded.

"It is for sale at the booksellers in order to help students prepare. It's a common practice."

"I see." He took the paper and looked it over.

"Do you mean to say you never did this?"

"No need to. I felt confident enough in my knowledge to tackle whatever was given on the exam."

There was a hint of arrogance in his statement, but Julia could forgive it. She'd often been accused of pride when she'd only been giving a sincere assessment of her abilities.

He continued to study the paper. "I see there are two parts to this test. First, translate a paragraph from a known Latin text. Second, answer seven grammatical questions." He handed the paper back to her. "I assume you won't know in advance which paragraph you will be asked to translate? You will need to ensure you have built a broad vocabulary."

"I know which text the paragraph will be taken from. That is always announced in advance. It will be Cicero's *De Oratore*. Unfortunately, I haven't been able to locate a copy in any of the secondhand bookshops." To buy a new copy was beyond Julia's reach, but she didn't feel she had to spell that out for him.

"You are in luck," he said cheerfully. "I own a copy. It is at my chambers. I will bring it next time."

"Wonderful!" Julia exclaimed. "That is my first big problem solved."

"As for the grammatical questions, they are straightforward, but they won't be easy. Each one calls for a long and detailed answer. You will need a good vocabulary for that, too. You'll need to recognize the principal parts of many types of verbs, not to mention being able to decline a good number of nouns and adjectives."

This need for declension—giving the various inflections of each word according to gender, number, and case—was a daunting task. Julia began to grow uneasy, in part because she knew that to receive the help she needed, she was going to have to admit just how much she didn't know.

"I suppose you have already attempted to answer the questions given here?" her mentor asked.

"Yes." Julia pulled out another piece of paper. "I have done all of it—with the aid of a dictionary," she admitted sheepishly.

She handed over her work, on edge as he read through it. He laid the two papers side by side on the desk, comparing the Latin paragraph with the translation she had written.

She watched him as he worked, his face in profile to hers. It was a nice profile, with a straight nose and a chin that was in good proportion to the rest of his face. Not wanting to risk getting caught staring, Julia looked away, searching for something else to look at. Her gaze settled on the exotic chess set, reminding her again of her ultimate goal. "Did that chess set really come from Africa?"

"I beg your pardon?" He looked up in surprise at this non sequitur.

"There is a chess set in that curio cabinet with an African design. I don't suppose Mr. or Mrs. Barker have actually traveled to Africa?" If they had, Julia was prepared to give them much credit and possibly even ask them some questions.

But Michael only shook his head. "My brother-in-law invests in many companies that trade worldwide. I believe that was a gift from one of his clients."

"I plan to go to Africa."

"Do you?"

She was not pleased at his look of disbelief, but it was a reaction she'd seen plenty of times before from others. "I'm going as soon as my medical studies are complete. I plan to be a medical missionary."

"Why would you want to do that?"

"Because God has called me. And if the Lord calls you to do something, it isn't wise to fight it."

A furrow deepened his brow. "Are you certain this is *God's* calling? How can you know that for sure?"

"Do you doubt the existence of God, or my ability to discern His will for my life?"

"I don't know either of you well enough to answer that question." His response managed to be sardonic and to steer clear of giving a direct answer.

"Are you not concerned about what God thinks of you?"

"I don't trouble myself much about God." His tone changed to flat and hard-edged. "It's not something we need to discuss. I made a commitment to help you in your endeavors, and you made a commitment *not* to interfere with mine. Did we not have this understanding?"

So many objections bubbled up in Julia's heart, so many things she wanted to say. Both Michael and his sister seemed intent only on material and social gain. This room was stuffed with objects, yet there was not one that hinted at spiritual inquiry. She actually felt sorry for them, despite these outward trappings of success. Without a spiritual life, what was the point?

What was in his soul? That was the important question. For now, he was looking at her intently, awaiting a response to his question. *Did we not have this understanding?*

Yes, they did. And Julia did not want to jeopardize it. Clearly she had touched a nerve, whether it was about God or the medical school or something else altogether.

"I did not mean to tread on any toes," she said. "I merely thought Africa might be a common interest for us. I forgot this is not your home."

His shoulders visibly relaxed, as did his expression. "Latin is our common ground for now, wouldn't you say?"

Julia could only nod in agreement.

He pointed to the paper on which she had written her answers to the examination questions. "When translating this paragraph, I think you could have done a better job with this phrase." He set before her a blank sheet of paper and a pen. "Let me tell you what I would have done. As my writing hand is still not fully functional, you will need to take this down yourself."

Despite the troubling detour their conversation had taken, Julia soon became convinced she had done the right thing by requesting these lessons. Michael understood the language very well, and he was adept at explaining its concepts. After reviewing the paragraph and enlightening her on some of the rhetorical devices it contained, he moved on to the grammar questions. Although he did not hesitate to point out her mistakes, he did not belittle her for them. That was all she could have asked—to be treated simply as a student willing to learn and not as a woman attempting the ridiculous.

It was hard to believe she was working with a man actively engaged in trying to close the very school she wished to attend. Perhaps it was too great a contradiction for her mind to comprehend. Or maybe his work did not reflect his personal feelings? Although he had scoffed at the idea of her becoming a missionary, he had never derided her desire to become a doctor. What would it be like as a barrister to defend a client's point of view that one didn't agree with?

She was debating whether to raise this topic or leave it for another day when the grandfather clock announced the hour of four with a series of delicate chimes.

Michael closed the Latin book. "That's all for today. I have business at Parliament tonight."

"Parliament?" This arrested her attention. "Do you involve yourself in politics?" She had not thought much about politics— aside from following the debate on whether women should be in medicine—until she'd come to London. Many of her fellow students and teachers read the newspapers thoroughly to keep up with everything that happened day by day.

"As a barrister, I have to pay close attention to what our lawmakers are doing."

He rose and was helping Julia up from her chair—the two of them standing for that moment very close together—when Corinna entered the room. She must have just come home, for she was still wearing her coat and gloves.

"My apologies for barging in," she said. "I thought you'd be done by now."

Michael stiffened under his sister's unfriendly gaze. "We are just finishing up."

All the warmth that had been in the room dissipated in the presence of Mrs. Barker. Her look of consternation when she saw the table strewn with books and papers told Julia that Michael had probably not consulted with his sister before removing the other items.

Determined not to let this woman dampen her spirits, Julia said brightly, "Thank you for allowing us to use your parlor for this lesson, Mrs. Barker."

"It was no trouble."

But something in her gaze did indeed look troubled. Julia couldn't help but think she was worried about more than returning the parlor table to its previous configuration.

Turning to Michael, Julia said, "The lesson was most illuminating. I feel ten times more confident already." She extended her hand, then remembered he was in no condition to return the gesture.

"Our next lesson will be at two o'clock on Wednesday. I'll bring my copy of Cicero, and we can review it together."

Julia thought he intentionally directed a note of defiance toward his sister. Although he was bound to have reservations about tutoring a would-be student to the medical school, he seemed determined to do it.

Whatever his reasons were, Julia was glad.

Collecting her book and papers, Julia said her good-byes and allowed a footman to show her to the door. She might have tried to get in another word or two with Michael, but he stayed behind in the parlor with his sister.

As she walked home, Julia thought over all that had happened. By getting Michael to agree to these lessons, she was receiving excellent help with Latin. Perhaps it was an indication that the medical school would survive, for why would God provide this means to help her conquer the matriculation exam if she would have no way to study medicine? She had not yet been able to truly discuss the lawsuit with him, but this was only the first lesson. She would remain vigilant for an opening.

Above all, she was intrigued by Michael himself. He had flatly refused to discuss spiritual matters. His underlying anger relating to the subject was unmistakable. Could she somehow reach him and turn him to God? To win a soul would be more important than anything else she could do. It might also be the tougher challenge, but she would welcome it.

Michael worked his way to the front of the visitor's gallery in the House of Lords, looking for a place to squeeze in. A large crowd had come to hear the Earl of Westbridge give a speech against the repeal of the Contagious Diseases Acts as a preemptive strike. It was rumored that a bill to repeal the act would be presented before the House of Commons later this week.

Michael saw John Kelso, a newspaper reporter on Parliament proceedings, and made his way over to him. Kelso gave him a nod of greeting and moved over to make room on the bench. "Can't say I'm surprised to see you here, Mr. Stephenson. Keeping up with your client?"

"You could say that. I'm surprised to see so many others here, though," Michael added as the two of them were forced to move over when another man commandeered a portion of the bench.

"His lordship is gaining lots of notoriety with this libel suit," Kelso pointed out. "Not that he doesn't have enough already. As does the legislation itself. It should have been named the *Contentious* Diseases Act."

Kelso was still chuckling at his own joke when the lord chancellor took his place and opened the proceedings. Michael looked over the House of Lords as everyone settled into their seats. A good portion of the room's red leather benches were filled, signaling the peers' interest in tonight's agenda. Ostensibly there would be a debate following the speech, but Michael didn't think it would come to much.

The next hour dragged on interminably, as other items of business were covered. There was little of interest to Michael, although Kelso, busy at his profession, took copious notes with his pencil and notepad.

At last, Lord Westbridge was given leave by the lord chancellor to speak. The earl tottered to the speaker's podium. Nearing seventy, he had a shock of white hair, wire-framed glasses, and wore a suit that, although modern enough in cut, somehow evoked the midcentury. He paused, took a moment to adjust his glasses, and began.

His speech was little more than a tirade in favor of keeping the act, setting forth a long list of arguments against repeal that consisted of everything Michael had heard before. The act protects the troops, who protect our nation. Why do we wish to imperil our sovereignty by allowing diseased women to infect our honorable soldiers? The very existence of our empire is at stake! His lordship even took time to mention how the women gained from this, too. Their diseases were caught and cured, making them happier people. Never mind that syphilis was never really cured. Nor that this entire argument tacitly accepted that there would always be prostitutes and that there was no reason to change that, so long as the women could be kept "clean."

Throughout this diatribe, there was not one mention of his own son, nor of the libel suit. That, at least, was wise. Tamblin had counseled his lordship to keep away from that subject. Every person in the audience, as well as most of the people who would read Kelso's report tomorrow, knew it already.

Michael grew more irritated as the speech went on. Why was he even here? Wasn't it a waste of time to keep rehashing this bill over and over, since it would probably be defeated in the House of Commons anyway? Although some members had begun to advocate the repeal of the acts, they were still in the minority.

And yet next to him, Kelso's pencil worked steadily. "Wonderful press," he murmured. "Readers will eat it up."

The earl finished his remarks to appreciative applause, and some people shouted, "Hear! Hear!"

There followed the debate, which was little more than a series of statements by other eminent peers reiterating what the earl had just said.

Heartily glad when it was over, Michael rose from the bench. There was nothing to be learned here tonight. Crouching low so as not to block the others' view, he sent a quick gesture of goodnight to Kelso and left the gallery.

The evening was fairly mild for March, so Michael ignored the line of cabs and directed his steps toward the street. He turned over many things in his mind as he walked back to his chambers. For all the earl's bluster about wanting to keep this legislation because of the good it was doing, Michael knew tonight's performance was just for show. His lordship wanted only to use the act to bludgeon an opponent over something entirely unrelated. The old man was angry because his estranged daughter wanted to pursue medicine instead of living the life she'd been born into. The earl probably refused to consider the sad truth that, win or lose, he was hardly likely to win back the affection of his daughter in this way.

Not surprisingly, Julia Bernay had never been far from Michael's thoughts tonight. After all, the libel suit was really an attack against women like her, who were fighting for the right to earn a medical degree. If judgment went against the school, the damages the earl was claiming would be catastrophic. But even surviving that, the school might lose its clinical training privileges at the Royal Free Hospital, without which it would most certainly have to close its doors.

Yet Julia had an unshakable belief that she'd been called to do both missionary and medical work.

He kept remembering her words: *If the Lord calls you to do something, it isn't wise to fight it.* Everything about her spoke of absolute determination, from the way she'd coaxed him into another physical exam to the vigor with which she approached her studies. She gave the impression of being an unstoppable force. It was tempting, in light of this, to worry that his efforts to win this case would ultimately fail. After all, if there was a God who was personally interested in the school's success, who—or what—could ultimately withstand Him?

He shook his head to dislodge that foolish notion. He did not think the Almighty took sides when it came to the political wranglings of men. Just because Julia believed in the inevitability of her success didn't necessarily make it so. There were more factors in play than she could understand.

Michael did not want to lose this case. He'd worked too hard to get this far. But even so, he was beginning to suspect that if he were to win and further his career as he planned, he would still feel some measure of regret over the school's fate. That was something he'd just have to accept. For now, he had to concentrate on the goal of winning and not dwell on what lay beyond it.

CHAPTER

10

As promised, Edith took Julia with her on her next visit to the free clinic at Bethnal Green, one of the poorer neighborhoods in London. Edith explained that they'd been hesitant to allow her to work there at first, but in time—and with notes of recommendation from Dr. Anderson and others at the medical school—she had won them over. She was relegated to seeing only minor issues among the women and children, but that was a good start.

Julia was excited. Months of academic studies left her longing to get back to actual medical practice. This would also give her the opportunity to spend more time with Edith. Julia was impressed by her skill and dedication.

As they rode in a hansom toward their destination, Julia said, "May I ask you a question? You can tell me if you think it is too personal, and I won't bring it up again."

"You may," Edith replied, although she gave a little sigh with it. "I expect it's nothing that hasn't been asked of me already."

106

"It's about the libel case. Those things that Dr. Tierney said about your brother."

Edith gave a little nod. "I wasn't at the rally. At the time, I felt my relations with my father were strained enough; I wasn't going to make them worse by publicly supporting the CDA's repeal, even though privately I do. However, I wish Dr. Tierney had not said what she did, primarily because of all that has happened since."

"I would have thought you'd be insulted or angry, as his lordship was. He denies that syphilis is what killed your brother."

"You are asking me if what Dr. Tierney said was true." Edith turned cool blue eyes toward Julia. "In truth, I don't know. I was at finishing school in France when he died. My brother was far older than me and already overseas with the army before I could even talk. Throughout his life, I never saw much of him. I suppose he was a dashing army officer and all that, but to me he seemed vain and self-satisfied, and not a man of much integrity. I think the rumors of syphilis are as believable as the version of events my father gives, especially since my father was always blind to my brother's faults."

She turned to look out at the passing street. "I've decided to remain as neutral as I can in this whole affair, and the school has stood by me through all of this. My father thinks that by closing the school, he can get me to change my mind, come back home, and be a dutiful daughter. That is his other blind spot. I will not allow anything to stop me from my goal of practicing medicine." She pointed straight ahead. "And *that* is the reason why."

The cab had been moving into increasingly poorer neighborhoods and now stopped in front of the clinic. There was a line of people outside waiting to get in, all shabbily dressed. Some looked toward the door with desperate anticipation, while others slumped along the wall, glumly resigned to the long wait. Most eyed Julia and Edith with curiosity as they alighted from the cab.

When they got inside the clinic, Julia saw the reason for the line. The waiting area was already overrun with patients. Seated on plain wooden benches, waiting to be seen by the doctors, was a cross-section of the community. Young and old, from those who might be poor shopkeepers to many who looked like beggars. At a glance, Julia could see their ailments ran the gamut as well, from broken limbs and infected sores to colds, coughs, and more serious illnesses. There were pregnant women and others who held crying babies, vainly trying to soothe them.

The next few hours were some of the most intense and eye-opening that Julia had ever experienced. Nothing she had seen in her previous work in Bristol, nor her glimpse into the London hospitals, was close to this. One overworked doctor and a few staff members did what they could, but the need was clearly greater than they could handle.

"I cannot understand why it took so much effort to convince the doctors to allow you to come here and help," Julia said to Edith as they washed their hands after tending to a woman with a badly infected cut on her leg. "There is no shortage of business."

"Yes, the need is very great," Edith agreed. "I'm glad you wanted to volunteer your time today. I have a hard time persuading other students to come, even though it provides valuable experience."

"Is it because they are so busy?"

"Partly. But also, they have no great interest in helping poor folk. Most are aiming to build lucrative practices serving women and children from the better classes. And perhaps they have a fear of coming here."

Julia could understand that sentiment. The neighborhood was rough, and the people desperately poor. Not to mention that one would be far more likely to be exposed to contagious and potentially fatal diseases here. "I am not afraid," Julia declared. "I believe the Lord will protect me. I plan to go to the missions in Africa once I have my medical license."

This pronouncement drew a frown and a stern look from Edith. "Why would you waste your talents like that when there is so much need here in England?"

The question took Julia by surprise. She hadn't thought in those terms before. But she didn't have time to formulate an answer. Their conversation was cut short by a disturbance in the waiting area. Edith hurried out of the little room where they had been seeing patients, and Julia followed.

A woman was pleading with the harried clerk who took people's information as they came in. "My sister is too sick to come here!" She spoke with an accent that sounded Germanic or Slavic. "She is pregnant, seven months. She has a fever that has not left for three days. You must tell me what to do!"

"No one here makes house calls," the clerk responded harshly. "You will have to bring her to the clinic."

Julia glanced over the waiting area. There were a dozen people waiting to be seen, but none appeared to have life-threatening problems. "Perhaps you and I could go?" she suggested to Edith.

"You are willing to do that? Coming to this clinic is one thing, but going deeper into the slums is quite another."

"I don't mind."

Edith looked at the waiting patients. She must have drawn the same conclusion as Julia, for she turned to the woman and asked, "How far away is your sister?"

"Ten minutes! Only ten minutes!" came the answer. "Please say you will come!"

"You are likely to find only more people with problems, more than you could ever hope to take care of," the clerk warned them.

But Edith simply replied, "We have to start somewhere."

They collected their coats and the medical bag Edith had brought with her to the clinic, and were soon following the distraught woman down the narrow street.

Michael sat in Tamblin's office, the two of them waiting while Lord Westbridge perused the statement Michael had obtained from the doctor at the private asylum. The old man muttered to himself as he read, but the tenor of the sounds indicated satisfaction rather than displeasure. Tamblin leaned back in his chair, steepling his fingers and looking content as he waited for his client to finish reading.

The earl tossed the report on the desk. "This is very good. I don't see how a jury can deny the truth of this statement."

"Right you are," Tamblin replied. "If we should need it, this statement will certainly bolster our case."

"*If* we should need it?" Michael repeated. "Surely this will be the cornerstone of our argument."

Tamblin leaned forward, pointing toward the report. "While we don't doubt the veracity of this statement for a moment, we cannot rely on the jury to reach the same conclusion. Certainly not if the defense tries to throw a cloud over the events surrounding the death of his lordship's son."

The earl shifted in his chair and emitted a grunt of pain. This might have been a reaction to the mention of his son's death, or it might have been in response to some physical malady. He often complained of arthritis. "Please explain your reasoning, Mr. Tamblin."

Tamblin said smoothly, "In order to be assured of success, we must ensure the case does not rely on each side trying to prove whether Dr. Tierney's statements were true or false. In fact, we must use every tactic at our disposal to prevent the defense from even approaching this topic. We must focus the arguments solely and completely upon whether your lordship's good name and reputation were harmed by Dr. Tierney's recklessness in making such statements in a public forum."

The earl nodded in understanding and approval, but Michael found Tamblin's words unsettling. "There is no doubt his lordship's reputation was maligned, but—"

"Precisely!" Tamblin exclaimed. "Of that there can be no doubt whatever. Stephenson, if you want to learn how to win your cases, pay close attention to what we do here. The defense must not be allowed to rest their argument on a matter of mere facts such as they might or might not pertain to his lordship's son."

"That is brilliant!" the earl enthused. "Mr. Stephenson, you could not have found a better mentor."

Tamblin gave a smile of humble pride. "I am honored by your high opinion of me, sir. I shall continue doing my best to earn it."

The earl's vanity was stroked by Tamblin's obsequiousness, but he did not appear completely satisfied. "We have everything we need, including the perfect plan of attack. The only remaining question is, why hasn't a date been set for the trial?"

"The wheels of justice move slowly, sir," Tamblin replied. "Remember that the attendant publicity over the months will only amplify our case."

The earl grunted again, this time in a show of impatience. "Be that as it may, I want us to move forward—and soon. The wheels of justice always move faster if the judge is given the right sort of prodding." He rose unsteadily from his chair, leaning heavily on a wooden cane. "As far as I'm concerned, we have more than gained our point. Now I want vindication. I will expect a report from you next week regarding what progress you have made in this regard."

"You may count on it, my lord," Tamblin replied.

Tamblin walked out with the earl to escort him to his waiting carriage.

Michael went to his own office and sank into a chair, deep in thought. In the two years since Tamblin had invited him to share these chambers, Michael's practical knowledge of common law and his skill in the courtroom had grown exponentially. He'd always been cognizant of how fortunate he was to have been taken under Tamblin's wing. The worth of the tutelage from such a distinguished barrister, not to mention the important contacts he'd made that could advance his career even further, was incalculable.

For all these things, Michael was extremely grateful. Although they sometimes accepted cases where Michael thought the opposing party had the better claim, he knew this was a fact of life all barristers faced. Whoever your client was, you made their case to the utmost of your ability. Today was the first time, however, that Michael had felt an honest doubt about Tamblin's approach.

He rubbed his eyes, still trying to fully grasp the implications of this meeting. Tamblin's proposed line of prosecution—to focus solely on the damage to his lordship's reputation—might have pleased the earl, but was it really the proper way to go? It would be legal, for Tamblin was a stickler for staying within the bounds of the law, but it would take all of Tamblin's finesse in the courtroom to lead the judge and jury down this path. One would expect that if a person was suing for libel, the focus should be on proving the falsity of the statements rather than simply their malignance. This was something Michael intended to ponder carefully. He wanted to be convinced of this plan if he was going to contribute to its success.

For now, he didn't much like that he'd spent those days traveling to the asylum and working up the report, only to have it set aside as backup. Especially since he had so many other demands on his time, doing the devil work for Tamblin as well as attending to his own clientele. The legal system might move slowly, but that didn't mean barristers were idle. There were constant summonses, trials, and mountains of associated paperwork. The time Michael had lost recovering from the accident had set him very much behind. He currently had three briefs on his desk to attend to, plus an appointment at court this afternoon.

Setting aside for the moment his worries over the libel case, Michael spent the next hour reviewing his newest briefs and attempting to make a schedule for the week ahead. But he could not keep his mind on his work. His head throbbed, and the scars on his neck had been itching all day. The itching was a sign that the cuts were healing, but that didn't make the sensation any more pleasant.

Tossing his pen down in frustration, Michael rose from his desk and looked out the window toward the park-like area attached to Gray's Inn, known as the walks. Tender new leaves rustled in the trees, while the gusty March wind swirled the brown remnants of last year's crop along the footpaths. He tugged again at his collar and remembered Julia's recommendation of the chemist on Gray's Inn Road who sold an ointment to treat the scars. He decided to stop there on his way home from the courts. It seemed ironic, though, to remember this bit of advice after spending a morning engaged in the business of attacking the school she hoped one day to attend.

He packed up the papers he needed for his court appearance, grateful that the walk over to the Royal Courts of Justice would afford him some fresh air. He hoped the exercise might help his brain feel not quite so addled as he contemplated many conflicting concepts at once.

Solvitur ambulando—It is solved by walking.

Perhaps that Latin proverb was something to share with Julia at their next lesson.

Julia and Edith followed the woman, who had told them her name was Hettie, down the rough streets of Bethnal Green.

As they walked, Hettie gave them more information about the woman they were going to visit. The sisters had come here two years ago from Poland. Her sister's husband had died just six months ago in an accident at the dockyards. Hettie had never married but supported herself with piecework—sewing shirts from precut cloth for a clothing merchant. Now she was helping to support her sister and her sister's two children as well.

They found some relief from the buffeting wind as they turned down a narrow, crooked alley. Julia could easily imagine the opposite effect in summer: the hot air would be still and oppressive. Edith had given Julia a scented handkerchief to use as they went through the more foul areas, and they both pulled them out now to offset the rank smells of rotting food scraps, dead vermin, and urine. Hettie didn't seem to notice the smells as she hurried on.

They stopped at a building that was little more than a crumbling pile of bricks. Hettie opened a flimsy, ill-fitting door, and they stepped inside. In the gloom, for there were no lamps, they followed Hettie up a dangerously rickety staircase to the second floor.

The only light in the hallway came from a tiny window set high up on the wall. Two doors stood on either side, each presumably leading to tenants' rooms.

Hettie opened one of the doors, calling out something in Polish as she ushered Julia and Edith inside.

It was a pitiful scene. The apartment consisted of one room. Feeble rays of daylight barely penetrated what was left of the sole window. Half the window's glass had been broken out, replaced with crudely fitted pieces of wood that blocked the light and did little to keep out the drafts. The walls were bare save for a rough wooden crucifix by the door.

A woman lay in a saggy bed against one wall. Two children were there as well: a small boy stood next to the bed, looking anxiously at his mother, and a little girl of about two sat at the foot of the bed, playing with a rolled-up bit of cloth as though it were a doll.

The sick woman looked at Edith and Julia with glazed eyes. "My sister says she has brought two doctors?" It came out as a question, as though she'd misheard.

"We are here to help you," Edith told her. She set her bag on a battered table near the bed and opened it.

The boy immediately went to the table and tried to look inside the bag. "What's in there?"

"Things that will help your mother," Edith replied, pulling out a stethoscope. "But you mustn't touch anything, because we don't want to damage something that could help her, do we?"

The boy withdrew his hand, which had been reaching out to touch the bag. "No, ma'am."

"Come here, Sam, there's a good boy," Hettie said, taking a seat on one of two stools that were the only furniture in the room for sitting. Sam went and stood by her side, and she wrapped an arm around him.

"What's your name?" Edith asked the woman in the bed.

"Sybil." The word barely came out through dry and cracked lips.

"Well, Sybil, we are going to have a look at you. You don't mind, do you?"

Sybil did not speak, but the fear in her eyes as she looked at Edith's face was unmistakable.

"I had smallpox several years ago," Edith said. "I can no longer catch it or spread it."

This seemed to allay Sybil's fears. She did not protest when Edith gently pulled aside the thin, worn blanket covering her in order to place a stethoscope over her heart.

Edith did a thorough examination, including the woman's abdomen, which was swollen with her seventh month of pregnancy. Julia offered a few suggestions where she could, drawing on her previous work as a nurse. She also ensured that the little girl, whose name was Jemmie, was kept out of the way so Edith could work without interference.

When they had finished examining Sybil, Edith and Julia conferred together.

"She has a fever," Edith said, "but I do not think it is influenza. Or cholera, thank God. The skin pallor, among other things, points to a more low-grade fever."

"I agree," Julia said.

It was good news. A serious illness could do irreparable harm to the baby.

Edith mixed up a draught of some of the items she'd brought with her, and they were able to coax Sybil to sit up enough to take it.

Now more alert than when they'd come in, Sybil studied the two women with interest. "Are you really doctors?" she asked.

"We will be," Edith answered. "We are in training."

"I've never heard of women doctors."

"You do believe we have helped you today, don't you?" Edith asked as she set the glass aside.

"Oh yes!" Sybil reached out to take Edith's hand. "Will you come back when it is time for me to have my baby?"

"There is a maternity clinic close by," Edith pointed out. "It is attached to the workhouse, but they accept other patients. They will be able to help you when the time comes—"

"No!" Sybil shrieked, clutching tighter to Edith's hand. "The women who go there to give birth, they all die. It is the killing fever there."

Julia grimaced. Sybil was referencing puerperal fever, the bane of maternity wards.

"I do not fear for myself, for God in heaven will receive me, and I will see my beloved Johann again. But I will not leave these beautiful children orphans. I cannot!"

Her terror was palpable. Picking up on her mother's anguish, Jemmie began to wail. Sam was silent, but tears slid down his face.

Sybil stretched out her hands, and Hettie scooped up Jemmie and placed her in her mother's arms. Immediately Sybil began crooning to the child, soothing her. Sam came over to the bed, leaning in to get some of his mother's loving caresses.

"It's shocking how cavalier they can be with people's lives," Edith murmured. "I must implore Dr. Anderson to speak to them, for I know they will not accept it from me."

Julia knew she was talking of the workhouse hospital. Despite growing evidence that puerperal fever could be stopped from spreading if doctors and all other medical personnel simply washed their hands thoroughly between patients, many places still had not instituted the procedure.

The act of soothing her children had calmed Sybil, but still she turned to look at Edith and Julia with pleading eyes. "You will come, won't you?"

The birth was two months off, and with all the demands on their time, it would be hard to say with certainty that they would be able to get here when the time came. Julia could see Edith was probably thinking the same thing. But it was impossible to refuse Sybil's imploring gaze.

They said, nearly in unison, "Of course we'll come."

CHAPTER

11

As Michael waited in the Barkers' parlor for Julia
to arrive, he noticed Corinna had already cleared the
table of its usual assortment of items. Perhaps she didn't
want anyone but her moving them about. He couldn't understand
why she needed so many decorative things. Perhaps it was just
something women liked to do.

Walking over to the curio cabinet, he studied the African chess
set that had caught Julia's eye. He tried to conjure up a picture
of her plying her medical practice there. What would that look
like? Would she remain in one of the towns, or venture out into
the wilderness? From what he'd seen of her, he had no doubt
she was intrepid enough to attempt the latter. But did she truly
understand the dangers?

Hearing the doorbell, he turned in anticipation, expecting
the butler to escort Julia to the parlor. Instead, he was surprised
to see Corinna leading her in. Julia looked surprised, too, but
Michael saw her lips twitch. Catching her eye, he smiled back.

An unexpected and peculiar feeling of happiness filtered through him at the sight of her.

"I'm just on my way out," Corinna announced. "However, the servants are nearby if you should need anything."

It was phrased as helpful, but as she'd noticed the way Michael and Julia had just traded smiles, Michael was sure it was her way of advertising that the two of them would not really be alone. Her parting glance at Michael—a warning to behave himself—confirmed it.

It was another reminder that Corinna was anything but pleased by the situation. Michael was glad this year's winter social season was a busy one. There were plenty of events to keep his sister occupied outside of the house, and she was taking advantage of them. Her baby was due in July, and she would likely stop going out a month or two beforehand. Therefore, she would miss a good portion of the high summer season.

"How is the wound?" Julia asked, approaching him.

"Healing well," he assured her. "The ointment you recommended is doing a wonderful job. Very soothing."

"Excellent." But her focus was still on his neck, as though she were about to ask to see it for herself.

This was not something Michael was ready to face again. He remembered too vividly her previous examinations. The sensation of her cool, practiced touch. When she had scrutinized the cut on his forehead, bringing her face close to his, he hadn't feared that her prodding would cause pain. Rather, he'd been uncomfortable at her nearness.

Was it because she was a woman? Even though women were now able to become licensed physicians, they were primarily limiting their practice to other women and children, and this seemed to Michael a proper state of affairs. Fear about overstepping the bounds of propriety had never been as all-consuming to him as it was to his sister and many others in society, but he had to admit that having a woman so close, in a professional context, might not be advisable. Especially when he recalled his reaction when she had delicately run a hand along his hairline, ruffling his hair—and his composure.

He quickly strode over to the table, picking up the book he'd left there. "I brought something for you. It's the volume of Cicero we spoke of at our last meeting."

She gave a murmur of delight as Michael held the book out to her, accepting it with reverential awe.

"Don't worry, it's not a priceless artifact. It is well used, and you may find various notes written in the margins."

"Nevertheless, I promise to take good care of it." She began leafing gently through the volume. "I see what you mean about the notes. I believe I might find them helpful."

"Scrawls of a schoolboy who knew little more Latin than you do now. But you're welcome to any wisdom they might impart." He was oddly gratified to see the corners of her mouth turn up at his joke.

As they sat down at the table, he said, "Have you been working on the conjugations list we drew up during the previous lesson?"

"Yes, here it is." She pulled a sheet of paper from the book she'd brought with her. "Twenty verbs written out in the imperative mood and the perfect subjunctive."

Michael took the paper and glanced down at it. He frowned and shook his head. "One thing I can see right away that you will want to work on is your penmanship."

"I admit that is not my strong point." She looked appealingly unabashed. "However, I did try to make it legible. Can you not read it?"

She leaned closer to him, so that they might peruse her work together. Once more Michael noticed there was no cloud of floral scent wafting around her. She was scrubbed clean and fresh. Unpretentious in any way.

He forced his attention back to the paper. "It's an interesting style. Forthright and, well, *energetic*."

She laughed. "No one's ever read that much into my handwriting before. Are you sure you've never been a schoolmaster? I think you would have been a very good one."

He found himself distracted by her laughing eyes and the freckles on her nose. It was aggravating how she managed, without trying, to disturb his concentration. "I'll keep that in mind if my work in the legal profession ever dries up."

"Ah, right. I suppose your work keeps you busy?"

"It does." Michael answered with some apprehension, for she was leaning forward, looking at him intently.

"Have you ever had to represent a client whose position you strongly disagreed with?"

Oh no. He could see where this line of questioning was going, clear as day. "Many times."

His direct, affirmative response appeared to catch her off guard. "And does that not bother you—even in the slightest?"

He regretted that his quip had reminded her that his professional activities were indirectly pitting them as adversaries. He was also irked at her insinuation that there was something unethical about him or his profession. "It's not my job as a barrister to make moral judgments. I will leave that to the Church."

This blunt answer ought to have silenced her, but she continued on, undaunted. "Have you felt that way about any *recent* cases?"

She peered at him with frank openness, as though she actually expected him to answer that question. He felt some of his annoyance dissipate, because really, how could he blame her for wanting to use any opportunity to influence him? But he had to put a stop to it.

"Miss Bernay." He spoke her name in an admonishing tone. "If we were in a court of law, I'd say you were leading the witness. You know we can't discuss this."

She looked a little deflated. "I understand." She made as if to return to her work but then paused. "May I just say one thing? Not about the lawsuit."

He regarded her warily. "Yes?"

"There is more to the Church than passing judgment on people." She spoke quietly. Earnestly. "It's about finding the peace that comes with Christ. About the soul's rest in knowing a loving God."

For several long heartbeats, Michael could think of nothing to say. Her rock-solid belief in this loving God was undeniable, but he couldn't share it. He cleared his throat. "Shall we return our attention to Cicero?"

It was a truce, and she accepted it with a nod. "What shall we learn today?"

Her bright eagerness was hard to resist. Michael pointed toward the book. "I've placed a marker at page fifty-four. The second paragraph is a good one for practicing translation. Why don't you work on that while I review this list you wrote up?"

"Right." Julia turned to the book and began reading, and Michael could almost physically feel the atmosphere of the room return to normal.

While she pored over the paragraph, Michael checked her list of verb conjugations. It was actually a refreshing mental exercise to review the intricate mechanics of the language. The Latin phrases he used daily as a barrister were dry and rote. Reading philosophical and poetic texts, with their varied nuances, enlivened his imagination again. As he watched, Julia began to sketch out a translation. She opened the Latin dictionary to look up a word she didn't recognize, and Michael realized just how much he was looking forward to spending time in the classics again.

She looked up from her work. "I'm a bit confused here." She pointed to the text. "If I'm reading this correctly, the verb shifts to present tense, which seems odd."

"I'm glad you noticed. That's one of the reasons I chose this paragraph. This is called the 'historic present.' In a narrative that is set in the past, Latin authors often used the present tense to create a vivid effect. As you see here, they might even switch from past tense to the historic present within the same sentence."

"Ah, I see what you mean," Julia said, as she reread the sentence.

"So tell me how you would translate it."

She looked several times between her notes and the text. "'When it had been . . . reported to the general that they were trying to march through our province, he hastened'—although that is literally 'hastens'—'to set out from the city.'" He nodded, and she smiled in triumph. "It does make it feel more immediate, doesn't it? You can sort of feel his rush to set off."

"Exactly." He picked up the volume and skimmed through it, looking for another example. "Try this paragraph. You will spot the historic present here as well."

They spent the rest of the hour reading through various places in the text, although they had to stop frequently for her to refer to the dictionary. Michael could easily have given her the definitions, but he felt she would absorb it better if she looked up the words herself. Along the way, they discussed points of grammar that arose.

Michael was disappointed when the clock struck the hour. Their time had been enjoyable, despite the rough beginning. But now there were pressing matters at work to attend to. "Time to end our lesson for today."

Julia closed the books, although it seemed she felt the same reluctance as Michael.

After helping her up, Michael began to walk toward the door, but Julia stayed where she was. He turned and looked at her expectantly.

She said, "I assume Miss Maynard suffered no harm after the accident on the Underground?"

Startled, he answered, "Yes, she is well. Did you have a specific reason for asking?"

She shrugged. "Sometimes the shock of an incident doesn't really manifest in any noticeable way until later. At the time, Miss Maynard seemed fine from a physical standpoint, but she was quite distraught. Exceedingly so."

Michael grimaced, remembering her lurid descriptions at the dinner party. "Yes, I know."

"I got the impression she is very fond of you. I suppose you might be considering marriage someday? Perhaps soon?"

He blinked. He had the sense that she'd been doing some homework—beyond the Latin—since their last lesson. "Do you make it a habit to ask impertinent questions?"

"I suppose my medical training makes me more forthright than I ought to be."

Despite the semiapologetic tone, Michael sensed she was still expecting an answer. "Have you any plans to get married?" he countered.

"I've told you already, I plan to become a medical missionary. I've no time for marriage." She said it in such an offhand way, dismissing an important life event. "But I suppose you plan to marry Miss Maynard?"

Michael marveled at her temerity to even ask. He had no idea what she was fishing for. It was possible she was merely curious. But really, he didn't owe her an answer at all. He was about to tell her as much when she looked past him.

He turned and saw Corinna standing at the parlor door. How much of this conversation had she heard? From her frown, she might have heard all of it. Or she might have heard none of it and would have been scowling at them anyway.

Her demeanor remained frosty even after Julia had gone.

"A word with you, please," Corinna said, as Michael went to the hallway and reached for his overcoat from the coat rack.

"Corinna, I can't stay. I've got a court summons this afternoon, and I'm meeting a new client."

"I would like to know why you can't answer a direct question about Laura—even if it was asked with such impertinence."

"Precisely because it *was* asked with such impertinence," Michael replied, taking his sister's words for ammunition. "Given that Miss Bernay is invested in the fate of the medical school, there is always the possibility she might try to use personal information against me in some way."

"It's not *that* personal. At least, it won't be once the notice of your engagement gets into the *Times*."

"Well, we're not there yet," he reminded her. "Lord Delaford asked me to wait, and that's what I intend to do."

He put on his gloves and hat and made for the door.

"Are you sure that's why you're waiting?" Corinna's voice was accusing as she called after him. "Or is there some other reason?"

This stopped him cold. He turned around. "Will you stop badgering me! Everything is on track. However, if you think going against the viscount's wishes is the way for me to secure Laura's hand, I'll gladly do it."

Corinna recoiled at his abrasive tone, but her response was as forceful as his. "Just be careful that you're not allowing anything—or any*one*—to waylay our plans."

Our plans.

She would never let him forget how important this match was to her. Michael's heart grieved to see her insecurity, despite how far they'd come. But they were no longer on shifting sands, even if Corinna seemed to think so.

"We've had this discussion before, remember?" Despite his chiding words, he spoke in a gentler tone. "Miss Bernay saved my life, and I am rendering her a very small service in return. That is all."

"I'm grateful to her, of course, but that doesn't stop me from worrying. After all, what do we know about this woman? Where does she come from? What is her family?"

He had to admit Corinna was right about that. He blew out a breath. "I don't honestly know." He had taken Julia's statements about herself at face value and not asked for details. "I will ask her the next time we meet. In the meantime, you needn't worry. Easter is just a few weeks away. After that, when the Season is truly under way, I expect things with Miss Maynard will move swiftly."

By the time Michael left, Corinna was mollified, but now it was Michael who was unsettled.

It was true that he knew virtually nothing of Julia's background. That was something he would rectify. Interestingly, she'd had no qualms at all about asking Michael all manner of personal questions.

Corinna had intimated that Julia had designs on him, but Michael found this hard to believe. To be sure, there was a growing camaraderie between them—so long as she wasn't needling him about God or the libel suit. Now he could add prodding about his marriage plans to that list. But she insisted she was going to Africa and had every intention of remaining single. Michael was pretty sure she was fanatic enough to be telling the truth. He couldn't help thinking it was a shame that a woman like that should dedicate herself to spinsterhood. A woman that beautiful and clever would be a good catch for the right sort of man.

Someone who wasn't intimidated by her candor and independent streak. Someone like—

Michael pulled up short, as though the physical stop could help him rein in his thoughts. Despite Corinna's warnings, he couldn't believe the distraction Julia caused him was intentional. But whether intentional or not, he could not allow her to interfere with his life. Julia seemed to be an open book, but he would do well to delve a little deeper.

"I can hardly believe we are here," Lisette said to Julia, as they arrived at Dr. Anderson's home on the night of the *conversazione*. "It seems like our unofficial start to medical school, doesn't it?"

Julia agreed. As a manservant led her and Lisette upstairs, Julia was filled with anticipation for the night ahead.

Dr. Anderson met them at the parlor door. "Welcome to you both."

"This is truly an honor," Julia said.

"Yes!" Lisette exclaimed. "To be invited here, when we are not yet students of the school, is such a privilege."

"Perhaps this will motivate you to study hard and ensure you pass that entrance exam," Dr. Anderson replied with a smile. "I hope you will find the evening profitable."

A half-dozen ladies were already in the parlor, including Edith Morton. She introduced Julia and Lisette to the others while Dr. Anderson went to greet a few more guests who'd just arrived.

After a while, Dr. Anderson called for everyone to be seated. Julia noticed there were still a few empty chairs.

"I believe you will find tonight's discussion very illuminating," Dr. Anderson began.

That was as far as she got, however, before a little boy rushed into the room, accompanied by a tall redheaded man wearing a bemused expression.

"Mama!" the boy cried, launching himself into Dr. Anderson's arms.

She laughed as she received the boy into her lap, although she said with gentle disapproval, "Alan, what are you still doing up?"

The man lingered at the door. "Apologies, my love, but he wanted to say good-night to you before going to bed. He has absolutely made up his mind on it. I can't think where he gets his stubbornness from."

He spoke with a Scottish brogue. Julia had heard a lot about Jamie Anderson, all of it good. Co-owner of a large and prosperous shipping line, as well as a board member of several important organizations in London, he was a successful man in his own right. Yet he never resented his wife's notoriety, which gave her a far more prominent position in the public eye. He supported and encouraged her efforts. Julia thought it must be a rare man who would do that. And now here he was, being a doting father as well.

Dr. Anderson sent a look over her son's head, her smile returning the playful accusation of her husband. "I think he gets his stubbornness from the same place he inherited his red hair."

Her husband laughed.

Lisette sprang from her chair and took Mr. Anderson by the arm. "You will be joining us tonight, won't you?"

It seemed a very forward gesture, but Julia knew by now that this was simply Lisette's nature. She did not have the English reticence about physical contact.

Mr. Anderson took it in stride. "I'm not staying if you plan to discuss vivisections or other horrors," he countered, although it was clear he was only teasing. He allowed Lisette to bring him into the center of their circle.

The boy squirmed in his mother's arms. "What's vivee . . . vibee . . ."

Dr. Anderson stroked his hair. "Never you mind. It's bedtime. Here's your hug and kiss." She gave him both with a mother's effusive tenderness. "My sweet baby," she murmured, almost in a whisper, giving him a tight squeeze before releasing him. "Now, you must run along with Papa and go to bed."

The boy threw his arms around his mother's neck and planted a last kiss on her cheek before wriggling out of her lap and running to take his father's hand.

"We won't be discussing vivisection," Dr. Anderson called out to her husband as he led the child toward the door. "In fact, I've asked Millie and Henry to join us tonight."

"Have you? Sounds intriguing. I'll be back in ten minutes."

"How astonishing," murmured one of the other students as she watched father and son leave the room.

"What's astonishing?" Dr. Anderson asked with a smile. "That our son obeys his parents?"

"No, that you have such a kind husband who allows you to continue in your career."

"There are a few out there."

"*Very* few," Lisette declared stoutly. "Most men want to keep women 'in their place' and suppress the good they could do in the world. I plan to remain single so I can control my own destiny."

It wasn't the first time Lisette had voiced this opinion. Julia could sympathize with it. At times, it did seem as though the odds were stacked against women. Several other students echoed Lisette's sentiments.

Dr. Anderson raised a hand to quiet them. "There were plenty of people—women, mostly—who were surprised or even angry when I got engaged. I had only just qualified to practice medicine, and the naysayers told me my career was over before it had even begun. And yet in the ten years I've been married, I've been able to grow my practice, open new clinics, and help establish the first school of medicine for women in England."

"But it was a hard fight, wasn't it?" Lisette pointed out.

"I'm not denying that I had many obstacles to overcome. It was supremely frustrating at times. I needed a great deal of patience as well as persistence. Others tried to force their way into this profession through sheer belligerence, but over the years I have found that tempering my dogged determination with professional courtesy and congeniality has yielded far better results. There are now more medical men who perceive me as a colleague than as an enemy. I encourage you all to take the same approach I did."

"You are such an inspiring example to us," one of the other students gushed. "I'm working hard to become a doctor, but I would also like to have a family someday."

"I still say good luck finding a man who will allow you to do that," Lisette scoffed. "By the laws of England, you and everything you own will be his property to do with as he likes."

From the parlor door, a cheerful voice said, "I hope we are not late."

Julia turned to see that this comment came from a petite woman who had her arm wrapped through that of a man wearing dark glasses.

Dr. Anderson went over to give her a warm hug. "You are right on time, Millie. Miss Blanco has just brought up the question of married women and property. Something you are both eminently qualified to discuss."

Since Julia and a few other students did not know these newcomers, Dr. Anderson introduced Millicent and Henry Fawcett, her sister and brother-in-law. Despite being blind, Mr. Fawcett seemed to have a good sense of where the people around him were located. As he was being introduced, he insisted on shaking everyone's hand.

Jamie Anderson returned to the room while the introductions were being made, and gave his in-laws a warm greeting.

"Mr. Fawcett is a member of Parliament and a champion for women's causes," Lisette whispered to Julia.

As the Fawcetts were being seated, Dr. Anderson told the students, "Mr. Fawcett is a proponent of the Married Women's Property Act. If passed, it will allow women to retain control of their own property and earnings."

"I'd vote for the Act if I were a member of Parliament," Edith declared.

"I'd be happy just for the privilege to vote at all," another student chimed in.

"Women's suffrage—something else this country sadly lacks!" Lisette spoke with such fervor she nearly rose from her chair. "But how can it change? So long as men run the government, they will never be persuaded to share that power with women."

"I don't like the idea that men and women must always be at enmity," Millicent Fawcett said. "Why is it so hard to picture us all working together?"

"Like you and Mr. Fawcett?" Julia asked. She was growing in admiration for this couple.

"That's one way," Mrs. Fawcett answered. "We must allow that in some marriages, men and women may have entirely separate careers." She indicated the Andersons. "Or their work may be intertwined, as with me and my husband. Other women may decide to remain unmarried to pursue a career, and others will marry and prefer to focus on home and family. Can we truly fault any of these choices? What we should be advocating is simply for the right of women to be able to decide for themselves what is best for their lives."

"Well spoken, my dear," Mr. Fawcett said, giving his wife's hand an appreciative pat. "You can see why she is my chief speech writer."

Mr. Anderson scratched his chin in an exaggerated gesture of thought. "So the topic for this evening is women and the law?"

Dr. Anderson said, "In fact, I asked Henry to come tonight so he could explain to us the details of the new sanitation bills that were presented last week. I thought we could discuss their timing and possible impact on public health." With a smile she added, "But this has certainly turned out to be a much livelier discussion."

The conversation did eventually turn to the sanitation laws, but later that evening as Julia and Lisette were walking home, it was the topic of marriage that dominated Julia's thoughts.

Not that she had any plans to get married. But that was because she didn't think her missionary work would be compatible with being a wife, not because she thought there were no men who would be supportive of their wives having a career. After all, hadn't her sister Rosalyn married such a man? Rosalyn and Nate were even now touring northern England in a production of Gilbert and Sullivan's operetta *H.M.S. Pinafore*. Rosalyn was performing in the chorus and Nate worked backstage. Together they were happy and living the life they loved. Before now, Julia had supposed their arrangement was an aberration from the norm, but she was beginning to see that there were others forging new paths as well.

As she contemplated these things, she thought about Michael's possible marriage to Laura Maynard. What type of wife would she be? Probably a society matron like Corinna. Julia didn't think Michael would be content in such a marriage, even though it seemed to be his objective. He needed someone who would be a match for him in intellectual pursuits as well.

Unfortunately, questioning him on the subject had only caused consternation to both brother and sister. Did Corinna think Julia wanted to interfere with Michael's marriage plans? That wasn't her intention. She was simply curious to know what was motivating him to make that choice, but they had seen it as prying into their affairs.

Perhaps Dr. Anderson's advice for success was something Julia could apply in her dealings with Michael and Corinna. Maybe she'd come up against their brick walls because she'd been too blunt with her questions. *Patience is a virtue*—this was something she'd heard over and over again growing up in the orphanage. As a child she'd disliked that saying, thinking that to have patience meant waiting around and doing nothing. But as an adult she'd learned that it often meant to trust God's timing, not her own. She would not stop pressing to achieve her goals, but when it came to her dealings with people, she might do better to tread more lightly.

CHAPTER

12

I THOUGHT WE WOULD TRY something different today,"
Michael said. After several weeks of lessons, he could see she
was ready for a new challenge.

Julia faced him with eager attention. "Do you mean we shall
do something other than noun declensions, verb conjugations,
and vocabulary drills?"

"Precisely. You have a quick mind and are adept at memoriz-
ing many things."

She preened at this compliment. Until he'd met Julia, Michael
had never seen a woman whose pride in knowledge outweighed
her vanity about her personal appearance. There was nothing
at all artful in her dress or in the way her hair was done up in
a simple bun at the back of her neck. And yet she was alluring
without benefit of decoration. Too often during these lessons,
those freckles on her slender nose had distracted him so much
that he'd lost a train of thought and had to stop midsentence.

As they were threatening to do now.

Michael determined to bring the one thing she *was* vain about down just a notch—if only to bring his own thudding heart back to normal. He said in his best schoolmaster voice, "You cannot expect rote memory to get you successfully through the exam, and certainly not when it comes to actually using Latin later. The important question is how well you can apply your knowledge to actual sentence construction."

She straightened a little, her slender shoulders squaring at the challenge. "How do we work on that?"

That was something else he'd noticed about their time together. She often used the term *we*, as though these lessons were something they were pursuing together, like a team, rather than the more obvious case of student and teacher.

Michael took out a piece of paper. "*We* know you will be asked to translate from Latin into English for the examination. You have done this tolerably well with the texts I've given you. However, I believe the best way to build fluency in the language is to translate from English into Latin." He set the paper before her. It had three paragraphs printed on it. "Tell me how you would translate this."

She looked down at the paper, absently reaching for the Latin dictionary as she began reading.

He reached to stop her. "Without the dictionary."

His hand—now free from the splint and bandages—rested on hers briefly. Her skin felt cool beneath his, soft and delicate, and yet he knew from experience that they were sensible and strong hands. Even this light contact brought back vivid memories of her practiced touch when she'd examined him. He was unprepared for the burst of pleasure it gave him.

Julia's eyelids fluttered opened a little wider, as if she, too, had felt some unexpected sensation.

Fighting the urge to trace a finger along her skin, Michael

withdrew his hand. "This is something my teacher at Harrow gave us for practice. The sentences are structured to challenge the translator in the use of verb tense and rhetoric, as well as vocabulary."

"And you've kept it all this time?"

"I found it as I was going through a few dusty old books from my school days that I never got around to parting with."

He spoke casually, not wanting to admit that he'd purposefully kept those books. They were like tangible memories from a happier time. Back when his life was a lot simpler.

It was a pleasant little story, too, briefly describing two small groups of travelers who meet as they are going in opposite directions along a country road in spring. They stop, greet one another, and have a brief conversation before traveling on their respective journeys. Intended as a didactic device, the syntax of the piece was a little tortured, but there was a line that Michael had always found intriguing, whether in Latin or English.

Julia, apparently arrested by the same sentence, read it softly aloud: "'They now continued on their way, and yet the young man in the wagon looked back, once more, at the westbound travelers. As they rode into the valley, their wagon was framed by the wildflowers in the field, a hint of color that was to be their lives, and the young man wondered whether he ought not to have taken the other route after all.'" She looked up at him. "That's quite a nice image, isn't it?"

"Yes." He grappled with his thoughts. He had perhaps been foolish to bring in this paper. He'd forgotten just how profoundly this little passage had affected him when he'd first read it in school. He'd fancied that the young man in the story had seen a beautiful maiden sitting in that wagon, and that was what made him wish to turn back. It was a typical daydream for a lad of fourteen, but as he recalled it, Michael remembered he had always pictured the girl as a brunette with laughing eyes and a determined lift to her chin. And perhaps a few freckles, too.

He cast around for something to get his mind off that old daydream. "Are you hungry?"

"Famished," Julia replied with gusto. Seeing his look, she said, "I seem to be too busy to stop and eat these days."

He stood up. "I'll see if there is some tea at hand. In the meantime, why don't you have a go at translating that?" He paused at the door. "Remember, no dictionary."

She nodded, apparently not seeing anything unusual in his sudden departure, and immediately became absorbed in the work.

Even though he was ostensibly seeking one of the servants, he was relieved to see no one in the hallway. He needed a quiet moment to take a deep breath and regain his composure. How could this woman have such an effect on him?

"May I help you, sir?"

Michael nearly jumped as the footman seemed to materialize from the shadows. "Yes, will you bring us some tea? And a few cakes, if there are some at hand."

"Certainly, sir."

The footman thus dispatched, Michael took another few moments alone before returning to the parlor.

When he went back in, Julia was still concentrating on her task. Her pen was paused over the paper, and with her other hand she was tapping a finger on her cheek.

It's a simple gesture, he told himself. *Plenty of people do the same.* But he could not recall a time when it had made him notice an appealing mouth so close by.

He returned to the seat beside her. "How are you progressing?"

She pushed the paper toward him. "I believe I've gone as far as I can. I'm afraid I can't think of the words for *hogshead* or *wildflower*." She laughed. "Seems an odd juxtaposition, doesn't it?"

"Indeed," he replied, smiling a little. Now that he had composed himself, he was braced to discuss the passage without getting caught up in memories. He read over what she had written and was impressed that she'd gotten as far as she had. Perhaps she would be ready to pass that exam in a few months after all. But there were still some gaps. "I believe you used the gerund here when you intended the pluperfect."

He had her write out the correct tense of the verb and pointed out a few other minor errors. They also took time to discuss two of the rhetorical devices in the piece.

"On the whole, this is tolerably good," he concluded, just as the maid arrived with the tea service.

It wasn't exactly profuse praise, but Julia responded with a smile of pride nonetheless, just as she'd done earlier. "May I look up those other two words?" She indicated the closed dictionary on the desk.

"Yes, that's a good idea."

The maid set the tray on a nearby table. There were cakes and, Michael was happy to see, sandwiches, too. Corinna's staff was well-trained to handle any request at a moment's notice, and by now they knew how much he enjoyed cold beef sandwiches.

The tea, too, was flavored with orange, another favorite of Michael's. He saw Julia inhale deeply as its scent reached her, but she did not look up until she had found the words she was seeking in the dictionary and written them down.

"You are quite disciplined," he observed.

"Years of practice. At the hospital, my meal often had to wait until more critical tasks were completed." She closed the books and stood up.

The maid was still standing next to the table where she'd set the tea tray. "Shall I serve you, sir?" she offered.

Michael suddenly found himself at a loss. He was not entirely sure of the protocol in this situation. Although he'd taken tea at the club and in dozens of fine homes, he'd always been the visitor being served. He glanced over at Julia. She also looked unsure what to do.

"Thank you, but we'll just serve ourselves," Michael told the maid.

She nodded and left the room, but not before something flickered in her expression that might have been disapproval.

"I've never been in the position of having to serve a lady before," he admitted. He didn't think the times he'd handed a cup to his sister counted.

"I'm honored to be the first." Julia sent a longing glance toward the sandwiches. "But I don't think we should stand on too much ceremony, do you? As we might both be said to be guests here?"

"Excellent point."

They seated themselves at the tea table.

"Might we pray first, before eating?" Julia asked.

Pray? Michael could not remember the last time he'd heard grace before a meal. It had probably been before his mother died. He was not comfortable with the idea, but he could not refuse her request.

Julia bowed her head. Michael did, too, but instead of closing his eyes, he watched her as she prayed.

"Dear Lord, we thank you for this food and for your bounteousness to us. May your hand of blessing be upon us and upon this house. Amen."

The prayer, which was brief but elegant, moved him. Or perhaps it was the expression on Julia's face as she prayed. He saw peacefulness there. However proud she was of her personal accomplishments, she seemed to have true humility before her God. There was generosity in her choice of words, too. *May your hand of blessing be upon us and upon this house.* Julia had to be aware that his sister was providing this location to them unwillingly. It had been abundantly clear in Corinna's attitude every time she'd seen Julia in the house. But Julia had prayed this prayer anyway.

She poured the tea, and they each helped themselves to the sandwiches and little tea cakes. As they ate, Michael realized this might be a good time to ask Julia about her background. He'd promised Corinna to do this several weeks ago, but the time had never felt right. Besides, any worry on his part over her possible ulterior motives had lessened as he'd seen her genuine determination to learn Latin. She came to every lesson with her homework painstakingly complete and a single-minded focus.

Now he wanted to find out about her not from suspicion but because he was personally interested. "May I ask you a question?"

Julia swallowed the bit of sandwich she'd been chewing. "Of course."

"Where are you from? How is it that you were able to come to London to study? At our first meeting, you mentioned having a generous benefactor, yet it seems you were supplied with everything except a Latin tutor."

Julia wiped a crumb from her mouth with a napkin, but Michael had the distinct impression the action covered up a smile. "Grammar, Mr. Stephenson," she chided. "I think that was *three* questions, if we count that last declarative sentence as a question."

"Perhaps you think I'm prying. But you can understand why I'm curious."

"I don't mind. I'm happy to tell you. The truth is, I lost my benefactor only days before that accident on the Underground."

"Who was he?"

"It was a lady, actually. Perhaps I should go back a bit." She took a sip from her teacup before continuing. "My two sisters and I grew up in an orphanage in Bristol. Actually, it's in an area just north of Bristol called Ashley Down."

Michael could scarcely believe it. She had a level of poise he would not expect from someone with such a background. She had always displayed reasonably good breeding, even if she was a tad too direct at times.

"You look surprised."

"Yes, well, considering where you are now, a student at Queen's College with plans to study medicine . . ."

She nodded. "I suppose my story is a bit unusual. I've come a long way, with the help of God." Having finished her sandwich, she took another sip of the orange spice tea. "The first thing I should tell you is that the orphanage is supported entirely by prayer. Mr. Müller, the founder, never solicits donations or money. He only sends his requests to God."

"That seems a risky way of managing things."

"Yet the prayers have always been answered! Money, clothing, *food*." She picked up a tea cake. "Even furniture and other items. They always seem to arrive just as they are needed."

If this was true, it would go a long way toward explaining Julia's strong faith. Michael nodded noncommittally, taking a bite of his own sandwich as he waited for her to continue. She did—after she finished off a tea cake.

"At the orphanage, the boys are apprenticed out at age fourteen. The girls stay on until they are seventeen, but during those last few years, they work at the orphanage in various roles, including overseeing the younger children. They are even paid a small stipend for it. I was assigned to the infirmary. That's when I began to realize I had an aptitude for nursing."

"Is there a lot of sickness at the orphanage?" Michael envisioned it as a soulless and unsanitary place. Maybe even a breeding ground for typhoid.

She held up a hand. "Please don't get the wrong impression! The buildings are very clean and orderly. But with two thousand children, there will always be someone under the weather. Not to mention the usual scrapes and sprains from raucous playtimes—"

"Did you say two *thousand?*"

"That's right."

"Supported only by prayer."

She caught the disbelief in his voice. "I suppose it seems surprising for those who have never tried it. But it works."

Michael wasn't ready to contradict her, and in any case, she continued her story without waiting for his reply.

"There was a doctor in Bristol who visited our little sick ward sometimes. I used to pester him endlessly with questions."

"That seems hard to believe."

She grinned. "He was impressed with my abilities, so he contrived to get me into training as a nurse after I left the orphanage. I was younger than the age they usually accept, but they made an exception for me on the strength of the doctor's word and by ensuring that I worked only with women and children. As I gained experience, my interest in medicine grew. A few years ago, when the laws were changed to allow women to qualify as doctors, I knew that's what I wanted to do with my life. Then last year, Mrs. Staunton, who was always a generous donor to the orphanage, offered to pay my way to medical school. It was another case of God answering prayer, because I did not ask her for money—she offered it. I had nursed her little boy through a very bad bout of the flu, and she was grateful to me for that."

"But you said earlier that she is no longer your benefactor?"

"That's true," she replied sadly. "I'm sorry to say her husband's bank failed, and they are without any funds to give." She added cheerfully, "I still have enough to live on, though. For a while."

"For how long?"

She shrugged. "Sufficient unto the day. I know God will provide other means when I need it."

That answer sounded as precarious as the idea of the orphanage surviving only by prayer. More troubling to Michael was the news she conveyed about her benefactor. "It seems wrong somehow that the Stauntons should be in these financial straits if they were answering prayer by giving you money."

"Are you suggesting God somehow fell short, causing or allowing the bank failure? No!" She waved a hand to accentuate the word. "Sometimes bad things happen in this world. But we can always look to God for a way up and out. It was a blow for them, to be sure. I pray every day for their recovery. I know God will give them the help they need. The Bible says we are to continue 'instant'—that means steadfastly—in prayer, so that's what I do."

Michael was silent for a few moments, considering her words. It had been many years since he'd thought or even heard so much talk about prayer. His mother used to pray with him and Corinna every night before bed, but it always seemed to be for vague, general things. Not the kind of specific requests Julia talked about. He toyed with the rim of his teacup, remembering the prayer she'd spoken before they ate.

"When you prayed for this house, I suppose you were including the people in it, as well?"

"Naturally. I am grateful to your sister for allowing us to meet here."

"Even though she does it grudgingly and only as a favor to me?"

"Perhaps especially so. It shows me how much she loves you that she would agree to this despite her personal preferences. I respect that. My two sisters and I would do just about anything for each other. I believe there are few things in life more important than one's family—don't you?"

That was true. Family was so important that it impacted every aspect of Michael's life. Even areas where he would have preferred greater latitude.

When he didn't respond right away, Julia said, "It was merely a rhetorical question. You needn't answer if you don't care to."

"No, you're right, family is important. Corinna has done a lot for me over the years. More than most people realize. In fact, if it were not for her, I would not be teaching you Latin. Not for lack of a location, but because I would never have attended university."

Michael could see in Julia's expression all the questions she wished to ask. Maybe she hesitated because he'd asked her before not to pry. Perhaps it would be good if he told her. Easter was coming up, and afterward the social season would be in high gear. Corinna expected many things of Michael—things he knew he must do. Julia had behaved charitably toward his sister, even though Corinna's manner could be abrasive. But Michael wanted her to understand that Corinna had good reasons for behaving as she did.

"Corinna is the only family I have. Since you were raised in an orphanage, I suppose that means you lost your parents at a young age?"

"Yes."

"We have that in common, then. My mother died when I was nine years old, and my father died seven years later."

Julia made a murmur of sympathy.

"My father left many debts. We had to sell off everything to escape the creditors. Corinna was only nineteen, but she had been managing the affairs of the household since our mother died. Our father's spendthrift ways had put us in a precarious financial position, and though she tried to curb expenses wherever she could, in the end, it wasn't enough. We found ourselves, in essence, penniless."

"How terrible!" Julia stared at him, wide-eyed. "What did you do?"

"I was at Harrow when he died, and of course I was immediately recalled home. It took nearly a year to dispatch my father's estate and determine exactly how deep in debt we were. I was ready to go out and earn my living however I could. I had enough schooling to get a job as a clerk, perhaps at a bank or a solicitor's office. But Corinna was determined that I should go to university and that she would get me there."

"How did she do that?"

"By marrying David Barker."

Julia downed the last of her tea, but Michael was sure the look on her face had nothing to do with how the beverage tasted.

"I put it too coarsely. I don't wish to disparage Corinna in any way. Many would call it a marriage of convenience, but in fact, David loved her long before she consented to marry him. They had met a year or so before my father died, and David had been smitten with her from the start. And now, I think, they are reasonably happy."

"So it was Mr. Barker who paid your way."

"Yes, I suppose that is more accurate. From the moment they became engaged, he loved me as a brother and has always been generous with his money. He was as adamant as Corinna that I should go to university. He never had that opportunity. He worked himself up to riches, being the son of a dry-goods merchant, and has earned a lot of money through insurance and foreign investments. Some people just have a talent for business."

Julia tilted her head, studying Michael. "What do you think your life would be like if you were a solicitor's clerk?"

It was a question Michael had asked himself many times. "It would have been like sitting near a banquet without being able to partake of it. I've always loved the law and wanted only to be a barrister. Perhaps I may even be a judge someday. I tell you these things so that you might understand why I never balk at my sister's requests or aspirations—at least, not too much."

"Yes, I see. I agree that she is to be lauded for doing so much for you. But do you really think she had to marry into money to do it? I'm an orphan, but God provided money for me. He always finds a way."

"Perhaps Corinna was the means for how He provided," Michael countered. "As the Stauntons were for you."

"Did you ever go to God? Pray about the situation?"

Michael didn't need to answer. She saw it in his face.

"That's too bad. Perhaps that might have led you to a better solution."

"Yes, we saved ourselves by our own devices. We saw it as playing the hand we'd been dealt. I'm not going to second-guess our actions."

He had to believe Corinna's sacrifices had not been entirely self-serving. There had to be something spiritual in a sister's devotion. But these were questions he never felt qualified to delve into, despite the very fine education purchased for him by Corinna and David.

"You have sisters," he added. "As you said, you and your sisters would do anything for each other."

"*Just about* anything." She reminded him of that qualifier, which he hadn't really grasped before.

"'Just about'?"

"If the request goes against what I know to be right, I must remain true to my conscience, even if it might seem ungrateful to others. I believe that must end up being better for everyone."

"'To thine own self be true'?"

She looked at him blankly, and he realized she didn't understand the reference. Perhaps there had not been a lot of Shakespeare in her past schooling.

"It's from *Hamlet*. 'To thine own self be true, and it will follow, as the night the day, thou can'st not be false to any man.'"

"Oh, I see. That's lovely."

She looked at him with what he could only describe as admiration, much as she'd done during their lessons whenever he'd helped her grasp a new concept.

He'd done what he told Corinna he would do. He'd gotten the story of Julia's background. It turned out she was dangerous after all. Not because she deliberately intended to do him harm—that kind of attack would have been easy to repel. No, the problem was far more complex. He would have been better off not inquiring. To have kept a safe, ignorant distance. From her wide-eyed earnestness to the way her slender fingers absently brushed a crumb from her skirt, he was far too drawn to her. This was a stealthier encroachment on his heart. He had better retreat before it was too late.

He set down his plate. "Shall we get back to work?"

CHAPTER

13

J ULIA SAW THE MORAN FAMILY as soon as she entered King's Cross Station. Nearly everyone had come—Nate's mother, his sister Mary, his brother Patrick, and Patrick's wife, Hannah, all stood together, reviewing the board that listed the platform numbers for arriving trains. Well, they were *mostly* standing together. Hannah kept getting pulled from the group by Tommy, her energetic toddler. He would have raced off to look at everything in the station if she hadn't kept a firm grip on his little hand.

"Julia!" cried Mary, hurrying to meet her. Tugging her toward the rest of the family, she exclaimed, "I'm so glad to see you again. It's been ages!"

Mary was eighteen, and although she helped with the family business of taking in washing for wealthy households, she had plans to find what she called "proper employment" in an office or perhaps as a shop girl at one of the larger department stores.

"How is the job search going?" Julia asked as they made their way over to the others.

"Still working on it," Mary whispered in response.

"There's our stranger," Mrs. Moran said in her distinct Irish accent, giving Julia a hug as she and Mary reached the group. "We haven't seen you since Christmas!" The reproach in her voice was unmistakable. "Have you been eating properly?" She held Julia at arm's length and scrutinized her. "They're not working you too hard, are they?"

"It's a school, Ma, not an iron mine," Mary chided in a manner that, whether she intended it or not, hilariously echoed her mother.

"School has kept me so busy," Julia murmured, although she didn't really feel the need to defend herself. Mrs. Moran was a loving woman, but she had some old-fashioned notions. Her disapproval of Julia's missionary plans sometimes made their interactions uncomfortable. Before coming to London, Julia had planned to share a room with Rosalyn at the Morans' home while she completed her schooling. But then Rosalyn and Nate had gotten married, and Julia thought it better to stay in lodgings next to Queen's College. Her sister relished being part of this big, boisterous family—something they'd never had growing up. But Julia savored her independence more.

They all had the same goal today, however. They'd come to welcome Rosalyn and Nate back to London. The couple had been touring the East Midlands with a production of *H.M.S. Pinafore*, but now they were on hiatus since the theatres closed during Easter week. Nate's sister Martha was the only member of the family not here. The others explained that she'd not been able to get away from the seamstress's shop. With so many orders to complete before Easter Sunday, they were overloaded with work.

"The train arrives at platform three," Mary informed Julia. "We're on our way there now!"

Patrick scooped up his wayward son and placed him on his shoulders as they trekked toward the platforms.

Julia said, "I've heard there's a new show starting soon."

Patrick worked on the lighting crew at the Opera Comique, where *The Pirates of Penzance* had just ended its run. He nodded enthusiastically, causing his son, who had tight hold of his hair, to giggle. "We've been incredibly busy with setup and rehearsals. The new show is called *Patience*, and I'm sure it will be a great success. It's very funny—but then, we couldn't expect less from Mr. Gilbert, could we?"

"What's it about?"

Patrick pointed toward the platform, where the train was just arriving. "I'll tell you later."

Julia was glad to see her sister again, even though she'd likely have to endure Rosalyn's continued attempts to persuade Julia to change her mind about becoming a missionary. Rosalyn was fully in support of Julia becoming a doctor; it was the aspect of going overseas that troubled her. Rosalyn was terrified of losing a sister to the deep, just as they'd lost their father. Julia didn't know how to convince her not to worry—she could only pray that when the time came to leave, her sisters would have come to terms with it and be at peace.

The line Michael had quoted to her at their last lesson came to mind: *To thine own self be true.*

She'd thought about it a lot since then. In fact, many things about their last lesson together remained on her mind. She felt strangely out of her depth. They'd had nearly six weeks of lessons, and with each one, Julia's anticipation had heightened. His family history, sad as it was, moved her greatly. Not only for the struggle he and Corinna had endured, but for the way he was so dedicated to his sister in return. Julia didn't think anything would persuade her to give up her dreams—not even if her sisters asked her to do so. Was Michael giving up something for his sister? Or were they pursuing the same goals together? It was something Julia could not entirely discern.

The phrase from Shakespeare was intriguing. As she'd thought about it, however, Julia realized it was not entirely correct. Really, it was God to whom a person owed first allegiance. That was how to find one's true self. She would relay this to Michael, but his spiritual hunger seemed minimal, and that was perhaps the most disappointing thing about him. There were times when she thought she could see it, but then it would just as quickly vanish.

The Moran family kept a lookout for Rosalyn and Nate among the passengers spilling out of the train. When the pair finally came into view, Julia thought her sister had never looked more beautiful. Over the past year, she'd seen Rosalyn only a handful of times, but each time she'd been impressed by her sister's increasing boldness and self-confidence. A happy marriage and a satisfying career on the stage had made her less reticent and more outgoing. She was joyful, almost carefree, despite her half-serious moaning about their hectic and demanding touring schedule.

The whole family rushed forward to embrace the new arrivals, causing a general scuffle and much laughter as Nate and Rosalyn tried to return every hug.

Rosalyn held Julia for several extra seconds. "I'm so glad to see you. How well you look."

"Tell that to Mrs. Moran," Julia whispered. "She thinks I don't eat enough."

Nate detached himself from his mother's fierce grip and held out his arm toward Julia. "My scar is healing well, as you can see, Dr. Bernay."

It was a reference to the day they'd met, when Julia had been fascinated by the long scar that ran from his hand nearly up to his elbow, an army injury that, at that time, had not yet fully healed. Now Julia could see the scar had paled significantly, and Nate flexed his hand to demonstrate that the range of motion was returning. Julia couldn't help but think of Michael again and how embarrassed he'd looked when he'd accidentally held his splinted hand forward to shake hers.

"Julia is not on medical duty today," Patrick informed him.

Nate looked at his brother askance. "How do you know that?"

"Because she hasn't asked me once about my broken leg." He feigned a limp and gave a moaning, exaggerated grimace that made Tommy laugh.

Hannah poked her husband. "Perhaps she hasn't asked because you've been healed for over a year now."

"Oh, thank goodness," Nate said with a dramatic sigh of relief. "I thought maybe you'd managed to fall off that ladder again."

"Nate has missed having Patrick to tease," Rosalyn said.

"Patrick might have broken his leg *and* recovered in the time you've been gone," Mrs. Moran put in, but her teasing held disapproval. She was unhappy when Nate and Rosalyn hadn't been able to come home at Christmastime. They'd been touring up north, almost to Scotland. With Christmas being their only day off, there had not been enough time to travel to London.

"We're here for the whole week now," Nate reminded her. "Just as we promised."

"Let's not spend half of it at the station," Patrick said. "I know for a fact that Liza is putting the finishing touches on a wonderful supper. Where's your luggage?"

The brothers went to collect Nate and Rosalyn's trunks out of the pile being off-loaded from the luggage carriage.

"A whole week without working," Rosalyn said with a happy sigh as she wrapped her arm through Julia's. "Much as I love the theatre, this will seem like heaven. I hope we can spend lots of time together. There is so much to catch up on. So much *news*."

Julia had plenty of studying to do, even though Queen's College was on break for Easter. With only two months before the university examination, she had to make the most of every day. Michael had given her a hefty Latin assignment to work on, too. But she would spend as much time with her sister as she could. There was indeed much to talk about. Julia needed to inform her about losing her benefactor and ask her opinion about moving in with the Morans. She had even halfway made up her mind to tell Rosalyn about her lessons with Michael, although since she'd promised to tell no one, she was warring with her conscience over doing so. She would wrestle with the problem again when the time came.

It struck Julia that Rosalyn had put an interesting emphasis on the word *news*. Rosalyn was beaming.

"Is something changing? I thought your tour ran through August."

Rosalyn slid a sideways glance at Mrs. Moran and Mary, whose interest was also piqued by Julia's question. "Oh yes, the tour is going on as scheduled. I just meant that I look forward to hearing all about your studies. And that accident on the Underground! You didn't provide nearly enough details in your letter."

Despite her words, Julia was pretty sure she'd been talking of something else.

Seeing Nate and Patrick's jovial chatter as they approached with the trunks, Julia suddenly had a vivid mental picture of Michael walking beside them, joining in their lighthearted banter. He would like these two, she felt sure. But the brothers inhabited a very different world from his. Those two worlds were not likely ever to meet.

Julia was generally better at giving advice than receiving it, but now she craved Rosalyn's guidance. She knew many things about the physical body and that organ in the chest that pumped blood, but she knew so little about affairs of the heart.

153

❧❦❧

Later, after a lively dinner at the Morans' home, Julia and Rosalyn finally had a few minutes alone. When she'd heard how Julia's best dress had been ruined in the accident, Rosalyn had insisted on giving Julia one of hers. She'd pointed out that she owned more than she could use right now anyway, since she had to keep her baggage to a minimum while on tour.

"Here's one that Jessie gave me last year," Rosalyn said, pulling out a dark green gown from the large oak wardrobe in her bedroom. "I think this color will suit you."

Julia held up the dress, trying to gauge its effect as she looked at herself in the tall mirror next to the vanity table. It did look very nice. "It seems almost too elegant, though," she said doubtfully.

"Nonsense. It will be perfect for the Easter service. You can also wear it to the theatre."

"I have neither the time nor money for that, I'm sorry to say."

"I hope you'll make the time. Nate and I have secured four tickets to *Patience*, and I'd like you to have one. Please don't tell anyone else, though. It's a surprise. We're going to present it to Martha for her birthday tomorrow. She's wanted to go to the opera for ages."

"It sounds wonderful!" Julia exclaimed. "I only wish we were going to see *you* singing in it."

"It would be lovely to perform in London," Rosalyn admitted. "It may yet happen. These touring shows have given me invaluable training, and my singing has reached a quality I would never have thought possible just a few years ago. But in the meantime . . ." She pointed to the gown Julia held. "Try that on. We'll see if it needs alteration."

As she was changing into the gown, Julia said, "Getting the tickets—is that the news you were hinting at earlier?"

Rosalyn stepped behind Julia to button up the back. "Partly. There is more, although Nate doesn't want to tell his family until everything is settled."

Julia caught a glimpse of Rosalyn's face in the mirror and saw that her eyes were sparkling with excitement. "I won't tell anyone," Julia promised, turning to face her. "What is it?"

"Nate is going to ask for a job at the Savoy."

This was interesting news, for it had many ramifications. Patrick had told them over dinner that *Patience* would be moving in October from the Opera Comique to the Savoy, a brand-new theatre being built specifically for Mr. Gilbert and Mr. Sullivan's operas. It would have only the most modern furnishings and equipment, even electric lights—a first for any theatre—although Patrick told them they would still use limelights to illuminate the principal singers. Lighting was Patrick's specialty, and one that Nate loved as well. Julia could see why he'd want to work there.

"Does that mean you'd be at the Savoy, too?" That would be thrilling news.

Rosalyn smiled but gave a tiny shrug. "It's doubtful. Getting a spot *on* the stage is a lot harder to manage. Of course, I could always go back to work as a dresser. Speaking of which . . ." She stepped back to study Julia. "This is lovely on you. Just perfect."

She began to fuss with the gown, placing a few pins in the bodice where she said it would look better if taken in. Julia wasn't sure that was necessary, but she trusted Rosalyn's judgment on such things. She was just thankful to have something so nice to wear.

"You wouldn't really go back to being a dresser, though, would you?" she asked after Rosalyn had helped her back into her other clothes.

"No, I was only teasing. Still, after traveling this past year and a half, I'll be happy to be in one place for a while, no matter what I do. And the truth is, well, Nate and I want to start a family."

Julia's gaze went immediately to Rosalyn's stomach. "Are you—?"

"No! That is, I'm not sure. There have been a few signs. But if I am, I'm only a month or two along, I think. There will be time to finish up our tour."

"But if you have children, does that mean you'd give up singing? You've come so far, and you just said you want to sing on a London stage."

"We don't know all the details yet. We don't even know whether there will be an opening at the Savoy for Nate. We just feel that returning to London is the right decision."

"That's a big decision to make without a clear plan."

"Perhaps. But when you're doing what you know is right, the next steps become evident as you need them." She took hold of Julia's hands. "Surely this is something we've learned together over the years? Our exact path may not always be clear, but with God, the way is always certain nonetheless."

"You're right." Feeling unusually sentimental, Julia pulled Rosalyn into a heartfelt embrace.

There was a knock on the door. "It's me," Nate called. "Ma wants to hear me play, and I realized the fiddle was brought upstairs with our other things."

"Don't come in just yet," Rosalyn called back in return. "We'll be there in a moment." Turning to Julia, she said in a softer voice, "Don't forget, our thoughts about returning to London are secret for now."

Julia nodded, and Rosalyn opened the door for Nate. She decided not to broach the subject of coming to live here. Rosalyn would be overjoyed to have them all living together under one roof, but Julia wasn't yet convinced it was the right answer. She didn't want to raise her sister's hopes. She had money for the next few months, so there was time. As Rosalyn had pointed out, the best way forward would reveal itself in time.

Julia took comfort in that thought for other reasons as well. She'd been unsettled by her growing attachment to Michael Stephenson. Spending so much time with him only made the way more murky rather than clear. This conversation had been a good reminder not to be anxious, and perhaps that was all she needed. Besides, how could she talk directly to Rosalyn about it without breaking her promise to Michael? In addition, her sister was so blissfully happy that Julia suspected she'd be more likely to try to convince Julia to stay in England, seeing romantic possibilities in her relationship with Michael that could never come to pass.

As they made their way downstairs, Julia's gaze kept straying to the way Nate's hand rested on the small of Rosalyn's back. A protective, loving gesture. A thought tried to slip into Julia's mind—could there be a husband for the type of life she planned to lead? A fellow missionary, perhaps?

No. Somehow Julia was sure that was the wrong answer. She was destined to remain single, and she'd always been satisfied with this fate.

She just wished the pangs of happiness she felt for her sister didn't have this disturbing hint of longing as well.

All Saints Church was impressive decked out in its finest Easter array, from the gold vessels on the altar to the profusion of lilies in stands along the walls. In truth, All Saints was impressive every day, with its elaborate frescoes, marble decorations, and polished granite columns topped with carved alabaster capitals. It was known for attracting the better classes, and yet, over the past few years, Michael had seen an influx of respectable working-class people here as well. The seating was open; there were no reserved pews. This eclectic mix was precisely why David preferred to come here. The elegant surroundings and high-church service satisfied Corinna, so she and her husband found this church mutually agreeable.

The congregation was dressed in their finest clothes today. Michael didn't normally pay attention to these things, but he noticed Corinna's hat was especially becoming. She had likely chosen it to draw attention away from her less fashionable gown, which was loosely fitted to allow for her burgeoning stomach. She was about six months along now, and her growing middle was unmistakable.

This year Corinna might have lobbied to attend the Easter service at St. Paul's Cathedral, with the hopes of rubbing elbows with Miss Maynard and her brother, the Viscount Delaford. But as Laura and the viscount were spending Easter week at their ancestral estate in the countryside, Corinna was content to follow David's wishes and come here.

Michael was glad to forgo visiting another church today. Being familiar with the services here, he did not have to worry about where to sit or who to talk to. His mind was free to think of many things, even as he listened to Reverend Compton's sermon.

"If we are indeed risen with Christ, this Eastertide is a solemn call to us to 'seek those things which are above.' . . ."

Easter was perhaps the holiest day of the year in the church calendar, and Michael was here, as he always had been before, out of obligation. It was expected. It cemented the appearance of propriety. Although these reasons were no less true on any other Sunday, today Michael had an additional and far weightier motivation. He could not stop turning over in his mind the way Julia spoke so freely of God—as though she were on intimate terms with Him. Not in a pompous way, as though she had somehow earned or deserved it. She saw God as a father who was taking care of her and guiding her path.

If that was so, did that mean God had specifically led her

into Michael's railway carriage on the day of the accident? Why should that matter to *Julia's* life—even though it had mattered so critically to his own? And why should Michael have been so favored? An omniscient God would certainly know that any thoughts Michael had sent His way were scarce and not generally favorable. Not since his mother had died. That day had been heart-wrenching enough for a small child, but its sorrows had been multiplied by the troubles that had come after.

Yet here Michael sat, ostensibly worshiping the Creator but really casting about for any reasonable explanation for all that had happened over the past few months. He resented the way Julia's words had begun shifting his thoughts on the matter. It was more comfortable to think of her presence on that train as a lucky coincidence. He was not going to become a religious zealot who looked for signs everywhere. To ascribe a larger meaning to it would surely place Michael under a burden that he must repay. He had too many such burdens already.

Reverend Compton looked over the congregation with a smile as he concluded his sermon. "Eastertide is the time of new life. Let us then seek to lead the risen life of striving after higher and better things. Let us go on unto perfection looking unto Jesus, our risen Lord, setting our affections on things above, so that where our treasure is, there may our hearts be also."

Michael looked around him as the congregation rose to their feet. He thought he could discern between expressions of self-satisfaction and those of true joy. He wondered what others might be reading on his face. He felt more perplexed than joyful. Where were his affections, his treasure, his heart? He knew the answer, but he was not at all sure he liked it.

CHAPTER

14

THE THEATRE WAS FILLED TO CAPACITY. *Patience* was only a week into its run, but it was clear this was going to be as popular as Gilbert and Sullivan's previous shows had been. It poked fun at the vanity and pretentiousness of "aesthetics," people who indulged in high art for art's sake and thought art should eschew any moral or social message. The curtain had just come down on act one, and the theatre was buzzing as people rose from their seats for the interval.

Michael, Corinna, and David had been invited to join Viscount Delaford and his sister in their private box for this performance.

"Are you enjoying it?" Michael asked Laura. Although the opera's focus was on poets and the arts, he knew plenty of self-important people in other fields who were just as insufferable as the character Reginald Bunthorne.

Laura turned from scanning the people in the boxes on the other side of the theatre. She'd spent as much time watching the spectators as the show itself. "It's a delightful satire of the aesthetics. I think those people rather silly myself."

"I can't say I understand much about the aesthetic movement," David put in. "I did enjoy seeing those Dragoon Guards, though."

"That's because the Dragoons don't understand the aesthetics either," Corinna pointed out with a barely concealed eye roll.

"Do you really think the aesthetics are silly, Laura?" Viscount Delaford asked. "I should think you'd find the loose, flowing fashions of the ladies appealing, as being more comfortable than bustles and corsets."

Laura waved her fan and pretended to look shocked. "You really shouldn't mention such things in mixed company, dear brother." But she sent a glance at Michael that he deemed more than a little coquettish.

"How about we find some refreshment?" he suggested.

Now that the Season was fully under way, so were Laura's flirtations. Michael was not the only man so honored, but he was unmistakably high on her list, and he needed to ensure he remained so. It was time to stake his claim, as it were. He'd planned this for months, but he could never have foreseen the way his heart had fallen so completely out of the endeavor.

If there was one thing he had in common with the bluster-ous Bunthorne, it was an attraction to the one maiden who was very different from the rest. Julia was no milkmaid, as the title character in this show was, but she had a similar artlessness that was undeniably alluring. Something he should *not* be thinking about right now, as he took Laura's silk-gloved arm in his to walk downstairs to the lobby.

Perhaps he was thinking about Julia too hard. As they reached the bottom of the stairs, he noticed a woman on the far side of the lobby who might have been her, except for the elegant gown she wore.

He nearly tripped on the last stair as he looked again. It *was* Julia. She was chatting with three other young women, and she looked happy and more beautiful than he'd ever seen her.

"Is everything all right?" Laura asked, as he'd yanked her arm when he'd misstepped.

"My apologies," he murmured.

They paused, waiting for the others to catch up to them. "What a crowd," David observed, looking over the lobby. "I don't think we'll even be able to reach the refreshment room."

"I'm going outside for a smoke," Delaford informed them. "I'll rejoin you later."

As Michael and the others discussed what to do next, he couldn't resist looking at Julia again. He hadn't seen her since before Easter. Their next lesson was scheduled for the day after tomorrow. Although she'd been in his thoughts, he didn't realize just how intensely he'd missed her until her now. Or had he just not allowed himself to admit it?

"Perhaps the gentlemen might be able to get us something to drink?" Laura suggested. "I'm about to faint from thirst."

David surveyed the lobby. "We should take the right flank and skirt those pillars along the perimeter," he said, sounding like one of the Dragoons. "If we do that, we might gain the refreshment room—" He stopped short as something else caught his attention. "Oh, look, there is Jamie Anderson. Excellent. I've been wanting to ask him something."

He started forward but was arrested when Corinna took hold of his arm. "What are you doing?" she hissed. "You can't go talk to him."

David looked genuinely perplexed. "Why not?"

"Why not?" she repeated sarcastically. "Because as you've no doubt noticed, his wife, *Dr. Anderson*, is with him. It would be very bad to be seen in public with people who are Michael's adversaries in the libel suit. Surely not even you can be so dense as to not know that."

Corinna often spoke deprecatingly to her husband in private, but she rarely did so in public. Michael thought it likely that the physical changes in her body were affecting her emotional state. Even Laura, who'd begun to know her fairly well, looked alarmed, her lips pursing.

After years of marriage, David's skin was so thick that he didn't seem to notice the insulting barb in his wife's words. He said only, "Anderson and I have worked together on the board of the Working Men's Educational Union for nearly five years. I'm not going to ignore him in public simply because of a lawsuit that has nothing to do with either of us."

"What is the Working Men's Educational Union?" Laura asked.

"It's a charity that presents educational lectures on science and other topics to working men," Michael replied. "It's often their only chance for learning beyond the very basic teachings they may have gotten as children."

"There is a thorny issue concerning an upcoming lecture that I must get Anderson's advice about, and now is a good time to do it," David said. "Besides, Anderson has always made it clear that he doesn't involve himself in his wife's business affairs."

"Not directly, perhaps," Corinna pressed, "but think what this case means to Michael. To his career."

"London is not so big a town in some ways. I daresay that the longer Michael continues in practice, the more of these people he'll be involved with legally—either as clients or adversaries. Now, if you persist in clinging to me, my love, you'll simply have to come with me."

Although typically an easygoing man when it came to his wife, it was clear that in this instance David was not going to back down.

"David is right," Michael said. "I might refrain from speaking to them in order to avoid throwing any doubt on the integrity of the suit, but I see no reason why you two shouldn't go."

He knew this was the last thing Corinna wanted to hear. It always irked her to be contradicted. Michael could sympathize with her concern about damaging his prospects. But he did think she had overestimated the danger. And every now and then he felt compelled to take his brother-in-law's side.

David smiled. "Rest assured I shall not broach the subject of the lawsuit. I expect they'll be just as happy not to speak of it, either. This is a social evening, after all." He tugged once more at his wife. "Come along, Corinna."

"One other thing," Michael said, before they went. "You know of certain *other* matters that need to remain confidential."

At the moment, Julia and the Andersons were standing on opposite sides of the crowded lobby. He didn't think they were aware of one another's presence. He wasn't even sure whether Julia knew them personally, since she was not yet a student of the school. But he gave David this reminder on the chance that, if Julia did know them and spotted them, she might go speak to them.

"Understood," David replied.

Laura briefly pointed her opera glasses toward the Andersons to get a better look. "So that is the famous Dr. Anderson. I've never seen her before. She looks very nicely dressed. She even seems reasonably pretty."

Michael heard a note of surprise in her voice. "What did you expect? That she must be dowdy and ugly because of her choice of profession?"

"You must admit that for the most part, those kinds of women are indeed, shall we say, less than feminine."

Michael looked at Julia again. This time, his gaze caught hers. Her mouth widened a little in surprise. She would be wise enough to know they should not acknowledge one another in this public setting. He had no fear on that account. That wasn't why his heart was racing. It was because she was just the opposite of how Laura pictured such a woman. Even if dressed in her usual practical clothing, Julia would be, hands down, the prettiest physician to grace any hospital.

He tore his gaze away, lest Laura should see where his attention was focused. So far she had not noticed Julia, and he hoped to keep it that way.

Laura continued, "I once heard Dr. Anderson quoted as saying, 'The first thing a female medical student must learn is how to behave like a gentleman.'"

Michael was tempted to laugh at this clever turn of phrase. "I suppose that's what it takes to succeed in a man's world."

"Why should they want to?" Laura appeared affronted at the very idea. "Are you aware that even Her Majesty does not approve of women practicing medicine—at least in England?"

"She is entitled to her opinion, I suppose."

He could see this comment did not sit well with Laura and decided it was probably time to change the subject. Besides, David, who was by now in animated conversation with Mr. Anderson, was pointing at him and Laura, obviously talking about them. It was probably something innocuous about their having been invited to sit in the viscount's box, but still it made him uncomfortable. "We might be able to get you something to drink if we try going around the crowd the other way," he suggested.

They began to work their way through the crowd, Michael seeking a way that could avoid both the Andersons and Julia. But it seemed Laura's mind was still on the Andersons.

"Do you suppose Mr. Anderson really distances himself from his wife's business affairs? I should think that, given the amount of notoriety she generates, he'd want very much to be involved."

"Perhaps he feels she is capable of handling whatever arises."

"But to act on her own like that when she is married just doesn't seem right."

"I surmise that you are not interested in pursuing some sort of profession?"

"Heavens, no! I think a woman, especially one who is a wife and mother, has enough things to keep her life full and rewarding."

"Perhaps Dr. Anderson wishes only to help people."

"There are many ways to do that through charity work or donations."

Volunteerism and charities were laudable, but Michael could understand why a person would want to get involved in a way that would have greater impact. He supposed Dr. Anderson was earning a good living, too. Not everyone could afford to give their time for free. But more importantly, he could understand a person's driving need to make a real mark on the world. Wasn't that what he wanted to do? He'd never thought about whether women could have this drive, too, but clearly it was so. It was an arresting point of view that he'd not considered before becoming involved in this lawsuit.

They heard a man call out to them. "Miss Maynard!"

They turned to see a couple making their way toward them. Michael thought the man looked familiar, though he couldn't place him.

"Miss Maynard," the man said, taking her hand in his. "How lovely to see you."

"What a coincidence to meet you here!" Laura exclaimed, looking pleased.

"Not such a coincidence, perhaps. When Louise told me you'd mentioned coming to the show tonight, we thought we'd come too and see what all the fuss is about. We were lucky to get tickets, but then, we might have paid a bit more than the going rate." He looked proud at the admission that he'd been overcharged—or perhaps bribed a box office clerk? He turned his attention to Michael. "Mr. Stephenson, you may not recall me, but I was in your train carriage on the day of the accident." He extended a hand. "Arthur Browne. And this is my sister, Miss Louise Browne."

"So pleased," Miss Browne said exuberantly. "Miss Maynard told me all about the accident—what horror! It's a miracle you survived!"

"Did you all know each other before the accident?" Michael was still trying to piece together how Laura seemed to be on such familiar terms with them.

"Not at all!" Laura answered. "But Mr. Browne was so kind to take me home that day. He was concerned for my well-being, for we'd all been through such a traumatic time. He asked if Miss Browne might call on me sometime, so of course I said yes."

Something about the way the Brownes wore their very fine clothes, and in their manners that were just a hair off the accepted etiquette, told Michael these two were probably nouveau riche. Social climbers who took advantage of any opportunity to strike up a friendship with someone in the aristocracy. Laura didn't seem to mind; she clearly enjoyed their attentions.

"You're a barrister, I hear," Browne said to Michael. "Myself, I'm in the stock market. I invest in manufacturing, too. It pays to diversify."

"Isn't this show marvelous?" Miss Browne enthused. "My brother and I plan to attend the new exhibition at the Grosvenor Gallery next week. That is where those aesthetic painters have their shows, you know. I think I shall giggle if I see anyone dressed in the odd attire they are wearing on stage tonight!"

Her thirst apparently forgotten, Laura chatted happily with the Brownes about the exhibition and other upcoming social events. Michael did his best to appear engaged, but he kept thinking of Julia, wondering how she'd been able to come here tonight.

The bell rang, announcing that act two would be starting soon. The Brownes said effusive good-byes, but not before they'd elicited a promise from Laura that she would join them on a drive in the park tomorrow.

As Michael and Laura made their way back upstairs, he looked around for Julia. She was nowhere to be seen. He knew they had a lesson in just two days' time, but he would have enjoyed another glimpse of her in that dress.

CHAPTER

15

J ULIA ENTERED HER BOARDINGHOUSE, her mind filled with many things. She'd just posted a letter to Rosalyn and had taken the long way back in order to enjoy the lovely spring weather. She found she could think better when walking.

Solvitur ambulando. She smiled, thinking of the proverb Michael had taught her. *It is solved by walking.* It was ironic, given that more of her walk had been spent thinking over her night at the theatre than on solving any specific problems. How surprising it had been to see Michael there. It had been less surprising to see he'd been escorting Miss Maynard. She was sorry for that, unable to shake the idea that he deserved a different kind of woman. Or was she judging Miss Maynard too harshly? She didn't know her, after all. If Michael really was intent on wooing her, perhaps he saw something Julia didn't.

She made her way to the parlor, intending to spend some time preparing for her next Latin lesson. So preoccupied was she with her thoughts that, even after she saw the young lady seated by the fireplace, it took a few moments to comprehend what her eyes were telling her. It wasn't until Cara jumped up from the chair and threw her arms around Julia that she fully realized her little sister was in London.

Her heart did several somersaults, but whether it was from the joy of seeing Cara or dread that her sister might be out of work again, Julia didn't know. It was definitely the latter emotion that caused her to exclaim, "Caroline Bernay, what are you doing here?"

Cara pulled back and looked at her with bright blue eyes. She was the only one of the three sisters who had inherited their mother's coloring. "You needn't take that tone with me, dear sister. I'm visiting London with the Needenhams, and naturally I took advantage of the opportunity to come and see you."

The mention of Cara's employers in the present tense immediately relieved Julia. "So you are still working as a nursery maid?"

A brief flash of hurt crossed her sister's eyes, and Julia was immediately sorry she'd asked the question in such a negative way.

But true to Cara's mercurial nature, the look was quickly gone, and her warm smile returned. "How could I possibly leave the Needenhams? They would be in dire straits indeed. I am now officially the nanny. Little Robbie is four years old now. Such a handful! But he always does what I tell him to do." She smiled. "Eventually, that is. I certainly have a better time of managing him than anyone else."

This assessment was given with a toss of her head. Julia considered this little display of pride acceptable as satisfaction in a job well done.

"More than once, I can assure you, Lady Needenham has told me she would be absolutely lost without me," Cara continued.

"And yet, here you are." Julia could not help teasing her.

"Getting away from the house wasn't easy. They will only be

in London for two weeks. Miss Sarah Needenham—that's Sir John's daughter from his first marriage—is to be presented in court next week! So naturally they've come to town early in order to get her fitted up with exactly the best gown, suitable to the occasion and positively the height of fashion."

Cara sounded like she was reading aloud from one of the ladies' magazines she devoured at every opportunity. Julia had long ago despaired of ever getting her to read something useful.

"I'm sorry to say that we'll be going away again as soon as that's over. Miss Needenham will remain for the rest of the Season, though. She's staying with her aunt and uncle. But I must return with the Needenhams and little Robbie. Sir John absolutely detests London."

Sir John Needenham, baronet, preferred to spend most of his time at his large estate near Exeter. That had been a plus in Julia's eyes when Cara had gained the position of nursery maid there. Julia thought quiet country living would keep Cara safe and out of trouble. She was fascinated by big city life, the "mode," and everything else associated with wealth. Things Julia knew her sister was likely never to acquire.

"So how did you get the day off? I can't imagine Lady Needenham wants to have her toddler in tow when taking her stepdaughter to the dressmaker's shop."

"I'll tell you all about it. But as I only have this one day to myself, may we go for a walk? This is my first time in London, and I want to see as much of the city as I can!"

Julia thought about the myriad things she was supposed to be doing today. She was far too busy to spend an afternoon strolling around London sightseeing. And yet it was good to see her sister again. They could rarely spend time together. Cara was brimming with excitement, practically bouncing on her toes, and Julia knew she'd be an ogre to refuse the request.

"All right. But I need to arrange a few things first. It won't take long."

Cara followed Julia upstairs and offered lavish praise for her bedroom. Although it was small, it nonetheless boasted a writing desk and a window. Cara assured her it was nicer than the "little garret" she occupied at the Needenhams' town home. She then alternated between sitting on the bed and rising again to look out the window at the street below, plying Julia with questions about life in London. Julia tried to answer them while she penned a few hasty notes. Her sister's impulsiveness often had a way of changing other people's plans without notice, but Julia was still glad to see her.

As Julia sealed up the notes, Cara looked over her shoulder. "What's this?" she asked, reaching out to pick up Michael Stephenson's calling card. It had been lying on the desk next to Julia's Latin textbook. With a look of distaste, Cara added, "Is that *blood?*"

"That is a card of the man I helped on the Underground after the accident."

Julia had told Cara about the accident in a letter, although she'd left out the more gruesome aspects. Cara was getting a hint of them now.

Cara scrunched up her nose. "This seems a rather odd memento."

Julia took the card from her and set it aside. "We'd better get going if you want to see London."

Soon they were walking in the direction of Regent Street. Cara, unsurprisingly, wanted to window shop at the elegant stores that lined the famous avenue. Despite her stated desire to see as much of the city as she could, she wasn't moving very quickly. She was gawking at everything, from the elegant town homes to ordinary streetlamps. It was at one of these lamps that Cara paused, studying the wrought-iron designs around its top.

She sighed. "I wish we were staying longer. Some families remain in London for the entire Season. What heaven that would be!"

"And here I thought you would grow to enjoy the country."

"Oh, it's pleasant enough. I am even able to do some sketching while I'm outside with Robbie. But the city is more fascinating. How I would love to paint some scenes here!"

"Not everything in London is beautiful or picturesque," Julia said, thinking of the times she'd gone to the slums with Edith.

"It doesn't have to be picturesque, only *interesting*. Don't you love living here?"

Worried this train of thought might feed into Cara's more dangerous impulses, such as leaving her employment, Julia tried for a different tack. "So who is minding little Robbie? Or is he spending the day with his mother after all?"

Her interest in the streetlamp fading, Cara turned away, and the two of them began walking again. "I was able to persuade Aileen, the parlor maid, to do it. She has a soft spot for the lad. The rest of the family has been invited to spend two days in Kent at the home of a marquess. I believe there's talk of marriage between Miss Needenham and the marquess's younger son. He's handsome as well as rich, and he and Miss Needenham struck up quite a friendship when their families were introduced to each other at the Derby last year."

"You sound like a family confidante rather than the nanny."

"Miss Needenham may have spoken to me about it once or twice. We are just about the same age, you know." Cara sighed. "At times, I feel positively like Cinderella."

"At least you are not stuck in a corner among the ashes," Julia pointed out. "Here's Regent Street. You will have plenty of fine clothes and other items to ogle in this place."

Cara surveyed the scene with childlike joy. Finely dressed ladies walked along the sidewalk, several of them followed by footmen bearing their parcels. Others were seated in carriages, waiting as merchants brought out goods for their inspection.

As Julia looked at these women, she could only think that spending so much time and effort simply to acquire another set of gloves or a new hat—even supposing she could afford such things—seemed a colossal waste of time.

And yet Cara's thoughts were clearly running in a different vein. She pointed toward a shop several doors down from where they stood. "Is that a millinery shop? We must go there first!"

Later, after they'd looked into every shop on Regent Street, they walked south toward Green Park. They paused when they reached the square in front of Buckingham Palace to admire its imposing edifice.

"One day, I will go into that building," Cara announced.

The audacity of her statement surprised even Julia. "You will go to Buckingham Palace? Her Majesty is long past needing a nursery maid."

"Oh, I shan't go as a servant. I shall be a guest of Her Majesty. Or perhaps I shall be presented at a royal levee, just like Miss Needenham."

The idea was so outlandish that Julia didn't even try to contradict it. She said merely, "Shall we find a place to take tea?"

They found a little restaurant where they could get a cup of tea and some biscuits for a reasonable price. Julia would have preferred something more substantial, but her budget wouldn't allow it. Cara had less than a shilling, which was all the cash she'd had on her when suddenly presented with the opportunity to take the day off.

"Where shall we go next?" Cara asked when they had finished their tea and were back out on the street.

"Don't you need to get back to your employer?" Julia asked.

"Not just yet. Aileen knew this was my only opportunity to see you, so she assured me she would be happy to watch Robbie until after his supper. But I must be home to put him to bed, as he won't go to sleep for just anyone."

"I should think the Needenhams would be put out if their maid neglects her other duties."

Cara waved away that notion. "Sir John never troubles himself about domestic matters, and Lady Needenham is too caught up in everything relating to Miss Needenham's presentation to notice if the parlor didn't get dusted this one day. She dotes on Sarah as completely as if she were her own child. Of course, she brought her up from the age of ten, so that's understandable." She wrapped her arm through Julia's as they walked. "How I should love to go to the National Gallery! But I read in a tourist guidebook of Lady Needenham's that it is not open on Thursdays and Fridays except by special application."

"Have you developed a taste for fine art, then?" Julia knew Cara had a talent for drawing but hadn't properly considered that it would lead to an interest in studying the great painters.

"Oh yes! I have seen a few works here and there by the masters. But to be in a whole gallery devoted to them would be heaven."

"I know just the thing," Julia announced. "There is a gallery at the Foundling Hospital."

"That's a wonderful idea! I heard there are paintings by Hogarth, Reynolds, and Gainsborough."

Julia was not familiar with the painters Cara mentioned, but she had been wanting to pay a visit to the Foundling Hospital. Having been raised in an orphanage, she was curious to visit this one. "It's a bit of a walk, though. We'll have to go quickly, no dawdling."

It would have been faster to take an omnibus or the Underground, but since today they were doing the free tour, they would have to use their feet for transportation. They made good time, however. Cara's excitement to see the gallery apparently outweighed everything else.

When they reached the gates of the Foundling Hospital, the porter located one of the headmistresses there, who would serve as their guide. It did not take long for them to see that this was a very different place from George Müller's orphanage. Physically, it consisted of three large buildings surrounded by a high wall. Julia couldn't help but compare it to the five orphan homes built by Mr. Müller in Bristol, each surrounded by open fields. They learned from their guide that to be accepted here, a child must be less than a year old and illegitimate, except in the case of having a father who'd been killed in military service.

Several important painters had been patrons of the institution, which was the reason for the art gallery. Cara moved among the paintings at her own pace, passing some quickly, and lingering at others. "I like the portraits best," she told Julia, "especially the ones that truly capture the essence of the person's soul. That's what I want to do. I want to paint someone in such a way that the viewer has an immediate sense of what that person is like—whether good or bad, lively or languid."

"I see you've put a lot of thought into this," Julia said.

"Why shouldn't I? Anything worth doing is worth doing well. I'm sure you feel that way about your studies, don't you?"

Julia couldn't argue with that.

After a while, their guide informed them the gallery was closing for the day. "I hope you can come back sometime to hear the children's choir," she said. "They sing like angels."

As they returned to the main gate, they passed two long rows of children walking toward the dining hall for supper. The children were quiet and seemed intent on staying in line and getting to their destination. They hardly gave Julia and Cara a passing glance. One poor boy was being harassed by a larger boy in line behind him, who kept poking at his back and making snide remarks about his shorter stature.

"Do you suppose those are two of the boys who sing like angels?" Julia whispered.

She meant it as a joke, but Cara looked troubled. "How terrible. I don't think the children here are as happy as we were."

"I believe you're right. I've heard they're not allowed to speak at meals. Not one word, or they get punished. You, my dear sister, would not have survived a week."

Cara responded to this gentle dig with a smile, but Julia could see she was still distressed.

Once they were out of the gate, Cara said, "I'm glad we came here today, and not simply to view the paintings. When I first read about the fine works of art here, I was a little envious. We had nothing on the walls except for a few religious aphorisms at Ashley Down, but I wouldn't trade growing up there for here. Not for the world."

They walked on in silence, and Julia supposed they were both sending up silent prayers of gratitude for having—in the absence of their parents, which would have been best of all—a childhood home that had at least some warmheartedness.

As they walked, the modest brick building of the London School of Medicine for Women came into view. "I will begin my studies there in October," Julia informed her. "Would you like to see the inside?"

Cara's steps slowed. "It depends on what kind of medical things are in there."

"There are rows and rows of tall glass jars with pickled body parts." Julia spoke with dramatic and macabre emphasis. "Hearts and brains and eyeballs."

Cara gave her a shove. "Stop trying to scare me."

Julia laughed. "All right then, come on."

But they hadn't gone much farther before a carriage stopped right in front of them. Inside sat Edith Morton. Sam, the little boy from Bethnal Green, sat next to her, his dirty face smeared with tears.

"Julia, I'm glad to see you," Edith said breathlessly. "Sam says Sybil is having terrible pains. I think she must be going into labor sooner than we expected. Will you come with us?"

"Yes, of course," Julia replied. She turned to Cara. "This is an emergency. I have already promised to help this lady with her delivery, so I must go. I'm sorry to cut short our visit."

"I'll go with you," Cara offered.

"Dearest, that's not a good idea. It is likely to be—" Julia stopped. She was going to say *unpleasant*, but a quick look at Sam prevented her. She did not want to stoke his fears. "That is, we'll be busy, and it may take some time. Do you think you can find your way back to the Needenhams' residence?"

"You know I'll never find my way alone. Can't I go with you, and you can take me home afterward?"

"Please, we must hurry!" Sam begged. "Ma was yelling, and nobody knows what to do for her!"

"There is no time to be lost," Edith said. "Who is this?"

"This is my sister Cara. She's visiting me for the afternoon."

"I want to go," Cara said firmly, her natural sense of adventure beginning to outweigh any hesitation over being involved with *medical* things. "Maybe I can help."

Julia was torn. Seeing her indecision, Edith said, "Perhaps she can ride with us and then take the cab home from there. I'll pay the fee if cost is an issue."

It did seem like the best option. Julia relented, although she still had misgivings as they got into the carriage and raced toward Bethnal Green.

CHAPTER

16

A s the cab made its way along the dingy streets, Cara soothed the crying boy. "You mustn't be too alarmed," she told him. "My sister will make sure everything turns out all right."

Soon Cara had managed to calm him down. She even taught him a little game with hand motions. As the two became absorbed in this, Edith looked over their heads at Julia. "She has a knack for working with children."

Julia nodded. That had always been one of Cara's strongest traits. She knew how to speak to small children in a manner they would listen to and accept.

The carriage stopped at the run-down tenement. Edith was the first to get out, and she held out her hand to Sam. "Come along."

But Sam turned to Cara. "Are you coming, too?"

He said it with such hopefulness that Cara seemed at a loss. She looked from Sam to the filthy street outside. She had been so caught up in playing with him that this seemed to be the first time she truly noted their dismal surroundings. Her nose crinkled at the smell of refuse. Somewhere a dog barked, and a baby was crying. Two men lounging at the door glowered at the cab, their interest in the strangers tempered by mistrust.

Even the cab driver was beginning to look uneasy.

"I must go," Cara said to Sam. "You see, there is another little boy waiting for me—"

Sam clung ferociously to her hand. "Please!"

They seemed to be at an impasse. Then, from inside the building, a woman let out a scream of pain.

"It's Sybil," Edith said. "Her contractions must have started." Evidently deciding the boy was safe with Cara, she hurried into the building to address the greater emergency.

Still seated in the carriage with her sister, Julia tried to decide what to do. She needed to help Edith, but she could not leave Cara here.

"Make up your minds, then," the driver said gruffly, sending another worried glance at the two unsavory men by the door. "Stay in or get out, but this cab is leaving."

Another child wandered out of the building, a little girl barely old enough to walk. She looked dazed.

"Jemmie!" cried Sam. He tugged at Cara, pulling her out of the carriage with him. He led her over to the little girl. "Jemmie, don't cry." Just having Cara with him seemed to give him the strength to comfort his sister.

Cara turned back to Julia. "You see, I can help."

Edith's head popped out of the second-story window. "Julia! She is very far along, and I don't like the position of the baby."

There was nothing for it but to allow Cara to stay. Julia jumped down from the carriage.

"Your skin, not mine," she heard the cabman mutter before he quickly drove away.

For better or worse, Julia needed Cara. But she wasn't going to leave her here on the street. "Come upstairs with me," she directed. "You can watch over the children there."

Cara scooped up Jemmie and took Sam's hand as naturally as if she were a mother herself, and they followed Julia up the stairs.

Julia and Edith enlisted the help of Hettie and Doreen, another friend of Sybil's, to locate things they needed and to bring up water from the community well and as many cloths as they could spare. The room was filthy, and the water was cold. While Julia understood Sybil's fear of dying of puerperal fever in a hospital, remaining here had big disadvantages. At least Edith had been able to bring soap and a few other supplies. It would have to do.

As the labor progressed, Edith appeared more and more out of her depth; her clinical work at the teaching hospital had been primarily in the surgical wards, so her experience in midwifery was minimal. After years of working at the hospital for women and children, it was Julia who had the skills needed for this situation.

Julia lost all sense of time. When at last they'd escorted the baby girl safely into the world, Julia let out a sigh of satisfaction.

Edith wiped her forehead and sent Julia a tired smile. "I don't know what I'd have done without you."

"You would have managed," Julia assured her. "You are clever and resourceful, which surely are the two things most needed for a physician."

Edith shook her head, still regretting her lack of experience. "I suppose I should have taken the opportunity to spend three months at the lying-in hospital in Dublin. But there were things here in England that were more pressing."

"Do you think you'll go next year?" Julia asked when Edith did not elaborate.

"Perhaps." But the way she said it made it sound unlikely.

They put the babe on Sybil's breast, and Julia was relieved to see that the mother, although exhausted and malnourished, was able to produce milk to satisfy the child. With the help of the other women, they were able to get Sybil cleaned up and comfortable.

Cara stood in the doorway. "Is it all right to bring in Sam and Jemmie? They're anxious to see their new little sister."

Before Julia or Edith could answer, Sam burst through the door and ran over to the bed, crying out for his mama. She gave him a weak but happy hug. Cara followed, holding Jemmie, who appeared more asleep than awake, her head resting on Cara's shoulder. Cara laid the child gently on the little pallet in the corner that functioned as the children's bed.

"Oh, my poor sweet Jemmie," Sybil said, giving her daughter a tender glance. "She will miss her mama's milk from now on, but I fear I won't have any to spare."

Hettie and Doreen fussed about the bed, keeping Sam at arm's length while he scrutinized the baby.

Cara looked out the window at the darkness and said worriedly, "What time is it?"

Edith pulled out a watch from her pocket. "It's past eight."

"Oh no!" Cara exclaimed. "The housekeeper will have my hide for not getting back when I promised."

"Yes, we need to get you home," Julia agreed.

While they'd been in the tenement, they'd been surrounded by constant noise: men and women talking, or arguing, or laughing; children running up and down stairs; babies crying. Now as Julia looked out at the street below, she felt a twinge of worry. Walking here in broad daylight had not given her much apprehension, but darkness gave the area a sinister feel.

Edith evidently felt a few qualms herself. "I wish I'd had the presence of mind to ask the cabbie to come back in a few hours."

"I'm not sure he would have done it," Julia answered. "He did not seem to like coming here."

Edith nodded. "It can be rather daunting."

As if to punctuate her remark, they saw a man being tossed out of the building next door by a burly fellow who shouted, "If you dare show up here again, I'll do more than just cuff ya!"

The hapless fellow stumbled to his feet and ran off.

"Why don't I walk with you as far as Columbia Road?" Doreen suggested. "After that, it's constables and cab stands on every block."

"Doreen grew up in this neighborhood," Hettie explained. "You will be safe with her."

The women accepted this offer gratefully and gave a few final instructions to the new mother and Hettie.

"Will you come tomorrow?" Sam asked as Cara hugged him good-bye.

Cara looked distressed at the question, unwilling to lie.

"Sam, come over here and help me," Hettie called. "Your mama's hair is in a tangle. Let's help her comb it out."

His attention immediately returning to his mother, Sam went to the bedside as he was bidden. The others took the opportunity to slip out of the room.

"You'll write to tell me how they are all getting along, won't you?" Cara asked as they made their way down the stairs.

Julia assured her she would.

Following Doreen's lead, they went up the alleyway and turned onto a wider road. The streetlamps were sparse and not very bright, leaving much of the sidewalk in murky shadows.

"'I will never leave thee nor forsake thee,'" Julia murmured to herself.

Doreen appeared not the least bit daunted. "This is my time of day," she told them. "Darkness is as good as daytime if you know where you're going. And what to avoid."

She led them confidently along block after block of run-down houses, dingy taverns, and secondhand shops. There were plenty of people on the streets, and no one seemed to pay any mind to four women. Julia even began to feel at ease.

It wasn't until they reached a particularly seedy-looking gin shop that the trouble began. The sound of a fierce argument was clearly audible through the open door, and through the shop's grimy window, they could see a commotion.

"What's going on, Fred?" Doreen asked, as a man slunk out of the doorway.

"Myrtle's got everyone in an uproar. Says the bobbies is up in arms 'cause a toff was beaten and robbed. Now they're out for blood. I recommended everyone makes themselves scarce, but they're too busy arguing over who mighta done it. I say it's better to save yourself first and worry about the particulars later."

He gave a nervous glance up and down the street before walking off in the direction Julia and the others had just come.

Inside, the shouting got louder, and one of the men struck the woman so hard her knees buckled. She moaned, her hands covering her face, and cringed, evidently expecting another blow.

Gasping in anger, Doreen ran inside.

Feeling it wasn't any safer out on the streets, Julia and the others followed.

"Leave Myrtle alone!" Doreen shouted at the man, shoving him out of the way.

Julia was amazed at her bravery. The man was so surprised that he merely stood there, gaping at her.

Julia and Edith went to Myrtle, raising her to her feet. Julia gently pulled her hand from her cheek and inspected the wound. She'd have a bad bruise tomorrow, but at least the skin wasn't broken.

Still reeling from the blow, Myrtle tried to speak. "We gotta get out of here! I'm telling you—"

"Shut up, girl," the man said. "No one's listening to you. But who's this?" he asked, his attention diverted to the newcomers.

"These are *doctors*, Bob," Doreen answered. "They came to help Sybil deliver her baby."

"Lady doctors? I ain't never heard of that."

"There are plenty of things in the world you don't know about," Doreen retorted. "But you leave them alone. I'm helping them get home."

"What's the hurry? We're a congenial lot. Have a spot of gin first." He sidled over to Cara, who stood near the window. "I've got a little ailment I'd like to ask you about."

"We all do!" another man chimed in, and the men guffawed.

"Cara, come over here."

Julia injected quiet authority into her voice, hoping that would keep the men at bay. It wasn't enough, however. When Cara tried to comply, another man reached for her and caught hold of her sleeve. It tore as she tried to wrench free, and he grabbed for her waist.

From outside came the clatter of approaching horses, drowning out the other noises in the street.

"Thank heaven, it's the police!" Cara exclaimed.

Her words set off panic inside the shop. Men and women scrambled for the back exit, even as the police wagon drew to a halt and half a dozen policemen jumped off. "They're getting out the back!" one called, and two of the bobbies disappeared around the side of the building in pursuit.

The others raced into the shop, brandishing nightsticks. "Everyone over here!" one of them shouted, circling around those who hadn't made it to the exit and forcing them into a corner.

Cara tried to push her way through them to the constable who was giving orders. "Sir, thank you for coming! We were just—"

But another policeman took rough hold of her arm. "Come with me, and no talking."

Julia saw the shock on Cara's face as she recognized what was happening. They were getting rounded up like prostitutes or thieves. It was understandable. Aside from the fact that they'd been found among the suspects, after the hours they'd spent in the dirty tenement and the messy business of childbirth, they must have looked as disreputable as the others.

Edith said, "Constable, you're making a mistake. We are honest citizens—"

"You can explain yourself to the magistrate," he answered, forcing her into the corner with the others.

One of the two policemen who'd gone around the side of the building came in the back door. He was dragging a woman with him. "The others got away, but I managed to catch this one," he reported.

The woman cursed and struggled against his hold. "You ain't takin' me in. I ain't done nothin' wrong. You ain't gonna subject me to that disgusting examination."

The policeman shoved her forward, but that was a mistake. Quick as a flash, she drew a knife from her boot and lunged at him. He tried to fend her off with his nightstick, but she struck his hand. Julia saw the blade sink into his flesh. The woman withdrew the knife just as fast, and the policeman cursed in shock and pain.

She was a wily opponent. She'd planned the attack so that his instinctive response would be to step to one side. This freed her path to the door, and she took it. But she kept brandishing the knife, facing everyone in the room.

None of the policemen moved. Julia was surprised at this. Were they afraid? They watched the woman intently, and yet also ensured none of the other women tried anything similar.

The woman kept backing away, every muscle tense as she prepared to make a final bolt for the back exit. She was almost at the door when the last policeman came through it. Seeing what was happening, he pulled out his nightstick and struck her across the back with a forceful blow that sent her sprawling forward. Julia couldn't tell whether the stick had landed on her head as well. The woman hit the rough wood floor with a sickening thud. The knife fell out of her hand and clattered to the ground mere inches from her face.

"Assault with a deadly weapon," the constable said, picking up the knife. "She'll be lucky if that 'disgusting exam' is the worst thing that happens to her."

The policeman she'd attacked was still howling in agony, holding his bleeding hand.

Julia started forward but was immediately restrained. "I can help him!" she insisted.

"Don't come near me!" the wounded man growled. He pulled a rag off a nearby table and began to wrap it around his hand. Knowing what she did about germ theory, Julia cringed at the thought of that filthy rag on an open wound.

"Get 'em in the wagon before they try something else," the constable ordered the other men.

They began to lead off the women two at a time. "Where did that little blond one go?" one of them said.

Julia looked around in confusion. Sure enough, her sister was nowhere to be seen.

"Cara!" she shouted. How had she managed to slip away? "Cara!"

"Little chit musta slipped out during the knife fight," the constable growled. "I'll search the building just to be sure she's not hiding somewhere."

Julia and Edith were forcibly taken to the wagon along with the other women. "I can't leave my sister!" Julia protested as a policeman pushed her inside the wagon.

"Don't worry. If we find her, we'll be sure to bring her along later." His voice was hard and menacing. Julia had never been afraid of policemen until today. It was a shocking and unnerving feeling.

There was nothing she could do but pray as the police van hurtled toward the station, leaving Cara behind.

CHAPTER

17

T HE WOMEN CLUNG to the wooden benches nailed to
either side of the wagon's interior, trying to keep from being
thrown to the floor as the vehicle turned a corner. The
woman who'd been knocked unconscious had been tossed into
the van like a sack of potatoes. Doreen said her name was Eliza.
Julia was trying to keep both herself and Eliza from pitching
around the wagon.

Her heart was in as much turmoil as her body. Where had
Cara disappeared to? Julia didn't know which was worse—the
thought of her sister being caught and manhandled by policemen, or fear of what could happen to her if she was left to roam
the cruel streets alone.

"I'm sorry about your sister," Doreen said. "I shouldn't have led
you into that gin shop. But when I saw Bob being such a brute
to Myrtle, I just had to stop him."

"You're a good one to risk yourself for me," Myrtle said. "I'm

189

worried about Eliza, though. She got the worst of it. Do you think she'll be all right?"

Doreen's compassion did not extend that far. "Serves her right for attacking that bobby. He was right about the kind of treatment she'll get for that."

"No, Doreen," Edith remonstrated. "Nobody deserves to be struck down like a dog."

Doreen sniffed. "All I'm sayin' is, it's better if you just go in, let 'em do their worst, prove you're clean, and then you can leave."

Never had Julia thought her life would be personally affected by the Contagious Diseases Acts. "Has this happened to you before?"

"Twice." She grimaced. "It ain't pleasant. But there are worse things."

"But you're not a prostitute!"

"No. But I used to be a maid to one of the higher-priced ones. Sometimes that got me rounded up by mistake."

Faint light from the streetlamps came through two small, barred windows. Julia could see Edith's brow furrowed in concentration. Was she worried they'd be subjected to the exam? "Don't worry," Julia said. "Once we get there, we'll explain who we are. When they hear you're the daughter of an earl, they'll be horrified at what they've done and let us go immediately."

"I'm not going to tell them."

"What?"

"I'm not going to let my family connections decide my fate. I will stand or fall on my own merits, not because of my birth."

Doreen stared at her. "You're the daughter of an earl?" She looked for all the world as though she wanted to curtsy right there in the cramped wagon.

"You will not treat me any differently," Edith snapped. She probably didn't realize how aristocratic she sounded; a sign that her breeding could not be set aside entirely. "It's not my lineage

190

that makes me good or bad. It's what I do with my own life and abilities."

"But . . . an *earl*, though!" Doreen was not about to let this go. "Does that mean you live in one of those big, fancy houses?"

"I used to. But now I rent simple lodgings near the medical school. The way you are acting right now is exactly the reason I didn't tell you before."

The wagon came to a halt, bouncing a little as the policemen jumped off. This was followed by the sound of footsteps coming around the back of the van and the bolt being slid out of its lock.

They were led to a cell—a dank, dark room about twenty feet square. Julia instinctively pulled out a handkerchief, holding it to her nose until she could acclimatize to the smell of unwashed bodies and the foul odor emanating from the bucket in the corner.

The cell already had two occupants. One of them—a tall, lean woman with frizzled gray hair—gave them a malevolent, confrontational stare, as though she were trying to assert her supremacy. The other—a smaller, younger woman—sat in the corner, her shoulders slumped. She looked up when they came in, her eyes meeting Julia's with a mildly curious expression before dropping down to stare once more at her worn boots.

Two policemen came in behind them, carrying Eliza. Without a trace of ceremony or care, they deposited her on a bench against the wall.

"Wait—don't we get a chance to speak to the stationmaster?" Julia asked, as the policemen made to leave.

One of them glared at her as though she'd asked a rude question. "You will all get your turn." Pointing to Myrtle, he said, "You first."

Myrtle lifted her chin in a show of dignity that was not entirely successful and went out with him.

"What're you in for?" said the gray-haired woman, addressing

191

Julia and the others after the cell door had slammed shut. Her voice was raspy, as though worn out from overuse.

"For delivering a baby," Edith answered crisply.

The woman's eyes narrowed, but something in Edith's defiant manner kept her from saying more.

"What about you?" Doreen challenged.

"For minding our own business. Unfortunately, we just happened to be standing in the street while we was doing it." She must have decided Edith's answer was an equivocation and answered in kind.

Julia noticed the use of the word *our* and the way the young woman in the corner hugged herself a little at the gray-haired woman's response. It seemed they'd been brought in together, although it appeared neither wanted much to do with the other.

Edith went to Eliza's unconscious form and began examining her, lifting her eyelids to check her pupils and searching her head and neck for skull or cervical injuries. Julia crouched next to the bench while Edith placed two fingers on Eliza's neck.

"Pulse is weak," Edith murmured. "No sign of consciousness. I'm worried for her."

The door creaked open, and a policeman pushed Myrtle back into the cell. "You're next," he said to Doreen.

The gray-haired woman smirked as Doreen went out. Julia saw her eyeing Edith's frock, which although simple and functional was clearly made of quality material. "I guess they're saving the best for last."

"What did they ask you?" Julia asked Myrtle.

"The usual things." She began pacing the cell, her fists clenched. "If I ever see that Bob Logan again, I'm gonna give him a big piece of my mind. And maybe my fist, too. All I was trying to do was warn him, and now look what's happened. If I get consigned, I'll be stuck in jail until the next assizes, and then what'll I do?"

"What do you mean, 'consigned'?" Edith asked.

But Myrtle didn't answer. She paced back and forth, consumed with her own agitated thoughts.

Julia had the same question. She wished she could ask Michael for advice. He would surely know what to do.

The gray-haired woman crossed her arms and gave Edith a condescending smile. "New at this, are you? Allow me to fill you in. If the magistrate decides there's enough evidence to consign you, you'll be remanded to jail until the trial. Unless you got the brass for bail. Otherwise, you get to cool your heels in prison until the assizes."

Once more the young woman in the corner twitched. Julia had a hard time controlling her own worried reaction. She didn't know how much bail would be, but she had no spare money of any kind.

"I see," said Edith, receiving this information with detached interest, as if none of this applied to her. Perhaps she wasn't worried because she had money to pay bail, if needed. Edith could say what she wished about not wanting to depend upon aristocratic privileges, but she had an independent trust fund that allowed her to live well, if not lavishly. It would presumably provide what she needed in such an emergency.

Doreen wasn't gone long. Unlike Myrtle, when Doreen returned to the cell, her movements displayed calm resignation.

Julia asked the policeman, "Has anyone else been brought in tonight?" Even with everything else going on, Cara was never out of her thoughts.

"If there had been, you'd know about it" was the gruff reply. "All the ladies end up in this cell."

He summoned Edith next. When they'd gone, Doreen came up to Julia and whispered, "If I was you, I wouldn't tell anyone at the station about your sister. She could get in worse trouble for evading arrest."

"Surely not!" Julia protested.

Doreen nodded solemnly. "People have been sentenced to six months in prison for less."

It was another grim vision of what could happen, and it would be Julia's fault for allowing Cara to go with her to that unsafe neighborhood. Her sister was tender and naïve, often given to daydreaming and flights of fancy. These traits had irritated Julia over the years, but she would never wish to see Cara brought to the harsh realities of life by being thrust into a prison and crushed like a flower underfoot. She said earnestly, "Thank you for the warning."

Turning away, Julia went to the window, although it was too high to look through. She had been praying for Cara to be found and pulled in from the streets, but now she didn't know what to pray for. Reflexively she clasped her hands together and murmured, "Lord, you know what's best. Please keep her safe."

She'd meant this as a private moment, forgetting that the older woman was still watching them closely.

"Oh, a godly one!" said the woman sarcastically, raising her hands in mockery. "Well, don't bother sending up any prayers. He don't pay no mind to the people in the slums."

Although startled by this outburst, Julia didn't hesitate to answer. "On the contrary, God hears every prayer, holding both rich and poor in equal consideration."

The woman's sour expression showed what she thought of that answer. "I'm sure it was your pious ways that got you here. But I suspect it'll be your *money*—not your prayers—that gets you out. Oh yes, I got a good look at that one." She stretched a bony finger toward the cell door, referring to Edith, who had just left for her turn with the stationmaster. "She's got someone keeping her, that's for sure—though Lord knows why, with a face like that. How about you?"

"These are good women!" Doreen exclaimed. "Not grifters or whores. Be quiet!"

The woman advanced menacingly. "Care to make me?"

Doreen held her ground, tensed for a fight. Julia pulled her back, putting as much distance as she could between them and the other woman. The last thing they needed now was an altercation. "Please don't get insulted on my account. Ugly words don't change the truth."

Doreen still looked riled up but held her peace. The gray-haired woman looked pleased with herself, as though she'd won this round.

Edith was back in less than five minutes, looking as unruffled as when she'd left.

Julia pulled her to the far side of the cell, whispering to keep from being overheard by the gray-haired woman. "What happened?"

"He asked my name and place of abode."

"And how did you answer?"

"I said my name is Edith Morton and I live in Boswell Street, Bloomsbury."

"But even with this information, he didn't make the connection of who you must be?"

Edith shrugged. "London's a big city. I imagine there are plenty of women with the name Edith Morton."

Julia sighed in exasperation, still speaking under her breath, "But there are not too many who are the Honorable Lady Edith Morton, daughter of the Earl of Westbridge."

"He didn't ask if I had an honorific, so I didn't offer it."

"I don't imagine they would, given the circumstances," Julia replied through gritted teeth.

"Well, then, it's their fault for not doing a thorough enough job, isn't it?" Edith delivered this criticism of the Metropolitan

Police with an air of disdain that made her sound exactly like the daughter of an earl.

"This is foolishness," Julia said. "With a word, you could probably get us all out of here."

"You may tell them what you like about yourself. Say whatever you like, if you want to leave," Edith returned. "For myself, I am very interested to see firsthand what happens to women like these. Don't you see? This is what our struggle is about. Everyone, high and low, male and female, should be treated equally under the law. My father thinks I cannot survive outside the protection of our rank and station. I am determined to prove otherwise."

"And if the magistrate orders you to undergo a physical examination?"

Edith blanched a little, although her answer was bold enough. "Then they will see how utterly wrong and useless these laws are. It will further our cause."

Julia thought over these things as she was led to the station-master's desk. She understood Edith's desire to stand on her own two feet, but she also thought there was a flaw in her approach. She had not told them she was a student at the London School of Medicine for Women. Surely that would have been better than saying nothing at all, wouldn't it? That she was on the verge of qualifying for her license was something she'd accomplished on her own. Why would she not say that? Julia thought that perhaps Edith *wanted* to be treated in the worst possible way, to experience for herself the horrors she'd heard about. But that indicated a kind of morbid fascination Julia could not understand. She had no compunction about telling the complete truth. She had no important family lineage giving her privilege, and she didn't think she'd hide it in any case.

The station chief was a harried man who looked a little bleary-eyed, as though he'd been on shift too long. He barely looked at her as she came to a halt in front of his desk, but remained with pen poised, ready to write.

"Your name and place of lodging." He barked it out as a command rather than a question.

"Julia Bernay. Eleven Harley Street."

His head came up sharply, and he gave her a good look for the first time. "Did you say Harley Street?"

"Yes. I am a student at Queen's College, and I live in lodging next to it."

He set down his pen. "You're a student at Queen's College? What were you doing in Bethnal Green at night?"

"Helping to deliver a baby."

"Well, that seems to have been everyone's job tonight! Must have been a whole fleet of babies being born."

"Perhaps, but we were all delivering just the one."

Her attempt at pleasantry got no response. His voice remained cool. "And why should you want to go all the way to Bethnal Green to deliver a baby?"

Julia told him about being a nurse, about her preparation for the London School of Medicine for Women. She even told him Edith was already a student there, but he still didn't make the connection between Edith and the libel suit. Perhaps the case was only momentous in the eyes of those who had a stake in its outcome.

"So you see, we are innocent of any wrongdoing. We were guilty only of being in the wrong place at the wrong time."

He grunted. "Unfortunately, that's enough guilt to keep you here. You were in the company of one woman who is suspected of robbery, and another who attacked a policeman with murderous intent. We cannot rightly let you go until you explain all this to the magistrate."

"So we must remain here tonight?" Her heart sank at the thought.

"We'll take you all over to the court in the morning. The magistrate will decide whether you are to be dismissed or remanded to trial."

"Can you do anything for Eliza, the woman who was knocked unconscious? She needs medical attention."

His eyebrows lifted. "Why can't you give it to her, seeing as you're so qualified?"

"I mean, she ought to be taken to a hospital."

"She is a danger to others. We are not taking her to a hospital. There will be a doctor along in the morning."

Once she'd been returned to the cell, Julia told Edith what had happened.

"That was exactly what he told me," Edith said.

It was disappointing, but at least she and Edith would be able to watch over Eliza. She would also be here in case they brought in Cara. Julia resigned herself to a long, sleepless night.

Michael was awakened by a loud knocking on the outer door. He fumbled in the dark for a match to light the oil lamp, his mind scrambling to think what could be the matter. Whoever wanted him at this late hour could not be bringing good news. He could only think the worst—that something had happened to Corinna or David.

By the time he'd made his way to the door, Rawlins was already there, unlatching the bolt. Michael watched as his valet opened the door about a foot and peered out into the dark passageway. "Who's there?"

To Michael's surprise, he heard a woman's voice on the other side of the door. "Please, sir, is Mr. Michael Stephenson here? I must speak to him right away!"

Rawlins turned to look at Michael for instructions. "It's a woman, sir. And a man is with her."

Before Michael could respond, the woman poked her head through the door. "Are you Mr. Stephenson?"

Michael tightened the sash on his dressing gown and ran a hand through his hair. But there was no way to look presentable after being roused from bed in the middle of the night. "I am. Who are you? Have you come from the Barkers?"

But even as he asked, he couldn't think why they would send two servants to deliver a message. Certainly they wouldn't send out a young girl like this, for she looked no older than twenty. Her clothes also looked very damp. He couldn't account for that, as both the day and evening had been fine.

His mention of the Barkers did not even seem to register with her. She rushed forward and said, "Oh, thank God we've come to the right place!"

By this point Rawlins had also admitted the man. He was a grizzled older gentleman with shabby clothes, holding a tattered hat in his hand. He remained just inside the door while Rawlins kept a suspicious eye on him.

Michael looked at the woman, still flummoxed. "May I ask what your business is with me?"

Looking at him with wide, hopeful eyes, she said breathlessly, "My name is Caroline Bernay. My sister is Julia Bernay. You know her, I believe?"

The mention of Julia brought all sorts of new questions to mind, and no less worry. "I know her. But why—"

She launched into a rapid-fire explanation. "I don't live in London. I'm only here for a week. I'm a nanny—oh, that part doesn't matter. I was spending the afternoon with Julia, and we went to someplace called Bethnal Green to help deliver a baby, but we were out late and got caught up in a fight and—oh! Now she has been taken off by the police!"

CHAPTER

18

"Y OU HID IN THE WASHING KETTLE?"

Michael was still trying to comprehend the chain of events that had brought this woman to his house. At the moment they were seated by the fire, along with Mrs. Ames, the head charwoman for these buildings. She had a small set of rooms nearby and had been good enough to come when Michael sent the request via Rawlins. He didn't think it was right to have a woman here in the middle of the night without another lady present.

Once Mrs. Ames arrived, Michael had taken a few quick moments to excuse himself and quickly dress. He'd at least gotten Cara to realize there was nothing they could do for her sister at the moment. He'd persuaded her to have a cup of tea, get dry and warm, and tell him what had happened.

"It was a large copper kettle. It must have belonged to a professional laundress. I'm glad there wasn't water in it, although what had been left at the bottom was enough to ruin this frock." She looked woefully at her skirt.

The man who had brought her here, who'd introduced himself only as Harry, seemed to find this more amusing than distressing. With a little grin, he said, "Good thing there wasn't more water in it, or you'd have looked like a drowned kitten for sure, 'stead of just damp around the edges."

At least by now the warmth of the fire had dried her skirt, although it was dirty and wrinkled from the experience.

"How long did you stay in the kettle?" Michael asked.

"Oh, such a long time. I waited until I couldn't hear anyone moving about."

"And when you left, what did you do?"

"I knew I needed to get to a better neighborhood where I could find someone nice to help me. But I had no idea which direction to go. I cautiously made my way to a street and tried to decide which way looked more promising. Far down the street I saw a post box. The bright red stood out so prettily in the gloom, so I decided to go that direction. After that, I followed my nose." She said this last part with a little giggle.

"Your nose?" Mrs. Ames repeated.

"My son's a baker," Harry said. "He was baking bread for the morning customers."

"I could smell it a block away." Cara breathed deeply and sighed, obviously reliving the happy memory. "I knew a baker would be the sort of person who'd help me."

Michael shook his head. "I don't follow your logic."

She looked at him as though he were a little dense. "Who could be bad if they make something that smells so wonderful?"

He was finding it hard to believe this was Julia's sister. They seemed such opposites, whereas he and Corinna were more like birds of a feather.

201

"Right you are," Harry said. "At least when it comes to our bakery. We bake good quality bread, no alum added. We don't cheat no one if we can help it."

Michael rubbed his face. He still could not believe this conversation was happening in his chambers in the wee hours of the morning. "So you went into the bakery . . ." he prompted.

"The shop was still closed, but I went around back and found the door to the oven room. That's where I found Harry."

"I help my son when I can, though I can't do so much of the hard labor anymore. My back's not what it used to be. When she told me she needed to get to Gray's Inn, I offered to take her."

"And how did you think to come to me?"

"I know Julia saved your life on the Underground. I saw your calling card on her desk, and that's how I knew your address. Gray is easy to remember because it's a color, even if it's a drab one."

"My card?" Michael had no idea how Julia might have acquired one.

"It was from the accident, I think. There is dried blood on it."

"Oh." It was an intriguing thought, to imagine her finding the card on the train and deciding to keep it.

"Since you are a barrister, you can help her get out of jail!"

"It doesn't exactly work like that, I'm afraid. But I will go to the court tomorrow and see what can be done. Most likely they will release her."

"Do you really think so?" Cara responded hopefully. "If you say it, I believe it, for surely you know the laws."

She seemed a trusting soul—first with this man Harry and now with him. Michael found himself growing uncomfortable under her admiring gaze. She expected quite a lot from him.

"I'm sure Julia will be able to prove her innocence. In fact—" Michael snapped a finger as he realized he'd neglected to consider one very important detail. "In fact, they may have gotten released immediately. Once the policemen discovered they had brought in a member of the aristocracy, they might well have let them go."

Cara looked confused. "You can't mean Julia."

"No, I am speaking of Edith Morton—or more properly, Lady Edith Morton, as she is the daughter of the Earl of Westbridge."

Cara stared at him in surprise. "*Lady* Edith?"

"She didn't tell you?"

"No hint of it. Julia called her 'Edith,' and of course with those smallpox scars on her face, who would have thought . . ."

"Blue blood does not make a person immune to disease."

"I know, but . . . I mean, why . . . ?"

Michael could see questions filling her mind too quickly to voice aloud.

"Lady Edith wishes to become a physician and succeed on her own merits, not simply because of an accident of birth."

How ironic that he sounded as if he were taking her side. Which, to be honest, he supposed he was. Or he would, if he had a choice. But the earl was his client, and Michael's professional ethics demanded he set personal opinions aside and put forth every effort to win the libel case. The strain of this was increasing by the day. It would be a relief when the case was finally tried and he could be done with it.

"Does that mean Julia could be home already, at this very moment?" Cara's voice held a new hopefulness.

"It's possible."

"Then we must go there at once!"

Now Michael regretted he'd said anything about Edith. This had only turned Cara's head the wrong direction. "I believe we should take you home instead. The boardinghouse where Julia lives will be shut up tight, and it would be unwise to rouse them."

"But if she's there!"

"If she's not, we may create a whole different set of problems with the school authorities," Michael countered. "Whether she's there or at the jail, she should be safe for the night. On the other hand, the later it gets, the more difficult it will be to explain your absence to your employers. I would not want to see you put out of work with no character."

"I don't care about that!" she insisted.

Once again Michael thought about how different she was from her sister. Cara was led by her feelings, whereas Julia had a mountain of common sense. He realized his best chance of persuading Cara was to appeal to her emotional side—the part of her that had begun to see Michael as a rescuer. "You said you trust me, did you not? Do you believe I can give you the best counsel in this situation?"

Although he truly did believe this was the best course of action, there were other reasons for taking it that he did not divulge. To go looking for Julia at her lodgings in the middle of the night—even at the behest of her sister—could cause a scandal that would damage both his personal and his professional reputation. If he truly thought Julia was in any physical danger, he would not hesitate. But as things stood, he had to be more circumspect.

He told himself that coaxing Cara to his plan was truly for everyone's benefit. Even so, it pained him to see her so easily swayed by his words. Looking at him with sincere innocence, she responded, "I suppose we should do what you think is best."

There was nowhere but the floor to sleep. Eliza was still unconscious on one bench, and the gray-haired woman had claimed the other. "I was here first," she told them in a manner that dared anyone to fight her for it. She made no mention of the girl in the corner who'd arrived with her.

The girl had drawn her knees up and was resting her head on them, her arms wrapped protectively around her legs as though trying to keep warm. She looked lonely and not a little scared. Perhaps this was her first time in jail, although her companion had clearly had lots of experience.

Julia decided to sit by her. The girl raised her head in startled surprise, as though she were used to being ignored. Julia didn't speak right away but gave her a friendly nod.

In a short time, the older woman was asleep, her mouth open and occasionally letting out a grunting snore.

The floor felt uncomfortably damp, but that might only have been the cold seeping up through the hard stone. The days were warm now, but the nights still held a distinct chill. Myrtle and Doreen sat together against a wall, their arms linked for warmth, their eyes closed. Edith had taken up her vigil next to Eliza.

Julia bowed her head, thinking of Cara, praying fervently to ward off fear.

At one point she opened her eyes and noticed the girl was looking at her curiously. Speaking softly to keep from disturbing the others, she said, "My name's Julia. What's yours?"

"Gwen."

"Did you come here with her?" Julia indicated the woman asleep on the bench.

Gwen nodded. "That's my Aunt Henrietta."

"Is she really your aunt?" Julia remembered her sister Rosalyn's terrible tale of arriving in London alone and being picked up by a woman named Aunt Molly, who was really a procuress for a house of prostitution.

"I know what you're thinking, but it's not like that. She's my mum's sister. Raised me from the age of five, after my parents died."

Henrietta didn't seem very loving for an aunt. But there was no need to point that out to the girl. She asked gently, "Why are you here?"

Gwen gave a worried glance toward the bench, but Henrietta was asleep. Gwen didn't return her gaze to Julia but focused once more on her feet. "Caught stealing. My aunt says it's my fault. I was supposed to talk to the shopkeeper and keep his attention turned away from my aunt so he wouldn't notice she was pocketing a little clock."

"Sounds like it was your aunt who was in the wrong. Does she often steal?"

"We have to eat."

Something in this answer made Julia think the girl was simply parroting her aunt. Julia's heart went out to her, sympathetic to her tough situation.

"But you don't want to steal, do you?"

"No." The single word was laden with hopelessness.

Gwen looked over at Edith, who was seated on the floor next to the bench where Eliza was lying. Her shoulders were slumped, and she looked like she was dozing.

"I suppose you're some kind of gentry, too, like she is," Gwen said.

"Not at all. I was raised in an orphanage in Bristol."

Gwen's mouth fell open in surprise but closed again as she gave a sad nod of understanding. "Poverty can make people do all sorts of things."

"That's true, but it's not why I'm here."

Continuing to speak in quiet, whispered tones, she told Gwen about how she'd come to London and what she was doing here. She explained how at the orphanage they had been taught from an early age to trust in God and that He would provide all their needs as they asked in prayer.

Gwen listened intently. Unlike her aunt, she did not react with scorn at Julia's mention of God. "Do you really believe that?"

"I do."

It had been good for Julia to say these affirmative words aloud. Surely God would protect Cara, keep her safe from harm. He was a loving Father.

"I've often thought about God," Gwen confessed. "But we are not church people. In fact, my aunt rails against God a lot, saying terrible things. She says ever since she was a little girl she's been told what a terrible sinner she is."

"Sometimes when people are raised in condemnation, they feel they must live up to it."

Gwen's eyes opened wide. "I never thought about it that way."

"He will help you, too, Gwen. Would you like to pray together?"

Gwen cast another glance at her aunt. When she replied, it was barely a whisper. "Yes, I would."

Julia took Gwen's hands, chafing them a little to counteract the cold. Together they bowed their heads. Julia prayed for Gwen, and then she prayed individually for everyone in the cell. She did not hesitate to pray for Henrietta, as well, and she felt Gwen start in surprise. Julia took her time with the prayer, feeling Gwen relaxing as she spoke. Julia's own heart eased, as well. She had done all she could. She would have to leave the rest in the Lord's capable hands.

When they were done, Gwen whispered, "Thank you."

She gave a deep sigh and leaned on Julia's shoulder. Eventually, the two dropped off to sleep, warmed by each other.

Somehow Rawlins had managed to locate a four-wheeler cab, which was good, since they needed a vehicle large enough for Michael, Cara, Mrs. Ames, and Harry. They dropped Harry off at his son's bakery before going to Belgravia, a wealthy neighborhood south of Hyde Park. The carriage pulled to a halt on the street where Cara said she was staying.

"Is this the place?" Michael asked, wanting to be sure. Cara had been unable to remember whether the address was 122 or 124, and Michael had no wish to awaken members from the wrong household at this hour.

"That's the one!" Cara said, pointing. "I knew I'd be able to spot it by the lovely flower boxes above the bay window."

By the glow of the streetlamps, Michael could make out the flower boxes with red and white blooms spilling out of them. Cara might not have a head for numbers, but she clearly had an eye for visual details.

"Let's get you inside, dearie," said Mrs. Ames. Michael was grateful she'd been willing to come along to lend an air of decency to Cara's late-night return. No one would have believed she hadn't spent an illicit night alone with a man if Michael took her to the door. Mrs. Ames had a far better chance of success.

Cara did not seem eager to leave the carriage. Looking at Michael, she said, "You will send me word as soon as you can, won't you? I'll be sick with worry until I know what has become of Julia."

Michael had answered this question a dozen times already, but he understood her anxiety. "I will get you a message directly. Or better yet, I'll bring her myself."

"Thank you. I knew you were a good man the moment I set eyes on you." She reached out to take his hand. "I know you will make sure my sister is safe."

She was placing too much confidence in his abilities, assuming that because he was a barrister, he could clear any legal obstacles in Julia's path. Michael knew this was far from true. But he also knew he intended to try his hardest to make it so.

Mrs. Ames and Cara left the cab. Michael watched as they went through the wrought-iron gate and down the steps that led to the servants' entrance. Mrs. Ames was gone for what seemed to Michael a very long time. Was there a problem? What if they did not allow Cara back into the house? Michael didn't want to imagine what he would do if he suddenly had charge of a single young lady. He supposed he'd have to depend on Mrs. Ames's kindness to keep her for the night.

But at last Mrs. Ames reappeared. Michael was relieved to see her coming up the steps alone.

"Is everything all right?" he asked as she was helped into the carriage by the cab driver.

"They were very put out, as you might expect. But we told the housekeeper what had happened, and she was willing to let Cara back, albeit with a harsh reprimand."

"You really told them everything?"

"I figured I could be honest with the servants. If Cara's employers had been at home, it would have been quite a different matter. Thank heaven they are out of town until tomorrow. The housekeeper said Cara is the only person who can keep their little boy in line. He adores her."

Michael leaned back against the carriage seat. One problem was solved for now, but the larger question of what was happening to Julia—and what would happen to her tomorrow—could not yet be answered. He could only wait. Tired as he was, he knew he would get no more sleep tonight.

CHAPTER

19

MICHAEL HAD BEEN to the magistrate's court before in the course of his work, but it depressed him every time. There was always an air of gloom that had more to do with the people than with the dingy, cavernous space with its peeling plaster and battered wooden benches.

Men and women who'd been detained by the police on suspicion of various crimes were seated in the front benches, women on the left and men on the right. The dozen or so male prisoners here today were, as usual, a dodgy-looking bunch, all of them wearing sour, scornful expressions.

Looking at the women's side, Michael spotted Julia immediately. His first reaction was deep concern that she'd been placed in this predicament. And yet he was amazed to see her sitting with her back tall and straight, looking undaunted by her circumstances and apparently unharmed despite a rough night. She was seated in the middle of the row, with Lady Edith to her left. The two of them stood out easily from the others, primarily by their demeanor. Lady Edith was watching the proceedings with interest, almost like a spectator at a play. If either of them was worried, they didn't show it.

Because their attention was focused on the magistrate and the case currently being heard, the women did not notice as Michael quietly took a seat at the back.

Michael had visited the magistrate's clerk first thing that morning and learned that Julia and Edith were still in custody. From the position of their names on the docket, he knew it would be a while before their names would be called. He watched as several of the men were brought up on various charges. Nearly all were remanded to jail to await trial. This magistrate was not one of the lenient ones.

A handful of journalists were in the courtroom. For most of them, court reporting was their regular assignment. Michael had known they would be here, but he also knew it wouldn't make his position any easier. He would have to carefully parse out his representation of the women as being for this affair only. Although it had nothing to do with the ongoing libel suit, the reporters might attempt to make a connection anyway, once they discovered one of the defendants was Lord Westbridge's daughter.

Two women were called up and charged with shoplifting. After hearing the testimony of the shop owner and the policeman, the women were remanded to prison to await trial. As they were being led out, the younger of the two threw a sad glance at Julia. In response, Julia gave her a sympathetic smile and clasped her hands together near her heart. Was it a sign of empathy? Of prayer? Whatever it was, the young woman looked as though she were trying to gather courage from it, even though the fear on her face was unmistakable. Michael felt sorry for her. The police had labeled her an "accomplice" to the older woman, but Michael suspected she was no more than an unwilling pawn. He'd seen many such cases. There was a chance she'd be pardoned at trial, but she wasn't going to have an easy time of it until then.

The court usher announced the next case, reading out Julia's name along with the others in round, ringing tones. They had all been charged as accessories to violent theft and assault. An attorney was there to represent the victim, who could not be present due to his injuries. According to the attorney's statement and the testimony of the constable, the two people most likely to have committed the crime weren't even in the courtroom: a woman who'd been brutally injured while resisting arrest, and a man who had escaped. This seemed further corroborated by the testimony of the defendant Myrtle Hodges, who knew both of the prime suspects.

The magistrate then turned his attention to Lady Edith. "You were found in the suspects' company when the police arrived to make the arrest, shortly after the crime was committed. Can you explain to us what you were doing in that particular gin shop at that time?"

"I'd be happy to, your worship," said Edith. She was using the customary and proper term of address for a magistrate, but Michael heard a hint of irony in her voice. It only added to what he knew about this woman: by all reports, she enjoyed questioning authority.

Her description of events matched what Cara had told Michael, although she was more concise and didn't use the hyperbole Cara had indulged in at times.

"So you see, we were innocent bystanders, nothing more," she finished. Pointing toward Julia and a woman called Doreen, she added, "If your worship will also question these two women, they will confirm this version of events."

"Thank you, I am aware of my job." The magistrate referred to the papers on his desk and then looked out over the courtroom. "It says here that Mr. Michael Stephenson, barrister at law, wishes to speak for the defendant Julia Bernay."

Michael rose to his feet. "Yes, your worship."

There was a rustle and murmuring in the courtroom as he made his way to the table at the front reserved for legal counsel. He felt a pang of delight as Julia's lovely mouth widened into a grin of joyous surprise. Edith, on the other hand, glared at him as though unsure whether he was friend or foe.

"Yes, I am here on behalf of Miss Julia Bernay. She is entirely innocent of anything to do with the assault and robbery in question. Last night, she went to Bethnal Green in order to assist with a difficult childbirth. She and these two women had been passing by the gin shop on their way home and entered it with the sole purpose of helping out a woman in distress. It was all exactly as Lady Edith Morton has just described."

The collective gasp that filled the courtroom when Michael spoke Lady Edith's name was exactly what he expected. Everyone stared at her in wide-eyed shock. There was no movement except for the pencils of the newspaper men, who were writing furiously while simultaneously staring at Edith—an amazing feat of dexterity.

Lady Edith clenched her fists and turned a furious gaze on Michael. Why had she been trying to hide this information? He couldn't imagine she wished to remain incognito due to shame at her actions.

Understanding dawned in the magistrate's eyes. Like everyone in London's legal circles, he would be familiar with the libel suit and the famous Earl of Westbridge. He must have finally put this together with Edith's name and appearance.

"The title that Mr. Stephenson gave when referring to you—is this correct?" the magistrate demanded.

"It is the title I was assigned at birth, your worship."

The room was abuzz as people chattered to one another about this amazing development. Michael distinctly heard a woman with a cockney accent tell her friend, "Aww, what a shame that is—she got all that birth and breedin' but 'er face is ruined by the pox." Someone else said, "The daughter of an earl, gone slumming in Bethnal Green! What is the world coming to!"

"Usher! Come here!" the magistrate barked.

A man approached, looking singularly uncomfortable.

"Why does it not state on these papers the full name and title of this woman?"

"She never told us, your worship! How could we have known?" He looked as though he would have liked to throw Edith a glare for putting him in this spot but was too afraid of the consequences.

"I am the daughter of an earl," Lady Edith said, "but does that make a difference in the eyes of the law?"

The magistrate slammed a hand down on the desk. "It makes a great deal of difference! You might very well have saved yourself a night in jail."

"So I can get off scot-free because I am a member of the aristocracy?"

"Careful," Michael advised, speaking softly. "This magistrate does not tolerate impertinence of any kind in his court."

"I'll take that under advisement," she whispered back, but she sounded not the least bit concerned.

The magistrate glowered at her. "This is a court of law. We do not talk of 'scot-free.' We are here only to assess whether there is probable cause to commit you to trial. You may rest assured we will do our duty entirely as the law dictates. Mr. Stephenson, have you anything more to add to your statement?"

"No, your worship." Michael had done what he could. Now he only hoped the magistrate would release the women.

After carefully adjusting his spectacles, the magistrate made a great show of taking his time to reread the official documents concerning this case as well as the notes he had made during the testimony.

The murmuring among the spectators continued. Everyone was ogling Edith. She stood with her arms crossed, staring defiantly over the courtroom. Michael halfway thought she was daring the magistrate to commit her to trial. By contrast, Julia was looking only at Michael with a warmth in her eyes that made it hard for him to breathe. Clearly she was placing her trust in him. He could only hope he deserved it. There was no evident case against them, but Edith's actions weren't helping their cause.

Finally the magistrate looked up and announced his decision. "The defendants Julia Bernay, Doreen Collins, and Edith Morton are discharged."

He didn't use Edith's title. This was probably a deliberate response to her refusal to lay claim to it.

Michael gave a sigh of relief. He saw the women do likewise, despite the bravery they'd all shown. Doreen did not look entirely happy, though. She exchanged a worried look with Myrtle.

The magistrate pointed at Myrtle. "You will stay. I have more to ask you."

Julia looked at Michael with tears in her eyes. "Thank you! How did you know we were here?"

Edith said coldly, "Does my father know about this?"

"No," Michael answered, although a glance at the busily scratching pencils of the reporters confirmed that it wouldn't be long before he did. "I'll tell you outside," he said, as the usher motioned for them to follow him to the exit.

"We can't go!" Edith hissed. "What about Myrtle?"

Michael said, "You must admit the magistrate has good reason to question her further. You never met her before last night's altercation. There may be extenuating circumstances you are not aware of."

Despite this counsel, Edith looked ready to dig in her heels.

"Edith, please," Julia implored, seeing the growing consternation of the magistrate and the usher.

"You can do more for her as a free civilian than as a prisoner," Michael urged. He wanted nothing more than to get these women out of the courtroom.

This argument seemed to convince Edith. She said quietly to Myrtle, "We won't forget you."

Doreen nodded, adding, "Soon as we get out, I'm coming straight back to the gallery." Myrtle gave them all a grateful look.

The usher led them out a side door to the hallway. They could just hear the magistrate beginning to question Myrtle again before the usher shut the door.

Doreen took hold of Michael's hand and pumped it vigorously. "Thank you, sir." She added swift good-byes to the other women, promising to keep them informed of what happened to Myrtle, before returning to the courtroom through the visitor's entrance.

Julia turned eagerly to Michael. "How did you know we were here?"

"Cara told me."

"Cara! When did you see her? What happened to her? Is she all right?"

"She is safe and sound. She managed to get help and find me. She is now back at the Needenhams' residence."

"Thank God!" Julia was radiant with happiness. "He has answered my prayers."

Michael would have preferred that Julia could have said her prayers at home and not in a jail cell. "With all due respect, Lady Edith, what were you thinking, to allow them to hold you all night? Surely with a word or two of explanation, you might have gotten all of you released."

"You may refer to me as Miss Morton," the lady answered archly. "As to why I did it, I found the experience quite instructional. How am I going to help these people if I have no real idea what they face in their lives?"

"I should think there are plenty of ways to do it without the risk of getting committed to trial."

"You are free to think what you like," she responded. "I don't intend to argue the point. You offered us your assistance, and I respect that. Although, given your connection to Julia, I should say I am not surprised."

Startled, Michael looked at Julia. Had she broken her promise about keeping their lessons a secret?

Julia gave a tiny shake of her head to answer his unspoken question. "She means how I helped you on the day of the accident."

Edith looked between the two of them as if some intuition told her there was more to their connection than Julia was admitting to. "I must be going. Mr. Stephenson, I know you will understand if I say that the less time I spend with you, the more I will like it."

"Yes, Miss Morton, I understand completely."

They made their way down the long hallway to the main doors. Outside, the sun was bright. The ladies squinted, their eyes unused to such light after their time in jail and court.

"Shall we go?" Edith said to Julia, motioning toward the street corner, where a line of hansom cabs stood waiting at the cab stand.

"Thank you, but I will make my own way," Julia said. "I want to visit Cara and make sure she is all right."

Edith nodded. "I am going back to the police station. I want to see what has happened to Eliza and ensure she gets proper care. As Mr. Stephenson said, I might manage to do some good as a civilian."

It was a deprecating twist on Michael's words. Although he had benefited greatly from having Lord Westbridge as a client, he was sorry that its corollary must be that the man's daughter perceived him as an enemy. He could see why Julia was friends with this independent-minded woman.

"We are still going to visit Sybil tomorrow, are we not?" Julia asked her.

That took bravery, Michael thought, to return to Bethnal Green after what they'd been through.

Lady Edith sent another appraising glance between Julia and Michael. Her distrust of him was evident. Michael didn't like to think she might transfer that mistrust to Julia by association, but the possibility was clearly there.

"I'll see you tomorrow, then," she said to Julia and walked off toward the cab stand.

Julia turned all her attention to Michael. "Did Cara give you her address? I never got it from her yesterday."

"Yes, I know the address. May I take you there?"

She looked hesitant. "I couldn't ask you to drive me all over London."

Her brown eyes looked into his. Her smooth cheeks looked feather-soft, even though they were smudged with dirt from her night in the jail.

"It's no trouble." The words came easily, despite the many items of business he needed to handle today. "But are you sure you don't want to go home first and get some rest? You've had a trying experience."

"No, I'm anxious to get to Cara and set her heart at ease." She looked down at her dirty frock. "I know I look a sight, but I expect I'll have to go in the servants' entrance anyway, since

I'm visiting their nanny. What is the correct protocol for that? In the past when Cara and I have been able to see one another, we always did it on her day off and met somewhere away from her employer."

He'd been so busy looking at her that he hadn't realized she'd asked him a question. He scrambled to figure out what it was. Protocol. Right. He cleared his throat. "We'll work it out when we get there."

Michael helped her into a cab, conscious of her nearness as they settled onto the narrow bench.

Once the carriage was in motion, she said eagerly, "Please tell me what happened last night. I can't imagine how Cara found you!"

Michael shared with her everything he knew, including the details Cara had given him about her escape and how she'd ended up at his chambers.

Julia shook her head. "It's astounding. And yet I think everything worked out for the best."

"Including your night in jail?"

To his surprise, she said, "Oh yes. It was, in fact, a triumphant night. I was able to minister to a lost soul. To give her a word of hope and encourage her to return to God. I hope she will keep those things in her heart as she faces what's ahead."

"You just spent a night in jail, with the possibility of being sent to trial for serious crimes even though you were innocent, and the main thing you can say is that you're happy you were able to talk to someone about God?"

The words came out sharply. After the hours he'd spent worrying, her breezy statement rankled him.

Her mouth flattened. "All right, I admit it was not a pleasant night. It would have been easy to give in to fear. If you had seen the way they treated that woman Eliza . . ." Her face drew tight with pain at the memory. "Most of all, I was so worried for Cara. If anything had happened to her, it would have crushed me. And it would have been my fault for getting her into that mess."

Michael was sorry now that he'd chastised her. He saw plainly that her cheerfulness did not replace deep empathy.

"I don't worry so much on my own account," she continued, "but Cara has always been flighty and unequipped to face hard situations."

"Perhaps she's stronger than you give her credit for."

"Well, she made it through last night, and she had the ingenuity to find you. Perhaps she is." She wiped away a tear. "But speaking to Gwen about God's love and grace—that was like a balm to me last night. To give glory to Him. How else does one truly survive life's worst situations?"

Michael looked away, ostensibly to watch the passing buildings, not wanting her to sense the truth about his life. His answer for harsh, bitter times had always been to place a guard around his mind, toughen his heart, wall off his feelings. He used unyielding stoicism to survive disasters, even on days when it felt like swimming through icy waters or running through fire. Thus far, the strategy had worked for him. But grinding his way to success had never given him the kind of satisfaction he saw right now shining in Julia's eyes.

"Here we are, nearly to her street," he said, eager to change the topic.

The carriage passed by the open gate of a small park bordered with brick walls.

Julia exclaimed, "There she is! In that park with Robbie. Driver, can you stop?" she called, leaning dangerously out of the cab.

The cab came to a halt. Without waiting for Michael or the driver to help her, Julia got down from the carriage and doubled back toward the gates of the park. Michael paid the cabbie and walked swiftly to catch up to her.

As they walked through the gates, he saw Cara and a boy tossing a ball back and forth. Julia shouted her name, and Cara turned just as the boy threw the ball. It whizzed past her as she broke into a run toward her sister.

CHAPTER

20

JULIA CLUNG TIGHTLY TO HER SISTER. They'd had plenty of disagreements growing up and were generally about as compatible as oil and water, but at this moment, Julia had never been so glad to see anyone. "Oh, my dear Cara, I was so worried for you!"

"And I for you!"

They were only brought out of their fog of happiness by Robbie crying out in irritation, "Now look what you've done!"

They separated, both wiping tears from their eyes, to look at the boy. He was pointing to a row of bushes. "The ball went under there!"

"I'll help you," Michael offered. He got down on his hands and knees, looking under the bush. "I think I can just reach it."

He moved in closer, extending his arm under the shrubbery, looking most undignified. Julia was amused and intrigued to see how naturally he interacted with the child.

"I knew Mr. Stephenson would get you out of jail," Cara said, beaming. "And now he is rescuing Robbie's ball, too!"

Her eyes shone with admiration. Or perhaps it was only an effect caused by her tears of happiness. Either way, Julia could see her sister was quite enamored with Michael. Julia could not blame her. After the events of last night and today, her own estimation of him was higher than ever.

Michael got to his feet and held out the ball. "Here you are, Master Needenham."

The boy was only four, but someone—could it really have been her flighty sister Cara?—had drilled some manners into him. "Thank you, sir," he said with deferential politeness. He even gave Michael a little bow, which was absolutely endearing.

"Robbie, I see that Master Reese has arrived with his dog," Cara said. "Why don't you go play with him?"

She pointed to where a large, energetic dog was dragging a boy into the park. The boy was shouting commands at the dog, to which the creature paid no heed. The nanny who trailed in their wake wasn't any help. She looked afraid for the boy, but even more afraid to go near the dog.

"Napoleon!" Robbie cried out in excitement—Julia presumed this was the dog's name—and ran over to join them.

"He does love dogs," Cara explained to Michael and Julia. "Poor little tyke. He really wants one for a pet, but Sir John says dogs should only be kept for hunting and not allowed in the house."

Seeing that the boy was happily chatting with his friend, Cara put her arm through Julia's. "You can't think how tormented I was last night worrying about you! You must tell me everything! Was it horrid in the jail? Did they mistreat you? I've heard such lurid stories about those places!"

Julia could see her sister's mind running in all sorts of misguided directions. She also knew it would take some time to give her a complete account. She looked at Michael. "You should go. I know you are so busy. We have already caused such an imposition by coming to you for help."

"Well, how else was I going to get you out of jail?" Cara protested. "You don't know how I agonized over what to do!"

"You did exactly the right thing," Michael assured her. To Julia, he said, "To be honest, I'd like to stay and hear your story. Once Cara told me you'd been arrested, I had a bit of a hard night of it myself."

He said this with the air of giving a confession, and Julia was surprised to see an unusual vulnerability in his eyes. It struck her how deeply he'd been worried for her. This knowledge, added to the way he was looking at her just now, caused an odd tickling sensation near her heart. She said, somewhat breathlessly, "I'm glad you want to stay."

"Excellent!" Cara exclaimed, and tugged her toward a nearby bench.

Michael remained standing. He looked as though he were keeping one eye on Robbie. Cara seemed to have forgotten all about the boy in her excitement to hear Julia's story. As Julia told them everything in detail, she also cast her gaze toward the boy from time to time, but he was happily engaged with his friend and the dog.

"What adventures we both have had!" Cara exclaimed when Julia had finished. "It sounds like they were very quick to let you go once they found out about Edith. *Lady* Edith, I mean. Imagine that! If I were an earl's daughter, I wouldn't hesitate to let everyone know it."

"She has her reasons," Julia said and looked at Michael, wondering if she should say more.

He didn't seem inclined to broach the subject of the lawsuit. He said merely, "Lady Edith wants to distance herself from her father. To make her own way in the world."

"Why, doesn't she like her father?" Cara *tsk*ed. "It would be too bad to have a father and not get on with him. I'd be thankful just to have a father, whether he was an earl or a commoner. Our father was a ship captain, but he disappeared some years ago. We don't know for certain where he is. But I expect Julia has told you these things already."

This rapid, breathless way of talking was normal for Cara—and, Julia was sorry to note, so was the content. For years her little sister had clung to the belief that their father was still alive somewhere. Nothing in what she'd just said hinted that she was yet mature enough to accept that he was dead.

"Are your parents still living?" Cara asked, her gaze fixed on Michael with interest.

"They are not," he answered with a sad smile.

"I'm sorry to hear it. Were you very young when it happened?"

"Not so young. But not yet out of school."

"And do you have brothers and sisters?"

"A sister."

Julia thought back to the times she'd asked Michael the same questions. He was answering Cara more directly and, Julia thought, with more evidence of emotion behind the words. Was it Cara's artlessness that made it easier to breach his walls? Or had something changed?

Cara said, with the air of speaking to a good friend, "Then I'm sure you understand, just as Julia and I do, why families should always stick together."

The same thing had gone through Julia's mind as she'd gotten to know Edith. It hadn't been a direct thought, the way Cara was stating it now, but rather a vague, troubled feeling. Cara had put it into words.

"That kind of enmity hurts more than just themselves," Cara went on. "Think about it—if she had said who her father was, maybe everyone would have been released! Or maybe Lord Westbridge would have gone there himself to get his daughter out."

"No, his lordship would *not* have gone there," Julia said, not wanting Cara to start imagining unrealistic scenarios. "And in any case, there are plenty of ways to solve a problem other than having a father come rescue you."

Her rebuke stemmed from deep-seated frustration at her sister's constant daydreams about their long-lost father. She was tempted to feel bad when she saw the hurt on Cara's face, but she would not apologize for speaking the truth. "I do not say, however, that Edith did the right thing in hiding her rank. If we had been freed last night, I could have gone looking for you."

"Don't go down that path," Michael put in sharply. "The worst possible thing would have been for you to go wandering those dangerous streets alone at night."

"But she would not have been alone!" Cara responded adamantly. "She would have gone looking for you first, surely? Just like I did?"

"I would have done nothing of the sort," Julia protested, her face growing hot. "That would have been too presumptuous."

"But are you not friends? He was so eager to help last night that I just assumed . . ." She looked between them for confirmation.

It was a question that Julia could not imagine how to answer. There did not seem to be any word to correctly describe their relationship. Not friends, but no longer mere acquaintances. Not after all the time they'd spent together over these past weeks. But she could not explain any of that to Cara. She sent an embarrassed look toward Michael, worried he might think she'd told Cara about the Latin lessons. But she had kept her word and not told anyone, not even her sisters.

Michael turned his gaze away, as though he, too, was unsure

how to answer. His attention snagged on something in the distance. "Robbie looks out of his depth," he commented.

The boy was on the ground, pinned down by the dog, whose nose was rammed into Robbie's coat pocket. Robbie was shrieking in the way boys do that makes it impossible to tell whether it is from delight or terror.

Cara jumped up from the bench, shouting as she ran toward him, "Robbie, what are you doing? Oh!"

Julia ran after Cara. Michael followed more slowly, heartily relieved for the distraction. The conversation had veered into dangerous territory. At the same time, he realized it was a landscape he wanted very much to explore. But he had to talk to Julia alone first. Her expression after Cara had asked if they were friends had been most interesting. There had been a blush on her cheek, he was certain of it. He had to know if she was beginning to feel as he was.

By the time Michael reached them, Cara was caught up in the tangled heap of child and dog, trying to push the animal away. He took hold of the dog's collar and pulled him off the boy.

Cara dragged Robbie to his feet. "What on earth happened?"

Now it was plain the boy was laughing. "I was . . . teasing Napoleon . . . with this bit of candy," he gasped between giggles. "When I put it in my pocket, he tried to get it."

The dog was still wriggling excitedly. To calm him down, Michael led him back over to his owner. After the nanny thanked Michael profusely, she took her young charge and the dog away from the park, exclaiming that it was time to go home.

Cara crouched in front of Robbie, busily dusting him off. "Look at the dirt on your clothes," she chided. "And you've torn your coat! There'll be the devil to pay if your mother sees it."

Her angst rolled off the boy. "Is it tea time?" he asked. "I'm hungry."

Cara licked a thumb and used it to wipe a smudge of dirt off his face. "You might not be so hungry if you'd eaten that sweet instead of teasing the dog with it."

She sounded just like a stern mother. In the short time Michael had known her, he'd seen her curious mix of flightiness and resourcefulness. Now he could add something else to that list: when she got down to the business of mothering, she could do it as well as anybody.

Having returned Robbie to some semblance of order, Cara stood up but kept a firm hold of the child's hand. "Have you the time?" she asked Michael.

He checked his pocket watch. "Nearly three."

"We have to go," Cara said, her sadness clearly mixed with anxiety. "I must find him clean clothes and get him something to eat before the Needenhams arrive. They'll be furious with me if they see him in this state. Robbie, where is your ball?"

The boy pointed to where it lay about twenty yards off.

"Run and get it, will you?"

Robbie raced off to retrieve his ball, and Cara turned to give Julia a hug. "I probably won't see you before we leave London. Miss Needenham will be presented in court tomorrow, and we're taking a train to Exeter the following day. You will write to me, though, and tell me how things are going? And you will send my love to Sybil and especially to little Sam and Jemmie?"

Julia promised she would. Once more Cara drew her close and whispered something in her ear. Looking startled, Julia whispered something back. Wanting to give the sisters a moment of privacy, Michael strolled toward the little fountain in the center of the park and feigned interest in the tiered waterfall that topped it.

He didn't turn back until he heard Robbie say, "Here is the ball! Can we go now?"

"*May* we go now," Cara corrected him. She took Michael's hand and clasped it warmly. "I am so grateful to you! I would say that at last my sister owes me something—but I know you are the one we are indebted to."

"You don't owe me anything. It was my pleasure to help a lady in need."

Michael meant every word. The bizarre events of last night had not been a burden or an imposition, as Julia had fretted. Instead, it had been a refreshing break from the rigid path he'd been following. In fact, it had opened his eyes to the truth that his life had changed from the day Julia had come into it.

She'd slowly grown on him, stolen steadily larger portions of his thoughts—and his heart. For years he'd allowed no emotional attachments to anyone, aside from Corinna and, to a lesser extent, David. Last night, after the torment that came with the knowledge that Julia was in danger, he could no longer deny to himself what she meant to him.

He was painfully aware that falling in love with Julia would only cause endless and perhaps insurmountable difficulties for both of them. But at this moment, he didn't care what trouble she might bring his way. Not if he discovered that she loved him in return.

CHAPTER

21

THE LITTLE PARK WAS EMPTY of anyone else now. Michael and Julia were, for the first time since he'd met her, truly alone.

He was curious what the two sisters had discussed in whispered tones before Cara left them. Whatever it was, it left Julia unsettled. She didn't want to meet his eye.

"Right," she murmured, making a motion as if she were dusting her hands. "I should be going. You have your work to get back to, and I must make my explanations to the house matron for not coming home last night, not to mention apologizing to Dr. Chase for missing the natural history examination this morning—"

"Wait." Michael stepped close to stop her. He'd never seen her agitated like this before. Perhaps the strain of the night and the resulting tiredness had subdued her usual air of indomitability. He was seeing a rare glimpse beyond her self-assured façade. "Surely those things can wait a little longer. It's pleasant here; why not take a few minutes to enjoy it?"

Finally, she looked up at him, trying unsuccessfully to push an errant lock of hair back into its pins. "After a night at the jail, I am terribly bedraggled."

Julia Bernay, worried about how she looked. Now Michael was sure she was not her usual self.

He reached up and tucked one last strand of hair behind her ear. "I've never seen anyone who could manage to look bedraggled and yet so pretty at the same time."

Her eyes widened. "You are too kind."

He noticed, with not a little satisfaction, that her words came out a touch breathlessly. At this moment, as they stared at one another, Michael wanted very much to ascribe her agitation to something other than the trials of the past twenty-four hours. They stood so close that he could see a tiny quiver of her lips as she smiled. Sunlight, filtered and dappled through the leafy trees, danced over her face.

"Please stay," he coaxed.

After another pause, she nodded. But the way she searched his eyes first, and the way they moved in quiet unison to sit together on the bench, told him that something important had just happened.

They sat without speaking, looking out at the well-manicured little park. A gentle breeze rustled in the trees and teased the flower beds. The little fountain gurgled, and birds chirped as they splashed in it. This walled enclave felt intimate and private, as though they were removed from the rest of the world. Julia was mere inches away from him, and he savored this nearness. Her hands fidgeted in her lap, and he wanted nothing more than to reach out and take hold of them. But he was not going to risk doing anything to rush—and possibly upset—the quiet bond building between them.

He was glad he held back, for she sighed, her shoulders relaxing and her hands growing still, as the peacefulness of the park touched her. "It's so lovely. I feel as though, sitting here, all the cares of the world could be set aside, if only for now."

"I was just thinking the same thing."

"What you did for me—and most especially for Cara—words cannot express. . . . My sisters and I relied on each other through all the terrible times in our childhood. Now that we are grown, things are changing, and yet our care and concern for one another never changes. But I know you understand these things."

"I do." Julia's oblique reference to Corinna pained him, because he knew how much his sister would object to what he was doing just now. "I realize, to my chagrin, that I never asked you about your parents. Cara spoke of your father's disappearance?"

Julia's hands begin to fidget again. "That's because she won't accept that he is dead."

"Perhaps I should not have asked."

"It's not that I mind speaking about it." She turned to face him. "I get upset at Cara sometimes, that's all. The question of what happened to our father has been a source of disagreement between us for years. He was the captain of a merchant ship, traveling most often to South America and the Caribbean. They made stops in America sometimes, too, although those were suspended when the American Civil War began in 1861. A little over a year later, the ship disappeared."

"Sank, do you mean?"

"That's what the owners of the shipping company said. They determined it was lost in a hurricane. We were so young when it happened, all three of us under ten years old, so we had to accept the story the adults told us. But later I began to doubt the truth of it. Based on where the ship should have been at the time, it would have been well to the south of the hurricane. I began to fear that my father had not died but had abandoned us."

Michael closed his eyes briefly, feeling an almost visceral reaction to her words. He knew the pain of losing a father. He knew the irrational feelings of guilt felt by the child who'd been left behind. "Why do you think he abandoned you?"

"It's a rather long story. Are you sure you want to hear it?"

She asked the question earnestly, perhaps remembering how he'd tried in the past to stop any discussion of personal matters. But Michael also saw a sadness that he wished he had the power to wipe away.

He said gently, "Yes, I would."

"I should say that what I'm about to share . . . well, I've never told it to anyone."

Michael felt as though she were putting her heart into his hands. "I'm honored" was all he could say.

"Here it is, then. The day before our father left us for the last time, he was at the pub near our house, having a pint with his friends. My mother sent me to fetch him and tell him supper was ready. This was my favorite thing to do, because it gave me a few precious moments alone with my father. He was away so much that whenever he was home, we all competed for his attention. But during his last few visits home, he'd grown more surly. Short-tempered. He'd once been so lighthearted, but that seemed to be eroding away. Children pick up on these moods without understanding their cause. Like many children, I suppose, I began to think that my sisters and I were the cause of it. I began to doubt whether he even loved us."

Michael was well acquainted with this feeling. He'd suffered through his father's bizarre behavior after his mother died. He and Corinna had even wondered whether they'd somehow caused her death. Wondered if they were responsible for the way he was growing distant and unreachable.

"When I got to the pub, I paused before going in. I'd gotten a rock in my shoe, and I sat down on the edge of a horse trough to get it out. While I was doing that, my father stepped out the door. There was a man with him, but it wasn't anyone I knew. They didn't see me at first, because there was a stack of crates between me and the door. But Father was clearly upset about something. 'It was the biggest mistake of my life,' I heard him say. 'I wish to heaven I could be free from the whole lot of them. I had such plans for my life, you know. And it was nothing like this.'"

Julia was looking forward as she talked, her eyes focused on the bubbling fountain, but Michael had the impression she was seeing that last day with her father very clearly. "I think he was talking about us—his family. He and my mother squabbled about money. She was never good at economy. She was supposed to spread out the money he left her over the time he would be gone, but she never could manage to do that. We always ran short."

Michael shook his head. "He might have been talking about any number of things, not necessarily your family."

"Perhaps. But then the man said, 'Well, you have no choice, now. Do this thing, and you'll at last be free of them.' My father said, 'But will I ever really be free? And the suffering it will cause—' And then I stood up, and my father saw me. 'What are you doing there?' he yelled. He grabbed my arm and shook me, his face red with anger. 'How long have you been listening?'"

Julia spoke with the same raspy harshness that her father must have used. Michael hurt for her, knowing how deeply a parent's sharp words could cut a child's heart. He wasn't surprised when she said, "That was the first time I'd ever been afraid of my father. I insisted I'd heard nothing, mostly from fear of what he might do to me. The other man left, but not before saying to my father, "Stay the course, Bernay.'"

"And then?"

"We walked home. My father said not one word the whole way, and he was very short with us that evening. He was gone by morning, his ship leaving with the four o'clock tide." She rubbed a thumb and forefinger over her eyes, perhaps to ward off tears. "We never saw him again."

"I'm very sorry," Michael said, knowing the words were inadequate.

"Cara always felt he was alive somewhere, wanting to return to us but not able to for some unknown reason. I took his disappearance as proof that he'd abandoned us—that he wanted to be free from us, even though he knew we'd be hurt by his leaving."

"Do you still feel that way?"

"I don't know what to think. I'm ashamed to admit there are times when I fall prey to the same foolish hopes that Cara has nurtured. But then I tell myself it can't possibly be true. At best, he did mean to come back, but his ship really did sink, as we've been told. And really, why should we doubt it? The ship and the entire crew were never seen again. If only we *really* knew what happened . . ."

Michael thought this over. "How alike our stories are. While there is no doubt my father is dead, there are mysteries surrounding his death. And yet, even if we were to know everything, would the pain of loss be any less? I don't think so. It would remain just as bitter. Just as terrible."

He spoke from the depth of his being, even if these were not the consoling words he ought to be sharing right now. "I'm offering you small comfort," he said apologetically.

"I do feel better for having shared it, though." Julia reached out to take his hand. A friendly gesture, filled with warmth and support. "Will you tell me about your parents? How was it that you and Corinna were left in so much trouble?"

He looked down at their clasped hands. "I think that, in order for you to understand, I may have to go back a ways."

"I want to hear everything."

"All right." He inhaled—the kind of deep breath he always took before plunging into deep water. But he began with the simple, straightforward facts, as though slowly wading in. "My father was the son of a bank clerk, but he had a flair for business and soon earned a lot of money in investments—railroads, mostly. He had no social connections, but my mother was allowed to marry him anyway because he was rich. They were intensely happy. She raised Corinna and me with all the tender care a child could wish for. But she died when I was nine years old. Corinna, who was just twelve, became the *de facto* mistress of our home."

Julia gave a murmur of sympathy. Knowing what he now did about her life, Michael heard the depth of understanding behind it.

He wanted to tell her everything. He wanted to share the burdens on his heart. Although he and Corinna had shared these trials together, each had borne their own burdens separately. They had not truly discussed what was in the depths of their hearts, only what steps to take next, what actions were necessary to survive. They'd given support to one another, but not true comfort.

"In a sense, you could say I lost my father at that time, too. He became distant to us in every way, often leaving us for months at a time and barely interacting with us even when he was home. He began making bad business decisions and unwise investments. As Corinna got older, with her responsibilities at home, she came to understand what a terrible state we were in financially. She tried to hide it from me and did her best to outwit the creditors. I was sixteen, away at school, when our father died. He fell from a horse, which he'd been riding late at night at full gallop over a field. From the tracks in the mud, it was clear he'd been jumping the horse over fences and hedgerows. This was unusual, because he was a mediocre horseman and never did such things. Some say he was purposefully trying to kill himself."

He sent Julia a sideways glance, trying to discern what she was thinking. Often the mention of a parent's suicide was enough to make people want to distance themselves. After all, madness was believed to run in families. But her expression was soft, filled with compassion.

"I can see now why you were so hesitant to discuss your family with me," she said. "I'm sorry for the things you suffered. What did you do after he died?"

"It soon became clear that we'd have to sell everything we owned, and not even that would cover all my father's debts. The scandal of his death, the whispers of madness and suicide, made us outcasts in society as surely as the loss of money had. This was hardest on Corinna. My mother had a connection to the aristocracy through a first cousin. That, plus my father's wealth, would have been enough to gain Corinna an invitation to be presented at court. But all that was lost. To this day, she's never gotten over it."

Julia nodded thoughtfully. "That explains a lot of things."

"About why Corinna acts as she does? Yes, I suppose it does."

"Yet she seems to have done very well for herself."

"She married David within a year of my father's death. Like my father, he was a self-made man with no social connections. I was ready to go out and earn my keep, of course, but David insisted on paying my way to finish at Harrow and go on to university. He knew how much that meant to Corinna as well as me. He adores her. Heaven knows why."

"Some men are drawn to feisty women."

He heard the teasing in her voice. He loved how the corners of her mouth made a little downward turn just before they lifted in a smile. "Yes, I suppose they are."

After sharing these terrible stories, to be making even this hint of a joke was a good thing. A sign that the burden, if not entirely lifted, had at least eased a little.

The sun was waning now, casting longer shadows in the park. As Julia looked at him, smiling, Michael's thoughts began to move in a different direction. He wanted nothing more than to close that very short distance between them and kiss her. He felt his own heart skitter at the thought, and he fought to catch his breath. How would she respond? Would it ruin this moment of understanding between them, or seal the bond?

He was going to find out.

Michael placed his right arm along the bench behind her back, resting it there but not touching her, and waited for her reaction. He'd telegraphed his intention clearly enough. Her lips parted slightly in surprise. He ran a finger along her cheek, lightly tracing those lovely freckles. She shivered at his touch, but he knew it was with pleasure. He saw it in the way she returned his gaze.

He didn't move, not just yet. The anticipation was unbearable, but he took time to savor it anyway, drinking in the sight of those full lips. He knew the import of the irrevocable step he was about to take. He knew there would be consequences. He chose instead to think only of the reasons his heart was telling him why this was right.

Whatever nervousness Julia felt, she handled it in typical Julia fashion—by meeting it head on. She leaned in, closing the gap herself. Taking hold of his coat lapels to pull him closer, she pressed her lips to his.

Oh yes, he loved this woman. He knew it without a doubt. He could guess that she'd never been kissed before, and yet she was so bold, as though she were claiming this kiss. Claiming *him*. He could feel her pouring herself into it, and he responded in kind.

He wrapped his arms around her, drawing her close, reveling in the elation that overwhelmed him.

How much time passed before they parted, breathless, Michael could not have said. It pained him to stop, although he found immediate solace in the pleasure of looking at her. She gazed at him wonderingly, her eyes reflecting the same amazed joy that he was feeling.

"Julia." He didn't know what to say next. He only knew that he loved the sound of her name. Loved being able to speak it out loud.

He was not prepared to hear her say, "Michael, what . . . does this mean?"

Michael's eyebrows lifted. "I think it's pretty clear what this means." His eyes were gray and intense, but his mouth held a hint of a smile. "I think *you* know, too, as you are the one who kissed me."

It was true. She had kissed him. Not only invited it but acted impulsively to ensure it happened. And she'd done it shamelessly, right here in this public place. Thank heaven the birds and squirrels were the only ones who'd witnessed it. She sent a quick glance around just to be sure. They were indeed alone.

"Not that I minded at all," Michael continued, reaching out to take hold of her hands. "I am discovering I rather like bold women."

This compliment only caused her heart to sink even more. How could she have done this? She knew full well it had not been entirely her idea. He had intended to kiss her. But she had foolishly jumped in, wanting so badly to know what it would be like to kiss him. Now she knew: it was so rich, so wonderful that it went into realms beyond description. And that was a big problem.

This was most definitely *not* in her plans. It could not mesh with everything she'd been striving for. Michael, too, had dreams he was pursuing with equal vigor. Dreams that were in no way compatible with her own.

He began caressing her hands, distracting her, clouding her mind when she desperately needed it to be clear. Why could she not pull her hands away? Her body was rejecting all orders from her brain. "That was wrong of me," she insisted.

"Why?" he challenged. "Why was it wrong?"

"Because you are going to marry Laura Maynard."

"No!" he responded vehemently. "I don't deny I was pursuing the match. But there have been no promises made. Somewhere, deep in my soul, I knew it was not right."

She shook her head, wishing there were some way to calm the wild beating of her heart. "But your plans—your career and mine. I cannot reconcile them."

Placing a hand gently on the back of her neck, he tugged her closer. "This is how we reconcile them."

He kissed *her* this time. She might have stopped it, but she could not bring herself to pull away. The need to kiss him was irresistible; the pleasure it brought was too good to deny.

When they parted again, he drew her into an embrace. She rested her head on his shoulder, feeling his warmth as they sat in silence. But before long, worries began to press through the happiness.

"Surely one day you will regret this," she said.

"Never. We are right for each other, Julia, despite what you or I or anyone else might think."

She pulled away. "Then *I* will regret this. I can't turn my back on the things God has called me to do."

He looked confused. "I'm trying my best to understand your faith, to understand God. If He is as good as you say, how can He be such an ogre as to deny two people who are in love?"

In love.

She must have repeated the words aloud, or perhaps her expression showed how deeply she'd been struck by what he'd just said, for he answered her.

"Yes, Julia, I love you," he declared. "Tell me you love me, too. I know you do."

Julia could not speak right away. Her mind scrambled to make sense of how, exactly, they had come to be in this situation. She had purposely drawn near to him, benefitting from the Latin lessons and thinking that by spending time with him, she might find some way to help the school. Or to help *him.* She never dreamed he would embed himself so deeply in her heart.

As the silence grew, a glimmer of doubt appeared in his eyes. Honesty won out, for Julia could not hurt him with a lie. She said soberly, "Yes, I love you."

He stood up, bringing her with him, planting a gleeful kiss on her cheek. "My love, it is customary to smile at times like this."

"But this still doesn't change our circumstances," she protested.

"On the contrary, it changes things very much. And what hasn't changed, will."

He tried to kiss her again, but this time she stepped back. She did not like doing so, not when everything within her wished to do the opposite, but as unpleasant as it was, someone had to think clearly. "Michael, it can't work. We have been brought together for this brief time, but it won't last. Our lives will be going in opposite directions."

"You don't have to go to Africa to practice medicine."

"I do in order to be a missionary. I cannot abandon God's calling."

He turned his gaze away, frowning. Despite his earlier words, he still did not understand her devotion to a spiritual life. Nor could she comprehend—or accept—a life without God at the center of it.

"The important thing is to trust God and to keep Him first. If we compromise on that, we will never get to the right answer."

Michael rubbed his eyes, his frustration evident. "So then what do we do?"

"We cannot trust feelings only. I once heard a saying: 'Decisions made in the heat of the night fade in the cold light of dawn.'"

It seemed appropriate to say that now, as dusk was rapidly approaching.

"My love for you is not going to fade," he said. "I promise you that."

"Since you are convinced, you will not mind if I suggest that we both take several days to think things over—separately."

He stared at her in disbelief. "So that we can try to talk ourselves out of it? It won't happen."

"In that case, a few days won't matter," she insisted. She was not going to back down on this stipulation. "And not just to think, but to *pray*."

He recoiled at the word. It was ever so slight, but Julia saw it.

"If you are seeking to understand, start with prayer. The Lord said, 'Seek, and ye shall find; knock, and it shall be opened unto you.' He was talking about spiritual insight."

It was only a fraction of the things she wished she could share with him, but it was a start. She was heartened to see him take some moments to reflect on her words, not rejecting them out of hand.

"All right. I will pray. I will carefully think things over." He said this with a gravity that convinced Julia he was telling her the truth. Whether he thought it would make a difference was another matter. She saw a gleam of defiance in his eyes. He stepped toward her, placing his hands on her waist. "While you are also doing those things, will you think about this, too?"

This was exactly why she needed time away from him. When he was this close to her, there was only one direction, one answer her heart would heed, and it was not one that made any sense at all.

Despite her misgivings, she lifted her face to his, accepting his kiss. It was sweet and tender, urging her to keep her heart bound up with his. Making her wish there was some way he could be right. But she could not even imagine how that could be.

ICHAEL STEPPED OUT of the copyist's shop near
the law courts. He'd come on this errand primarily
to get away from his chambers and enjoy a walk on
this sunny day. It also freed his mind to think of Julia. It had
been two days since he'd seen her, but she was never out of his
thoughts.

Corinna had been surprised to learn the Latin lessons were not
taking place this week and hadn't made much effort to conceal
her pleasure. Michael wasn't ready to tell her how short-lived
her happiness might be. He'd said only that a full caseload this
week had prevented the meetings. It was true that he had plenty
of work to do. He had thrown himself into it as best he could,
meeting all obligations even if his mind wasn't fully absorbed
in the tasks.

He and Julia had agreed to meet back at that little park tomorrow afternoon. He'd spent these days considering what to do.

Julia deserved an opportunity to train as a physician. But what if the medical school here in London was forced to close? Would she travel to the continent or perhaps even America to get training? He might survive a few years' separation. But would she love him enough to give up her dream of becoming a missionary? Should he even ask that of her?

He'd done his best to send up prayers, and not only because he'd promised Julia to do so. He wanted to arrive at a solution where they both could be at peace. He still couldn't believe God would separate two people who were in love. Or was what they wanted inconsequential in light of the Almighty's greater objectives? That thought only confused and angered him. His grasp on spiritual matters was tenuous at best, and it was clearly not good enough to answer any of these questions.

He was so intent on trying to untangle this knot of imponderables that he was annoyed to see Tamblin striding toward him.

Tamblin didn't look too happy, either. "I'd like a chat with you, Stephenson."

"I'm just on my way to deliver these copies to Chancery," Michael said, hoping to put him off.

"It can wait. We have something more pressing at hand. Why don't we take a walk—say, over to the Embankment? What we need to discuss is too personal to risk being overheard by the clerks at Gray's Inn."

Michael had an inkling of what this "chat" would be about. They walked at a good pace, speaking only of general matters until they reached the river.

Once they were strolling along the Embankment, watching the busy boat traffic along the Thames, Tamblin stated what was on his mind. "Word has reached me about an event that could be troublesome for us and for Lord Westbridge—who, please recall, is our most important client."

"I assume you are referring to my appearance at the magistrate's court?" Michael hoped fervently that nothing of what had happened afterward had become known to them.

"Why didn't you tell me you went there to defend Lady Edith? Did you not understand the conflict of interest? I thought you a better lawyer than that."

"I was not there on Lady Edith's behalf. Her presence was incidental to my purposes."

"Which were?" Tamblin turned an angry gaze on him.

"There were two others with Lady Edith at the time of her arrest—Miss Julia Bernay and a woman who is a resident of Bethnal Green, where they were arrested."

He began to give an account of how the women had ended up in front of a magistrate, but Tamblin interrupted him. "That much I know already," he said impatiently. "But why were *you* there?"

"Miss Bernay is an acquaintance of mine," Michael answered, well aware that *acquaintance* was a deceptively mild description. "Her sister came to me and told me what had happened, and I went to the court to see what I could do to help."

"And yet you knew Lady Edith was there, too?"

"I did. But I was not going to allow innocent women to languish in prison because of it."

The look on Tamblin's face showed how much he disagreed with that assessment. "Don't you think the magistrate would have freed them anyway, on the strength of Lady Edith's word?"

"Because she would invoke the privilege of aristocracy? Perhaps you are not aware that Lady Edith neglected to mention to the authorities that she was an earl's daughter. It might not have come out at all if I hadn't used her title during my remarks to the magistrate."

"That's preposterous," Tamblin exclaimed.

"Why do you think the whole business got as far as it did? Lady Edith never said a word. I think she *wanted* to spend a night in jail. If so, it takes this new upperclass craze called 'slumming' a bit too far, don't you think?"

"That is neither here nor there," Tamblin sputtered in annoyance. "The point is that you entered a public hearing, knowing full well what damage it could do to our case and, by extension, our reputation. Furthermore, I want to know why you have never told me about this Julia Bernay. Apparently there are things about your 'acquaintance' with her that have import on our case. That she is preparing to go to medical school, for example."

"How do you know that?"

"It was in her statement to the police! It's public record now."

"She wants to go to the school, but she is not there yet. How can there be a conflict of interest?"

"How did you come to be acquainted with this woman? Did you meet her on the Underground?" Tamblin motioned toward Michael's neck. "That nurse who saved your life. It was Julia Bernay, wasn't it?"

Michael drew in a sharp breath. He supposed he should have known that Tamblin, one of the best legal minds in England, could have easily tied together those disparate pieces of information.

A fruit seller approached them, carrying a basket of apples. Michael bought one from her, taking his time to select the right coin from his pocket. It was only an excuse to keep from answering Tamblin, but the man wasn't fooled.

"Don't you suppose one might reasonably consider you beholden to Miss Bernay after what she did?" he said to Michael as soon as the fruit seller had moved on to other potential customers.

"It wasn't something she could have planned."

"Don't equivocate. The question is whether she has yielded influence over you since then."

She had. Of course she had. But not in the way Tamblin was thinking. Or maybe it was, for being with her had certainly made him look at everything differently, including the libel suit. He'd accepted her request—it seemed almost like a dare—to teach her Latin because some part of him knew, even then, that he wanted to spend more time with her. He'd thought he could keep their meetings from seeping into other aspects of his life. He'd been wrong.

"Shall I recuse myself from this case?"

Tamblin slapped his hand in annoyance on the low wall where they were standing. "The mere fact that you ask that question shows me how far this has gone. But the answer is no; you shall not recuse yourself from this case. You shall recuse yourself from any further contact with Miss Bernay. Whatsoever. Permanently."

"No, sir!" Michael exploded. "That is too much to expect. I will not do it."

"You don't have a choice, counselor." Tamblin's voice was low now, almost threatening. "This directive does not come from me. It comes from Lord Westbridge."

"And what makes him think he can direct my personal life in such a high-handed fashion?"

"After hearing about the incident at the magistrate's court, his lordship wanted to know who this woman was and why you would go to such lengths to help her."

"Well, now he knows. Why doesn't he just allow me to recuse myself?"

"After all the work you've done on this case, and all you know about our strategies for pursuing it? No. He wants to ensure he has your loyalty above everything else."

"She saved my life, Tamblin."

"You do not understand how far he will go to have his way. He has every detective in London at his beck and call. He's done some personal research into your life, too, it seems. This morning he met with me, irate over this affair at the magistrate's court. But more than that, he'd uncovered some disturbing information about your family."

"If you're speaking of my father, that's public knowledge. Has been for years, including every possible permutation on every rumor."

"It's not about your father. It's about David Barker."

Michael stared at him. "The earl objects to a man who comes by his wealth through honest hard work? Surely even his lordship understands that many such people exist in England nowadays."

Tamblin's eyebrows raised. Michael thought it was a reaction to his sarcastic comment, until he said, "You really don't know, do you?"

There was a note of sympathy in his voice that, mixed with his earlier demands, hinted at a new menace.

"What don't I know?"

"It's a serious situation, Stephenson. But I shouldn't be the one to give you the news. Have a talk with Barker. Do it today. Then tell me what you intend to do."

Michael stood outside the Royal Exchange, waiting for David. After his conversation with Tamblin, he'd gone straight to David's place of business. Whatever was going on, whatever the earl and Tamblin knew, Michael was certain Corinna did not know it. Since their father's death, they had not kept secrets of any magnitude from one another. Therefore Michael decided it would be best to speak with his brother-in-law privately.

He'd been informed by David's clerk that David was at the

Exchange, meeting with a new client. Michael had been waiting for perhaps a quarter of an hour when he saw David come through the main entrance. He was accompanied by another man, a prominent banker whom Michael recognized from his club. They paused and shook hands before the banker continued on his way. If this was David's new client, he had done well indeed.

David placed his hat on his head with a satisfied tap, his face displaying his usual air of geniality. Michael could not imagine this man harboring some terrible, dark secret. It just wasn't in his nature. Michael was determined to get this cleared up.

Calling out David's name, Michael hurried up to him.

"Hullo, this is a pleasant surprise," David said, smiling. "Don't tell me business has brought you here. None of my clients are under suit at the moment, and I should like to keep it that way."

"It's not business. I must talk with you about something else."

"I was just heading home. Why don't you come with me? I've received an order of excellent cigars from Cuba. You really should try one."

Michael shook his head. "This needs to be private. I have to ask you a very personal question—and I wouldn't do it if it weren't critically important to all of us. Is there something about you, or your background, that you haven't told me?"

David's smile faded. He glanced around to see who was in their immediate vicinity—a sign of nervousness that aroused Michael's fears. The area was bustling. Businessmen came and went from the Exchange, and messenger boys threaded their way among them to deliver important missives at various buildings throughout the financial district. An omnibus had just pulled up and was disgorging passengers.

"Let's drive to the park," David suggested.

Once they were in a cab and under way, David asked, "Who

told you to ask me about my past? How much does this person know?"

Michael explained the conversation he'd had with Tamblin. "I have been as honest with you as I can," he finished. "I hope you will be so with me."

David looked down at his hands, which were clenched together in his lap. He said, heavily, "Yes, I will tell you everything."

They got out of the cab at Hyde Park Corner and walked into the park. There were many people out enjoying the day, but they were widely dispersed along the paths and the green fields of the massive park. Michael and David had space to speak confidentially.

"Suppose we take a seat." David pointed toward a bench that had just been vacated by a man and woman. The pair walked off arm in arm with a casual lightheartedness that Michael envied. He had a premonition that everything he'd worked for all these years now hung in the balance. Even worse, the love he'd known for a scant few days might slip from his grasp as well.

"Warm day, isn't it?" David took out a handkerchief and pressed it to his brow, but the tremor in his hand betrayed that he was feeling more than the late-day sun. "I'm sorry it has come to this. There are things I should have told you and Corinna, but I never did. I kept telling myself there was no point, that I had atoned and it was all behind me. But I see now I was wrong."

Atoned? "What haven't you told us?"

"I was born in a workhouse. I don't even know who my father was."

This introduction already gave Michael an understanding of why David would lie about his past. The stigma of the workhouse could never be fully erased. Certainly not in polite society. And if he was born out of wedlock, it would be nigh on impossible.

David looked at him with a combination of guilt and fear, as if he expected Michael to lash out in anger or disgust. Certainly it was tempting, for this knowledge would devastate Corinna and her dreams of respectability. Such a response would be futile, though. Michael had to stay levelheaded and approach this situation as logically as possible. David was his brother-in-law; that fact could not be changed. They must simply go forward as best they could.

Michael said calmly, "How did your mother end up there?"

Gratefulness for this compassionate response glimmered in David's eyes before he continued. "She was heavily pregnant when she arrived at the workhouse door. She told them her husband had died and she had nowhere else to go. I'd like to believe her story was true. Or it may have been a lie she told as a grasp at some small shred of dignity. A few years later, she was dead."

He paused again, this time to blow his nose with his handkerchief. "Allergies, don't you know," he muttered.

Michael stayed silent, allowing David this moment. It could not have been easy to relive these memories of his past—or even admit to them.

"It was a cruel, heartless place, as you might imagine. I ran away when I was eleven. I tramped my way to Manchester, where I fell in with a bad lot. They taught me pickpocketing, housebreaking, and most especially, the joys of alcohol. I got happiness from drink, but it didn't quench my anger. You can never really 'drown your sorrows,' as they say, if there is an endless supply."

Michael nodded. It was not difficult to imagine a young man's rage at such a lot in life.

"Late one night, three of us infiltrated a crowd at a local fair. Two boys would cause a distraction while the third did the pickpocketing. Must have been hundreds of people there, most of whom had had plenty to drink. I'd been drinking, too, although I knew better. I generally waited until after the work was done, but not this time. It was getting to where I couldn't go too many waking hours without a drink. As a result, I was sloppy at the pickpocketing. When my mark realized what was happening, he raised an uproar. There were bobbies nearby, and they came after us. I ran off down a side street, pushing people over in my desperation to escape. At one point, I shoved a man out of my way—and directly into the path of an oncoming carriage."

This horrific tale, coming from David, was almost impossible to believe. David paused, leaning forward and looking at the ground, giving Michael time to take it all in. Or perhaps to compose himself as he confronted memories he had hoped to keep buried. "It was an accident, but that didn't lessen the impact of those carriage wheels. I was convicted of manslaughter and sentenced to twelve months hard labor. But I was a changed person before I ever got there. I was in jail for weeks before the trial. Those weeks, coming off the liquor, nearly killed me. The tremors, the fever. I decided it would be a fitting way to die. I didn't die, though. I stood trial, and after my conviction, I worked every day of those twelve months at the prison. Not for one day did I forget the sight of that man's mangled body.

"I came out of that prison at age fifteen, hardened but penitent, too. I begged God to forgive me. The prison chaplain saw my genuine remorse. He found me a position with a dry-goods merchant. You wouldn't think good people would want anything to do with me, but that man and his wife gave me a chance. I learned the business during the day, and they taught me reading and arithmetic at night. Improved my speech and etiquette. In time, I came to think of them as my parents, and they never objected to my calling them that."

He leaned back, once more wiping his brow with the handkerchief. "Now you know my story. I hope you can find it in your heart to forgive me for hiding it."

"Why didn't you tell us?"

"Michael, I love your sister. I suppose that, as her brother, you wonder how anyone could love her." He managed a wry smile. "And yet Corinna means more to me than anything else in the world. When your father died and I saw what straits you were in, I knew this was my opportunity, and as any determined suitor, I took it."

Michael thought back to those days when David was courting Corinna. Everything he had said was true. Michael had known full well why Corinna married him. But she was determined to do so, and all had agreed it was for the best.

"I wanted nothing more than to gain her hand and to help you both," David continued. "But I was afraid she would never marry me if she knew my true history. For one thing, she might worry that I would give myself over to drunkenness again. To be honest, I fear this as well. That is why I am a temperance man and find my pleasure instead in good cigars."

"There were times when I wondered about that," Michael admitted. He'd assumed it had something to do with David's charity work. Many of those charities promoted temperance among the working classes.

"But really," David continued, "the most pressing concern to me was Corinna's great desire to regain her place in society. Such a woman would surely never marry me. If my true history were known, who would ever receive us into the best circles? I care nothing for those things, except that Corinna does, and therefore her desires are mine as well."

Michael thought back to the man he'd seen David with earlier. His newest client was a man of eminent respectability. "It would hurt your business, too."

"That is true," David agreed. "And then how should I be able to take care of Corinna in the way she both craves and deserves?"

This was the point around which everything now centered.

"Michael, what can we do to keep this from becoming public?" David asked quietly.

"Tamblin has told me the information will remain confidential so long as I continue working on the libel suit—and break off all contact with Julia Bernay."

David's brow wrinkled. "That seems excessive. Why would he make such a stipulation?"

"I think the earl wants to quash the medical school and anyone who has even the slightest connection to it. He doesn't want me spending time with someone whom he sees as being in league with his daughter."

"Why doesn't he just remove you from the case?"

"He fears I would change sides and help the defense. That would be an unconscionable breach of ethics on my part, but his lordship doesn't trust anyone. Now that this information about me and Julia has come to light, I think he trusts me least of all."

"Well, I trust you implicitly," David declared. "I know you are a good man, and you would not do anything to hurt your family. I beg you not to tell any of this to Corinna. Especially not now, in her delicate condition. She would be devastated, and who knows what effect that could have on her and the baby?"

"I agree," Michael said grimly. "We will keep this between ourselves."

"I'm sorry you cannot see Miss Bernay anymore. I know you feel beholden to her after what she did for you. Perhaps you might be able to help her another way, rather than tutoring her yourself."

If Corinna had suspicions about Michael's growing attachment to Julia, she must not have voiced them to her husband. David clearly assumed Michael's association with Julia went no further than the lessons.

A kind of numbness began to steal over him as he considered

the choice he had to make. But really, he had no choice. After all of Corinna's sacrifices and all David had done for them both, how could he do anything to put them in jeopardy?

But what it was going to cost him in return was too unbearable to even ponder.

CHAPTER

23

J ULIA PACED UP AND DOWN THE PATHS of the little
park, waiting for Michael's arrival. These past few days, her
mind had been in turmoil despite her efforts to think ratio-
nally. Her prayers had given her some comfort, but she could not
bring her mind around to an answer that felt right.

She thought of Dr. Anderson, who was proof that a woman
could be married and still carry on a career in medicine—and an
exceptional career at that. But Dr. Anderson's work was here in
London. Julia's missionary work was going to take her far away.
That dream had become a burden that lay heavy on her heart. If
she gave it up, would she be putting a man above her faith? She
kept vacillating between the choices presented to her, making up
her mind to one but then deciding just as fervently for the other.

The park had other visitors today. There was a nanny pushing
a perambulator, accompanied by a little girl. On a far bench sat
an older gentleman who looked like he was dozing in the sun.
Whatever happened between Julia and Michael today, it would

not include kissing under the trees. She told herself this was a good thing—that it would help her remain strong. She had to ensure her decisions were based on God's will, not on unreliable feelings.

She kept watch on the entrance to the park, but there was no sign of Michael. It seemed odd that he hadn't shown up yet. Perhaps something had detained him at work. She could not imagine he'd be late for this appointment. Not after his fervent declarations to her before they'd parted.

Nevertheless, each passing minute seemed to confirm that he had changed his mind after all. Grief began to well up within her at the thought. And yet wasn't that why she'd suggested this period of separation? Wouldn't it be best to find out now, before they'd made irrevocable decisions? It brought her back to the conviction that they should not be swayed from their cherished but very different ambitions.

But what if he did come, and what if he tried just as fervently to persuade her to stay? Could she resist his appeal?

Julia strode faster along the path, breathing deeply, forcing her mind to be sensible and reject the folly of daydreams. As far back as she could remember, she'd lived her life with important goals that had nothing to do with finding romantic love. She was not going to succumb to the foolish notions that were too prevalent among her sex—her sister Cara being a case in point. When Cara had whispered in her ear—right here, in this very park—how glad she was to see Julia had fallen in love, Julia ought to have taken that for the danger signal it was and not allowed things with Michael to get as far as they had. But she had not heeded that warning, and now she had impossible choices to make.

Reaching the end of the path, Julia turned abruptly to retrace her steps and saw Michael at the gate, looking at her across the length of the park. When he started forward, it was with a solemn deliberation that told Julia, even from this distance, all she needed to know.

She gulped air, clenching her fists and tensing every muscle, as though by reinforcing her physical strength, she could shore up her emotions. She refused to be weak. It had never been in her nature, and she wasn't about to start now. If only her legs, which were alarmingly unsteady as she walked, would get the message.

They both came to a halt when they were still several feet apart.

His expression was distant, cool. But there was also a hesitancy in his eyes. Perhaps he was holding back, waiting to see her reaction first? That was not something she would have expected, given how adamant he was at their last meeting.

"I thought you might not come," she said.

"Of course I came. I had to come." He spoke with a heaviness that made it sound like a burden. "I have to tell you that we cannot meet anymore."

Julia gasped. His words only confirmed what she'd seen in his demeanor the moment he'd arrived, and yet for him to blurt it out left her stunned.

"I—I see." She lifted her chin and squared her shoulders—anything she could do to give the appearance of calm detachment. "As a matter of fact, I think that's best, too. While I'm grateful for the many things you've done for me, we cannot expect, being on such different paths in life, that there could be anything between us, except perhaps for mutual admiration—"

"Julia." He stopped her rambling with one word.

She crossed her arms and looked away, afraid he might see the silly tears creeping into her eyes or notice the ridiculous trembling of her lower lip. She bit her lip to keep her weakness from showing. She ought not to be tempted to cry. Perhaps she ought to be angry at the way he was so coldly reversing everything he'd said and done at their last meeting, but she could not find anger anywhere within her.

Michael closed the gap between them, startling her with his swiftness. He did not take her in his arms, although she thought—more foolish fancy!—that he looked very much like he wanted to. Standing mere inches away, he spoke softly and urgently. "It is I who must be grateful to *you*. I can't leave you thinking that I don't care, that my feelings for you have changed in any way. I thought I could, and perhaps that might have been better for both of us. But I see now that's impossible." His eyes were beseeching. "Will you allow me to explain?"

The feeling in the pit of Julia's stomach told her that further discussion wasn't going to make anything better. But her legs were still irritatingly untrustworthy, so now was not the time to try to walk away.

She sank onto a nearby bench. Michael joined her, leaving plenty of space between them. He even sent what Julia thought was a nervous glance around the park before he did so. "Is something wrong?" she asked. "I mean, aside from . . ."

She couldn't finish the sentence.

He didn't answer. He looked as though he were trying to decide where to begin.

"Just spit it out."

If her voice was caustic, it was because her nerves were stretched to the breaking point. She regretted her tone when she saw him wince. But he carried on anyway.

"Julia, there are circumstances, which I can't explain, that make it imperative we spend no more time together."

"You don't have to explain."

He turned toward her. "I love you, Julia. Please believe this has nothing to do with my feelings for you. With how much I want . . ."

His voice trailed off as Julia closed her eyes, squeezing them against the threatening tears.

"There are vital things at stake, regarding my family's well-being, that I cannot ignore. You may not understand the reasons for my actions, but I know you can understand the motivation behind them. We talked before about the importance of family."

Julia understood perfectly. He was going to marry Laura Maynard. He needed an aristocratic wife. Perhaps that was all that was needed to make Corinna's return to society complete. Michael had clearly explained how much he owed to his sister.

"There is nothing more important than family," she agreed, but the sentiment rang hollow in her heart. Perhaps it would have been better to believe he'd merely come to his senses, realized he ought to be putting his career and his social ambitions above a passing attraction to a woman who did not fit his agenda. Far worse to think he loved her still, yet chose duty above the leanings of his heart. It rebuked her, for she'd been so close to doing just the opposite.

If she left now, Julia knew she had just enough strength to walk out with some semblance of dignity. She stood up. "I should go."

He rose swiftly to follow her. "Wait! There is one more thing. I want to keep helping you—with your lessons, I mean. I can at least pay for a tutor."

"I would prefer you did not do that. You have fully discharged any debts you might have owed me."

She did not slow her steps—not until his gentle hand on her arm stopped her.

"How do you repay a person for your life?"

The tender sincerity in his voice almost did her in. She met his gaze directly, although she knew it would put her scant bit of self-composure in peril. She wanted to look once more at his face—the gray eyes, the scar that was only partly covered by his hairline. The mouth that quirked at odd moments when he found something amusing. Everything that she would miss so terribly.

"There are many things in life that can never be repaid," she said. "At those times, we can only store the gratitude in our hearts and never forget when someone has given us a profound and invaluable gift."

She was referring to herself as well, what he had done for her and most especially for Cara. From the look in his eyes, she felt that he understood.

It was hard to walk away, but Julia did it. Somehow, she kept her legs moving forward. She had to believe, with her analytical mind, that no matter how the decision was arrived at, it was the best one for them both. But somewhere, deep inside, her irrational heart was refusing to fall in line.

Watching Julia walk away was the hardest thing Michael had ever done. This woman had come to mean so much to him, and yet she was simply leaving his life. And he had to allow it.

He would have preferred if she'd gotten angry at him, reproached him, told him what a terrible man he was. It might have been vanity on his part, but he'd even braced himself for the possibility that she might break down in tears, heartbroken.

Her cool acceptance was harder to bear. She hadn't even pressed him for details. He thought it entirely possible that even if he had come to this meeting with a full marriage proposal, she would have turned him down anyway. She was placing her goal of being a missionary above everything else. And who was he to argue? Perhaps the Almighty really was directing her path. Had Michael just played his part to ensure it happened?

No. He could not believe that. Not when he considered that the decision was driven by the hatred and bitterness of the old earl.

He stood in that spot for a long while, giving her time to leave the park and get far enough away that he would not risk seeing her again. He felt battered and bruised enough already.

In time, the old man on the far bench tottered off, too. He probably lived close by. Still, Michael couldn't help but feel a little nervous about his presence. Now that he knew the Earl of Westbridge had a network of detectives working for him, he was inclined to see people on every corner who might fit the bill.

Trying to shake off those thoughts, Michael began the long walk back to Gray's Inn. Movement was what he needed now. Anything to keep him from being overtaken by sorrow or giving in to self-pity. Better to stoke his anger and indignation at being trapped into this position. Trapped by the needs of his sister, by the secrets his brother-in-law had kept, and above all by the plotting of a man who would stop at nothing to get what he wanted.

By the time he'd reached Gray's Inn, it was late enough in the day that he could reasonably suppose the clerks had gone home. He knew Tamblin would be gone, as he always gathered on Thursday evenings with a group of barristers and law students to discuss the most interesting cases of the week. Michael was glad for this. He had no desire to see Tamblin today.

He was about to go up the steps toward his residence when one of his clerks, Bob Masters, came out the door of the business office.

"So there you are, sir," Masters said. There was a rare note of censure in his voice. "Did you not remember you had a meeting this afternoon with the attorney for the copper mine?"

Michael rubbed his forehead in frustration. "No, I suppose I didn't."

He could add dereliction of duty to his ever-growing list of faults.

"I told him you'd been called away on urgent business for a

very important case. I phrased it in such a way that I could see he surmised it was the libel case. Then, of course, he was not so put out, because he admires his lordship."

"You're an excellent clerk, Masters. You know how to lie without actually lying."

Masters beamed. "All in a day's work, sir. Although I supposed that was where you were, anyway—with his lordship. On account of today's news."

"What news?"

"You mean you haven't heard? The date for hearing the libel case has been set. It will be May twenty-fifth."

"No, I hadn't heard."

"We're ready, though, sir," Masters said cheerily. "Everything is all set to win this case, eh?"

"Yes," said Michael, not caring what his clerk might think of his glum attitude. "Yes, it is."

CHAPTER

24

JULIA WAS SITTING IN THE OFFICE of the reverend Dr. MacKenzie, who was the director of the missionary society that Julia planned to join after she got her medical license.

She had sent a letter to the society months ago—not long after she'd arrived in London—requesting an opportunity to meet with Dr. MacKenzie. The fact that they had finally answered her letter only yesterday seemed to her fortuitous. A chat with them might raise her spirits. Now more than ever, she had to keep her mind and heart steadfastly focused on the future.

For nearly an hour, Dr. MacKenzie described their missionary stations in southeast Africa. He showed her the large map of Africa on his wall, with the locations of the camps marked with red circles. He told her about the schools and the practical skills they were teaching the natives, from sewing and cooking for the girls to building and farming for the boys.

"That's all very interesting," Julia acknowledged, "but what can you tell me about the medical clinics?"

"Medical clinics? Oh yes, there are clinics at every camp. Two physicians travel between them to attend to the worst cases." He opened a ledger book on his desk. "What sort of contribution may I put you down for?"

"I will help wherever I'm needed. I'm already qualified as a nurse and working to become a doctor. That will take three years, but I thought I might begin corresponding with your medical personnel now, if possible. I'd like to get their advice on what areas of medicine I should study that will be of particular use in the field."

"I must have misunderstood you." Dr. MacKenzie picked up a sheet of paper that was lying next to the ledger book. Julia recognized it as the note she'd sent some months ago. "When you asked to speak with me regarding how you could contribute to our mission, I thought you were interested in making a financial gift."

"I apologize for the misunderstanding, but I'm in no position to give money. I am a student with limited means."

"So when you said 'contribute,' you meant . . . ?"

"Contribute *myself*—and my skills, of course! I intend to become a licensed physician before joining the mission." She smiled at him, hoping to see some form of gratitude or interest.

Dr. MacKenzie shook his head, his hands moving in an accompanying negative gesture. "No, no, no. That's impossible." He snapped the ledger book shut. "We do not send female doctors."

"But you already have—Dr. Jane Waters."

The mention of Dr. Waters only deepened the scowl on the reverend's face. "Dr. Waters is no longer affiliated with us. She left the mission, but not before causing a lot of bother and setting back our work considerably."

"I beg your pardon?" Julia was unaware of this development.

"She brought unfounded accusations against our men, claiming they were somehow derelict in their duties. In fact, everything was going very well. But she had the audacity to think that she, newly arrived on the continent and barely out of medical school, could tell our seasoned missionaries how they ought to run things."

"Surely her goal was only to make things better," Julia protested. She didn't know Jane Waters but felt compelled to rise to her defense. "Perhaps, being just out of school, she was bringing more current information—"

"What she brought was disrespect and an egregious lack of protocol!"

This seemed an overly harsh assessment, but Julia had no way to refute it.

"After some consideration, therefore, we have adopted new guidelines. Our female missionaries will limit themselves to teaching reading to the children and domestic skills to the older girls."

Julia could hardly believe this. "Domestic skills," she repeated flatly.

"And the Gospel, first and foremost, naturally. If your desire is to spread the Gospel to the uttermost part of the earth, as our Lord commanded, then shouldn't that be your priority? You told me you've spent this past year at Queen's College. I believe that has more than qualified you for missionary work. Why wait another three years when you can go right now? You need only complete our training program, which covers theology and the practical details of how the mission camps function and what we expect from our missionaries. That takes only a few months."

"With all due respect, sir, why would you *not* want me to acquire extra medical training that could be invaluable in the field?"

"Miss Bernay, I have been a director of missionary work for nearly thirty years. There are very few things that I have not seen or dealt with before." His smile was condescending. "You must believe me when I say I know what works best. There is no confusion or strife when everyone stays within the bounds of their specific responsibilities."

Julia rose from her chair. "I'm sorry, sir, but I won't give up on becoming a doctor."

"It's your decision." He did not seem terribly disappointed by her words. Before she left, he said, "Take some time to prayerfully think over what I've said. I believe you will begin to understand and agree with what I am telling you."

Julia made it to the chemistry lab at the same time as Lisette and Colleen. The students were performing a variety of exercises today. This was normally very interesting work, but Julia was still in turmoil over Dr. MacKenzie's words. She slammed her chemistry book on the laboratory table.

"Careful, you'll break the beakers!" Lisette admonished. "What's the matter?"

"I just had a meeting with the director of the missionary society."

"That would make me testy, too," Lisette quipped.

Colleen was more receptive. "What happened?"

As they set up their experiment, Julia explained what had transpired at the meeting.

"It's no wonder he got angry when you mentioned Jane Waters," Lisette said. "She got in trouble for exposing the mistreatment of the natives in the camp. If she were a man, maybe they would have listened to her, called her a reformer. As it is, they called her an agitator and meddler and basically forced her out. But Dr. Anderson says Jane has gone to Cape Town and established her own practice, which is flourishing. She'll have her revenge. Her work will impact thousands of people. She'll be making better money, too, I'll wager."

"I'm glad her practice is doing well, but making money isn't the primary goal."

"Of course it is! We are rendering an important service. Don't we deserve proper compensation?"

"What I meant was, Jane Waters also wanted her life's work to glorify God." Julia had read some articles Jane had written for a Christian paper before she'd left for Africa.

"Religion and medicine don't mix," Lisette said. "Not real medicine, anyway."

"That's not true," Julia protested. "What about all the nurses in France and Germany who are nuns?"

"It is still their medical knowledge that heals people," Lisette insisted. "The rest is peripheral. If you want to be a real doctor, you must set aside religious superstitions. When did those ever help anybody? It's science that provides genuine answers."

Julia was aware that Lisette did not pursue any kind of religious life, but she hadn't realized until today that she was so hostile to the idea. "I can't agree with you there. The spiritual realm has a greater impact on the physical than we can ever know. We ignore it at our peril. I always believed that my faith was what led to my desire to help people, not that I'd have to set it aside first."

"There is a movement underway to send women doctors to India," Colleen offered. "They are needed to care for the Hindu women who observe the custom of keeping separate from the men and refuse to seek care from a male doctor. Perhaps you could go there."

It was not an idea Julia had ever considered. Her thoughts had been on Africa ever since she'd read a pamphlet about it years ago. She wished to minister to spiritual needs as well as physical. What better place to do it than in Africa, where millions of people had never heard the Gospel of Christ? On the other hand, if the door was open in India, perhaps she should look into it.

"You must not try to convert them, though," Lisette warned, effectively halting this new line of thought. "They have strict rules about that. These are high-caste Hindu ladies, and neither they nor the men want someone trying to change their religion."

They went back to their work, but Julia was still agitated. It felt like the two options she'd explored today were equally untenable: to be a missionary but not a doctor, or to be a doctor but not a missionary.

Should she give up the idea of becoming a doctor? No. She was certain this was God's will for her life; therefore she ought to concentrate on that first. Rosalyn had given sound advice: move forward on what one did know, and trust God for the rest.

But would it even happen if the school was forced to close? Julia thought of the libel case, of the disappointments in the earl's life that had led him to pursue such a course of action. To lose his son must have been very hard indeed. She supposed he would want to preserve his family legacy in any way he could.

"My father thinks that by closing the school he can get me to come back home and be a dutiful daughter," Edith had said. But if his lordship truly wanted to win back his daughter, he was going about it in entirely the wrong fashion.

Perhaps Julia's efforts had also been misdirected. She'd once thought she might influence the outcome of the lawsuit through her interactions with Michael. Not only had that scheme been a failure, it had been a disaster for her heart, as well. Michael was fulfilling his obligations and doing what he felt was right. Julia would not hesitate to do the same. If she was going to have any impact at all, she had to go right to the source.

She would talk to the earl himself.

Michael rose after a sleepless night, completing his morning routine and eating his breakfast with a weary soul. In the quiet of his room, he sat unwilling to move. Then, for the first time he could remember since his mother died, Michael truly prayed. He offered it up in sincerity, pouring out his heart with no reservations. It was nothing like what he'd attempted during Easter or later, when Julia had asked him to pray. With all that had happened, and especially losing Julia, he supposed he ought to give up on the idea of prayer altogether. But he was determined to give it one more try.

He did not think it a very good prayer in terms of whatever proper words or phrases ought to have been in it. All he could do was say what was troubling him. What was he going to do for Julia? What *could* he do? He had to do something, even if he never saw her again—which in his heart he still refused to believe. The prospect was unbearable. He told that to God, too, while he was at it. If he was going to get things off his chest, he might as well cover everything. He spoke out loud, just as if he were talking to a person sitting next to him.

"Amen." He knew enough about prayer to end with that.

The room settled into silence. He waited, but no great revelation burst into his brain. He felt marginally better for having expressed his troubles verbally, but it did not appear that any divine guidance was forthcoming. The Lord evidently knew when a prayer was offered in desperation from an unbeliever. Michael could only hope that Julia's prayers, whatever they were, would be answered. She, at least, deserved it.

As he sat there, the frustration began to creep back into the few recesses it had vacated. Feeling suddenly restless, he stood up, walked over to the window, and looked out. The day was gray

271

and drizzly, yet it perfectly matched his mood. He donned his coat and grabbed an umbrella. There was nothing to do but try to walk off this agitation. *Solvitur ambulando.*

He walked across the courtyard at Gray's Inn, past solid brick buildings, past the venerable old dining hall where once Shakespeare's company had performed *The Comedy of Errors.* Past all the things that were symbols to him of success, the proof that he'd buried his family's unpalatable past and was gaining what he wanted from this world. He walked out the gate without a backward glance.

On Gray's Inn Road, he turned left simply because there seemed to be fewer people in that direction. Michael had walked down this road countless times. He knew every way to reach the City and the courts. His surroundings were blurred by the rain and familiarity as he walked, so wrapped up in his thoughts that he saw little else.

Thunder boomed overhead, though it was barely distinguishable from the rumble of traffic on the cobblestones. The wind picked up, too. Michael turned up the collar of his coat but did not pause as he continued down the street. As the drizzle became stronger, he walked faster. Not to outrun the rain, but in a desperate bid to outpace his restlessness.

He was still so wrapped up in memories, worries, and self-recrimination that he was almost surprised to find himself standing at the corner of Leadenhall Street, where many of London's important businesses were located. He paused, trying to decide whether to go left or right. The heavens opened in earnest.

Even Michael had to admit this was enough. He ducked into the doorway of the nearest building, a massive edifice with its entryway recessed under a cover of arched stone. He was content to wait it out, knowing a downpour like this was not likely to last long.

He watched the rain splatter on the road, heard it gush out of a nearby downspout. A few people rushed by under the scant protection of their umbrellas. Cabs and carriages continued on, their horses inured to the rain.

Michael breathed in deeply, finding this deluge almost refreshing. London was a dirty, smoke-filled place, with soot everywhere. A rain like this settled the dust, even if the price paid was more mud.

Gradually, as the rain slacked off, a sign on the building across the street caught his attention. It was the headquarters for the Peninsular and Oriental Steam Navigation Company. The firm co-owned by Jamie Anderson. An idea began forming in Michael's mind.

Going in to see Anderson was not something he as a counselor would have advised a client to do, given Anderson's wife's connection to the lawsuit. Walking across the street and into the P&O offices might be inadvisable, especially with the court date looming. Michael disregarded all these considerations. This had nothing to do with the lawsuit. It had only to do with Julia.

Gray clouds were still overhead, but in Michael's mind, a bit of sun had broken through.

The P&O headquarters was a large and busy place, but Michael soon found a clerk who could show him to Jamie Anderson's private office. Everything in the room befitted the owner of a successful shipping enterprise: in addition to the large desk, there was a table covered with maps, papers, and even a yard-long model of a steamship. A bookcase, filled with shipping registers and other related books, dominated one wall; paintings and prints of ships covered the others.

Anderson received Michael courteously, although his surprise was evident. Once they were seated with the door closed, Michael explained his reason for coming. Doing so wasn't easy. The plan was simple enough, but detailing what he had in mind without revealing the depth of his feelings for Julia—that was the challenge. Countless hours in the courtroom had made him proficient at displaying the right expression for any circumstance. But what had been easy to do for his profession was far more difficult when the matter was personal and so near to his heart.

His aim had been to give the impression of merely having a friendly interest in Julia. Based on the thoughtful way Anderson was studying him, however, Michael didn't think he'd been entirely successful.

"I want to be sure I understand clearly," Anderson said. "You want to find a way to anonymously fund Miss Bernay with a tutor so that she can pass the preliminary exam that will enable her to begin medical studies."

Michael understood what Anderson was really asking. "I know this sounds surprising coming from me. But yes, that's what I wish to do."

"May I presume, therefore, that you don't believe certain legal actions pending against the London School of Medicine for Women present an existential threat to that institution?"

Michael donned the polite, barrister smile that he used whenever he had to answer a client's request in the negative. "I'm sure you understand why I am not at liberty to discuss that particular case. But I will point out that Miss Bernay has no connection to the lawsuit—nor, at this time, does she have any official connection with the medical school. My aim is only to help her be successful in her goal to acquire higher learning. What she does with the knowledge she gains is entirely her own business."

All of this was legally true; and ethically, it was on solid ground. But to Michael's ears, he sounded like some attorneys he knew who overstated an argument in a vain attempt to add credibility to a questionable defense.

"You are providing this aid merely as a *friend*? Nothing more?" The slightest lift of a brow telegraphed Anderson's real meaning.

The question hit home. Michael exerted every ounce of self-control to keep from shifting in his seat or showing any other sign of how uncomfortable he was. "You could say that."

But Anderson had already gleaned his answer. He leaned back in his chair and said casually, "I understand your point about separating a . . . *personal* connection, shall we say, from what is going on in the larger context of current events. I have had to do plenty of that for the past ten years, so I sympathize with your situation."

He paused, and Michael nodded in acknowledgment.

"My wife had already gained a good bit of notoriety before we'd even met. I never begrudged her any of that, nor did it prevent me from falling hopelessly in love with her, even though plenty of people warned me I'd regret it."

Another pause as Anderson looked at him. Michael kept his expression neutral and mildly interested, as though not catching the undercurrent in Anderson's words.

"She and I had a pact right from the beginning," Anderson continued. "Our professional lives would be carried on independent of one another. I told her I meant to be a successful man of business, neither interfering with her pursuits nor being interfered with by her—except, of course, for the very natural conversations and advice we might informally give to one another as husband and wife. And, of course, we would cheer each other's successes as well. She readily agreed, and we adhere to that rule to this day. From time to time, someone will try to urge me to publicly support—or interfere with, depending on the person and the issue—something my wife is trying to accomplish. I tell them they are wasting their time by coming to me. What Dr. Anderson does in the public sphere is entirely her own business. The result of all this is that ten years on, we are still incredibly happy."

There was one photograph in the room that was not related to shipping. It stood in a frame on Anderson's desk. He nudged it a little so that Michael could view it clearly. The Andersons, along with their two small children, a boy and a girl, were seated together, looking the very picture of contentment. Michael felt a stab of . . . what? Self-pity? Sorrow? Jealousy? All the emotions he could not and would not allow himself to indulge in.

"I like to think that we are proof that marriages built on mutual support of separate pursuits can happily exist," Anderson went on. "We are not by any means the first couple to do so, and yet I think such examples are still too rare. I should certainly like to see more of them. Wouldn't you?"

A lifetime with Julia was something Michael would contemplate with immense happiness. If only it were possible. Since it was not, he had to steer the conversation back on track. "Perhaps in the future more men will be as forward-thinking on this subject as you are." He paused long enough to allow Anderson to receive the compliment and acknowledge it with a slight tip of his head. "Now, about getting this money to Miss Bernay . . ."

Anderson didn't press the point. He picked up his pen and pulled some paper from his desk. "Yes, let us devise a plan. I don't believe it will be too difficult to find some plausible pretext for getting her the money. But won't she suspect it came from you anyway?"

"Not necessarily. She isn't surprised when gifts seem to fall on her out of the blue. She's already ascribed many such incidents in her life to blessings from God." He tried to add an ironic air to his words, to project that he himself did not believe them.

"I suppose this makes you an agent of God?"

Michael stared at him, nonplussed. He'd been many things over the years—son, brother, barrister—but that was certainly one description he would never have applied to himself. "I'm sure you know plenty of people who hold a far different opinion of me."

Anderson laughed. "What a shame that I shall not be able to disabuse them of that notion, since you are determined to keep your identity in this matter confidential."

Michael held out his hands in a gesture of mock defeat. "It's a burden I shall have to live with."

After a grin in response, Anderson began to tap pen on paper, thinking. "The school has many generous patrons. I'll approach a few of them for ideas and let you know something in a day or two. How can I reach you?"

"I think a letter to me in care of the Carlton Club would be the best way."

Anderson made a quick note. "Very good."

He stood up, and Michael followed suit.

As they walked to the door, Michael paused to take a closer look at the model ship.

"That's our newest," Anderson said, beaming with pride. "I went to the shipyard in Glasgow just last week to have a look at her. She launches in two months' time."

Michael's eye traveled over the full bookshelves. "Looks like you have been doing this for a long time."

"Over twenty years. The company was founded by my uncle, but that doesn't mean I was handed this position. I started as an assistant and worked my way up."

"I suppose you know a lot about shipping worldwide—not just to the orient?"

"Naturally. It's part of the job." He eyed Michael and said with a smile, "You're not by chance looking to change professions?"

"No, but . . ." Michael realized, with a sudden sense of things coming together, that there might well be a second reason he'd been led to come here. It could be a wild goose chase, but he would never know if he didn't ask. "If you can spare a few more minutes of your time, I'd like to ask your advice on another matter. One that relates to merchant shipping."

"Be happy to," Anderson responded amiably. "What would you like to know?"

CHAPTER

25

T HE EARL'S HOME WAS TWO MILES from the train station. Julia decided to walk the distance, since the money she'd spent on the train ticket was all she could spare. It had been raining all week in London, but here the roads were reasonably dry. The gray clouds overhead appeared threatening, but it was windy, too, so Julia thought there was a good chance they would blow over.

She got directions from the station attendant, who pointed her toward the road leading out of the far end of the village. Repinning her hat against the breeze, she set off.

Julia was no stranger to walking, and the distance was easily covered. She knew she was at the right place when she reached two stone pillars framing a wide entrance to a private drive. The house itself was barely visible, being set back among stately oak trees. Although evidence of the earl's large household staff was everywhere, from the perfectly tended hedges to the raked gravel drive, Julia saw no one about. The elegant wrought-iron gate was open, so she did not hesitate to walk through it, striding purposefully up the long drive.

Despite her resolve to come here and speak to the earl directly, Julia couldn't help feeling daunted as the mansion came fully into view. It was massive and imposing, with a semicircular set of stone steps leading up to the wide front door. Flowers and statuary abounded on the green lawns around the house. She marveled that Edith was so willing to leave this opulence behind.

As she approached the door, Julia imagined finely dressed women holding their skirts delicately as they walked up these same steps, accompanied by gentlemen in silk top hats. It was a testament to how vividly the place spoke of grandeur and wealth, for she was not normally prone to such daydreams. She reached the door and, not knowing what else to do, rapped on it soundly.

The wind rustled the trees and brought a sprinkling of raindrops to her face. A very long minute or two elapsed, during which the rain began in earnest. Julia was about to knock again when the door finally opened.

Tall and dignified in his black coat and stiff white collar, the butler looked at Julia and then glanced beyond her, as though looking for a carriage or any other conveyance that might have brought her here. Seeing she was alone, and clearly had arrived on foot, his expression took on a suspicious frown as his gaze returned to her. "May I help you, madam?"

"Is Lord Westbridge at home?"

"May I ask what brings you here today?" he countered.

"I am here on business for Lady Edith."

The name had a visible effect on the butler. His head drew up in surprise. "Are you saying she is known to you personally?"

"Yes, that's what I'm saying." She could not believe they were having this conversation while she stood in the rain. "May I come in?" she prompted. "It is rather wet out here."

With the air of conceding to a burdensome request, the butler stepped back, motioning Julia forward. Once she was inside and the door firmly shut against the weather, he said, "Wait here, please."

She watched as he crossed the cavernous entry hall, heels tapping on the tile floor, and disappeared through a door at the far end.

As the minutes stretched by, Julia imagined the conversation going on between the butler and the earl. "She says she is here on *business*, my lord," the butler would be saying, scrunching his nose a little. "Business?" the earl would reply, to which the butler would utter, in half-whispered tones, the forbidden name: "For Lady Edith." The earl would be flabbergasted. Or maybe irate. Or more likely, unyielding in his refusal to speak to her.

At this thought, Julia decided to remove her coat. She placed it and her hat, which was wilted from the rain, onto a narrow side table. It was a positive action to demonstrate that she wasn't going to be put off from her purpose. She was fully prepared to force her way in to the earl's study if need be, like the knights of old storming castle walls. Now that she was inside the gates, so to speak, she could not be turned back.

In the end, however, extreme measures were unnecessary. The butler returned and announced, "His lordship will see you."

She followed him back down the hall, and he ushered her into a large library. Bookcases two stories high held hundreds of leather-bound volumes. A sofa and leather chairs were comfortably arranged near an impressive stone fireplace. Tall windows looked onto the expansive garden. Julia immediately thought that if she were ever asked to describe her idea of heaven, it would look just like this.

Except she might not have included the scent of cigar smoke hanging in the air. Or perhaps it was a pipe. It wasn't altogether unpleasant, giving the impression of masculinity and the lord of the manor. It was not something she was well acquainted with, having only been exposed to it while on occasional visits to Mrs. Staunton's home in Clifton. She'd noticed it once or twice at the Barkers' residence, too.

And there was the lord of the manor himself, standing next to a chair that he must have been occupying before the butler had alerted him of Julia's arrival. He was staring at her coldly. "State your business, madam."

"Good afternoon, Lord Westbridge," she said, refusing to be cowed by his gruff manner. "I've come all the way from London, and I thank you for taking time to speak with me."

He advanced toward her, moving slowly and stiffly. "How long you stay has yet to be determined. You say you have come on business for the woman who calls herself Edith Morton. She has sent an ambassador—someone who hopes to win me over, perhaps." Upon reaching Julia, he stood very close, staring down his nose at her. "Has she finally seen the error of her ways? Does she wish to make amends?"

Julia took a deep breath. "Not exactly, my lord."

"Ha! I suspected as much." With an angry wave of his hand, he turned aside. "My daughter wishes only to annoy me. She refuses to act in a sane and reasonable manner. She is determined to remain a laughingstock, bringing shame on all of us."

"Hardly a laughingstock, sir. She is an intelligent and thoughtful woman, and proving to be an astute physician as well." She studied his movements as he walked toward the far end of the room. What was ailing him? Gout? An old injury of some kind? Perhaps it was arthritis, for he moved as if his entire body was in pain.

"A physician." He spoke the word with disgust. "I have outlived my wife and my son. Now all I have left is a daughter—who isn't my daughter. She wants to help the world but neglects her real duties. She sends some sort of apologist in her stead." When he reached the large windows, he took out a handkerchief and wiped his brow, his hand shaking a little. The sweating, and his apparent weakness, was a stark contrast to his forceful manner. "Well?" the earl barked. "What have you to say, then?"

"The truth, sir, is that Lady Edith does not know I am here today."

"What!"

Julia spoke quickly, before he could launch into another tirade. "I came here because I believe she would be willing to patch things up with you, if you would only agree to meet her halfway."

"Impossible." The earl seemed prone to brief and declarative statements, the kind that brooked no argument. "And who are you, that you take it on yourself to come on her behalf yet without her knowledge?"

"I am a student at Queen's College in London. Next year I will begin my studies at the London School of Medicine for Women."

"I knew it! You're another of those females who simply will not understand your place. Why are you in London, or for that matter, gallivanting around the countryside, annoying your betters? You ought to go back home to your family."

"I'm afraid I cannot do that, sir," Julia answered. "I have no home to speak of, and two sisters who are also making their own way in the world. I did not have the luxury of rich parents."

"If you are anything like Edith—and it appears you are—it would not have done you much good anyway," the earl replied without sympathy. "She spends her time demeaning herself and our family name by consorting with all manner of base people. She might have married the man who will inherit my title when I am gone. I don't see why she should have the least objection. They are not even so closely related, for all that people make a bother about such things nowadays. He's her second cousin, once removed. Who could object to that?"

"Perhaps the problem is that she doesn't love him?" Julia suggested.

"She hardly knows him! If she would spend some time with him, she'd see he's a perfectly agreeable, sensible man. As much as I hate that my son's death has caused our family line to end, I will admit my heir is a good man for the inheritance. But no, she has to go off and make a public spectacle of herself with all these causes. Women in medicine! Women's suffrage! Schools for the poor!" He spoke each of these things as though they were the most absurd ideas ever conceived.

During this tirade, Julia noticed a writing table with pen and paper on it. She went over to it and quickly began writing.

This arrested the earl's attention—probably more than her protests might have done.

"What are you doing?" he demanded.

"This is information about a liniment that I think might be helpful to you." She kept writing as she spoke. "These ingredients should be available from a chemist. I'm including the proportions, as well as information on how to burn the pokeroot first."

She tried to extend the paper toward him, but he shooed her away.

"I do not need instruction from you!"

"Very well, I will leave it here." She set the paper on the desk. "I will also say before I go that it is a shame when families cannot be together. I lost both my parents before I was nine, and so never had even the possibility of that happiness. You and Edith ought to make up and not allow petty grievances to keep you separated."

"Do you think I am the cause of this trouble? She is separating herself from me! Disrespectful creature."

"Far from being ashamed of your daughter, you ought to

be proud of her. She has a gift for helping people, and she is using it. At the Royal Free Hospital, I saw her save the life of a young boy. She was astute enough to see the signs of internal bleeding, and she immediately took measures to keep the child from dying. There were licensed physicians in the hospital that day—all men—but none of them saw those critical signs. It was Edith."

"Stop!" the earl ordered. "I will not be lectured at in my own home." He vigorously pulled the rope to call for a servant. "I don't know why I even agreed to see you."

But Julia wasn't ready to concede just yet. "The boy's parents are extremely grateful that Edith made medicine her choice of occupation. What is the life of a boy worth?"

The earl stood, glaring at her, the red in his face reaching all the way up to his white hair. "I know very well what a boy's life is worth. I am glad to know how good Edith is at healing *other people's* children."

The bleak coldness of his words penetrated Julia's heart. She had not persuaded him; just the contrary. By reminding him of the son he had lost, she had inadvertently poured salt on his wounds.

The butler entered the room.

"Show this woman out," ordered the earl.

The butler sent a glance toward the window. Outside, the rain was pouring down steadily. "Now, sir?"

"You heard me!"

The earl spoke so sharply that any ordinary person would have jumped. Julia certainly did, even though she had no fear of this man. But the butler was no doubt used to his master's ways by now. He turned toward Julia, clearly intending to show her the door.

"Good afternoon, your lordship. Thank you again for seeing

me today." Despite her misstep, she was determined that being tossed out into the rain was not going to quell her pride.

Her polite words only angered him more. "Good afternoon!" he responded, loading those two words with so much vitriol that Julia almost felt sorry for him.

She followed the butler to the front hall, where he helped her into her damp coat. As she made her way down the muddy lane, she prayed. She guessed that not too many people prayed for this man—especially if he'd treated them as he'd done her. It certainly was not the outcome she'd been hoping for. She prayed she had not been wrong to come here, and that even if she had, that some good might come of it.

"Wonderful news," Lisette said, speaking as usual without preamble as she entered the student laboratory and approached the table where Julia was working.

Julia looked up from her microscope, irritated at being interrupted just as she'd gotten a good focus on this blood sample. The university examination was a little over a month away, and she still had so much information to master. Keeping her full attention on her studies had been hard enough, between worry over the upcoming trial and her continuing battle *not* to think of Michael. "What news?"

"Didn't you receive one of these in the mail?" Lisette thrust a sheet of paper toward Julia.

"I've been here all afternoon." The house matron delivered mail to the students' bedrooms, but Julia had spent the greater part of the day studying in the laboratory. She glanced down at the paper. It was a printed notice.

"The medical school is offering free tutoring," Lisette said. She began to give more details, but Julia was already reading the notice with astonishment.

The London School of Medicine for Women

Now offering tutoring sessions free of charge to candidates who will be sitting for London University's Preliminary Examination in June with the express purpose of enrolling in the London School of Medicine for Women.

All topics covered: Latin, Algebra & Geometry, English Language, English History, Natural Sciences, Chemistry.

Groups of 1–4 will be formed as needed.

Inquire at the London School of Medicine for Women during regular business hours. Must present proof of registration for the June examination.

Julia read it through twice, still unable to believe it was true. How astounding that this offer should come just when she needed it. "Has the medical school ever done this before?"

"Not to my knowledge."

"Why do you suppose they are doing it now? And how can they afford it—especially with the uncertainties of the lawsuit?"

"Perhaps that is *exactly* why they are doing it!" Lisette raised one arm dramatically in the air, fist clenched. "It's an act of defiance, to show the almighty Earl of Westbridge that *yes*, the school will survive, and *yes*, it will be filled with qualified students!"

Julia doubted this was the motive. But whatever the reason, she was thankful. "How many ladies do you think are sitting for that exam?"

Lisette shrugged. "We are a small but illustrious group. I don't think everyone will ask for the tutoring, though. Some women have hired their own tutors already and do not need more help. I do, however. I will sign up for English history—that is my worst subject. Such dry, boring stuff." Having been raised primarily in France, Lisette's lack of knowledge or interest in English history was understandable. "But you will sign up for Latin, yes?"

"Yes!" Julia answered enthusiastically. "Plus anything else I can."

Lisette threw an arm around her. "*Mon amie*, we are going to pass this exam with honors—maybe even get a prize! You know there are two prizes being offered by the medical school, don't you?"

"Indeed I do." The prizes were cash gifts to be applied to tuition. It would go a long way toward making ends meet next year. Julia did not truly hope to win one of these. Having come from so far behind on schooling, she'd long since decided she'd be content just to earn reasonable scores.

"I have a new theory," said Lisette. "You know those prizes are funded by some of the school's more generous patrons. Maybe they want to make the competition more lively, so they are paying for the tutoring!"

"How do you come up with these ideas?" Julia teased, shaking her head. Although she and Lisette had their disagreements at times, Julia admired her tenacity and drive.

Lisette murmured aloud as she perused the notice again. "'Proof of registration . . .'" She looked at Julia. "You have registered for the exam, haven't you?"

"Of course!"

"Then shall we go to the school and see about signing up for tutoring?"

"Yes. Let's go today."

This was a blessing to savor, even if for Julia it felt bittersweet. The tutoring from Michael was gone—and so much more—yet here she was being presented with a new set of opportunities. It was a reminder yet again to keep her eyes—and heart—on the dreams God had given her.

CHAPTER

26

THE TUTORING SESSIONS were a major boost to Julia's studies. Every day, from late in the afternoon until nearly nine o'clock, she and a handful of others worked with teachers who were experts in their fields, breaking up into small groups as needed. The medical school had even set aside a classroom for the purpose.

For two weeks now, the Latin tutor had drilled Julia on declensions, conjugations, and vocabulary. It was effective for learning, even if it was all done by rote. He did not have Michael's enthusiasm to seek out deeper, richer hues of meaning in the texts. But he was teaching her what she needed to know for the exam, and she was grateful.

For the next two days, however, Julia had to set the lessons aside in order to attend the trial. Although she could not allow herself to believe that the libel suit could signal the end of the school, she had to acknowledge the situation was serious enough to warrant her prayerful presence.

She knew she would see Michael there, of course. As she entered the courtroom, she caught her first glimpse of him since the heartrending moment when she'd walked away from him in the park. He stood at a table near the judge's desk, deep in conversation with Mr. Tamblin. It was the first time she'd seen Michael in his barrister's wig and robes. He looked so different and formal, emanating unmistakable gravitas.

His gray eyes were just the same, though. Her heart did a painful jump when he looked up and his gaze met hers. Julia longed for some sign of acknowledgment, however subtle. Some indication of the previous warmth they had shared, or even of the regret she'd seen in his eyes on the last day they'd met. But she saw only the impersonal coolness one might show a stranger. Perhaps he'd found it easy to go on with his life. If so, they had made the right choice. Even if it pained her to admit it.

Michael did not hold her gaze for long. Mr. Tamblin said something, and Michael turned to reply. He did not look her way again. He had a job to do, and by all appearances, he was more than ready to do it. Did he not regret that either, even knowing what it might do to Julia's future? She swallowed the lump in her throat along with her disappointment.

Lisette, who had come with her, tugged her toward the visitors' benches. They had to squeeze together on the end of a bench near the back, because the courtroom was packed with spectators.

"Do this many people normally come to watch a trial?" Julia asked her.

"Everyone has come to see the lady doctors," Lisette replied, making a face. "Like we're strange creatures or monkeys in the London Zoo. Look at how they're staring at Dr. Tierney and the others."

Sure enough, most people in the crowd were watching as Dr. Tierney and Dr. Anderson entered the courtroom accompanied by members of the school's board of directors and their legal counsel. Everyone in the group looked very solemn. All did their best to ignore the sea of onlookers and refused to acknowledge the jeers and whistles sent their way.

Julia felt a nudge as Edith sat down next to her, just managing to find enough space to fit on the edge of the bench.

"I wasn't sure whether you'd want to come," Julia said.

Edith's expression was grim. "I wouldn't dream of missing it."

There was a fresh round of excitement as the Earl of West-bridge made his entrance. His gait was slow, and he leaned heavily on a cane, but any physical weakness he showed was offset by the lift of his head and his haughty expression. He walked to the front of the room and joined Michael and Mr. Tamblin.

The jurors filed in, taking their seats in the jury box. Everyone was seated now except the usher, a large man standing in front of the judge's high desk. He wore a gown but no wig, and he held a long staff.

"Silence in the court!" he bellowed, punctuating the command by banging his staff on the floor. A hush fell over the room. Directing everyone to rise, the usher announced the judge.

Julia had not been able to imagine why the trial was scheduled to take two days, but before long she began to understand. The opening proceedings alone, including swearing in of the jurors, reading out the cause for the libel suit, and many other formalities, took what seemed an eternity. Or was it because she was so intensely aware of Michael's presence in the courtroom? She watched him from the corner of her eye. He appeared somber and wholly attentive to his duties.

Mr. Tamblin's opening remarks were lengthy, citing references to legal precedents that meant nothing to Julia. He included many Latin phrases, too. Some words were easy to translate, but whatever legalities they referenced were beyond Julia's realm of knowledge. Although he also covered in detail the actions and words of Dr. Tierney that had brought about this case, that did not seem to be the primary focus of his remarks. He seemed to spend more time discussing the *reasons* for libel laws, their history, and their import. He spoke of the ways they protected people's reputations, and how especially right and proper that was when it came to attacks on a peer of the realm. After a while, Julia began to think this sounded more like a university lecture than a discussion of this specific case.

Her sentiments were echoed by Lisette, who at one point murmured with exasperation, "I don't understand what is happening. The prosecution has not even tried to offer a rebuttal of Dr. Tierney's statements. Instead they keep blathering on about how important and noble his lordship is. And he is eating up the attention."

Lord Westbridge did indeed look exceedingly content to be the center of attention. He often sent an imperious gaze over the courtroom, as though to assert his authority. But there was one place he seemed to be deliberately *not* looking, and that was toward the back benches where Julia and the other students were seated.

Julia glanced at Edith. Surely it was difficult for her to sit through this. There was no sign of sadness on her face, however. Only anger. "Look at him, acting for all the world as if he were *holding* court, instead of sitting in one."

Even though the earl had treated Julia badly when she'd visited him, it still made her sad to hear Edith speak of her own father in such harsh terms.

"I hope the defense ensures our side of the issue is clearly laid out for the jury," one of the other students whispered nervously.

"We will prevail," Julia answered with conviction.

This drew a look of surprise from Lisette. "What makes you so sure?"

"We will prevail because we must," Edith said before Julia could answer. But the dark look she sent her father showed that she was not speaking from a place of optimism, as Julia had been, but from warlike determination.

The proceedings continued at a lugubrious pace until finally, the judge declared the court adjourned until tomorrow.

"How do you think it is going?" Julia asked Edith as everyone began to spill into the corridor outside the courtroom.

"It's impossible to say. I think we'll know better tomorrow, when we are able to present our defense."

There was a flurry of movement a short distance away. The earl, who was exiting another door of the courtroom into the crowded hallway, seemed to have stumbled. Julia heard Edith emit a soft cry as he fell to his knees. Several people rushed forward to help him up. Over the course of the afternoon, Julia had thought more than once that the earl's energy appeared to be flagging. Now he looked positively haggard. Michael and two other men led him to a bench, where he could sit and catch his breath.

"Someone needs to help him," Julia said.

"There are a dozen doctors here," Lisette replied and added with a sniff, "A pity they are all women."

Julia glanced at Edith, expecting a similar reply, but to her surprise, she saw that Edith's expression was anything but dismissive. Everything in her manner signaled a desire to rush to him. Surely this must be as much from filial devotion as from her instincts as a physician?

"Why don't you go to him?" Julia encouraged.

Her words had the opposite of her intended effect. Edith's expression shuttered. "No. He has fought my becoming a doctor at every step. I'm not giving him the benefit of my expertise. Or my pity."

She turned on her heel, but as she walked away, Julia saw her heave a tremendous sigh, and her shoulders shook a little.

I will go to him, Julia thought. But before she could move, her attention was arrested by the expression on the earl's face. He was waving away the people hovering around him, exclaiming that he was fine, but his gaze was fixed on his daughter's retreating form. And for a moment—just a moment—Julia saw in his eyes the very same sorrow and longing that she'd just seen in Edith.

There must be something there, she thought. *There has to be.* She just had to figure out a way to make them both see it.

She was so caught up in these thoughts that she barely realized her feet were closing the gap between her and the earl until he pointed an unsteady finger at her and said, "Stay away from me! You've caused enough trouble already. You're lucky I didn't bring action against you for trespassing on my property!"

Michael stood next to the earl, and his eyes widened in surprise at these words.

"I was given leave to enter your home, as I recall," Julia returned evenly, wanting to reassure everyone within earshot that she was no lawbreaker. "How are you feeling? Are you dizzy? In pain? Did you try the liniment that I left you instructions for?"

She reached out to lay a hand on his forehead, but he batted it away. "I will not be treated this way!" he bellowed. "I will be *respected!*"

Michael drew her away. "I think you'd better go, miss. I'm sure you mean well, but you are only upsetting him."

He spoke as if she were a total stranger. Startled, she looked up at him, silently chastising him for his aloofness.

But then, seeing that everyone else's attention was on the earl, who was complaining and calling out for his physician, Michael's expression softened. He whispered, "Did you really go to his lordship's home?"

She saw a hint of perplexed amusement. It was a look she'd drawn out of him many times during their lessons. She felt a burst of joy to see it again. "Why yes, I—"

"Here is Dr. Adams, sir!" Mr. Tamblin cried out in relief, as a gentleman carrying a medical bag rushed up to the earl.

"Sir, I warned you about overexerting yourself," Dr. Adams admonished. He began checking the earl's vital signs, exactly as Julia had wanted to do.

The earl allowed him to do it, although he said sourly, "Don't scold me, Adams. Just get me home." He addressed the doctor as if he were a servant instead of a private physician.

"Stephenson! Come help us," Mr. Tamblin ordered.

Michael's gaze lingered on Julia for a long moment. Enough to nearly melt her heart. He still cared for her; she could feel it in the heat of his gaze before he finally turned away.

Julia took a moment to gather herself. There was nothing more she could do here. She turned and hurried down the long corridor, exiting the massive doors to the street, looking for Edith.

"Edith, wait!" Julia called as she caught sight of her friend half a block away.

Edith didn't stop. Even when Julia caught up with her, she kept walking purposefully, not acknowledging her presence. But Julia matched her stride for stride.

"What just happened in there?"

"Don't lecture me about not helping him. There were plenty of licensed physicians available to give him whatever he needed."

"That's not why I came after you," Julia insisted.

They reached a corner, but Edith seemed so desperate to get away that she didn't even slow down. Julia yelped and grabbed Edith's arm, yanking her backward to prevent her from walking right into the path of an oncoming carriage.

The carriage raced by with a thunderous clatter, throwing

mud and a loose rock into the air, nearly hitting them. Julia felt Edith shaking as the enormity of what she'd almost done struck her. She stood still, gasping for breath, pulling her arm free but still not looking at Julia.

Julia took advantage of this moment, before her friend decided to move again. "I saw your face back there. I saw what it took for you to walk away."

"You don't understand anything about it."

"I also saw something you didn't. It was the look he gave you as you were leaving."

Edith gave a bitter laugh, but her hand trembled as she adjusted her short coat, which had gotten pulled askew when Julia stopped her flight. "I wouldn't have to see that. I can imagine it quite well."

"You're wrong. It was full of sadness—tenderness, even. Longing—"

"If he *longs* for something, it was lost years ago. I have chosen this path, and I'm not turning back. If this verdict spells the end for the school, then I will finish my studies in Vienna. I will show him I am not defeated. In fact, I should have left before now."

Julia seized on her words. "So why haven't you gone to the continent? I know it's not through fear or lack of desire. You speak fluent German, and you've mentioned how much you'd like to one day visit the land of your mother's ancestors. And yet you stay here. You even turned down an opportunity to spend three months at the excellent lying-in hospital in Ireland."

"Leave me be." Seeing a break in the traffic, Edith took the opportunity to cross.

"I know the reason can't be lack of money," Julia continued, doggedly following her. "I would guess that for some reason, you were determined not to stray too far from the home counties. Now I wonder, why is that?"

"You're right. I ought to have left sooner. My father wants to push me across the channel—or even the Atlantic. This is not a man who misses me. Clearly he would like me to go as far from him as possible. Well then, I will oblige him."

"But if you could make a truce with your father, wouldn't you want to?"

By now they had reached the other side of the street. Edith halted and turned on Julia. "Are you working for him? Did he hire you to try to win me over?"

"You know that's preposterous!"

"Is it? It doesn't matter. I do know you are friends with that barrister—the one who has been so instrumental in hurting the school."

"I was trying to *help* the school."

"I think you were only trying to help yourself. I have seen the way he looks at you. If you can't end up pursuing medicine, you might have an excellent career as a barrister's wife. Or paramour. Perhaps that's been your goal all along. It's certainly easier than working for a living."

"Edith, you know me!" Julia admonished, shocked at her cruel words. "How can you say such things?"

"Because I want you to stop pestering me. Now, will you let me be?" Edith's voice and posture were hard and unyielding, everything about her an impenetrable wall. Julia had pushed her too hard, and like a wounded animal, her friend had turned on her. Once more, her overly direct manner had done more harm than good.

"I'm sorry you feel that way," she said gently. "I won't bother you again."

There might have been a flash of regret in Edith's face, but it was quickly concealed by a little smile of prideful satisfaction at having gained her point. Without another word, she turned and walked away.

Julia made her way home slowly. Had she really misunderstood what she'd seen in the courthouse today? Had she been wrong in thinking that father and daughter even *wanted* a reconciliation? She couldn't shake the feeling that she'd been right. Yet there seemed no way to bridge the gap between them.

Edith's words about Michael troubled her, too. Had their attraction to each other been too obvious? Was it possible that anyone else had seen it? Everything in her life was in a jumble. The school, her friendships, and her heart—all seemed in jeopardy.

It was a long, prayerful walk home. It was all she could do, but today, it was impossible to take solace in it.

CHAPTER

27

DAY TWO OF THE TRIAL. After the way Tamblin had laid out the case for the prosecution, there seemed little doubt the jury could do anything except find the defendants guilty.

Michael was heartily glad it would soon be over. He'd done everything required of him, and it had taken a huge toll on his conscience. So much in his own life depended on this case succeeding, but he could never forget that Julia's dreams depended on the school's survival. After the day he'd ended up at Anderson's company, Michael was beginning to believe that prayers could bring results. When it came to the trial, though, he couldn't bring himself to pray for either outcome. He decided it was better to leave his petitions unsubmitted.

Today, he was impressed by how carefully the counsel for the defense was parsing out Dr. Tierney's liability from that of the medical school. They may well have thought it was their best way of preserving the school. They had not been able to present any solid evidence to back up Dr. Tierney's comments about the state of the earl's son when he died. Nor had they been able to fully refute the claims of damages done to the earl's reputation. Michael privately thought Tamblin had blown it out of proportion, but that had been their strategy all along.

The defense was now addressing the jury, summing up the responses from his careful questioning of the witnesses. "So you see, gentleman, the London School of Medicine for Women holds no official position at all on the Contagious Diseases Acts. Indeed, as we have just demonstrated, there is a difference of opinion even among the school's board of directors."

"No surprise there," a man sitting behind Michael said to his neighbor. "When has a group of women ever agreed on anything?"

"Except when they agree on how to bankrupt a husband by shopping for too many luxuries," the other man replied with a laugh.

The two men had made many such deprecating comments over the course of the afternoon. Michael was pretty sure they'd only come for the sport of jesting about the women. They'd kept their comments low enough not to gain the notice of the usher or the judge, but they were close enough that Michael could hear them.

Still addressing the jury, the counsel for the defense went on to sum up the statements of the witnesses by repeating—in detail—all their assurances of their respect for Lord Westbridge and their distress that he or anyone else should think they had attempted to throw a disparaging light on him.

Michael studied the men of the jury, trying to discern their thoughts. Most wore sober but neutral expressions. A few looked stone-faced at the barrister, leaving no doubt in Michael's mind which way they would vote. But several were nodding thoughtfully and throwing the occasional sympathetic glance toward the women seated in the dock.

Looking at the medical students seated in the audience, Michael thought back to Laura's comments at the theatre. What would she think now? To Michael's eye, they looked no different than any other group of women. Some were dressed stylishly, and others more simply. Some were pretty, and some less so. But none would have arrested attention for appearing out of the ordinary.

Except for Julia, of course. She was the most beautiful woman in the room. Michael was careful not to glance at her too often, although he could always tell when her gaze was on him. It had been hard to keep his composure. The incident after yesterday's session had nearly done him in, especially when he heard she'd gone to his lordship's home. What had she been thinking? Trying to influence him, no doubt. It must have done no good, although he couldn't help but admire her for the attempt.

The judge addressed the jury. "Gentlemen, you have heard the evidence brought forward in this case. It now devolves on you to weigh that evidence and pronounce upon the guilt or innocence of the accused."

After giving them more words of instruction, the judge dismissed the jury for deliberations. Michael had kept his part of the bargain. What would happen next was out of his hands. His only regret was that when this was over, he would no longer have the exquisite torture of seeing Julia, if only from a distance.

The jury returned in less than two hours.

"Have you reached a verdict?" the judged asked.

"We have, your honor," the foreman replied.

Julia waited, barely able to breathe, as apprehension tugged at hope. The school *must* win this lawsuit. She had prayed more during these past two days than she could ever remember. She was convinced the defense had made a good case. Surely God would take care of the rest. He would not let them down.

The foreman said gravely, "We find in favor of the plaintiff."

No. Julia could not believe it.

Immediately the room was abuzz as the spectators voiced either protest or approval. Those closest to Julia gasped in stunned disbelief, just as she had.

"Silence in court!" commanded the usher. He had to repeat the warning before the noise subsided.

"Continue," the judge directed the foreman.

"We find for the plaintiff. We assess damages in the amount of one pound."

The room erupted again—some people shouting with laughter, others with indignation. Julia was confused. One pound was an insignificant sum in this context. Did this mean the school was safe after all?

"The jury finds for the plaintiff, with damages in the amount of one pound," the judge repeated. "As the jury has found for the plaintiff, the Court assesses all court fees to be paid by the defendants."

"Oh no," Lisette moaned. "After all the months this case has dragged on, the court costs are bound to be ruinous."

Edith pointed toward the jury. "Why do some of them look surprised? They had to have known this would be the result of their verdict."

Julia sent a worried look toward the defendants' table. They were among the few people in the courtroom who were silent. They had fought for a decade or more to establish the school and keep it running. This was a terrible blow, and yet they were facing the worst with grim fortitude. The exception was Dr. Tierney, whose face was red from barely suppressed anger.

The earl had been as easy to read as an open book: his smile of triumph when the verdict was read; his consternation when the foreman announced the award of one pound; the way he leaned back in satisfaction when the judge assessed the fees to the defendants.

The most inscrutable person in the courtroom was Michael. Was he happy with this outcome? Did he have any regret over his role in defeating the school, knowing what it would do to Julia? It was impossible to guess. She stared at him, silently willing him to meet her gaze, which at last he did. As their gazes held, some emotion began to flicker in his eyes. Before she could decipher it, the moment was lost. He was forced to turn and acknowledge Mr. Tamblin, who had reached out to shake his hand.

There was no way for Julia to catch even a glimpse of Michael in the swirling crowds after the courtroom was dismissed. Edith, too, was quickly gone, stalking off alone. She hadn't spoken one word directly to Julia today; her anger over yesterday's events had not abated. Today, however, Julia did not pursue her. She needed time, as they all did, to consider what these events meant for their futures.

After the crowd from the trial had filtered out, Julia sat for a long time on one of the red-cushioned benches in the great hall. It was a magnificent place, with a soaring arched roof, stained-glass windows bearing coats of arms, and an intricate mosaic marble floor. It looked like a cathedral. She admired its beauty, but the Royal Courts of Justice was a shrine to the works of men, not God. *Had justice been done here today?* She could not believe it had.

The great hall still hummed with activity. Julia watched barristers in robes and wigs walking by on their way to other courtrooms, often accompanied by clerks or clients. There was no sign of Michael, though. Perhaps she'd been wrong, or even hypocritical, to look for an indication that he felt remorse for her sake. After all, if she loved him, shouldn't she feel some bit of happiness for a success that gave a critical boost to his career? Her heart only grew heavier as she pondered these questions.

Julia could not remember a time when she had doubted her calling. She'd been sure about where she was going and how she would get there. But over these past few months, her plans had unraveled. She'd lost her patron. Her scheme to attain Latin lessons, which she'd considered a godsend, had brought only trouble and heartache. She'd been rejected by the missionary society. What was she going to do? She could not embrace the idea of going to India, but it probably didn't matter. Today's verdict meant she might never become a doctor anyway.

Tears crowded her eyes, stinging as she blinked them back and heaved a long, despondent sigh. If she closed her eyes, she saw Michael. If she opened them, she saw his world, which had been so terribly at odds with her own. At last, taking a last swipe at a stray tear, Julia stood up. It would do her no good to linger here. She had never been one for self-pity, and she wouldn't allow herself to start now.

Outside on the busy street, she passed a vendor selling farthing pinwheels to a woman and her son. The boy looked a lot like Sam. It reminded Julia that she'd promised to visit Sybil today in order to check on the baby. She sighed again. It was a long walk to Bethnal Green, and she was tired after a sleepless night. She wanted only to find some tea and a quiet place to think. As she stood there, arguing with herself, she remembered something Mr. Müller used to say: if an answer from God is a long time coming, the best way to pass the time is to keep busy helping someone else. Her future was uncertain, but there was still plenty for her to do in the here and now.

She turned back to the street vendor and bought two pinwheels. Her heart lightened a little as she imagined the joy these colorful paper trinkets would give to Sam and Jemmie. She walked east, catching sight of St. Paul's Cathedral before turning northward. She passed the court for criminal trials, known as the Old Bailey, and Newgate Prison, which loomed next door. She prayed for Myrtle and for Gwen. Their trials would take place in a few weeks. Julia prayed they would find justice and, in Gwen's case, leniency.

There was one last stop she made on her way. At the shop of the baker who'd been so kind to Cara, she bought fresh bread. She also bought apples and a small meat pie from street vendors near the shop. She'd have to give up several dinners for this extravagance, but it would be worth it.

Sybil and the baby were in satisfactory health, considering their living conditions, as were the other children. Sybil and Hettie worked together doing piecework to support them all. It was a hard life, but Julia was impressed by their resilience. They received her simple offerings with such joy that she might as well have brought a feast.

Julia had always taken satisfaction in helping others, whether tending to physical needs through nursing, or to spiritual needs via prayer and sharing the gospel. Today, however, was the first time she felt others had truly ministered to *her*. The visit had turned into an impromptu party of sorts and given a lift to her downtrodden soul.

She looked around the simple room, which seemed more cheerful than when she first saw it. A fresh breeze coming through the window helped, as did the bright red pinwheels that the children were fanning with delight. Hettie had brewed tea to enjoy with the meal. Doreen had joined them, too, bringing a spoonful of tea leaves to add to the pot so there would be enough for everyone.

"You will surely be a doctor one day," Hettie insisted after Julia told them about the trial and its outcome. "You have a gift for healing. Today was bad, but God is with you. You speak to us all the time about the power of prayer, yes?"

"Yes."

"So what has changed?"

Julia felt her eyes grow misty even as she smiled at Hettie's question. "You're right, Hettie. God has not changed." She held out her hands. "Shall we pray together?"

They did. Sybil prayed for Edith, for they all were sad to learn it had been her own father who'd been fighting the school. Even Doreen joined in, adding a simple prayer for Myrtle that touched Julia's heart. At first, Doreen had staunchly refused to talk about God, but over the last few weeks, she had softened as Julia had continued to stress God's love and forgiveness.

After the prayer, Doreen said, "I don't mean to tell the Almighty how to do His business, but do you think maybe your handsome barrister friend can help Myrtle, too—like he helped us?"

Julia's breath caught. One detail she hadn't shared was the role Michael had played in the trial. She hadn't been able to bring herself to talk about him. Even now, the mention of him sent her heart in contradictory directions. "I can't promise that, I'm afraid."

Doreen sighed, but accepted this with a nod. "I suppose he only works for the finer set."

"Something will come through for Myrtle, I'm sure of it," Julia assured her.

When it came time to leave, there was still a half hour or so of daylight left, so Julia wasn't worried about the walk home. The narrow lane was as grimy and unwelcoming as ever, but it seemed less threatening today. Perhaps this was because Julia had grown accustomed to it. It was bustling with people, filled with noise as children played and dogs barked. No one paid her any mind.

Doreen's mention of Michael had been the only damper to an otherwise uplifting visit. It seemed impossible to think of

Michael without sorrow. She could not hold any anger against him, though. She loved him too much for that.

Julia felt a sense of melancholy returning as she made her way up the lane. Uncertainty still tugged at her heart, along with a feeling that maybe the answer was within reach, if only she could discern it. She paused when she reached the street corner, feeling an urge to turn around to take in the scene again before moving on. At one doorway, a mother was consoling a crying child. At another, a husband and wife were arguing. At a third, a young girl sat listless on the stoop to her decrepit home. Above them all, lines of laundry hung between the buildings. From bedsheets to petticoats, they formed a wall of white that flapped in the breeze.

"Lift up your eyes, and look on the fields; for they are white already to harvest."

Julia inhaled sharply at the memory of these words from the gospel. She'd once heard in a sermon that as Jesus had spoken this admonition, He might have been pointing to the crowd eagerly coming to see Him, as many people wore white garments in those days.

These are all people in need of help.

She had known that, of course. She'd seen it vividly during her visits to the charity clinic and the slums. There was poverty and misery throughout London, but Julia had never anticipated the way it would impact her heart. These people lived in a Christian country, and yet many did not truly know God. Nor was spiritual need limited to those in poverty; Julia knew this from her dealings with many others, including fellow students and the daughter of an earl.

Julia understood now. Even if she never became a doctor, there were people here whom she could help in the way that counted most. She thought of the admonition to seek first the kingdom of God, and the promise that in doing so, all other needs would be met.

London was a mission field, and it was big enough for a lifetime.

Friday night dinners in the great hall of Gray's Inn were always well attended, but this week the meal had turned into a victory celebration.

Michael sat with a half-dozen colleagues, all of whom had congratulated him heartily for his part in winning the libel suit. Everyone agreed this could only launch him to greater things. "You shall have all the briefs you want after this," one man assured him.

"Tamblin was the lead barrister," Michael reminded them.

"Yes, but we all know he will be called up for a judgeship soon, and no longer able to practice. Besides, your part in the case did not go unnoticed."

"It will be a good one for the law books," said another man. "The way the case was pursued at trial was not what people were expecting."

Michael looked around the ancient oak-paneled hall, which at the moment was filled with barristers and law students dining at rows of tables. Stained-glass windows on every wall bore the coats of arms of the Inn's most notable members over the centuries. This venerable place was steeped in history. Michael had long desired to make his mark here, but pleading a questionable libel suit was not how he'd envisioned doing it. The outcome of the trial still bothered him.

One of the men at the table voiced a concern that Michael had also been considering. "It does seem an extraordinary verdict, though—to find for the plaintiff and yet award so small an amount. What do you suppose they meant by it?"

"Perhaps they felt his lordship already has all the money he needs," one man offered.

"Maybe they didn't want to find the defendants guilty, but they knew they had to award to Lord Westbridge anyway," put in another.

"You gentleman seem to have missed the letter in the *Times* this morning," said John Findlay, one of the Inn's members whom Michael knew best. "There was a letter from one of the jurymen giving the whole story. I'm sorry I didn't bring it with me, but I'd be glad to sum up."

Michael was immediately intrigued. "What did he say?"

"He said everyone on the jury was of the opinion that the plaintiff ought to have provided clear evidence of the falsity of the defendant's claims regarding the death of his lordship's son. Nevertheless, they were split regarding which way to give the verdict, and they were not convinced that the excessive amount for damages requested by the plaintiff was warranted. The juror said they asked the clerk of court whether they could find the defendant guilty without assessing damages. They were told they could not. They then asked if assessing just one pound would carry expenses for court costs against the defender and were told it would not. So that is how they reached their decision. They were surprised, therefore, when the Court in fact assigned the expenses to the defense."

"The problem, then, is that the clerk did not give them correct information," said one of the men, to which everyone, including Michael, nodded in agreement. "What they ought to have been told is that damages of less than five pounds do not *necessarily* entitle the pursuer to expenses, but that it is still nevertheless at the discretion of the Court."

"Precisely!" said Findlay. "Given these circumstances, I do not think the verdict carries much weight. If I were counsel for the defense, I'd advise them to appeal based on the incorrect interference of the clerk of court."

"Findlay, why are you trying to throw cold water on Stephenson's victory?" one of the other men said. He raised a wineglass. "We still owe him a toast!"

But Michael had already come to the same conclusion as Findlay. When the meal was over, he pulled Findlay aside as everyone was leaving the hall. "Will you join me for a stroll on the walks?" he asked. "I'd like to follow up on something you said."

Findlay looked surprised but readily agreed. "I hope you did not take umbrage at my earlier remarks," he said, once they'd made their way to the gardens and chosen a path at random.

"Not at all. As we know, there are always multiple sides to every case, and even to every verdict. As you pointed out, the juryman's letter shows they were sympathetic to the defendants. However, it's not always easy to go against such a powerful figure, even in our most excellent legal system."

"That is very true."

"In fact, I think someone from the legal profession should write a letter to the *Times*, responding to the juror's letter as you did tonight."

Findlay stopped in his tracks. "You do?"

"Obviously it cannot come from me. But as you are a disinterested party and a respected barrister, I wonder if you might do it."

Findlay looked at him quizzically. "Why would you want to do anything to encourage their appeal?"

"Let me ask you a question: Do you think women ought to be allowed to be licensed as physicians?"

"Indeed I do!"

This was exactly the answer Michael expected. He knew Findlay was one of the more forward-thinking members of the Inn.

Findlay added, "I expect women will also enter the legal profession someday. I'm not against that either, but I will say it gives me some trepidation about winning future cases. Based on personal experience with my sisters, no one can argue a point like a woman."

He said this with a smile. Michael's heart twisted a little, remembering the day he'd thought the same thing about Julia. "Well, then, this letter could help lessen the sting of the verdict, in terms of the school's reputation among the public. It might vindicate them morally, if not financially."

"The thought had crossed my mind," Findlay admitted. "But I'm surprised to hear it from you."

"If I may speak confidentially . . ." Michael paused, waiting until Findlay nodded his assent, before continuing. "I am for women in medicine, too. I have done my best to live up to the tenets of our profession and win this case for my client, but all of that should have no bearing on the school's ability to continue its mission."

"Right you are."

"There's one more thing I'd like to ask you, if I may. I have heard you do pro bono work sometimes at the criminal court. I'd be interested in doing something of the same. I'm thinking specifically of two women currently in custody, although my scope might broaden in time."

Findlay gave him a friendly slap on the back. "Stephenson, before today I thought of you as someone driven to achieve personal success at all costs. But it appears I've been mistaken. You might be a man who favors truth and justice above personal gain."

"Just don't let the word get out."

This drew the laugh he'd intended, though Michael knew in his heart that Findlay had been right on both counts. He'd still be that first sort of man today, except Julia had changed him.

CHAPTER

28

J ULIA SAT WITH HER HANDS CLASPED in her lap, praying. Her eyes were wide open, though. She looked at the paper lying facedown on the table in front of her. As soon as the proctor finished handing them out, the Latin exam would begin.

This was the culmination of so much work. The matriculation exam would take place over the next three days. Latin was the first subject to be covered, and for Julia, this first hurdle was the most important. If she was successful, it would set the tone for the days to follow.

After the trial, Julia had immersed herself once more in her studies. She wasn't going to forget the truth that God had sealed in her heart that day—that she was already in the right place, fulfilling her primary calling. Medical training would only enhance that, and so long as there was a chance the school would stay open, Julia would pursue it. The trustees of the medical school had publicly declared that they would continue with the current term as scheduled, which would end in late July. The tutoring continued as well. The court fees were still being assessed, and the collateral damage, such as possibly losing clinical privileges at the hospital, was not yet known. The dust would likely settle during the long break between July and the next term, which did not begin until October. As she studied, Julia set a vision of herself passing the exam and beginning medical studies in October. She would not allow herself to think of anything else.

The room held over one hundred examinees, although only about twenty were women. Not all the women here planned to attend the medical school, however. Some had set their sights on other fields of study at the University of London.

They had all been seated together at the back of the room.

"Is this so we don't distract the men?" one of them had whispered sarcastically as they'd been directed to their seats by a university official.

"No, it's to keep us closer to the exit, so that if someone faints from the strain, she can be easily removed," Lisette had quipped in return.

Julia didn't really mind. She felt it was a triumph just to be allowed to test in the same room and vie for the same goals in education as the men.

After reviewing in detail the rules to be followed, the proctor gave the command for everyone to turn over their papers and begin.

The first hour was to be spent translating a passage from Latin to English. Julia quickly skimmed the text to get an overall feel for it. In spite of her nervousness, she couldn't help a tiny, aching smile. She wouldn't need the Latin words for *wildflower* or *hogshead* today. But she was still exceedingly glad she'd learned them.

Taking a deep breath, she inked her pen and began.

❧⁓✥⁓❧

"Congratulations on winning the lawsuit," Jamie Anderson said.

Michael was once more in the offices of the P&O Steamship Company. Even after receiving Anderson's note inviting him back here today, he wasn't entirely sure how he'd be received. "I trust you won't take it personally."

Anderson gave him a good-natured smile. "I've told you before that I don't allow my wife's affairs to affect how I do business."

"Still, the loss was a hard blow to the school."

"They haven't given up the ship just yet. The court costs are enormous, but the directors are actively seeking sponsors to help pay that debt. The harder work will be keeping access to clinical training at the Royal Free Hospital. But there are people with influence working on that, too. I think a certain letter in the *Times* is swaying some opinions." From the way he looked at Michael, it was obvious Anderson thought he'd written it.

"Yes," said Michael, "I saw that letter, too. John Findlay made some very good points."

Anderson nodded in understanding. "Well, if you know him, please send him my personal thanks for writing it."

"I will." Even though Michael could take no credit for that letter to the *Times*, he was glad he'd spurred Findlay to write it. "May I ask, have you learned anything more about Paul Bernay?" He was hoping that was the reason Anderson had asked him here.

"Yes, but not before running across a few obstacles. The man I spoke to at the Marine Casualty and Insurance Company was not particularly helpful. He told me only what was already in the public record: the ship was on its way to South America when it was caught up in the hurricane and sank."

"I suppose I expected that."

Anderson opened a large book, fully four inches thick, that sat on his desk. "However, I did find one piece of information from this shipping register. This lists the names of the captains and officers of the ships. I can't find Bernay listed anywhere as a ship's captain."

"How could that be?"

"I presume the Bernay sisters are mistaken. After all, they were very young when they lost their parents."

Michael shook his head. "Julia specifically remembers her mother telling them he was a captain. The directors at the orphanage must also have known his title, and no one ever told the sisters any differently."

Anderson shrugged. "I can't explain it. I only know that according to this register, Bernay was second officer during the ship's final voyage. This is still an important position, but it ranks third behind the captain and first officer. The second officer also has important duties regarding navigation. If the ship was off course, he would have been in some measure responsible for it."

Even reading the listing for himself, Michael found it hard to believe. He looked back up at Anderson. "Are we at a dead end, then?"

"Not necessarily. Since I was stymied working through the usual channels, I decided to try a different tack. I thought I'd see if we could find anyone who knew him personally."

"I had thought of that," Michael said, "but I haven't had time to begin looking."

"You might not have been successful, even if you had," Anderson replied. "It's difficult to find someone willing to talk to a complete stranger about a man who disappeared under mysterious circumstances nearly twenty years ago."

"You make it sound as though they might have something to hide."

"I did sense there were things the men at the insurance company were purposefully *not* divulging. So I asked an agent of ours in Plymouth to do some poking around. He's known and respected by the seamen there. He found a man, a former employee with my company, who was a friend of Paul Bernay. His name is Charlie Stains. He's long retired from sailing, but he helps run a home for old and invalid sailors."

"Is he willing to talk to me?"

"I sent him a letter stating that we are doing personal research on behalf of Bernay's children. He wrote back that he'd be willing to meet with you, although he can't say how much he'll know."

"Sounds like a circumspect fellow."

"Perhaps he is wise to be so." Anderson pulled out a piece of paper and handed it to Michael. "Here's his address. He also noted that he spends afternoons with other retired men at the tavern on the same street, and that's the easiest way to find him."

Michael accepted the letter, reading it briefly before carefully placing it in his coat pocket. "I can't tell you how grateful I am for your help."

"You're quite welcome. I hope the information will be useful in tracking down just what happened." As he walked Michael to the door, Anderson said, "By the way, I just received a note from my wife with news you might be interested in. The results of the university matriculation exam were posted this morning. That tutoring scheme was a complete success."

Michael could not keep himself from grinning. To know there was hope for the school and a possible lead on Julia's father were very good things, but the news that Julia had passed the exam was the best thing he'd heard today.

Julia stood looking at the long list of names posted on the board in the university's administration building. More specifically, she was reading her own name, which she'd found among those in the first division. The passing scores were divided into categories of honors, first, and second. Although Julia's scores had not been high enough for the honors division and the prizes, being among those in the first was a noteworthy achievement. She would receive a full report later, but for now it was enough to know that she must have done well in all subjects—including Latin—in order to make this grade.

"We will scrape by somehow, eh?" said Lisette, whose name was posted a few lines below Julia's. "There are more prizes awarded after the first year. We'll aim for that!"

"Yes, we will," Julia answered.

She would take one hurdle at a time, living as simply as she could to stretch the money she had left. God had brought her this far. He would not fail to provide in the future.

"We shall have a big celebration tonight!" Lisette took her arm as they walked away from the board, making room for the others eagerly searching out their standings.

"It will have to be a simple celebration," Julia countered. "We're saving our pennies, remember?"

"Ah, but this is the best kind—free! Have you read in the newspapers about the big comet? It will be visible for the next few nights. A group of us is going to Hyde Park tonight to see it."

Julia had read about the comet. It was a once-in-a-lifetime opportunity to view one of the wonders of the heavens. "Yes," she said, nodding in agreement, "that is the very best way to celebrate."

She would spend tonight admiring the handiwork of the One in whom she trusted.

The comet was every bit as spectacular as the newspapers had predicted. Its *coma*, or head, was bright, facing downward toward the earth; its long tail stretched upward in what looked like twin streams crossing the night sky. All around him on the viscount's yacht, Michael heard exclamations of wonder, along with laughter as the guests tried to out-do each other in finding grand enough words to describe it.

To these sounds were added the pop of a cork as Delaford opened yet another bottle of champagne. For this night of comet watching, he had invited thirty or so guests whom he'd described to Michael as his favorite people. They came from an interestingly wide section of society, from members of the aristocracy and their less noble cousins, to prominent businessmen, writers, and artists. One elderly artist sat in a cushioned chair, sketching the night sky and exclaiming that he hadn't seen anything this wonderful since the comet of '53.

All of London was outside tonight. Many had come to the Thames in search of the best view. The river was nearly choked with traffic, and crowds lined the Embankment. From his vantage point on the river, Michael could see that the rooftop terrace of the Palace of Westminster was filled with comet-watchers. One had to be a member of Parliament or the House of Lords to gain access to that prime location. The viscount might have gone there tonight, but this party with friends had evidently suited him better.

Michael stood at the railing, a little apart from the other guests. The viscount approached him, carrying two glasses of champagne. He extended one to Michael. "You seem quiet tonight, Stephenson. I hope you are not one of those morose fellows who thinks a comet is an evil portent."

"Not at all," Michael responded truthfully.

He had been thinking of Julia. After his meeting with Jamie Anderson, he'd gone to the university to view the posted results himself. He'd done so at the risk—or hope?—of running into her, but she had not been there. He had read her name, listed with those who'd taken firsts, as proudly as if he'd been her tutor for years and not just a few months.

Was she outside tonight, viewing this natural wonder? If so, he was certain she'd be thinking of the Creator who had made the universe and everything in it. She would be celebrating her great achievement. Michael wished he could be celebrating with her. He also wanted to tell her about the new work he'd taken on. The trials for Myrtle and Gwen would take place next week, and he would be representing them. Gwen particularly impressed him with her humility and her zeal to "live right," as she'd put it, when she got out of prison. He knew Julia would be overjoyed to hear it.

He accepted the glass from Delaford, then motioned toward the comet. "I suppose the sight has left me a bit speechless."

"Speechless? An amazing thing for a barrister!" Delaford laughed. "Whereas they are finding too many words." He indicated the other guests, who were still coming up with extravagantly redundant phrases. *A luminous band of silver lighting the heavens!*

Laura was among them, sipping champagne and occasionally taking a petit four from the table laden with food and drink. Clustered around her were members of London's young and fashionable set. The viscount, indulgent brother that he was, had allowed her to invite her own friends. These included the Browne siblings. Ever since he'd met them at the theatre, Michael had noticed them cropping up at many social events.

Arthur Browne was filling everyone's glasses with champagne. As Laura extended her glass for a refill, she noticed Michael looking at her. She fluttered her lashes, as though hoping to draw him to the group. Michael smiled in return, trying to send the message that he would join her soon.

"Laura has been having her fun this Season," Michael said, hearkening back to the conversation he and the viscount had had last March. So long ago, it now seemed.

"Yes, and she's even had a comet-watching party! Who could have predicted that?" Delaford took a sip of his champagne. "However, I think it is time to settle her future. Over these weeks, she has caught the eye of many gentlemen, but if you still wish to offer for her, I will not hesitate to give my permission. You will have to talk to her first, of course."

"Yes, I intend to do that soon."

Michael had been putting off the conversation, although he knew it was not fair to her. With every passing day, he found it more difficult to consider marrying her. He'd spent plenty of time with her, attending social events, doing his best to recapture the commitment he'd once had to this match. All to no avail.

He could not stop thinking that things between him and Julia were not yet settled. He had sent several messages to the Earl of Westbridge, requesting a private interview, for he could do nothing until he knew his actions would not hurt Corinna or David. But the earl had retreated to his estate after the trial and had not been seen since. He communicated with Tamblin and Michael regarding legal matters via letters written by a private secretary, but he had not responded to Michael's personal notes.

But even if Michael knew he'd never see Julia again, did it follow that he'd marry Laura? Was he being the worst kind of hypocrite, keeping Laura on a string as some kind of backup measure? That made him unworthy of any woman, and he was disgusted with himself.

"I will speak with her soon," he repeated. But this time, he knew what he would say.

Julia was glad she had come out tonight. Hyde Park was alive with people, despite the lateness of the hour. Standing next to the friends she'd made over the past year, Julia felt truly blessed. She gazed up with wonder. The comet was brighter and far more dramatic than she'd anticipated.

The heavens declare the glory of God, and the firmament showeth his handiwork.

Nearby, Colleen was chatting with Lisette. "Some say the comet is an ill omen. Perhaps some terrible calamity is about to happen."

"Well, it won't happen to us," Lisette answered stoutly. "Today is a day for *good* news. Julia and I are on our way to medical school."

"If it doesn't fold," Colleen said darkly.

Lisette continued as if she hadn't heard. "I also learned today that Dr. Tierney will be moving to America. There's a rumor the Royal Free Hospital stipulated she must leave the school or they won't allow clinical privileges to the students. But I think Dr. Tierney was planning to leave anyway. I heard she wants to go somewhere more democratic. She's fed up with the way the aristocracy runs this country."

Julia cringed, knowing Edith heard this remark.

But Edith merely said, "I hear the libel laws are more lax in America, too. That should help keep her out of trouble." Her voice dripped with sarcasm. Although publicly Edith had blamed her father for the lawsuit and sided with the school, her dislike of Dr. Tierney was palpable. Her stated reason was that the doctor's manner toward patients was too abrasive, but Julia suspected that Edith was also offended by the things Dr. Tierney had said about her family.

Julia pulled Edith aside so they could speak without being overheard by the others. "How is your father?"

Edith looked at her like she was daft. "How should I know?"

"I hoped you two might make up, now that the trial is over."

"You think I would go to him now?" Edith said indignantly.

"Now that he has won the suit and the school is scrambling to survive?"

"It's just that he didn't look well at the trial. Aren't you the least bit worried about him?"

Her question hung in the air for a fraction too long. Just long enough for Julia to see the same look of distress that had crossed Edith's face when her father had been ailing on the first day of the trial. A look that contradicted her cold response. "My father has made his choices in life, and I have made mine."

Julia said no more on the subject, but even after they'd rejoined the others and everyone's attention was once more on the comet, she was still thinking about it. It was true that father and daughter had each made their own choices. But in Julia's mind was born an idea to see if she could help them make some better ones.

Two days later, on a Sunday afternoon, Julia walked the road to the Westbridge estate. It was more familiar this time around. She prayed that her note, which ought to have reached Edith this morning, would have the desired effect.

Today the sky was clear, and the afternoon sun was hot. Dust billowed in the wind. She dawdled a little as she got closer to the main entrance of the estate, assuming Edith would have hired a dogcart at the station. Hesitating over whether to start up the drive, she looked to see if any vehicle was coming down the road.

She was almost too late. Edith had apparently not taken the train at all but hired a private coach directly from London. Afraid Edith might not enter the estate if she could stop Julia from doing so, Julia broke into an unladylike run. It wasn't easy, but at least her practical skirt was not as restrictive as the more fashionable gowns.

Julia was still about fifty yards from the house when the carriage caught up to her.

Edith stuck her head out the carriage window. "Stop!" she commanded.

Julia did not stop.

Edith repeated the command, more forcefully this time.

By now they had reached the final sweep of the drive to the arched front steps of the mansion. They had also attracted the attention of a gray-haired gardener and his young helper, who stood up from the flower bed where they'd been working and stared at them in surprise. An old dog lounging near them began barking at the carriage, though he seemed too old or well-trained to chase it.

Today there was no need to knock, as their approach had been anything but quiet. The large door opened, and both a footman and a maid raced out to see what had caused the commotion.

Satisfied there was no way for Edith to back out now, Julia stopped to catch her breath, wiping her brow. She looked up to see a face appear at the second-story window. It was the earl's.

It quickly disappeared as Edith got out of the carriage and stalked over to Julia. "What do you think you're doing? I told you that you have no right to interfere in my life."

"It's for your own good," Julia assured her.

"And just how will I be edified by listening to my father gloat in triumph, convinced that I've come back to beg for forgiveness?"

"Nonsense. He'll be overjoyed to see you. Just wait and see."

They didn't have long to wait. The old man walked out the door and stood at the balustrade, scowling at them. "I see you have finally admitted defeat. I knew you'd be back."

Edith balled her fists, preparing for an equally biting retort. Julia said quickly, "With all due respect, my lord, you knew nothing of the kind. You thought Edith was gone from you, and you were brokenhearted at the loss."

"What are you doing here?" the earl bellowed. "I had you removed from my grounds once before, and I'll be happy to do it again."

"But I brought your daughter to you, sir. She didn't want to come, but I told her you miss her as much as she misses you. After all, the two of you are all you have left."

"I came because I knew Julia would spout all kinds of lies about me," Edith said. "You won't have to kick her off your property, because we are both going."

She took hold of Julia's arm, as if she fully intended to drag her to the carriage.

"Well, good riddance to both of you!" the earl exclaimed. "I can see you want to continue spending your time with hoydens"—he waved his cane at Julia—"and people who slander our family. Well then, go right ahead. It's clear to me that I haven't got a daughter anymore."

Julia dug her heels in, refusing to budge. "That's all you want, isn't it? You don't care if Edith becomes a doctor. In fact, you're secretly proud that she has shown herself so clever and diligent that she could succeed in a man's profession. You only fear that she will leave you alone. You're afraid of dying alone. Especially now that your rheumatism has gotten worse."

"Will you stop talking!" The earl shook his cane at her, but this unbalanced him. He teetered to one side and would have fallen had not the footman and maid been there to catch him.

"Father!" Edith cried, racing toward the steps.

The earl regained his balance, although he didn't look entirely steady. He was still a forceful man, though, and his glare stopped his daughter halfway up the steps. "Don't come to me now," he warned. "Not if you plan to go away again. I will not stand for it."

It was delivered as an order, but as the words died away, his expression as he looked at his daughter, standing just a few feet from him, belied the harshness of it.

Edith saw it, too. "If I thought anything that Julia said just now was true . . ."

The hesitation in her voice was plain. It could not have been easy to open herself to the possibility of further attacks from her father. Julia had seen Edith's fearlessness before, as she went to the rougher parts of London to help people from all walks of life. Even in the way she tangled with the male doctors who would not listen to her suggestions. But what Edith was doing right now was perhaps braver than any of those things.

Julia held her breath, silently praying. The maid, footman, and gardeners also watched with intense interest. They must have been hoping for the same outcome Julia was, for each of them looked at Edith with warmth and sympathy. Even the dog, whom the gardener held unnecessarily by the collar, stood quietly, his head cocked.

The earl shifted a little, clearing his throat and readjusting his hold on his cane, although his eyes never left his daughter. "You are too much like me for your own good, my girl. Clever and pigheaded and proud—"

"Do you really think I'm clever?" Edith's interruption, and the vulnerable tone in her voice, showed she was willing to keep pressing at this tiny crack in her father's armor.

"I always thought you deserved to inherit the earldom more than John. I knew you'd do a far better job of it."

"I think that's the most wonderful thing you've ever said to me."

"Edith."

It was one word, but it came out with such tenderness that Julia felt tears moistening her eyes.

A split second later, the daughter was enveloped in her father's arms.

I N THE END, IT WAS NEARLY TWO WEEKS BEFORE Michael was able to arrange his affairs to allow for a few days away from London. He still hadn't talked to Laura. She had not made it any easier, for she seemed constantly engaged. This wasn't surprising, because the Season was at its height, and Michael decided that could wait. He wanted to get to Plymouth and speak to Charlie Stains about Julia's father.

The night before he left, he reviewed his copy of Bradshaw's railway timetable to double-check the departure time. He looked at the map and the calling points along the way to Plymouth. He could spare only two days away from his practice, but he realized he could take a short side trip to the town nearest the earl's estate. He decided it was time to see him face-to-face—even without an invitation. He was spurred on by his memory of how Julia had, amazingly, somehow done the same. Her example gave him inspiration and reproof in equal measures. He'd never in his life hesitated to chase what he wanted, and he'd be the world's worst fool if he let Julia be the one exception.

He had to know if he could reason with the earl. After all, now that the trial was over and the earl had officially won, what harm could come to his lordship if Michael and Julia wished to be together? Michael didn't know if he could persuade Julia to stay in England. All he wanted was a chance to try, and he would make the most of it.

And so, two hours after setting out from Paddington, Michael alighted from a trap he'd hired at the station near the earl's estate and walked up the steps to his lordship's wide front door.

Outside, everything appeared calm and serene, but when a footman opened the door before Michael could even ring, Michael could see that inside, the house was in an uproar.

"I beg your pardon, sir," said the footman. "I heard the carriage and thought it was Dr. Adams arriving."

Behind him, two maids scurried up the stairs carrying towels and tea and hot water. The butler passed them on the stairs, coming down just as rapidly.

Michael extended his card to the footman. "I came in hopes of speaking with his lordship."

"I'm afraid that's not possible," the butler said, reaching the door in time to hear Michael's words. "His lordship has fallen ill."

Michael heard a carriage making its way up the gravel drive. It had barely come to a halt when the door was flung open and the doctor jumped out, medical bag in hand. He took the steps two at a time to the door, giving a passing nod to Michael before he and the butler, by unspoken consent, hurried together up the stairs.

Michael was still mulling over the situation as he walked along the waterfront in Plymouth. Whatever was going on with the earl was clearly serious. Would he recover? If so, how long would it take? Michael regretted that he'd waited so long to see him, even though he didn't know how he could possibly have come sooner. It had been hard enough to spare these days as it was. He would just have to focus on the task at hand, which was to help Julia. She always spoke of trusting God for the next thing. Michael didn't know that he truly had that kind of confidence, but he would do his best.

The harbor was a busy place: pleasure yachts, military ships, and small fishing boats all jockeyed for position. Following the directions he'd been given by a helpful costermonger, Michael continued past a rope-maker's shop, looking for the Nine Bridges Tavern. He found it just past the fish stalls, on the corner of the harbor street and a narrow cobbled lane. Pulling open the weathered door, he went inside.

Two old men sat at the bar, talking with the tavern keeper, who was wiping down the counter. They had the lined and leathery faces of men who'd spent a life at sea.

"Is one of you by chance Mr. Stains?" Michael asked.

"Aye, that would be me," said one of the grizzled gentlemen. "But you can call me Charlie. You must be the man from London they said would be coming my way."

"Yes. My name is Michael Stephenson."

"How do you do?" Charlie extended a hand, and Michael shook it. The old sailor's hand was dry and callused from years of handling heavy ropes.

"I want to ask you some questions about Paul Bernay. I understand you knew him fairly well?"

"Now there's a name I haven't heard in a long time," the other man said. His look hardened to suspicion. "Why do you want to ask about him?"

"He's a friend, I think, Joe," Charlie reassured him. "Mr. Stephenson, suppose we take a walk? My creaky old bones could use some exercise."

Michael readily agreed. The tavern was small and dark, and it was clear they could not have a private conversation here.

They went outside and began walking along the harbor. "How are the girls?" Charlie asked. "Last I saw of them, they was just little things. Rozzie, the oldest, was only nine."

"All have grown to be fine women."

"I knew they'd be treated well at that orphanage. It had a good reputation, you know. The best possible, although it can't be rosy for any child to grow up without parents."

"That's true," Michael agreed.

"I wasn't here when their mother died. I was in the Indian Ocean with the P&O Steamship Company. It was my daughter, Lydia, who decided to take them to the orphanage. She was only nineteen at the time and worked day and night as a laundress. She knew she couldn't keep them, so she was determined to get them to the orphanage."

"Julia tells me her father was a ship captain, but the records indicate he was second officer."

Charlie nodded. "Their mother told them he was a captain."

"Why would she do that?"

"Marie was a lovely, kindhearted woman, but her head was always in the clouds. I think she was always spinning tales in her mind about Paul's prospects and what kind of life they'd all lead when he'd earned enough to be done with the sea for good."

Michael could see where some of Cara's personality came from. "I'm surprised no one ever told the girls the truth."

"Lydia thought she was doing them a favor by continuing the lie. She didn't think it would matter to the children whether their father had been captain or an officer. She was more worried they'd be heartbroken to know their mother had lied to them."

Michael thought she'd been wrong to do so, but he didn't want to put Charlie off by speaking ill of his daughter. "It was a kind sentiment."

"It's too bad he wasn't a captain. Mighta kept that ship from goin' down. I can tell you he didn't like his captain. Not many people did. He was a harsh commander."

"Julia has a memory from the last time she saw her father that I'd like to ask you about." He told Charlie the story Julia had related about the incident at the tavern. "Do you have any idea what the men might have been talking about?"

"Perhaps. Ah, here's one of my favorite places for watching the ships. Shall we go up there?"

They had reached the end of the harbor street, and ahead was a short path up a grassy hill. Charlie took the path with more agility than Michael would have expected. At the top of the hill, there was indeed an excellent view of the sea.

"A good place to be alone with one's thoughts," Charlie said. "Or to speak confidentially. Mr. Stephenson, I have a theory that Paul never went down with that ship. It's just bits and pieces I've put together from things I've heard over the years. Helping out as I do at the home for retired seamen, I hear a lot of stories. I can't say that any of my guesses are correct."

"Even so, I'd love to hear them."

"What first started me thinking Paul might be alive was a story I heard about an Englishman who lives in La Guaira—that's the port town near Caracas, Venezuela. The sailor who told me about him said the man is not 'all there' mentally. He spends his days at a tavern, playing checkers—that's our draughts, don't you know—with anyone who will humor him. Paul was an avid draughts player. The physical description sounded like Paul, including a burn scar on the left side of his face and neck from a gunnery accident. The woman who takes care of him says she's his wife. He goes by Pablo—the Spanish version of Paul—but everyone knows he is English. I began to think maybe this fellow is Paul Bernay. But perhaps you think that is too outlandish to be believed."

"I won't discount anything at this point," Michael said. "My first task is just to collect any information that I can."

"I heard one thing about that ship that would explain how it was so far off course when it went down. Some say the ship was involved in illegal activities. It was during the American Civil War, and Paul's ship mighta done some gunrunning for the South. I don't think Paul would have willingly gone along with that, but maybe he didn't have a choice."

"If the man in La Guaira is Paul Bernay, do you have any idea how he might have ended up there?"

Charlie scratched his grizzled chin. "That's the part I can't figure out. Especially as the ship would have been much farther north if it went down in that hurricane like everyone said. The gunrunning would explain that, but not how Paul got to La Guaira. It's a conundrum, ain't it?"

It certainly was.

"I'd sure like to know if I'm right," Charlie continued, "but I don't have any way of finding out. Perhaps someone who is younger and has the money could go to South America and discover the truth?"

"It might well be worth sending someone there," Michael agreed.

"I can't tell you how happy that would make me. I've often thought of those beautiful little girls. My own wife died when my daughter was young, but at least we had each other."

"The sisters became close, although they are very different from one another."

"They were then, too. Is Julia still the bossy one?"

Michael couldn't help but laugh, even though the remark made him miss her more than ever. "Yes, I believe she is."

"And how is it you're here? Are you a particular friend of Julia's?"

"I'm here as a legal adviser."

"Oh. I thought perhaps you had a more personal reason for doing this."

Michael only shrugged, not willing to say more.

"Look at me, being an old romantic," Charlie said, laughing at himself. "Well, Mr. Stephenson, I hope you find what you're looking for."

The long train ride back from Plymouth might have taken a mere five minutes, for all that Michael was aware. His mind was busy reviewing what he'd just learned.

There was a chance Paul Bernay was actually alive. But crossing the ocean to investigate the possibility was no small matter. Such a trip would require at least a month, considering there was a week or more of travel time each way, plus the days spent on land. The costs, too, would be greater than the Bernay sisters could afford. And even if they could, there was always the chance that the trip would yield nothing except further heartache from dashed hopes if the man were not their father. But what if this trip ultimately united a father with his daughters? There could not be a price put on that.

It was after eight in the evening when the train pulled in to London. Michael was hungry but decided to have a cold dinner at his chambers rather than to go to his club. He was not in the mood to interact with anyone just now.

When the cab pulled in to the courtyard of his building, Michael was surprised to see David's carriage standing there. He wasn't expecting a call from his brother-in-law.

David immediately got out of his carriage, waiting with a worried expression until Michael had paid the cabman and the cab had driven off.

"Is everything all right?" Michael asked. "Is something wrong with Corinna?"

"She's fine—at least as far as the baby is concerned. But she's very put out with you. You promised to dine at our house two nights ago. She was worried when you didn't come. She's written to you several times since then and became positively distressed when she got no answer."

At times, Corinna's constant efforts to direct his life were too overbearing. Now she was even sending David to check on him. He said in exasperation, "I went to Plymouth. I had business to attend to there. My apologies for missing what I'm sure was a lovely dinner, but my mind has been on other things."

"It's not just the dinner. Have you forgotten what day it is? Tonight is Lady Amberley's ball."

Michael let out a groan. Now he realized the reason for David's worry. Corinna was unable to go because of her advanced pregnancy, but for months she'd fervently hoped this would be the night Michael and Laura announced their engagement. She had done everything in her power to make it happen. But by now, Michael knew this wish of Corinna's would not be fulfilled.

"Corinna asked me to come by and see if anything was the matter. I learned from your manservant that you were out of town and not expected back until this evening." David looked at Michael anxiously. "You are going to the ball, aren't you?"

"I'm not even dressed, as you can see. I've just gotten off the train."

"There's still time. Nothing of import happens in the first two hours anyway."

"I will go, but the evening will not turn out as Corinna has been hoping for."

David grimaced, and Michael knew it was a show of disappointment on his wife's behalf. "If I get you there, I will at least have done my duty. Beyond that, it is up to you."

They went inside, and Michael left David to have a smoke and read the newspaper while he changed into clothing suitable for the grand ball.

No, this night would not end as Corinna had dreamed. Michael ought to have warned her sooner, but he had not been able to bring himself to do it. But he knew he had to go; he owed Corinna that much.

From the moment the carriage drew near the Amberleys' mansion, Michael could see that the ball was going to live up to its reputation for grandeur. Lights spilled from every window, vying with the lanterns lining the drive. There was a line of carriages dropping off guests. Michael and David were not the only latecomers.

Inside the house, all was sparkling opulence. Flowers were everywhere in ostentatious displays. Attendants collected their hats and gloves and directed them toward the ballroom.

Michael entered the fray with a heavy feeling in his stomach. This was supposed to be the crowning night of the Season, and yet he could not foresee it ending well.

Michael recognized perhaps half the faces in the crowd. This was a larger number than he would have known even a year ago. His growing acceptance by society had enlarged his circle of acquaintances considerably. He had seen an increase in warmth toward him in the days since the trial. Tonight, however, he had the impression people were looking at him oddly. Smirking, almost.

"I have a distinct feeling that something is up—do you?" David asked.

"Yes, I was just thinking the same thing."

At last he spotted Laura. She stood in a little group that consisted of her brother as well as the Brownes.

Arthur Browne was speaking, and Laura's smile was wide—broader and more natural than Michael had ever seen. It had the effect of making her even prettier. He half-wondered why he hadn't seen that smile before. It must take more skill to draw it out than he had. With Julia, it had been easy to coax a smile. In fact, it had often come when he'd least expected it, such as when he was correcting her Latin or rebuking her in some other way.

His approach seemed to throw a pall over the group. Browne interrupted himself in midsentence. Laura's smile took on a different, somehow harder appearance.

The viscount came to Michael's side. "I'm sorry to say you are too late, Stephenson. I did try to reach you but was told you were out of town."

Too late?

Browne patted Laura's hand, and as she looked up at him, her smile lost the frostiness it had taken on at Michael's arrival.

The Brownes wore expressions of such self-satisfied smugness that the analogy of cats and canaries seemed wholly appropriate. Michael looked at Laura again, noticing now the way her arm was linked through Browne's. A surprising and interesting suspicion came into his mind, immediately followed by a sensation that somehow tied together astonishment, disbelief, and relief.

Delaford said, "If you had come earlier, you would not have missed the big announcement. My sister and Mr. Browne are engaged."

Ha ow could you do this to me?!" Corinna moved around the room in agitation. She wasn't exactly pacing, as her large belly prohibited that, but she was doing the best approximation possible.

Michael had braced himself for this reaction. If it was more intense than he'd expected, he could only blame it on the heightened emotions of pregnancy.

"Please calm yourself, my love," David urged. "You'll wear yourself out." He went to the sideboard. "Let me get you some water."

Corinna didn't even seem to hear him. She advanced on Michael, poking him in the chest. "How could you throw away all of the plans we had in place?"

"Her sudden engagement took me by surprise, but perhaps it is for the best that I don't marry her."

"Why? What's wrong with her?"

"Nothing! It's just that I don't love her. Shouldn't that count for something?"

As soon as he'd spoken, he knew that had been the wrong thing to say.

"*Love?*" she repeated, her voice shrill. "I don't recall that being an issue before. In fact, you seemed quite content at the prospect of marrying Laura. At least until that accident." She nodded, wagging her finger at him. "That woman got to you. Is that where you were these last few days—off gallivanting somewhere with *her?* Is that why you didn't even have the decency to tell me you were going away?"

She was speaking for all the world like a cheated wife.

"No, I was not with Julia. I won't be seeing her again."

"No? What's stopping you?" Now Corinna appeared just as suspicious in the other direction.

"What do you care?" he shot back.

This attack did not fluster her in the least. "You're right. I don't care. But I *do* care that you have thrown away your chance to marry Laura Maynard. If waiting for love had held *me* back, where do you think either of us would be today? Certainly not in this house, with you in a thriving career and us on the verge of regaining everything our father threw away."

It was the baldest statement she'd ever made, voicing that she'd considered her own marriage as one of convenience and nothing more.

David generally took Corinna's bouts of temper with un-quenchable grace. But this time, the raw selfishness on display, the truth that she'd seen David as a stopgap from ruin and nothing more, finally broke through his normally unflappable exterior. His hands shook as he set down the glass he'd been about to bring her.

Michael thought that, pregnant or not, Corinna deserved any stinging rebuke David could throw at her. But without a word or further look at her, David left the room.

"Now look what you've done!" Corinna accused.

"No. You will not lay the blame for that at my feet. Have you not even one ounce of thankfulness in your heart for that man? He has given you all this"—Michael motioned to the riches all around them—"but you treat it as some kind of birthright and heap contempt on him in the bargain. One day he may very well tire of such treatment, and then where will you be?"

She took hold of his sleeve. "I did it for you! Don't you have any thankfulness for *me?*" She spoke accusingly, but tears began to well in her eyes. "Everything I did was so that you could succeed. So that you would not live your life as a middle-class clerk. But you have no gratitude for me!"

For all of his aptitude at debate in the courtroom, Michael could find nothing to say. No rebuttal or explanation. Anger, guilt, and sorrow threatened to suffocate him, leaving him desperate for air. He turned and walked toward the parlor door, following in David's footsteps.

"Yes, why don't you just go away, too!" Corinna shouted at his back. "You don't care a whit about the sacrifices I've made!"

Michael did not pause.

But as he reached for the door, Corinna said, "Yes, I have all this. But you have something I don't have and have *never* had—the freedom to choose."

The desolation in her words lodged in his heart—exactly as she'd meant them to. Tears stained her face now, from rage or sorrow. Or both.

Michael couldn't bear to see it. He went out, shutting the door behind him.

To his surprise, David had not gone far. He was slumped on a bench in the hallway, head in hands, the picture of utter dejection.

Michael sat down next to him. "Please don't take her words to heart. Corinna is overly emotional right now."

David shrugged off the attempt at consolation. "She only said out loud what we all knew already. She married me out of sheer desperation—and self-preservation. I knew it even then. But I thought that given time, if I kept loving her every way I knew how, she would grow to love me, too." He took out a handkerchief, wiping his forehead and, Michael thought, using the action to take a stealthy swipe at tears. "I'm finally ready to admit it was a foolish hope all along. I've been nothing but a simple, lovestruck idiot."

"I'm appalled by my sister's actions and heartily ashamed for having fostered this. You are the best, most decent person I know. She doesn't deserve you."

The compliment glanced off his brother-in-law. "I kept repeating this Bible verse: 'Husbands, love your wives, and be not bitter against them.' I had this idea that if I kept saying it, kept trying to live it, that eventually, one day, the tide would turn." He shook his head. "But it wasn't enough."

"You have nothing to blame yourself for."

David sighed and continued speaking. "Even now, I suppose I ought to be, I don't know, storming out of the house or something. But I can't leave her. Not when I know she is ill. She has been having cramps and nausea, did you know?"

"No," said Michael, more ashamed than ever. Although to be fair, his sister always put up a strong front, refusing to show any kind of weakness.

Not that he'd given her much of his attention lately. In fact, he'd been avoiding coming here as much as possible. He'd used the excuse of allowing her to rest as the time for giving birth drew near, but really, it had been to keep from discussing Laura or his future plans.

"I still love her—and my child, who will soon be born. I love them both." David's words had a tender poignancy after all that had happened.

From the parlor, Corinna give a shriek of pain. Instantly they leapt to their feet and raced inside.

Corinna was doubled over, clinging to a chair with one hand and clutching her stomach with the other. "Please," she gasped, "get the doctor."

"I'm dying, you know."

The earl's words were slurred, but his bright, piercing gaze as he looked at Julia and Edith showed his mind was clear.

Edith had moved back home with her father, planning to stay with him at least through September. When Julia had arranged last week to visit them this afternoon, no one could have anticipated she'd be arriving just a few days after he'd suffered an apoplectic seizure. His current condition was stable, although his left side was partially paralyzed. This caused him endless agitation. He made a sound of frustration as he tried to sit up in bed with only one functioning arm to push himself up.

"You always did have a penchant for morbid exaggeration, Father," Edith chided as she helped him to the position he was seeking.

"And you're always trying to contradict me," the earl rasped. "With all your medical knowledge, you know what I'm saying is true." He pointed an accusatory finger at her. "*And* as a doctor, you would not hesitate to tell me plainly."

Edith gave the pillows behind his back one last tug into place, then straightened and crossed her arms. "I'm sure you don't address Dr. Adams in this fashion."

"Actually, I think he does," Julia interjected, remembering the first day of the trial, when his lordship was barking orders at his physician.

"And you are both straying from the point—which is an un-professional and, I might add, *womanly* thing to do."

Edith threw a quick glance heavenward. "You know we are doing everything we can for you, Father."

This was true. They had just spent several hours giving him the best therapy known for his condition. They'd bathed his hands and feet in warm water, and, returning him to his bed, had placed warm bottles of water at his arms and feet. These measures helped keep the blood flowing to his extremities. To ease the pain of the rheumatism, Edith had applied more of the liniment Julia had recommended to the earl at their first meeting. Stubborn as he was, he had ignored her suggestion. It wasn't until Edith came to live with him and personally oversee his care that he'd agreed to give it a try.

Now that he was back in bed, he seemed more comfortable, if tired from submitting to all their attentions. He leaned back on the pillows, his eyes closing briefly. His right hand clutched the blanket. "Everything you can," he repeated, muttering under his breath. "It will be little enough in the end. Not even the best doctors can prevent the ultimate outcome."

The earl seemed to be a very different person since the rec-onciliation with Edith. It was as though his anger and deter-mination to pursue the lawsuit had been driving him, keeping him going despite his many physical ailments. Now there was nothing left to fight for. The stroke had been a further blow to his already frail health. Although clearly content to have his daughter back in his life again, the earl's demeanor had taken on an air of melancholy resignation. Julia had seen this before in elderly patients who had a sense, whether rightly or wrongly, that death was drawing near.

"That is a long way off," Edith insisted, tucking the blankets around his feet with more vigor than necessary. She turned to the nearby table where the medicines were set out and began to mix up a tonic for pain. Her movements were agitated and clumsy, nearly toppling one of the bottles. An indication of how much the idea of her father's death troubled her.

"She's right, sir," Julia said, both for Edith's sake as well as the earl's. "You are not done tormenting us yet." One thing she'd seen over these past few hours was that his lordship could be roused from moroseness by challenging words and jibes. His irascible nature fed on it.

He grunted in response. "Impertinent chit. Why do I put up with this?"

But he spoke halfheartedly, and Julia could see that this time, her efforts to galvanize him had failed. She sobered. "Sir, remember that, when that time does come, it will be a temporal end only. There is a greater destination—"

"Don't talk metaphysics!" the earl cut her off sharply. "I'm sure I will never get into that glorious heaven of which everyone speaks. Assuming it's even real."

"Father, how can you talk that way?" Edith admonished.

The earl didn't answer, only glared at the two of them. Julia was tempted to think she ought not to have brought up the subject, but how could she leave a person doubting God's salvation if she could help them?

"That is why we have a savior," Julia said. "If it were up to man to save himself, no one would make it. But God's love and grace is extended to all who will accept it."

Edith brought the tonic to her father's side. "Here, Father, drink this."

He waved away the glass, his attention still on Julia. He reached out with his good arm and took her hand. His grip was surprisingly strong, given his weakened state. "Are you saying you don't think I'm a lost cause?"

Julia nodded. "With God, there is no such thing."

He let go her hand. "You are being remarkably kind, considering . . ." His voice trailed off.

"Considering how you're always yelling at me?" Julia supplied with a smile, still hoping to raise his spirits.

He didn't answer. Edith offered the tonic again, and this time he accepted it. When he was done drinking, he fell back against the pillows, closing his eyes. It wouldn't be long before the medicine would cause him to doze off.

"Ah, well, I suppose the rest of it doesn't matter," he murmured, "since you're too busy saving the world."

"I don't understand. What doesn't matter?"

"Julia, let him rest," Edith said. "Don't press him."

But the earl wasn't done yet. "I told Stephenson he must never see you again."

"What?" Julia stared at him in shock. "Why?"

"It was a conflict of interest, of course! I couldn't have you trying to influence him, trying to win him over. Are you saying you didn't know?"

"No." Julia felt numb. She'd thought Michael had stopped seeing her of his own volition. He'd mentioned something about doing it for his family. Had he really just been bowing to this man's whims? No matter how powerful the earl was, surely Michael would not give in so easily. "I can't believe he agreed to that."

"He had his reasons. Those are not for me to divulge. Perhaps he will tell you, if you ask him." He eyed her. "Perhaps you don't think so well of me now. Will you revise your previous statement about those who are beyond hope?"

Julia swallowed, unable to speak, her mouth dry as cotton.

"I do not regret that lawsuit, if for no other reason than that woman Tierney is leaving the country!" He leaned forward, speaking with ferocity and shaking his fist. "What she said about my son was inexcusable! It was proven in a court of law!"

"Father, please!" Edith cried, urging him back down again. "You will bring more harm to yourself."

The earl leaned back, panting heavily from his exertion. He continued on, however, despite gasping for breath and perhaps fighting the sedating effects of the tonic. "I'm grateful to you, Miss Bernay. . . . You brought my daughter back to me . . . in spite of everything. If I've hurt you in any way, I regret it."

Julia's head was swimming. The call to forgive was battling with a tide of anger rising up within her that this man had come between her and Michael. They had not been allowed to decide their future for themselves. He had exerted control over their lives for his own benefit.

"I do not revise my previous statement." They were hard words to say, but Julia said them anyway. Because she knew it was right.

They sat in narrow chairs that the servants had set up in the hallway just outside Corinna's room. Michael knew David felt as helpless as he did, both men aware they could be of no practical use whatsoever.

Hearing his sister's periodic cries had been tough enough for Michael; he could see how much harder it was for her husband. David grimaced in misery at the sounds of distress coming from the bedroom. "I was aware that women experienced some pain during this ordeal, but I had no idea. . . . I feel so guilty."

"She'll get through it," Michael assured him. "Dr. Hartman will see to that."

Hearing footsteps on the stairs, Michael looked over to see Janet, the head housemaid, coming up the steps with a young woman he didn't recognize. The woman was wringing her hands, face twisted with anxiety as she followed Janet up the hall. Before either of the men could ask what was happening, the two women slipped inside Corinna's room, closing the door behind them.

"What do you suppose that was about?" David said. "I wish she had asked permission before going in there."

Michael heard the frustration in his brother-in-law's voice. The servants generally gave precedence to Corinna and looked to her for orders. It seemed to be the case even now, when Corinna was in no position to direct anything.

David got up and opened the door, but had not gotten halfway in before Corinna shrieked, "Go AWAY! Get OUT!"

He immediately backed out, looking utterly despondent. "She hates me now. She merely tolerated me before, but now she really hates me."

Michael could think of nothing to say.

Not a minute later, Janet and the woman came out again, accompanied by Dr. Hartman. He had his doctor's bag in his hands.

"Wait, where are you going?" David asked him, even as the two women hurried away down the stairs. "My wife—"

"*Nooo!*" Corinna screamed. It came out long and agonizingly, but she'd been making similar calls over these hours, so it was impossible to tell exactly who or what she was addressing.

"What's going on?" David demanded.

Dr. Hartman gave him an apologetic smile. "This has turned out to be a busy time for birthing. Another client of mine, Mrs. Asquith, is also on the verge of giving birth. She is further along in the process than Mrs. Barker and, I've been told, having some complications. I must go to her straightaway."

"But Corinna! You can't just leave her! Listen to her!" David's voice rose as he spoke, his emotions ratcheted up by his wife's cries.

"Everything is fine," the doctor replied. "Sometimes with the

345

first birth, the woman is surprised by the intensity of the contractions. Mrs. Barker is merely vocalizing this as a way to deal with what she's experiencing."

Michael could easily believe this. It was probably the first time Corinna had been confronted with a situation she could not control. For a woman like her, it could be as frightening as the actual pains.

"The baby is in a good position," the doctor continued. "I see no signs of trouble. But it will likely be several more hours yet."

"Several more hours!" David looked horrified.

"I'm sure he knows what he's talking about," Michael said, wanting to calm David even though he felt the same panic at seeing the doctor about to leave.

"I should be back well before I am needed. In the meantime, Mrs. Taylor will be here to watch over things."

Mrs. Taylor was the midwife who'd been assisting Dr. Hartman. She seemed capable enough, but Michael knew his sister's confidence lay more in her trusted physician than with this woman she didn't know.

Dr. Hartman handed a piece of paper to David. "Here's the address where I'll be. It isn't far from here. You can send for me if Mrs. Taylor deems it necessary."

David still looked aghast but didn't argue. The doctor gave a few more reassurances and then left.

"I can't deny help to another woman, of course," David murmured, looking down at the paper before pocketing it. "But I can't help being worried, can I?"

Mrs. Taylor bustled out into the hallway. She was short but broad, and from what Michael had seen of her so far, she always moved briskly and with purpose—just as she was doing now.

"You're not leaving, too, are you?" David said in alarm.

She pulled up to look at him. "Oh no, sir. I'm here for the duration. I just need to give some directions to the maids." Seeing David glance anxiously at the door, she added, "Mrs. Barker will be fine for ten minutes."

This reassurance didn't seem to penetrate the fog of David's worry. "She will be all right, won't she?"

"Pay no attention to the noise she makes. Some women like to raise a fuss, that's all. Don't you worry, we'll get her sorted out. They generally come 'round when the moment is upon them." Though the midwife was apparently trustworthy and efficient, there wasn't much to recommend her in terms of bed-side manner.

She went on her way, and once again David and Michael were left alone with nothing to do but wait.

David slumped into a chair. "Am I worrying too much? Am I being foolish? I want only the best for her. Have we done all we can?"

"I've been running that same question through my mind, as well. I think we should call in another medical professional. Just to be sure."

David brightened at these words. "Who do you have in mind?"

"Julia Bernay."

He blinked. "Why her? Don't we risk—" He shook his head. "Things are bad enough now with me and Corinna. I don't want to think what she would do if word of my past got out."

"We'll have to be careful, but I think it can be done. Julia is trustworthy, and she has a lot of experience in maternity wards. Plus, if we were to bring another doctor here, it would look like we don't have confidence in Dr. Hartman."

These were all true, and Michael had a gut feeling that Julia should be here. But even without any of that, he was simply ach-ing to see her again.

Seeing that David was still shaking his head, Michael added,

"Most of all, Julia is unfailingly honest. If something is wrong, she'll tell us. And isn't that what we really want?"

"Yes, it is," David agreed. This last argument seemed to win him over. "But will she come?"

Michael had been wondering that, too. He could think of so many reasons why he didn't deserve it. But if she would come, he could also tell her what he'd learned about the man in Venezuela who might be her father. Perhaps that might in some way make up for the rest.

"I don't know," he answered honestly. "But we will try."

Julia sat in a chair by the parlor window at her lodgings, ostensibly reading but not seeing the words on the page. Lord Westbridge's revelation that he'd been the one to separate her and Michael had left Julia so appalled and shaken that she'd been unable to decide what to do. Since returning home yesterday, she'd done little but simmer in agitation. She wanted to go to Michael, to confront him. What were the *reasons* his lordship had spoken of? Did she even have a right to know? Would it matter anyway? It was probably too late. Michael seemed to have made peace with the situation. Colleen, avid reader of the society columns, had mentioned several times over the past weeks whenever Michael's name had appeared in conjunction with Laura Maynard's. She'd been following them with interest since the accident. Surely any day now she'd inform them all of Michael's engagement.

Colleen was in fact reading the papers now. From the table across the room, she squealed in astonishment. "Julia, you'll *never* guess!"

"What's the news?" she asked dully, already angry with herself for the tears forming in her eyes.

"Miss Laura Maynard is engaged—to Mr. Arthur Browne!"

"What?" Julia stood up so sharply that the book flew from her lap and skittered across the floor. She raced to the table, looking over Colleen's shoulder as Colleen read aloud.

"'. . . Mr. Arthur Browne, whose success in the steel industry has placed him among the wealthiest of Britain's rising industrialists . . .'"

Julia didn't wait to hear more. She dashed upstairs for her hat and gloves.

Five minutes later, she left the house, moving so quickly through the door that she nearly ran into a man who was coming up the steps. "I beg your pardon," she murmured, barely slowing down until she realized she recognized him. It was a footman from the Barkers' home.

"I've come to deliver a message," the footman said, extending a sealed note. "I was instructed to wait for a reply."

CHAPTER

31

WHEN JULIA AND THE FOOTMAN ARRIVED at the Barkers' home, Michael opened the door before the servant could pull out the key. He looked tired. His coat was wrinkled, and he had removed his cravat. He drew her inside and for several moments simply looked at her. "I can hardly believe you came."

"I'll do what I can. Will she be willing to let me help?"

"Maybe not at first," Michael admitted. "But you are as strong-willed as she is. I know you'll find a way."

There was so much she wanted to ask him! But she could see his worry for his sister overshadowing his joy at seeing her again. Everything else would have to wait.

As they went up the stairs, Michael gave her a brief account of what had transpired over the past few hours. "David and I just want to be sure everything is all right and that nothing has been missed."

Julia was honored, and perhaps a little awed, that he had such faith in her abilities.

David met them outside the door to Corinna's room. "Thank you for coming." His hand was clammy as he shook hers. The poor man was in a cold sweat. "I'd take you inside, but the sight of me seems to set her off even worse."

"All women hate their husbands at this stage. Take heart; it will pass."

She saw a brief glimmer of hope in his eyes. "Do you really think so?"

"Julia has a lot of experience in these things," Michael reminded him.

"And many more things besides," David said, nodding. "After all, you saved his life." He tilted his head toward Michael.

"I don't think saving a life will be necessary today," Julia said, "but I will see how I can help." She couldn't know this for sure, of course, until she'd seen the patient, but David looked so over-whelmed with worry that she felt compelled to comfort him in some way. She reached for the door handle. "I'll just go in and see how she is. Introduce myself to the midwife."

"David and I want to know the absolute truth," Michael said. "I know you will be honest with us."

"You can trust me for that," she promised.

Julia had arrived during a quiet period between contractions. Corinna lay in a doze, propped up with some pillows, her hands loosely wrapped around her belly. The woman seated next to the bed was dozing herself, taking advantage of the chance for a rest. It was wise on her part, for both mother and midwife needed to save their strength for when it was truly needed. Julia went to the washstand, pleased to see there was soap and fresh water available, and quietly washed her hands.

When she was done, she looked around the room. The midwife

had everything in order: a pan for receiving the afterbirth, string and scissors for the umbilical cord, a jar of belladonna ointment, and some sweet oil. Everything was ready to attend to Corinna's physical needs. Based on what Michael had told her, Julia guessed that what Corinna might need most from her was help of a less tangible kind, such as comfort and understanding. Knowing what she did of Corinna, it could not be given in a patronizing way, but with simple honesty as well as kindness.

Corinna's eyes fluttered open, and she cried out as the contractions began again. Mrs. Taylor awoke, too, and began to rise from her chair. Both seemed to lay eyes on Julia at the same time.

Corinna cried out, "What are you doing here?"

"I'm here to help," Julia assured her.

"What insolence, to come here after what you've done! You're the reason Michael isn't marrying Laura!"

"I haven't seen Michael since the trial," Julia returned coolly. "Here, let's put the pillow under your back, like so. I think it will make you more comfortable."

"Stay away from me—"

Her protestations were cut off by her sharp intake of breath as another contraction overtook her.

"Now, then, Mrs. Barker, remember what I told you to do," Mrs. Taylor commanded, coming over to the bed. The instructions she gave sounded more like scolding than coaching. Julia could see that Michael had been correct when he'd described the midwife's brusque manner.

They worked together, helping Corinna through this round of contractions, and at one point, Julia briefly introduced herself to the midwife as a family friend. When Mrs. Taylor learned that Julia was a nurse experienced with childbirth, she was happy to give her the pertinent information concerning Corinna's condition.

Mrs. Taylor was of the opinion that the labor was proceeding well. Even though Corinna was vocal about her discomfort, painful contractions were not out of the ordinary. Julia thought Mrs. Taylor was probably correct, but still, she wanted to do an examination herself. This was not only for her own assurance, but so she could give Michael and David the accurate assessment they'd asked for. But she had to get Corinna's permission first.

Corinna had thus far tolerated Julia's presence, primarily because while she was in the midst of the contractions, she was in no position to do anything else. But gaining her trust was going to be another matter.

"Mrs. Taylor, would you be able to go out and speak to Mr. Barker?" Julia asked when things had quieted down again. "He asked specifically if you might step out periodically and give him a report."

"What a worrywart that man is," Mrs. Taylor replied. But she complied.

"Can you see now that I want only to help?" Julia asked Corinna when they were alone.

"Why would you want to do that?" Corinna was tired, so the protest came out with less force than earlier.

"Because Michael asked me to."

"Michael." Her voice was tinged with anger. But then she exhaled a long breath, as if in disappointment, closing her eyes briefly.

"He cares for you very much. He had only your best interest in mind when he asked me here. He did it because he knows we are both strong-willed women." She said this last with a bit of a wry smile.

"Mrs. Taylor is too," Corinna pointed out.

"But I don't think she really understands you, does she? She gives orders, tells you not to worry, and feels that is enough. She doesn't really know how to address the fears you have, deep down, that something terrible may happen."

"Don't presume you know what I think," Corinna snapped. But her eyes betrayed her.

Julia gently brushed some loose hair back from Corinna's face. "We really should braid your hair. You'll be glad to have it out of the way later."

"No! I don't like braids."

"This is no time for vanity." Julia went to the dressing table and snatched up the brush. Before Corinna could launch another objection, Julia began gently brushing her hair, settling for making the braid on one side, since Corinna was leaning heavily against the pillows. She knew the brushing would have a calming effect. Corinna tried to look as though she were barely tolerating it, but her shoulders relaxed and her eyes half-closed.

Julia began to gather the hair nimbly into a braid. "It's unsettling, I know, when faced with things that are out of our control. It can feel, perhaps, like being in deep waters, unsure of the current."

"Or walking over a precipice," Corinna murmured.

"Precisely." Julia was glad to see this hint that Corinna might be ready to open up to her. She cut off a bit of the nearby string and secured the braid. "One of my faults is that I am brutally honest. Not only can I help you, but I will answer all your questions, too. Will you allow me to do that?" She lightly squeezed Corinna's hand, giving her best reassuring smile, silently urging her to agree, until at last she saw acceptance in Corinna's eyes.

"Yes," said Corinna. "I will."

"She's been in there a long time," David commented. "On the other hand, we haven't heard Corinna yelling at her to leave, so that's a good sign, don't you think?"

"Undoubtedly." Michael had a feeling that the longer Julia stayed in the room, the better the news must be. If something were amiss, she would have told them.

It had been a risk bringing her here, but he knew he'd been right to do it. From the moment she'd arrived, Michael felt certain that nothing truly bad could happen. She'd come so quickly and been amazingly cheerful—not at all as though she thought he'd callously thrown her over and then gone on to successfully persecute the school that was so vital to all her dreams. And then to come help his sister, whose actions had been in no way friendly toward her! What a woman this was. Someone who truly held no grudges.

He heard Corinna emit another loud cry, but this one seemed to stem from alarm rather than pain.

Several minutes passed, during which they could hear a lot of bustling and talking going on in the next room. David stood by the door, straining to hear, attempting to decipher every sound. It was clear he was as mystified as Michael.

The door flew open, and Julia came out, looking purposeful but not necessarily worried. "It won't be long now!" she announced. "I rang for Janet. She'll need to alert Dr. Hartman that Mrs. Barker's bag of waters has broken."

"Broken!" David repeated in horror.

"That's a good thing," Julia assured him. "It has to happen before the baby can come."

She was about to disappear back inside the room, but Michael caught her arm. "Can you tell us anything else?"

"I think the baby's face may not be positioned in the most favorable direction, but at least it is willing to come out head first, so I don't think we'll have too much trouble." She smiled up at him.

"Thank you." This was just what he'd hoped to hear, and coming from Julia, he believed it.

He wasn't willing to release her arm just yet. It was too tempting to keep her near. How many long weeks had it been since he'd seen that smile, those freckles? The eyes that always had a spark of intelligent liveliness in them? He felt the warmth of her arm through her cotton sleeve and wondered how that could be, when he knew from experience that her touch was always cool. He'd never thought of her as a woman of contradictions, but perhaps this was one.

She studied him with equal fascination, her lips slightly parted. Michael recalled the way she'd been looking at him just before that incredible moment in the park when she'd pulled him to her for a kiss.

"There's Janet!" cried David.

Michael swallowed and stepped back as the maid hurried toward them. Julia turned to give her instructions and send her to Dr. Hartman.

David clasped and unclasped his hands, his gaze moving between Julia and the door to Corinna's room. He looked as though the weight of hopeful anticipation mixed with fear might crush him.

Julia gave him a pat on the shoulder. "Cheer up, Mr. Barker. You'll be a father soon." She might even have given him a friendly wink before she left them to go back to Corinna.

In contrast to David's fidgeting, Michael stood quite still, feeling bereft at her absence. But his heart was sustained by what he'd seen just before she'd turned to talk to the maid. It had taken great effort to pull herself back to the task at hand, just as it had him. Neither of them had wanted that moment to end. Michael had seen love in her eyes, and one way or another, once they were past the birth of Corinna's baby, he was going to do something about it.

❧◈❧

Dr. Hartman arrived just minutes before the baby was born. He and the midwife knew their business well, and in the end, Julia's best contribution was to stay close to Corinna, helping her through the process and explaining what the doctor and Mrs. Taylor were doing.

Julia had attended many births and always marveled at the beauty of seeing a new life, but she'd never been as personally thrilled as she was the moment Corinna's child made its way into the world.

"What a strapping, beautiful little boy you've got, Mrs. Barker!" the midwife exclaimed.

"A . . . boy," Corinna gasped, still short of breath. She sank back onto the pillows. "Oh, what a messy business this was." But she said this in a dreamy, offhand way, as though she were surprised to find herself here. And she was smiling.

Julia knew this was the moment. She went to the bedroom door and flung it open. David and Michael both stood there, obviously aware the big moment had arrived.

"Come quickly!" she said to David, eagerly motioning him into the room.

"Why? What's wrong?" he exclaimed, startled by the fervor with which Julia had given the command.

"Nothing. Go speak to her. Right now!"

David was understandably hesitant, for the room was still in disarray, and his wife had been cursing him for hours. But Julia knew there was a period after the birth when the new mother was overtaken with a feeling of absolute euphoria. This was the best time for the husband to be with her.

Julia pushed him forward. "Go on."

He approached the bed practically on tiptoe, looking ready to flee if necessary. Then he got a good look at his wife's face. Corinna was in the midst of that peaceful languor after the work of the birth is over. She hardly seemed to notice the doctor and the midwife, who were securing the umbilical cord and cleaning the baby. She gazed up at her husband and, as Julia had expected, the bliss she felt flowed naturally toward him. "It's a boy," she told him.

David beamed at her with pure adoration. "Oh, my love. Oh, my darling. How beautiful you are." He gently brushed a strand of matted hair back from her forehead, which was still covered in sweat, seeing only the beauty of the woman he cherished. He leaned down to place a kiss on her cheek, which she readily accepted. "I love you so much."

"Yes." It was not exactly a return of his declaration, but Corinna's gaze was warm and tender, and it was more than enough for David.

"It is time to go now," Julia whispered. "There is more to do, but I wanted you to be here for this moment."

David left the room in dazed elation, and Julia's heart sang. She prayed that the tenuous bond these two had forged would grow stronger with time. Her concern for their welfare was prompted not just by medical precepts or Christian ideals. Corinna and David meant the world to Michael, and that was enough for her.

"When I saw the look on David's face after he came out of that room, I was sure you had worked a miracle."

Julia chuckled. "It was only a matter of knowing the beauty of God's design and taking advantage of it."

The beauty of God's design. Michael loved those words. Julia had opened his eyes in so many ways to see how God had worked in their lives.

It was after midnight. Michael and Julia were making their way downstairs. They were finally alone. Corinna and baby were sleeping comfortably, and Mrs. Taylor had settled herself into a cozy chair to watch over them. David was also with them—the new doting father seated next to the crib, staring down at his sleeping son, drinking in the sight of him.

The servants had been dismissed for the night. Nevertheless, when Michael and Julia reached the parlor, he closed the door behind them to ensure their privacy.

Julia voiced no objection. In fact, she didn't even seem to notice. "Are those sandwiches?" she exclaimed, immediately spotting the food laid out on the tea table.

"I asked the servants to leave us something. I thought you'd be hungry."

"Indeed I am!"

It did Michael's heart good to think he had anticipated her needs. It seemed small recompense after all she'd done for him and his family.

Before long, Julia was eating and exclaiming that she'd never tasted better. Michael did not partake; he was content just to watch her, to enjoy the way she took delight in the food. Sitting in this room, he could not help but recall the hours they'd spent here, working on her Latin lessons. Even—or perhaps most especially—the times she'd poked and prodded at him, inspecting his injuries. All the times she'd been so near him, not realizing the effect she had on him.

Just like now, when she was wiping a crumb from the corner of her mouth . . .

"You're smiling," Julia said. But it was posed as a question.

Smiling? More likely grinning like a besotted fool. Michael brought his thoughts back around to the other reasons—besides the sheer pleasure of her company—that he'd wanted to see her again. "God is good, isn't He?"

He enjoyed how startled—and pleased—she looked. She said nothing, waiting expectantly for him to continue.

"I believe now in the things you told me." He paused, not finding further words to express himself, but she seemed to understand. "You might also like to know that Myrtle Hodges was acquitted of all charges."

She gasped in delight. "How do you know that?"

"I represented her. I defended Gwen, too, at her trial. She was recommended to mercy, and her sentence was reduced to three months. Her aunt, on the other hand, got eighteen."

"I'll have to do something to help Gwen when she gets out. I don't know exactly what, but . . ."

"We'll think of something."

"We?" She gave him a teasing look, the kind he loved.

"Well, you seem to have a calling to help these people. I began to see that I can perhaps be of use, too."

Her face was alight with joy. He wanted to spend the rest of his life doing all he could to bring that expression to her face and keep it there. "I saved the best news for last, though. I have been doing some research on your father."

"You have?"

"I was intrigued by your story, and I began to wonder if there was any way to find out what happened to him. With Jamie Anderson's help, I was able to track down someone who used to know him. Do you remember a man named Charlie Stains?"

Her brow furrowed as she searched her memories, but then she drew back and looked at Michael. "Wait a minute. Did you say you asked *Mr. Anderson* for help?"

He grinned. "Let me tell you everything."

She listened attentively, all the while looking at him with that lovely Julia expression. Attentive. Curious. Beautiful. There were so many words to describe her, and yet not enough.

Especially now, when she wore a dreamy expression, like a child who wanted to believe in fairy stories. "It seems incredible. Do you think it could possibly be true?"

"I think it's worth trying to find out."

"But to go all the way to South America." She deflated a little at the thought. "It's so far out of reach. The money and the time it would take . . ."

"Is this the same Julia Bernay who has told me so often about a bountiful God who supplies all needs?"

"Well, if I was truly convinced of it, I would have no trouble believing for the means. But this . . . is it folly?"

"Maybe sometimes we don't know for sure. Maybe sometimes we just have to walk out and see. I would gladly pay for you to go."

"No, I could not even think of asking—"

"I love you, Julia." He took her hand. "I'd take you there myself if I could. Of course, I'd have to marry you first. But then I could never come back to England, because Corinna would want my head on a pike. Even David, kindhearted man that he is, because I promised him—"

"What are you saying?" Julia looked confused, and yet also amused by his babbling. "Was that . . . a proposal?"

His heart sank. Like an idiot, he'd gotten carried away. He should never have said those things aloud. "I wish it could be. But as I told you that day in the park, there are circumstances that prevent me from doing so. Things I hope to change."

Once more, there was that hint of a smile playing around her lips. "What a good thing that his lordship has had a change of heart."

Michael was so caught up in the swirl of desire and disappointment that he thought he couldn't have heard properly. "I beg your pardon?"

"Lord Westbridge told me he was the one who forbade you to see me again. But you said it had something to do with your family."

"It was both." He hesitated, confused. "His lordship told you?"

"Yes, and he said he was sorry for it. He said you had your reasons, and you might explain it to me if I asked—"

"Wait!" It was Michael's turn to interrupt. "I appear to be missing some very important information."

"Ah, so you are. Here it is in a nutshell. I got Edith to go and talk to him, and they decided they did not want to fight each other anymore."

If Michael had thought Julia was a miracle worker before, he was sure of it now. He looked at her in wonder, feeling like a hopeful traveler standing on the brink of a brave new world. "Why do I think there is more to it than that?"

"I'll be happy to tell you all about it. It seems there is a lot to discuss." She reached out and gave an inviting tug to his coat collar. "But perhaps it can wait a bit?"

"Mmm, yes."

He allowed her to pull him in, reveling in the kisses of this irrepressible, dynamic, singular woman. Yes, there would be plenty of time to talk. For now, he wanted only to hold Julia in his arms and know she was truly his.

ICHAEL ENTERED THE NURSERY FIRST. Julia hung back at the door, not wanting to intrude. She was not yet a member of this family, although she soon would be. That was a small part of what they planned to share today. The room was quiet, which Julia took for a positive sign.

David had decided to tell Corinna everything, and they were unsure what the collateral damage might be. Michael and Julia had been waiting in the parlor for their signal to come up. Before going to see his wife in the nursery, David had given the servants strict instructions not to disturb them, and that when he rang the bell, the butler was to fetch Michael and Julia from the parlor.

They had waited most of the afternoon for that summons. Clearly, it had taken time for husband and wife to work through everything together. Although Julia and Michael had made good use of the time by discussing their plans for the future, they were also on pins and needles, wondering how the conversation in the nursery was going. Julia sent up countless silent prayers. At last, they'd received word to come upstairs.

Corinna sat in a large stuffed armchair, holding her son. She and David had tears on their faces. Were these tears of joy, sorrow, or acceptance?

The moment she saw her brother, Corinna jumped up from the chair. Cradling the baby with one arm, she threw the other around Michael's neck and began sobbing. Loud and forceful, as though releasing a torrent of pent-up feelings. By the panicked look on Michael's face, and the awkward way he half-embraced her while giving her a tentative pat on the back, it was clear overtly emotional displays weren't typical for them.

David didn't move from where he stood next to Corinna's chair. There was a low footstool pulled close to the chair, and Julia supposed he might have been sitting there as he and his wife talked things out. His eyes were glistening, but he wore a little smile that suggested happiness. Or relief, perhaps, at finally getting everything off his chest.

David had insisted on telling Corinna everything today, as soon as they were assured she was recovering from the birth with no ill aftereffects. He'd made up his mind to do it even before Michael and Julia told him that the threat of exposure from the earl no longer existed.

In the three days since the birth, Corinna had continued to be enamored with her husband and heartily in love with her son. Julia had tentatively offered to teach her how to nurse the baby, expecting Corinna might reject that idea and give the job to a wet nurse. To her astonishment, Corinna agreed to give it a try. The outcome was beyond what Julia could have hoped for. Nursing had a profound effect on Corinna's soul, bonding her and her baby in a powerful way.

Given that Corinna had been so content, it was surprising

that David wanted to test these new, tranquil waters so quickly. Julia thought it showed great bravery. Or perhaps, after many years of marriage, he understood his wife's moods well enough to know when to press his advantage.

"David told you everything?" Michael asked when his sister's sobs died down at last.

The baby gurgled and squirmed, objecting to being sandwiched in this awkward embrace. His movements spurred Corinna to release her brother. Murmuring softly to her son, she readjusted the little blanket he was wrapped in, carefully repositioning his head on the crook of her arm. She tucked the edge of the blanket under the boy's chin—a tiny gesture filled with incredible tenderness. Wiping away her tears, she returned her attention to Michael. "You must think I've become alarmingly silly."

Michael shook his head. "Don't apologize. You've had quite the week."

"David told me about his childhood. About escaping the poorhouse. And how he . . ." She paused, sucking in a breath. If it was impossible for her to finish that sentence, to say *how he killed someone*, Julia could understand why. No one would guess that David, so consistently mild and cheerful, could have once been a thief and a thug. Even if the man's death in Manchester had been accidental, it stemmed from a combination of circumstances David had helped create.

David's shoulders were slightly stooped and his chin a little bowed in a humble posture. Julia suspected he would never truly get over what he'd done, even though he had put forth every effort to atone for it. He watched his wife intently. Perhaps he worried that at any moment she might change her mind and decide to hate him after all.

"David told us everything, too," Michael said.

Corinna nodded. Did she notice Michael's use of the word *us?*

She sent the briefest of glances toward the door where Julia still stood, but did not meet her eye. "David also told me why you had to stop the lessons, and what it cost you to do it." She took another deep breath. "And here I accused you of selfishness." There was self-recrimination in her words.

"You only knew I'd thrown away a chance to marry well. To advance myself." Michael did not point out that it would have been an advancement for Corinna, too. In a way, it sounded as though he was excusing her actions, but Julia couldn't fault him. For years he'd struggled under the weight of his obligation to his sister; the events of these past few months had added an extra burden of guilt because he couldn't bring himself to do the one thing she wanted most.

Julia felt a surge of love for him. She was heartily thankful that God had brought them through these trying times with their honor intact. He had given them the best answer, as only the Almighty could do.

"My husband certainly had me fooled." Corinna's voice held more irony than malice, although it must have caused great upheaval of heart and mind to learn such incredible things about a man she thought she knew. "Here I'd thought of him as simplistically jovial—an unremarkable man who stumbled into success through luck and aptitude. He never gave the slightest inkling how intensely difficult his road has been."

As though drawn by the remorse in his wife's words, David closed the gap between them. Looking at them side-by-side, Julia thought they seemed easier in one another's company now. As though invisible walls had been broken down.

"Scripture tells us to forget those things that are behind," David said. "Yes, my life has been hard. I wanted to make yours easier." He reached out and lightly stroked his son's head. "And his."

Corinna's mouth trembled, and she blinked several times,

fighting tears. As a nurse, Julia had seen how women were often intensely emotional in the days and weeks after giving birth. There was usually a sense of elation, and sometimes, to their detriment, they could slide into deep depression. However, Corinna's natural fortitude and strength of will would surely enable her to survive these swings. She allowed her husband to coax her back to the chair.

"I don't think you know the best part of this whole affair, though," Michael said, once the baby had been tucked into his cot and Corinna had settled with evident relief into her chair.

"You're going to tell me you are getting married, I expect."

For the first time since they'd entered the room, Corinna squarely met Julia's gaze. It surprised Julia to see a shade of uncertainty in her eyes. Corinna knew there was a gap between them, largely of her own making, and that she would have to own up to this in order to bridge it.

Michael reached for Julia's hand and tugged her close to him, wrapping one arm around her waist. It was the first time they'd shown such an intimate gesture to anyone else. Julia's heart fluttered with nervous tension. It felt very public—even if there were only her future sister- and brother-in-law to see it.

David grinned and nodded in approval.

"I can see I'm outnumbered," Corinna said.

Michael gave Julia's hand an emphatic kiss before replying. "I love her. I can't help it. Some men are drawn to feisty women."

Julia smiled as Michael repeated the line she'd spoken to him just before they kissed for the first time.

"Quite right," David murmured, his eyes growing misty. He reached down to pat his wife's shoulder. "Quite right."

"I shall accept that as a compliment," Corinna informed him.

Michael rubbed his chin. "Perhaps I'd better rethink this. To have two such women in my life could mean trouble. Maybe—"

"It's too late now," Julia said, poking him in the ribs.

Michael's eyes lit with laughter. "You should like her, Corinna. She has many of your best attributes. Including first-class rib-poking. And speaking her mind."

"Perhaps I might learn to be a bit more diplomatic in that last part," Julia admitted with chagrin.

"Diplomacy can make the truth easier to receive," Michael replied with the air of conceding a point that exactly proved, with a barrister's finesse, the very point he was making.

Corinna seemed to be trying to join the frivolity, but a tension remained in her expression.

"There's something else I need to tell you," Michael said. "A bit of news I'm sure all of you will find supremely interesting."

He paused for dramatic effect. Julia joined the others in looking at him expectantly.

David said with a smile, "Don't leave us in suspense. What is it?"

"After I had to stop helping Julia with her Latin studies, I was determined to do something to ensure she got the tutoring she needed. But Julia adamantly refused to accept any money from me."

He paused briefly, perhaps to quietly—and tactfully—make it plain to his sister that Julia was never a fortune hunter. Corinna's eyebrows did raise in surprise, and Julia felt vindicated.

"I came up with another plan," Michael continued. "I arranged for a tutoring program to be offered at the school, something to help Julia get the training she needed. The program was supported by a lady interested in helping women who wish to pursue a medical career. In the beginning, I did not know her identity. Everything was arranged through an intermediary. But I have since learned that the lady in question is Lady Amberley."

"What?" Corinna sat bolt upright in the chair, her mouth

agape. A reaction that brought a satisfied smile to Michael's face.

"Shocking, isn't it? Unfortunately, her husband is disappointingly behind the times, so Lady Amberley must be circumspect in her support of this cause." He cupped a hand to his mouth and added in a stage whisper, "We won't even mention her thoughts on women's suffrage."

Julia stared at Michael, astounded to learn that the tutoring had been his idea. "Why didn't you tell me this before?"

"I wanted to tell you both at the same time. Corinna, you needn't fear that my falling out with Laura will exclude you from Lady Amberley's good graces in the future. Far from it. I think you'll find her more willing than ever to add you to her circle of close acquaintances."

This good news only brought a fresh round of tears. Corinna accepted a handkerchief proffered by David and began to dab her eyes and cheeks. "My plans seem so petty now, don't they?"

No one answered that. Nor would Julia even try. She had never been in Corinna's shoes and would not judge the worth of her dreams. She was glad only that God had met this desire of her heart. And He had done it—as improbable as it seemed—by way of Julia. Michael's love for Julia had not hindered Corinna after all. It had helped her.

"I'm glad to see you so happy," Michael remarked, as Corinna continued to wipe away tears. "We've got a wedding to plan for August fifteenth."

"But that's only a month away!"

"Gives us the three Sundays needed for the reading of the banns. It also perfectly coincides with the long end-of-summer recess in the courts and Parliament. Not to mention that we have to be back from our honeymoon in South America in time for Julia to begin medical school on October first."

"South America!" David exclaimed. "I think you'd better explain more about your plans."

Their plans! Where to start? God was opening so many doors for Julia, and the desires He had placed in her heart were being realized. But true to his promises, he was giving her even more than she'd asked for. As she and Michael sat down with David and Corinna to discuss the future, Julia felt great satisfaction to be completing this small family unit that was so fiercely dedicated to one another. To be able to pursue her dreams alongside the man she loved with all her heart was a prospect so rich, so full, it would take a lifetime to explore.

Epilogue

THEY STOOD ARM IN ARM at the ship's railing, looking over bright blue water toward the land. The north wind had at last died down, and the swells it had caused in the harbor had calmed as well. Rough waters had made landing too dangerous, so they'd had to wait. Now, after two days of being stranded within view of their destination, they were finally going ashore.

Most of La Guaira's buildings lay close to the harbor due to the mountains rising up sharply behind them. Just off the wharf stood the customs house, a long, nondescript building, and next to it, the harbor master's house. Beyond these lay the town's principal streets, lined with shops, taverns, and colorfully painted homes. Was her father somewhere in those buildings? They had come all this way in the hope that he was.

Julia and Michael had been married the Monday morning after the final reading of the banns. It was a quiet ceremony, with Corinna and David as witnesses. Their wedding occurred too late for them to catch the monthly departure of the Royal Mail packet to the West Indies. But by crossing the channel to Le Havre, they were able to board a German steamship that brought them all the way to La Guaira.

Later, in October, they would have a sumptuous wedding feast that included all their family and friends. But on their wedding day, after a simple wedding breakfast with Corinna and David, the newly married couple had taken a train to Southampton and boarded a ship for Le Havre. Because she'd expected to remain single, Julia had never dreamed of her wedding day. But even if she had, she'd never have imagined spending her wedding night drinking champagne with her husband while crossing the Channel. And yet it had been the stuff of dreams, for she was on a grand adventure with the man she loved.

Now, two weeks later, here they were. To be so close and yet unable to close the gap had turned Julia's heightened anticipation into an agony of waiting. The only thing that made it bearable was having Michael beside her. Together they had wiled away the hours much as they had during their days at sea: sharing memories from their lives and dreaming of the future. When they returned to London, they would live in Michael's quarters at Gray's Inn. The space was large enough to accommodate them both, and they agreed this would keep their living situation simple and allow Julia to focus on her studies. It was within easy enough reach of the medical school by walking or omnibus.

What would happen if they found her father, and if they should be able to bring him home, was something they would have to decide if that time came.

"Here it is," Michael said, as a boat to ferry them to the dock came alongside the ship. He turned to her, smiling. His face was tanned from days spent on the sun-soaked decks, his eyes warm and sparkling like the sea. "Are you ready?"

At last she was about to discover what had happened to her father. Or so she desperately hoped. Julia was suddenly finding it difficult to breathe. She reached up to caress the cheek of the man who had made this possible. "Whatever happens, I will be grateful to you for this journey for the rest of my life."

He gently kissed her palm, setting Julia's pulse racing. But he said playfully, "I'll remember to point that out to you during any future arguments."

It took another hour to reach land, clear the customs house, and find a cart and driver to take them and their baggage to the hotel. Despite the early hour, for it was just past seven, the wharf and streets were teeming with people. La Guaira was a town of several thousand people, and it seemed all were outside. As a port city, it drew people from around the world, and the air buzzed with a cacophony of different languages. Julia kept scanning the faces of everyone she passed, even though from the description Michael had gotten from Charlie Stains, it was unreasonable to expect any of them to be her father.

The hotel was small and plain, but the proprietor welcomed them cordially. He spoke mostly German and Spanish, and his English was barely intelligible. Fortunately, Michael had studied German at university and had brushed up on it by speaking to the German crew during their voyage. When Michael asked about the tavern where someone named Pablo was a regular, the innkeeper shrugged. He hadn't heard of such a man.

Julia could interpret the gesture without knowing the language. "Try again," she urged Michael. "Tell him every detail that Charlie Stains told you."

Michael began again, using what Julia could only assume was a different tack. This time, the innkeeper's response was different. He nodded as he replied.

"What does he say?" Julia asked excitedly.

"He said, 'If you are looking for a place where the sailors go, that would be on the other side of the town. It's dirty and dangerous, but the rum is cheap.'"

The sun was high overhead now, beating down on them mercilessly. Julia understood why there had been so much activity on the docks earlier today. The laborers had been getting in as much work as they could before the real heat set in. Now it seemed everyone had retreated to whatever shade or other respite they could find until the hot afternoon wore away.

Julia and Michael trudged down yet another dusty street. There was little movement around them, save for swarms of flies. Most of the dwellings they passed were low huts made of sun-dried mud and roofed with thatch. Occasionally they heard shouts in Spanish, but these came from women calling out to their wayward children, whose energy had not been diminished by the heat.

"We should go back to the hotel and rest," Michael said as Julia paused to wipe sweat from her brow.

She was ready to concede. It pained her to waste a single minute of their time here, but even she had to admit she felt weakened by the relentless heat.

"Ha, ha! I win!" cried a man's voice in English, startling them both.

The reply to this exclamation was a torrent of Spanish, spoken in a joking manner by someone younger than the English speaker.

The conversation was coming from behind a nearby building. It was built with mud walls like the other houses but was noticeably larger.

Julia and Michael followed the sounds around to the back, where they found an outdoor seating area, shaded from the sun's beating rays by a balding thatched roof. There, at a small, rough table, sat two men playing checkers. The older of the two looked up and caught Julia's eye.

At long last, she had her answer.

Author's Note

I love to include real people, places, and events in my novels. This book was no exception. One person that I included was Dr. Elizabeth Garrett Anderson, a pioneer in the field of women in medicine, who co-founded the London School of Medicine for Women. I addressed as accurately as I could the realities of what it took to become a physician in England at that time. Although the lawsuit in this story is fictional, it is partly inspired by an actual libel suit brought against a female medical student in the 1870s.

It may surprise some readers to learn that London's subway system, known as the Underground, began operations in the 1860s. We tend to think of it as a fairly modern invention. It ran with steam engines until the tracks were electrified around the turn of the twentieth century. Imagine riding in those smoke-filled tunnels!

In the first book in this series, *The Captain's Daughter,* I was able to present a picture of Gilbert and Sullivan's comic operas *HMS Pinafore* and *The Pirates of Penzance.* In this novel, we see their follow-up hit, *Patience,* which was a satirical look at a popular artistic movement called aestheticism. Although Gilbert and

Sullivan poked fun at many foibles of their time, their observations about human nature are universal, and their operas are still popular today.

There actually was a comet in June 1881, as occurs in this story. I based my descriptions on several accounts that appeared in local newspapers at the time. Then, as now, such celestial displays inspired awe and fascination, and huge numbers of people organized comet-watching parties to make the most of a once-in-a-lifetime event.

Julia grew up in George Müller's orphanage in Bristol. The story of Müller and his orphanage, which cared for thousands of children for about a century and was supported solely by faith and prayer, is well-known to many Christians. For those unfamiliar with this inspiring testament to God's love and care for His people, I highly recommend Roger Steer's biography of George Müller, titled *Delighted in God!*

By pursuing her dream of becoming a physician, Julia joined the ranks of many others who pressed the boundaries of what was acceptable for women to do. With the rapid advances in technology and the changing social norms, it must have seemed to a lot of Victorians that their whole world was in flux. Don't we often feel that way today, in the twenty-first century? In such times, I'm thankful for the reminder that the one constant in any age is God. He is the same yesterday, today, and forever. With God's help, Julia found her true calling, even though events did not unfold exactly as she'd expected. My prayer is that we can also make the most of our unique, God-given gifts—and, whether at home or abroad, we can share God's love and the Gospel with a world that surely needs it.

Acknowledgments

My abundant thanks to Dr. Nanette Lavoie-Vaughan, ANP-C, DNP, and to Cathleen W. Hemphill, RN, BSN, for sharing your valuable knowledge with me regarding some of the medical issues in this story. (Any mistakes are mine, of course, and a few of the stranger remedies described in the book reflect practices of the Victorian era rather than the present.)

I'm grateful to the awesome staff at the Wake County Libraries for your assistance, cheerful support, many interlibrary loan books, and for providing the excellent quiet room, where much of this book was written. I know Miss Julia Bernay would approve.

Jennifer Delamere writes tales of the past . . . and new beginnings. Her novels set in Victorian England have won numerous accolades, including a starred review from *Publishers Weekly* and a nomination for the Romance Writers of America's RITA Award. Jennifer holds a BA in English from McGill University in Montreal, Canada, and has been an editor of educational materials for two decades. She loves reading classics and histories, which she mines for vivid details that bring to life the people and places in her books. Jennifer lives in North Carolina with her husband, and when not writing, she is usually scouting out good day hikes or planning their next travel adventure.

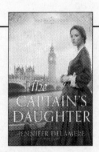

You May Also Like . . .

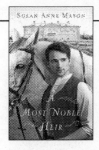

Stable hand Nolan Price's life is upended when he learns that he is the heir of the Earl of Stainsby. Caught between two worlds, Nolan is soon torn between his love for kitchen maid Hannah Burnham and the expectations and opportunities that come with his rise in station. He longs to marry Hannah, but will his intentions survive the upstairs–downstairs divide?

A Most Noble Heir by Susan Anne Mason
susananemason.com

At the outset of WWI, high-end thief Willa Forsythe is hired to steal a cypher from famous violinist Lukas De Wilde. Given the value of his father's work as a cryptologist, Lukas fears for his family and doesn't know who to trust. He likes Willa—and the feeling is mutual—but if Willa doesn't betray him as ordered, her own family will pay the price.

A Song Unheard by Roseanna M. White
SHADOWS OVER ENGLAND #2
roseannawhite.com

Vivienne Rivard fled revolutionary France and now seeks a new life for herself and a boy in her care, who some say is the Dauphin. But America is far from safe, as militiaman Liam Delaney knows. He proudly served in the American Revolution but is less sure of his role in the Whiskey Rebellion. Drawn together, will Liam and Vivienne find the peace they long for?

A Refuge Assured by Jocelyn Green
jocelyngreen.com

⬧ BETHANY HOUSE

Printed in the United States
By Bookmasters